Death and the Maiden

Also by Frank Tallis

LIEBERMANN PAPERS
Mortal Mischief
Vienna Blood
Fatal Lies
Darkness Rising
Deadly Communion

NOVELS
Killing Time
Sensing Others

NON FICTION
Love Sick: Love As a Mental Illness
Changing Minds
Hidden Spirits

Death and the Maiden

Frank Tallis

CENTURY · LONDON

Published by Century 2011

2 4 6 8 10 9 7 5 3 1

First published in Great Britain in 2011 by
Century
Random House, 20 Vauxhall Bridge Road,
London SW1V 2SA

www.randomhouse.co.uk

Addresses for companies within The Random House Group Limited can be found at:
www.randomhouse.co.uk

The Random House Group Limited Reg. No. 954009

A CIP catalogue record for this book
is available from the British Library

ISBN 9781846053573

The Random House Group Limited supports The Forest Stewardship
Council (FSC), the leading international forest certification organisation. All our
titles that are printed on Greenpeace approved FSC certified paper carry the FSC logo. Our
paper procurement policy can be found at www.rbooks.co.uk/environment

Mixed Sources
Product group from well-managed
forests and other controlled sources
www.fsc.org Cert no. TT-COC-2139
© 1996 Forest Stewardship Council

FSC

EXORDIUM

THE LORD MARSHAL AND the lord chamberlain, Prince Rudolf Liechtenstein, were observing Emperor Franz-Josef from the staircase. Their elevated vantage point afforded them a good view of the entire chamber. As usual, the monarch was dressed in a military uniform: dark blue trousers and a claret-coloured jacket with gold cuffs. He had three medals pinned high on his chest. He was standing erect, like a soldier on parade, stationed at the still centre of a slowly rotating spiral of humanity as various parties were presented to him. With every circuit, palace guests shuffled closer, drawn by the gravitational pull of his eminence. Each party was represented by a speaker who, when given a signal by Count Paar, would approach the emperor and make introductions. After a few words were exchanged, the group would move on, making way for the next.

Although there were a number of officers present — captains and colonels, proudly sporting their regimental colours — most of the men were civilians in sombre evening suits and white bow ties. The women who accompanied them were wearing ball gowns, some of which had been audaciously cut to expose the smooth whiteness of their backs. Lacy borders sank recklessly low, revealing the shapely convexities of the female form. A brunette sporting a corsage of jasmine and roses was making a graceful descent down the stairs. As she passed the two court officials she turned to smile at Prince Liechtenstein.

'Your Highness.'

He inclined his head and became conscious of a sweet fragrance.

'Who's she?' asked the lord marshal.

'You don't know her?' exclaimed the prince, a note of disbelief entering his voice.

The woman joined a group of men at the foot of the stairs.

'If I knew who she was I wouldn't have asked,' the lord marshal replied.

'Arianne Amsel,' said the prince. The lord marshal showed no sign of recognition and Liechtenstein was obliged to add: 'A soprano from the court opera. Have you never heard her sing? I don't believe it.'

'Do you really think I have time to go the opera?' said the lord marshal.

'She's famous for her role as Senta in *The Flying Dutchman* and she was most impressive in *Euryanthe* last year. Be that as it may, she may not be with us for much longer. Not very happy: keeps on complaining about Director Mahler. I'll introduce you.'

The lord marshal nodded and continued surveying the chamber.

On either side of the gilded double doors stood members of the Bosnian Guard. They were dressed in their distinctive garb: tunic, knickerbockers, ankle boots, tassled fez, and backpack. The lord marshal reflected that the backpack was no doubt essential for survival on the limestone slopes of the Dinaric Alps but surely somewhat redundant in the palace. More people were streaming in and joining the outer arm of the slowly moving spiral. The lord marshal returned his attention to the middle of the chamber.

'Look who's here.'

A bearded man in his late fifties, wearing a sash, was advancing towards the emperor.

'They say that Mayor Lueger isn't well,' said Prince Liechtenstein, 'but he looks healthy enough to me.'

'Healthy enough to fight another election,' said the lord marshal, before adding in a more subdued tone: 'Worse luck.'

'There's a general feeling of discontent around, don't you think?' said the prince. 'A feeling of dissatisfaction, a feeling that more could be done?'

'Who have you been talking to?' snapped the lord marshal.

The prince looked uncomfortable. 'Surely you don't object to a little enlightened discussion if it takes place among friends? You don't need to impress upon me the importance of discretion.'

'Look at him,' the lord marshal complained, flicking a finger disdainfully at the mayor. 'He thinks himself invincible.'

'And if things continue as they are, he very well may be.' Prince Liechtenstein shuddered theatrically. 'If only someone would show some initiative.' The two court officials stepped aside, permitting the *Hochmeister* of the Order of Teutonic Knights to pass. This venerable gentleman was wearing a white cape on which a large black and gold pattée cross had been embroidered. When the *Hochmeister* reached the bottom of the staircase the prince added, 'One might let it be known — tactfully, of course — that men of action could depend on our support.'

'Well, they could only depend on our support up to a point.'

'Quite so.'

'Thereafter . . .'

'Indeed. But you have the authority and means to deal with any complications should they arise. Isn't that so?'

Mayor Lueger was smiling — but the emperor did not reciprocate. The two men greeted each other somewhat stiffly, and the mayor began to present his party, a group of six gentlemen all in their middle years.

'The Anti-Semitic German-Austrian Writers' Association,' murmured the prince.

'How very embarrassing,' said the lord marshal. They watched as each of the men spoke a few words to the emperor before moving on. Finally, the mayor himself bowed and followed the band of writers to the less densely populated margin.

Unexpectedly, the emperor looked up in the general direction of his two courtiers. The lord marshal and Prince Liechtenstein both corrected their posture, but it was obvious that the emperor was seeking the notice of the lord marshal rather than that of the lord chamberlain. His Majesty was clearly unhappy. The lord marshal began to walk down the stairs but the emperor shook his head. Then, turning towards Count Paar, the emperor composed himself for the next presentation.

'This isn't good,' said the lord marshal.

The prince responded sympathetically. 'Yes, but at this precise moment there is nothing you can do. Come now. Where did that singer go? Let me introduce you to her. She's adorable.'

Part One

Death of a Diva

I

DETECTIVE INSPECTOR OSKAR RHEINHARDT — a portly gentleman with a turned-up moustache and world-weary expression — was standing on the pavement of a wide tree-lined road. The fog of the previous evening had persisted and the buildings on both sides were only faintly visible as shadowy cubes, spaced apart at regular intervals. It had been a slow and perilous journey by horse-drawn cab, visibility deteriorating as they gained altitude. Indeed, they had only narrowly escaped involvement in a serious collision next to the Kaiser Pavilion.

Rheinhardt turned to address his assistant.

'Search the grounds, Haussmann. See if you can find anything.'

'But, sir . . .'

'Yes, I know that conditions are far from ideal,' said Rheinhardt, 'Nevertheless . . .' The inspector removed a flashlight from his pocket and handed it to his disgruntled junior. Haussmann aimed the weak yellow beam at the cobblestones, revealing nothing but a slowly undulating blanket of fog. 'Oh, very well,' said Rheinhardt, persuaded to reconsider the wisdom of his order: 'You can accompany me. Perhaps it'll lift later.'

'Thank you, sir,' said Haussmann, much relieved.

A figure emerged from the mist. 'Who's there?'

'Detective Inspector Rheinhardt and my assistant, Haussmann.'

'Good morning, sir. Constable Drasche.'

The young man clicked his heels. He was wearing a long blue coat, a spiked hat, and a sabre hung from his waist.

'How long have you been here, Drasche?' asked Rheinhardt.

'Three hours or thereabouts.'

'I'm sorry for the delay. The driver could barely see the road ahead of him. Who's inside?'

'Frau Marcus, the housekeeper, and Fräulein Rosenkrantz's doctor — Engelberg. Frau Marcus called him as soon as she found the body. He was here before I arrived. He's not in a very good mood, sir.'

'Oh? Why's that?'

'He didn't want to be detained: said he had patients to see.'

The horse was restive and the driver jumped down from his box to give it some sugar.

'The dead woman,' said Rheinhardt. 'Fräulein Rosenkrantz . . .'

Drasche anticipated the inspector's question.

'Yes, it's *her*, sir. The singer.'

Haussmann's sharp features showed perplexity.

'Have you not heard of Ida Rosenkrantz, Haussmann?'

'No, sir. She's never sung at Ronacher's.'

Rheinhardt shook his head. 'Haussmann, she's not *that* kind of singer! She's an opera singer, a celebrated soprano. You'll recognise her when you see her. Her image is in every shop window along Kärntnerstrasse.'

'Even my tailor has a signed photograph of Fräulein Rosenkrantz,' said Drasche. 'He saw her in *The Flying Dutchman* and was smitten. I can remember teasing him about it.'

The restive horse — still nervous and unsettled — whinnied and stamped on the cobbles.

Rheinhardt pulled at his chin and emitted a low, pensive growl.

'Court opera singers are only appointed after they have been approved by the palace. I strongly suspect that protocol demands that the emperor — or at least the lord chamberlain, Prince Liechtenstein — must now be informed of Fräulein Rosenkrantz's demise.'

'You intend to go the palace, sir?' asked Haussmann, his eyes widening with alarm.

'No, of course not, Haussmann,' said Rheinhardt, a trace of testiness disturbing the otherwise pleasing fluidity of his baritone. 'We must contact Commissioner Brügel and it is *he* who will inform the lord chamberlain's office. Come, Drasche, you had better show us the way.'

They passed along a perimeter fence of railings (each of which was topped by a fleur-de-lis) and entered a small garden, where a paved pathway led between two beech trees to the double doors of a white stucco villa. Some of the windows were separated by gilded panels and a stylised statue of an eagle with angular outstretched wings perched above the entrance. All the ground-floor windows were illuminated.

Drasche opened one of the double doors and ushered Rheinhardt and Haussmann into the hallway. It was a bright space, with yellow wallpaper and floor tiles the colour of eggshell. Directly ahead, a carpeted staircase rose up before dividing into two smaller staircases, each reaching the second floor on opposite sides of the building. The air was fragrant with a smell similar to that of blooming hyacinths.

'Ah, there you are, constable,' said a man as he stepped over the threshold of an adjacent room. He was in his late fifties and wore a frock coat. 'I really must protest.'

Before he could continue, Drasche indicated his companions and said: 'Herr Doctor Engelberg, this is Detective Inspector Rheinhardt, from the security office.'

'Ah,' said the doctor, frowning. 'You've finally arrived.'

'Progress was slow on account of the weather.'

'You will forgive me for neglecting to observe the customary civilities, inspector, but I am obliged to make an immediate request. I have been here all morning and many of my patients are expecting domiciliary visits. If I am delayed for very much longer it will be impossible for me to see them all. Would you please take their needs into consideration?'

'You wish to leave as soon as possible,' said Rheinhardt. 'Of course, that is perfectly understandable. I will endeavour to conduct our business swiftly. Where is Frau Marcus?'

'In the kitchen. I was just attending to her. She is very distressed.'

'Should she be left alone?'

'Perhaps not.'

'Drasche,' said Rheinhardt. 'Would you be so kind as to sit with Frau Marcus?'

The constable took off his helmet and scratched his head.

'I'm not very good at that sort of thing, sir: comforting women in distress.'

Rheinhardt sighed.

'You don't have to *do* anything, Drasche. Just sit with her. Allow her to communicate her feelings if she wishes. But if she is silent respect that silence and do not speak merely for the sake of it.' Rheinhardt paused before adding: 'And be sure to make her a cup of tea.'

'But what if she doesn't want a cup of tea, sir?'

'Make her one, anyway. I can assure you that she will drink it.'

'Very good, sir.'

Drasche replaced his helmet, bowed, and departed with a noticeable lack of enthusiasm.

When Rheinhardt turned to address Engelberg, the doctor's hostility had been replaced by surprise and mild-mannered amusement.

'Excellent advice, Inspector.'

Rheinhardt acknowledged the compliment with a slight tilt of his head.

'And the body, Herr Doctor?'

'Upstairs.'

They began their ascent.

'What time was it when you received Frau Marcus's telephone call, Herr Doctor?'

'Around seven-thirty.'

'And what time did you get here?'

'No later than quarter to eight.' Rheinhardt's expression was sceptical. 'I rise very early, you see. I was already dressed and I live only a short distance away.'

When they reached the landing Engelberg opened the first of several doors. 'She's in here.'

They entered a richly appointed bedroom where gas jets flickered within globes of smoked glass. A four-poster bed occupied a commanding central position, its heavy curtains tied back with gold cords so as to reveal a counterpane embroidered with a medieval scene: against a backdrop of peacocks and roses stood a noblewoman who was holding a standard displaying three crescent moons. At her feet sat a docile unicorn and a good-humoured lion that seemed content to entertain a small white rabbit in the gap between its paws. Two purple stockings had been discarded on the pillows. The wallpaper was striped, burgundy columns alternating with green, with a repeated violin and laurel-wreath motif in raised silver.

Next to the window was a dressing table with a hinged oval mirror on which several bottles, an amber-coloured decanter and numerous small mother-of-pearl boxes had been casually laid out. Scattered among these items was a tortoisehell comb, several brooches, and a curious totemic object made of hair and beads. Rheinhardt inhaled.

The smell of hyacinths had intensified. He looked around and identified its source as a large egg-shaped pomander of fretted ivory; however, the inspector was also conscious of an acrid undertow. In the far corner he saw a wardrobe and beside it a washstand. Instead of the usual porcelain, the bowl and jug were made from a semi-transparent turquoise glass, encrusted with jasper.

The overall effect of the room suggested luxury and abundance. Yet there was something distinctly dissolute about the decor. The gemstones and sumptuous colours tested the limits of aesthetic toler-ance and awakened prejudices. Rheinhardt found himself thinking that he had entered not the bedroom of an operatic diva but a seraglio.

Engelberg crossed to the other side of the room and made a sweeping gesture. Rheinhardt and Haussmann followed and as they rounded the bed Fräulein Rosenkrantz's lifeless form came into view. The dead woman was lying on her back, positioned within the rectangle of a Persian rug. It was a pleasing effect, possessing the compositional virtues of a painting. She was wearing a pink silk dress overlaid with a lacy décolleté trim. Her complexion was pale and her plenteous auburn curls complemented a youthful face of exceptional delicacy. Fräulein Rosenkrantz's eyes were closed and the almost perfect ovals of her fingernails were tinged with a bluish hue. She was not wearing any shoes and her bare feet projected out from a sufficiency of petticoats. On the floor, next to the rug, was a phial. Its stopper had rolled beneath a bedside table on which more empty bottles stood.

'Herr Doctor?' said Rheinhardt. 'Did you move Fräulein Rosenkrantz when you examined her?'

'No. She remains exactly as found.'

'What about Frau Marcus? Did she move Fräulein Rosenkrantz's body?'

'I don't think so. As far as I know she made no attempt to revive or resuscitate her.'

Rheinhardt stepped closer.

'How did Fräulein Rosenkrantz die?'

'It would appear that she imbibed an excessive quantity of laudanum.'

'Intentionally?'

'That is certainly a possibility . . .'

'However?'

'I can think of no reason why she should have chosen to end her life. I take it you are aware of Fräulein Rosenkrantz's reputation? She was at the height of her powers. There are few who can claim to have conquered the hearts of the music-loving public so decisively. We have been robbed of a singular talent, make no mistake.'

'When was the last time Fräulein Rosenkrantz had cause to request a consultation?'

'Only two weeks ago.'

'With respect to . . .?'

'A touch of neuralgia but otherwise she was in excellent spirits. I can remember her talking excitedly about roles she expected to take next season.'

'So what are we to conclude, Herr Doctor? That her death was accidental?'

'That *would* be my opinion . . .' Engelberg's sentence trailed off into silence. He sighed and began again: 'That would be my opinion were it not for the fact that Fräulein Rosenkrantz once needed the services of a psychiatrist. In the spring I arranged for her to see Professor Daniel Saminsky.' Engelberg paused before adding: 'A colleague of some distinction. He once had the honour of attending the late empress, and has since been awarded the Order of Elizabeth.'

Rheinhardt twisted the horns of his moustache.

'What was the reason for the referral?'

'*Globus hystericus*,' Engelberg replied.

'Would you care to explain?'

'A hysterical phenomenon: typically, the patient reports the presence of a lump in the throat which produces difficulty when swallowing. Physical investigations reveal no obvious obstruction and the lump, or rather the perceived lump, is subsequently ascribed to psychological causes. *Globus hystericus* is not a diagnosis that we doctors commonly associate with suicide. And to the best of my knowledge Professor Saminsky's treatment was effective.'

Rheinhardt walked over to the bedside table, picked up one of the bottles and sniffed the pungent residue.

'Did you prescribe these tinctures?'

'No.'

'Then who did?'

'Professor Saminsky, I believe.'

'Didn't you say that Saminsky's treatment was successful?'

'That is correct. Nevertheless, he continued to see Fräulein Rosenkrantz for monthly appointments.' Engelberg raked his hand through his hair. 'No doctor can be absolutely certain of a patient's state of mind. If Fräulein Rosenkrantz was suffering from suicidal melancholia it not only escaped my notice, it also escaped Professor Saminsky's.'

Rheinhardt replaced the bottle.

'Herr Doctor, you say that Fräulein Rosenkrantz was fully recovered. Why, then, was she taking laudanum?'

'To hasten the onset of sleep. Difficulty sleeping was another of her problems. She has taken paraldehyde, sulphonal, potassium bromide and a host of herbal remedies. The laudanum has nothing to do with her *globus hystericus*.' Engelberg patted his pocket and removed a cigar. 'May I smoke, inspector?'

'Of course,' said Rheinhardt, taking a box of matches from his pocket and courteously providing a light. 'Herr Doctor, looking at Fräulein Rosenkrantz's body, does anything strike you as odd?'

'I'm not sure what you mean, inspector.'

'Her position,' said Rheinhardt. 'In the centre of the rug.'

Engelberg shrugged and surrounded himself with a yellow nimbus of smoke. 'Inspector, imagine, if you will, the following: Fräulein Rosenkrantz retires to her bedroom. She cannot sleep. She takes some laudanum but it has little effect. Those of a nervous character, as she undoubtedly was, are often less susceptible to soporifics.' He sucked at his cigar and flicked some ash into an onyx dish. 'She waits, but remains incorrigibly awake. Becoming impatient, she drinks another phial. Although she feels the laudanum isn't working, it most certainly is. She is no longer fully *compos mentis*. She cannot remember how much she has taken and she is confused. In this disoriented state she takes yet more laudanum, and the dose is now fatal. She sits on the side of the bed and removes her shoes and stockings. As she bends down she becomes dizzy. She slides off the bed and onto the floor. She rolls over, onto the rug, and closes her eyes.' Engelberg shrugged again. 'It might well have happened like that, inspector: an accident, a cruel tragedy of mischance.'

Rheinhardt lifted the counterpane and looked under the bed, where he saw a pair of brown leather ladies' shoes. He then examined the coverlet more closely, searching for small indications consistent with Engelberg's scenario. It was all very plausible, but when Rheinhardt looked again at Fräulein Rosenkrantz's body, positioned so neatly within the rectangular limits of the Persian rug, he could not quash a nagging doubt.

'Thank you, Herr Doctor,' said Rheinhardt. 'You have been most helpful.'

'May I leave now?'

'I must ask you to give Haussmann your details first.' The inspector glanced at his assistant. 'Then you are free to go. Once again, please accept my apologies.'

Rheinhardt bowed and left the room. He made his way downstairs to the kitchen, where he found Constable Drasche sitting next to a middle-aged woman whose eyelids were raw and swollen. Rheinhardt pulled a chair from under the large wooden table and noted with some satisfaction the presence of an empty teacup.

'My name is Rheinhardt,' he said softly. 'I am the detective inspector.' He sat down. 'It must have been a great shock.'

A prolonged silence followed, during which the housekeeper twisted a damp handkerchief.

'Terrible.'

'Frau Marcus,' said Rheinhardt, 'when did you discover Fräulein Rosenkrantz?'

'Seven-thirty.'

'I know that this is difficult but I must ask you to tell me what happened, precisely.'

Frau Marcus nodded and took a deep breath.

'I arrived here at seven o'clock and set about preparing mistress's breakfast: a boiled egg and some pumpernickel. When the egg was ready I took it upstairs on a tray, along with some butter. I knocked on the door — but there was no reply. Fräulein Rosenkrantz had told me yesterday that she wanted to rise early because she had a new role to learn, so I went in. I thought she'd fainted . . . and I knelt down on the floor beside her.'

'Did you touch her?' Rheinhardt interjected.

'Yes,' said Frau Marcus. 'I touched her face. It was cold. Horribly cold.'

The housekeeper shivered.

'Did you attempt to move her?'

'No. I was scared and thought it best to call Doctor Engelberg.'

'And you were right to do so. But are you quite certain that you did not move Fräulein Rosenkrantz? Please think carefully, Frau Marcus — it may be important.'

'I touched her face with *this* hand.' She raised her arm as if swearing an oath. 'Then I ran downstairs to telephone Doctor Engelberg.'

'What did you do while you were waiting for him to arrive?'

'I telephoned the police station.'

'And did you go back upstairs again?'

'No. By the time I had finished talking to the police, Doctor Engelberg was knocking at the front door.' Frau Marcus gave the handkerchief another twist. 'I took him up to the mistress's bedroom. He held a mirror under the mistress's nose — and then he said, "*She's dead.*" I already knew . . . no one is ever that cold. But it was still terrible to hear those words. He touched the back of her neck and told me that he thought she'd been dead for hours.'

Rheinhardt produced his notebook and scribbled a few lines. 'Where do you live, Frau Marcus?'

'The twelfth district.'

'And how long have you been working for Fräulein Rosenkrantz?'

'Two years.'

'Who else works here?'

'Only the gardener.'

'Fräulein Rosenkrantz has no cook? No laundry maid?'

'She had no need for a cook. She dines at the Imperial or the Bristol. I take care . . . I *took* care of everything.'

'Yet you do not sleep here?'

'No.'

'There is plenty of room.'

'I stayed here when mistress was ill. In the summer she had a lump in her throat — and some other,' she blushed, '*ladies*' problems. She was confined to her bed for weeks.'

Rheinhardt looked into the housekeeper's bloodshot eyes and felt a stab of pity.

'When was the last time you saw Fräulein Rosenkrantz?'

'Yesterday afternoon. She said that I could go home early. She wanted to work on the new role.'

'What sort of mood was she in?'

Frau Marcus hesitated. 'Quite irritable — but no more than usual. Not really.'

'Was that how she was?'

'Irritable? Yes, but her moods didn't mean very much. She could be irritable one minute and brimming with good humour the next. I suppose it must have been something to do with her gift. They say that, don't they, that artists are temperamental?'

'Indeed.' Rheinhardt wrote the word *irritable* in his notebook and tapped his pencil on the page. 'Did you observe any changes in Fräulein Rosenkrantz's behaviour that, on reflection, you feel might have been tokens of inner torment?'

The housekeeper shook her head.

'No.'

'What about over the last week or month? Did you see her crying, for example?'

'No more than usual.' Rheinhardt motioned for her to continue. 'She was easily moved to tears. It didn't matter whether she was happy or sad. I can't say that I noticed a difference.'

'Did she ever speak to you about what was upsetting her?'

'She wasn't very happy at the opera house. She used to talk about going to Munich. There was bad feeling between the singers. And she said that the director was very demanding. She used to call him *the tyrant.*'

'Bad feeling? What do you mean by that?'

'I can't say exactly. But my mistress would say something about so-and-so being jealous or so-and-so having spread a malicious rumour. And she would become upset.'

'Did she mention anyone in particular?'

'I can't remember names, but it was usually a woman. One of the other singers.'

Rheinhardt continued tapping his pencil on the notebook.

'Do you know whether Fräulein Rosenkrantz intended to receive any guests after your departure yesterday?'

'I don't think she did. She wanted to work on her new role.'

Rheinhardt smiled: 'What was it, incidentally? This role that she was so keen to start working on?'

'I don't know very much about opera. But I think it was an Italian name. Was it Lucca or Lucia?'

'Lucia di Lammermoor.'

'Yes, that was it.'

Rheinhardt recalled the principal elements of Donizetti's epic romance.

A beautiful young woman: madness, tragedy.

He closed his eyes and the photographic image of Fräulein Rosenkrantz's body came into his mind. Once more, he was made uneasy by the way she occupied such a central position within the borders of the Persian rug.

When he opened his eyes again, Frau Marcus was looking at him expectantly.

'You are quite sure,' Rheinhardt said softly, 'that you did not attempt to move your mistress before Doctor Engelberg's arrival?'

'Quite sure,' said Frau Marcus.

2

THE PIANIST OF THE Café Imperial began playing Chopin's Waltz in B minor. Liebermann recognised it immediately, a curious, wistful melody which trickled down the keyboard over a brisk left-hand part, executed on this occasion with staccato lightness. At the point where the ear expected repose, the melody suddenly began again, creating a peculiar impression of autonomy, as if the music possessed a will of its own and was determined to continue. This rallying quality produced in Liebermann's mind a corresponding image of a dancing couple who — in spite of being exhausted — revolved, just one more time, only to find themselves caught up in a waltz without end.

'Maxim, did you hear what I said?'

Mendel Liebermann was looking at his son with an expression of censorious displeasure.

'No, father . . . I didn't.'

Mendel sighed.

'I said, isn't it time you thought about getting married?' Liebermann was stunned and blinked at his father in mute disbelief. The subject of marriage had been assiduously avoided after Liebermann had broken off his engagement with Clara Weiss, the daughter of one of Mendel's oldest associates. 'You know how I feel about what you did.' The old man touched his chest and grimaced as if he was suffering from indigestion. 'Even so.'

They had never really discussed the broken engagement and, in a sense, there was nothing to discuss. Mendel's sense of duty and rigid principles precluded any possibility of sympathetic understanding. When his wife had pleaded their son's case, Mendel had been perfectly capable of grasping her argument: Maxim and Clara were fundamentally incompatible and the marriage would be unhappy. But such considerations were wholly irrelevant once a man had given his word. A man must *always* keep his word.

'No, father,' said Liebermann. 'I haven't thought about getting married again. Not since . . .' He paused, and summoned the courage to say her name. 'Not since Clara.'

Mendel took a mouthful of *guglhupf* — a sponge slice, sprinkled with icing sugar. 'Do you want to get married?'

Liebermann held his father's gaze and his reply, when it came, was indignant. 'To the right person, yes.'

'And is there anyone . . .?' The sentence trailed off as Mendel's confidence ebbed away. He was not used to speaking intimately with his son and making such an inquiry felt awkward.

'No,' said Liebermann, doubly discomfited by his father's frankness and his own duplicity. There *was* someone for whom he had very deep feelings, but he was not inclined at that moment to reveal her identity. He was as confused as he had ever been concerning Amelia Lydgate and he knew that he would be incapable of giving a coherent account of his troubled fixation. Besides, she wasn't Jewish.

'You're a young man, Maxim,' said Mendel, 'but not *that* young. When I was your age—'

'Yes, I know,' Liebermann interjected. 'You were married and had already started a family.'

'Well, you don't want to end up like your Uncle Alexander, now, do you? An ageing roué?'

'Father, many years must pass before I can be reasonably described as *ageing* and I can assure you, whatever you may think, my general conduct is far from dissolute.'

'I was just voicing a concern, that's all.' Mendel took a sip of Pharisäer coffee and, picking up a starched napkin, wiped a residue of whipped cream from his moustache. 'What happened . . . with Clara. I don't think what you did was honourable.' He waved his hand in the air, as if simply recalling his son's misconduct had fouled the atmosphere. 'Nevertheless, you are my flesh and blood and the thought of you being *unfulfilled* gives me no joy.'

Why was the old man talking to him like this? Had he finally found it within himself to forgive?

'But I *am* happy,' said Liebermann. 'I have my work, my friends.'

'Yes, these things are associated with a kind of happiness,' said Mendel. 'But not *true* happiness, not the kind of happiness that comes from marriage and children. These experiences are essential. They are sacred.' Liebermann flinched at this last word. The movement was so pronounced that his father noticed. 'It isn't so foolish, Maxim, to believe that we have been put on this Earth for a purpose.'

There were many subjects that Liebermann preferred to avoid when conversing with his father and religion ranked highly among them. He was greatly relieved when Mendel's train of thought was interrupted by the arrival of Bruno, the waiter.

'Herr Liebermann, another pharisäer?'

'Yes, Bruno, and another schwarzer for my son.'

'Herr Doctor Liebermann, you have hardly touched your *Mohnstrudel*. I trust it is to your satisfaction?'

'Yes, Bruno,' said Liebermann. 'It's very good.'

The waiter bowed and dashed off, vanishing behind the open lid of the piano.

'You remember Blomberg?' said Mendel. 'You met him at my lodge.'

'Yes, of course.'

'He has a daughter. Twenty years old. Very pretty.'

Ah, thought Liebermann. *So this is what it's all about!*

Liebermann shook his head. 'Not yet, father. It really is too soon.'

Mendel acknowledged his son's request with a brusque nod, and finished his *guglhupf* in silence. The B minor waltz came to a close, and the pianist, responding to a smattering of applause, began a second Chopin waltz: the languid E flat major. Their conversation continued in a desultory fashion until Liebermann, observing the time, announced that he was expected at the hospital.

'You'd better hurry along, then,' said Mendel. Liebermann had the distinct impression that his father was relieved to see the back of him. Bruno arrived with Liebermann's coat and soon the young doctor was standing on the Ringstrasse waiting for a cab. The hazy fog had still not lifted and the air smelled damp and autumnal. A woman wearing a feathered hat passed by and he found himself staring at her retreating figure. The slimness of her waist and the curve of her hips held his attention; interest slowly transmuted into desire.

Marriage, thought Liebermann. *Maybe the old man has a point.*

A cab drew up and he stepped towards it, but another gentleman had hailed the vehicle while Liebermann had been distracted by the woman in the feathered hat. Liebermann watched as the carriage pulled away and set off towards the looming mass of the opera house, his brain teeming with thoughts and the nervous melody of Chopin's B minor waltz.

3

RHEINHARDT AND HIS ASSISTANT were smoking cigars in the corridor outside the morgue. A sawing sound emanated from within, above which Professor Mathias's fragile tenor was drifting aimlessly. Somewhere in the pathological institute a chiming clock announced that it was six o' clock. The day had been long and Rheinhardt had eaten nothing since breakfast.

'I think it would be permissible for us to stop for some refreshment on our way back to Schottenring, don't you?'

'There's a new beer cellar that's just opened on Türkenstrasse,' Haussmann replied. 'They serve some very spicy *Weizenbock*. Knauss, a friend of mine, went there last week. He said it was good.'

'I was really thinking of something more substantial, Haussmann, something requiring the use of implements, such as a knife and fork.'

'Oh, I see, sir.'

'Boiled beef, fried onions, and dumplings, followed by a thick slice of *topfenstrudel*.' As Rheinhardt envisaged the meal his stomach produced a plangent wail that evoked images of eternal torment. 'I beg your pardon,' he added, positioning a placatory hand on the corrugated distensions of his waistcoat.

'This place also serves food, sir,' said Haussmann. 'Simple but wholesome. That's what my friend said. I'm sure you'd be able to get some boiled beef and dumplings.'

'Very well, Haussmann,' said Rheinhardt, suddenly feeling weak and seeing no purpose in prolonging the debate. 'That is where we shall eat. Türkenstrasse.'

'Rheinhardt!' It was Professor Mathias. 'Rheinhardt, come in, will you? I've got something to show you.'

The two men re-entered the morgue, where they discovered Professor Mathias standing by a bench next to the autopsy table. He was looking down at something that glistened beneath the beam of an electric lamp. As Rheinhardt passed Fräulein Rosenkrantz's corpse he saw that she had undergone a hideous transformation. All the skin had been peeled away from her chest and it now hung down from either side of her body like the loose flaps of an unbuttoned coat. Her breasts were still attached to these flaps and they drooped, piteously, over the lip of the table. Rheinhardt's gaze lingered on the neatly packed organs of Fräulein Rosenkrantz's thoracic cavity and he found himself swaying a little, unbalanced by the macabre spectacle.

'Are you all right?' asked Professor Mathias.

'Yes, quite all right, thank you,' Rheinhardt replied, drawing on his cigar for comfort.

'It's just, I can't help noticing,' continued Mathias, 'that you've gone green. Hasn't he, young man?' Mathias turned to address Hausmann. 'Oh, I see that you have too, dear fellow. Would you like some schnapps? It's good for queasiness.' The old man produced a bottle from a shelf beneath the bench.

'A very kind gesture, Professor,' said Rheinhardt. 'But we are on duty and must decline your offer.'

'You have no objection if I—'

'Do as you please, professor.'

Mathias filled a shot glass, threw his head back, and downed the contents in one gulp.

'Ah, that's better!' said Mathias. 'I'm feeling the cold more than I used to. The schnapps helps. Now, where were we?' He put the glass down and indicated the object beneath the lamp. It was the forepart of Fräulein Rosenkrantz's ribcage. Rheinhardt noticed that the sternum and all the projecting struts of bone were coated with a fibrous silvery material. Mathias's eyes bulged behind his thick spectacles. 'You said that you weren't convinced Fräulein Rosenkrantz's death was accidental. What made you say that, Rheinhardt?'

'There was something about the way she was lying on the floor that looked rather odd to me. It was as if she'd been' — Rheinhardt searched for an accurate expression — 'tidied up.'

'How so?'

'She was positioned in the middle of a Persian rug and her arms were exactly parallel to its edges.'

'Interesting,' said Mathias. The old pathologist reached out and, taking one of the ribs between his thumb and forefinger, demonstrated that a section of bone, distal to the costal cartilage, could be moved freely in all directions within its fibrous sheath.

'It's broken?' said Rheinhardt.

'It most certainly is,' said Mathias, turning to face the autopsy table. 'Now, take a look at these lungs. Enormous, aren't they? The secret of her success, I expect. I saw her in *The Flying Dutchman* last year: extraordinary power. You wouldn't have believed that a small woman could produce such a noise. Her voice soared above the orchestra.' The professor, inspired by this reminiscence, attempted to recreate the effect by singing in a wavering falsetto that cracked almost immediately and became a hacking cough. 'I'm sorry,' said Mathias, resting his hands on the side of the autopsy table. 'My asthma. It gets bad at this time of year.'

'You were about to show me something, Professor?'

'Fräulein Rosenkrantz is supposed to have ingested a deadly quantity of laudanum — is that correct?'

'Yes.'

'Yet there is no inflammation of the lungs and her pupils are only slightly contracted.' Mathias lifted one of the woman's eyelids, revealing a striking emerald iris with a distinct circle of darkness at its centre. 'She most certainly drank laudanum, but I'm not altogether sure that she imbibed enough to kill her.'

'There were many empty phials by her bed.'

'Which signifies nothing, Rheinhardt,' said the professor, dismissively. Then he placed a finger on the spongy exterior of the dead woman's left lung. 'What do you see here?'

'It's a different colour from the rest.'

'The distinctive cherry-purple of a contusion, corresponding with the break I showed you on the eighth rib. If Fräulein Rosenkrantz had had an accident before retiring, she would have experienced considerable discomfort. Of course, it's always possible that she sustained the injury, went to bed, and decided to treat herself with laudanum — although that would be most irregular. The pain and respiratory difficulties associated with a broken rib would almost certainly have caused Fräulein Rosenkrantz to call her physician with all possible haste.'

'But if Fräulein Rosenkrantz was disorientated she might have injured herself before losing consciousness.'

'In my opinion, it is quite difficult to break a rib by merely stumbling around a lady's bedroom.'

Rheinhardt stubbed his cigar out in a glass dish and exhaled a final cloud of smoke.

'In which case, how do you think the rib came to be broken?'

'It's only a theory, of course . . .'

'Nevertheless, I would like to hear it.'

'I strongly suspect that the rib was broken when someone applied pressure to her chest.'

'I beg your pardon, Professor?'

'Her lungs wouldn't have been able to expand and she would have suffocated. She might still have been conscious when it happened — or at least partially conscious. She wouldn't even have been able to scream. No air, you see.' Mathias stroked the dead woman's face and adopted a tender expression. 'She would have been helpless.'

'Forgive me, Professor, but are you suggesting that Fräulein Rosenkrantz was crushed?'

'In a manner of speaking — yes.'

4

'YOUNG MAN — YOU ARE occupying my seat.'

Liebermann looked up and discovered that he was being addressed by a frail old woman with rheumy, colourless eyes. Her face was deeply lined and her thinning hair had been lacquered and curled into a cobwebby mass through which the glass facets of the chandelier behind her were visible. She was leaning on a walking stick with a carved ivory handle, though her principal means of support was the arm of a pretty woman in a blue dress, whose flushing cheeks proclaimed her profound embarrassment.

'Great-aunt!' said the woman, the tone of her voice combining admonishment with desperation.

The dowager turned the whole of her body in order to look at her anguished relative. 'Whatever is the matter with you, Anna?'

'I'm sorry,' said the woman in the blue dress, smiling at Liebermann.

'What are you apologising for?' asked the old woman.

'This gentleman is in the correct seat, I am sure,' her great-niece replied. 'Besides, it hardly matters — we'll be able to see the stage wherever we sit.'

Liebermann stood up.

'May I see your tickets?'

The young doctor inspected the numbers and said, 'You are seated next to me — these two here — but I am perfectly happy to move along.'

'That is very kind, but—'

'No, I insist,' said Liebermann. Before the old woman sat down she stared up at him and squinted. She had very distinctive features. A thin mouth, hooked nose, and pointed chin. It was unlikely that she had ever been beautiful, quite the contrary, but once she must have been very arresting. She exuded a dry floral fragrance, like scented talcum powder. 'Allow me,' said Liebermann, taking her walking stick and offering her his arm. The dowager took it and he performed the necessary actions to get her comfortably seated in her preferred chair.

'Thank you,' said the woman in the blue dress.

Liebermann bowed. 'Doctor Max Liebermann.'

'Anna Probst — and this is my great-aunt Frau Baerbel Zollinger.'

Liebermann bowed again. 'Frau Zollinger.'

The old woman's expression did not soften. Anna rolled her eyes, and Liebermann, recognising that he could do no more to win Frau Zollinger's good opinion, returned his attention to the programme notes.

In due course the auditorium filled with patrons, the house lights dimmed, and the musicians appeared on stage. After some preliminary tuning, the conductor, who was wearing a white carnation in his lapel, entered through a door to the right of the stage and mounted the platform. When the applause had subsided he raised a very large baton and the air resonated with sublime harmonies.

The first piece was Mozart's B flat major Serenade for twelve wind instruments and double bass. Liebermann was particularly fond of the Adagio, the immaculate melodies of which floated smoothly above a pulsing accompaniment. It was music of supreme elegance. The second piece was also a Serenade, scored for a smaller wind band, by Johann Christian Brosius, a composer with whom Liebermann was completely unacquainted. The two pieces had evidently been programmed together because Brosius had incorporated several themes from

Mozart's B flat major Serenade into his own composition. When the final movement, a charming presto assai, came to its end, Liebermann clapped loudly. In due course the conductor signalled his intention to leave the stage, the applause subsided and the audience began to disperse for the interval.

'So, Herr doctor, it seems that you enjoyed the Brosius.'

Frau Zollinger was looking at Liebermann intently.

'Great-aunt . . .' said Anna, eager to prevent further embarrassment.

'Yes,' said Liebermann. 'I enjoyed it very much.'

'Over forty years,' said Frau Zollinger. 'Over forty years since I last heard that piece . . .'

'I must confess that prior to this evening I knew nothing of Brosius. Not a single note.'

'Oh, he had quite a reputation in his day. Brahms held him in very high regard.'

'Did he?'

'Well, that's what he said. But I was never convinced of his sincerity. He was a difficult man, Brosius: sullen, brooding, and prone to angry outbursts.'

Liebermann looked more closely at the old woman.

'You were acquainted with Brahms?'

'Yes. I couldn't stand the smell of his cigars.'

'Great-aunt,' said Anna, 'it is the interval. Doctor Liebermann does not want to hear about Brahms's cigars.'

Liebermann indicated with a gesture that he did not object to being delayed and invited Frau Zollinger to continue.

'He used to come to my soirées,' she declared.

'Brahms?'

'Yes. And Brosius. Once they came together. Of course, the real talent was his pupil . . .' Liebermann wasn't sure whether Frau Zollinger was referring to a pupil of Brahms or a pupil of Brosius.

He waited patiently. 'Brosius was technically accomplished, but young Freimark . . .' The old woman sighed. 'His songs . . . so clever, such careful attention to the meaning of the words. None of them were published, except "Hope". You must know "Hope"? His setting of Schiller's "Hope"?'

Liebermann was aware of a well-known song of that name and even thought he might have it at home in a volume titled *Klassiker des deutschen Liedes.*

'Yes,' said Liebermann. 'I believe I do know it.'

'A tragedy that he should have died so young. And even more of a tragedy that he should be remembered now for just one song.'

'Tuberculosis?'

'No. A fall — from a mountain — the Schneeberg: while staying with Brosius and Brosius's wife, Angelika.' Frau Zollinger shook her head. 'I never really liked her.'

Anna placed a restraining hand on her great-aunt's arm and asked, 'Where do you practise, Herr doctor?'

'The general hospital.'

She was about to say something else but Frau Zollinger carried on: 'The youngest daughter of a well-known portrait painter. She was a celebrated beauty. Brosius worshipped her. But I thought her vain and superficial. My husband used to reprimand me for being uncharitable.'

The old woman gabbled on a little more until her recollections lost coherence and eventually petered out. Seizing his moment, Liebermann excused himself and went to the foyer to smoke a Trabuco cigar. When he returned, Frau Zollinger was less talkative and he spoke instead to Fräulein Anna. It was not a very deep conversation, merely an exchange of pleasantries and some polite enquiries.

The second half of the concert was a delight: Beethoven's E flat major Octet and a Mozart *Divertimento.*

After the encore, an arrangement of a Brahms waltz, Liebermann helped Frau Zollinger to stand and offered to escort her from the building. Progress was slow and by the time they reached the cloakroom there was no queue, most of the audience having already gone. In the foyer Liebermann said, 'It will be cold outside. Perhaps too cold for Frau Zollinger? Wait here and I'll hail a cab for you.'

'You are most kind,' said Anna.

'Where are you going?' asked Liebermann.

'The ninth district, Bergasse 21,' Anna replied.

'Bergasse 21 — really?' He looked to Frau Zolliger. 'Do you know your neighbour Professor Freud?'

'Professor who?' asked Frau Zollinger.

'Freud: an esteemed colleague.'

The old woman's head wobbled a little on her scrawny neck to express the negative.

Liebermann crossed the foyer and went out through the double doors.

One of Mozart's melodies entered his mind, the exquisite opening theme from the *Adagio*, but not in its original form. Instead, he was hearing Brosius's arrangement. The melody was being carried by a flute instead of an oboe and the continuous pulsing accompaniment had been replaced by dissolving harmonies. It was actually quite haunting and as the fragment repeated itself Liebermann realised that Brosius's music had become lodged in his brain. He would probably still be hearing it in his head as he tried to get to sleep later.

A cab came rattling over the cobbles. Liebermann raised his hand and the driver pulled up.

As Liebermann was helping Frau Zollinger down some stairs, she muttered: 'He said to me — "*She's my muse*"'

'I beg your pardon?' asked Liebermann.

'Angelika. He said that without her the music would end.'

'Brosius? Well, he must have loved her very much.'

Frau Zollinger produced a dismissive grunt. It was obvious to Liebermann that she was not really talking to him but simply voicing her thoughts, recalling conversations that had taken place in the distant past. The music had revived old memories.

Liebermann opened one of the cab's doors and the old woman shivered as the chill air insinuated itself into her brittle bones.

'Your transport, Frau Zollinger.'

The old woman did not thank him and once again her great-niece was forced to apologise on her behalf.

5

Mayor Lueger was seated on a large leather armchair. His two
guests, Leopold Steiner and Hermann Bielohlawek, were also comfortably accommodated, and all three were smoking cigars of prodigious
length while quaffing pilsner. The remains of a ravaged *apfelstrudel*
were strewn across a silver serving plate on the table.

It had been rumoured for some time that the mayor was not well,
yet he showed no obvious signs of sickness or infirmity: quite the
contrary, in fact. He appeared robust and his cheeks were glowing.
In the ancient world he might have made a very acceptable philoso-
pher king. His thick dark hair was brushed back off a high forehead
and his full grey beard was cut squarely around the jaw. Women still
referred to him as 'handsome Karl' in spite of his age. He cultivated
a dashing and debonair image with assiduous care. The pomade on
his hair glistened and exuded a citrus fragrance that cut through the
pungency of the tobacco smoke. His clothes were bespangled with a
treasure trove of decorative accessories: an emerald tiepin, the thick
gold links of a watch-chain and large ruby cufflinks.

Lueger's eyes possessed the penetrating quality often associated
with greatness, but his gaze was not as stately nor as grave as it might
have been, on account of a slight flaw. One of his eyes was turned out
a little, giving the impression that many of his remarks were intended
to be ironic.

'It is not a matter of choice,' said Lueger. 'I *must* win the municipal council over. The construction of the second mountain-spring reservoir is of vital importance for the city. Moreover, if I succeed, I strongly suspect that it will stand as my greatest achievement in office.'

'What about getting rid of the English Gas Company?' said Steiner. 'That was a fine achievement and gave me inestimable satisfaction.'

'Or the electrification of the trams?' ventured Bielohlawek.

'And one cannot underestimate the importance of all the new schools,' said Steiner.

'Or the city brewery!' said Bielohlawek, raising his stein. 'A truly outstanding achievement!'

The mayor smiled indulgently at his friends who he suspected were, perhaps, a little drunk. They had been drinking for some time.

'The existing water supply is wholly inadequate,' Lueger persisted. 'It not only fails to meet the basic human need but it is also insufficient to do justice to the beauty of our city. Think of our magnificent fountains. Tell me, how often do you see them working?'

'I passed the Donnerbrunnen earlier today, as it happens,' said Steiner.

'Well?'

'Dry as a bone.'

'There you are!' said Lueger, satisfied. 'And when our fountains *do* produce water, they are singularly unimpressive. They spout so weakly that their ineffectual trickling makes the Männeken Pis in Brussels look like a cataract.'

'I thought the Männeken Pis was in Geraardbergen,' said Bielohlawek.

'That's a different one,' said Lueger.

'There are two?'

'Yes.'

'I didn't know that.'

Mayor Lueger paused to sip his pilsner. 'The council don't want to pay. I am ready to admit that the owner of the spring is asking a very high price. Even so, I will remind those dullards of the Roman king who sought to purchase nine books from the Sybil. He complained that she was asking too much and she responded by throwing three in the fire, before demanding the original sum for the remaining six books. When the king refused her, she threw another three books into the flames. The outcome was that the Roman king was forced to pay the original sum for only three books. I tell you' — the mayor leaned forward — 'if we don't accept the owner's terms of sale today then we will be creating problems for ourselves in the future. You mark my words. We will end up in a worse position than the Roman king.'

There was a knock on the door and a stocky bodyguard entered. He was dressed in the green 'court' uniform sported by the mayor's inner circle: a green tailcoat with black velvet cuffs and yellow coat-of-arms buttons. He was carrying a tray loaded with yet more pilsners.

'Ah, Anton,' said Lueger. 'Most thoughtful.'

The bodyguard collected the empty steins and replaced them with full ones before bowing and making his exit.

'A good man, eh?' said the mayor.

His companions drank to the bodyguard's health.

Steiner wiped the froth from his upper lip with the back of his hand and said: 'Oh, before I forgot, Karl, I think you should know that I've received another one of those ever-so-discreet communications from the palace.'

'About your comments?'

'Yes.'

'Who was it from?'

'One of the emperor's aides, Count Lefler. He asked me to consider whether my attack on the vivisection practices at the anatomical institutes was really wise.'

'Did he now,' said Lueger, adjusting his necktie.

'It was worded politely enough but it was clearly meant as a warning. He said that certain members of the medical faculty were deeply offended. You can guess who, of course.'

'Perhaps they're not so stupid after all,' said the mayor. 'Perhaps they can see where this is going?'

'Gentleman,' said Bielohlawek, 'I am a simple merchant, an honest trader. I am afraid that you will have to explain.'

'My dear fellow,' said the mayor, 'it's all very simple. If we can arouse a little public feeling, a little antipathy, then the hospitals will have to accept stricter controls. In due course, if we have more say in hospital affairs, we will be able to address the *other* problem. That is to say, the *principal* problem.'

'Oh, I see,' said Bielohlawek. '*Them.*'

'How did this happen, I wonder?' said the mayor.

Steiner became agitated. 'The Jewish doctors tell the Jewish bankers, and the Jewish bankers tell the emperor's mistress!'

'Now, now, Leo,' said Lueger, holding up a finger in mock admonition. 'I can't have you saying anything too disrespectful about the money-Jews. It was Rothenstein, remember, who allowed us to use all his land, at no cost, for the reservoir.' The mayor's errant eye did unstinting service for the cause of irony. 'You will recall, I hope, my fulsome praise last year: one of the best and a true citizen.'

'Rothenstein,' said Steiner. 'As if he couldn't damn well afford it!'

The company fell silent until the mayor spoke again — more softly this time, and more serious in tone. 'The emperor has the empire. But Vienna is mine. When will the palace realise this?'

6

'DEATH AND THE MAIDEN?' said Rheinhardt.

Liebermann flicked through the pages of the songbook until he found Schubert's early masterpiece, which occupied only a single page and looked easy to play. He saw octaves, minims and quavers, nothing that a beginner couldn't tackle. Yet he knew that this simplicity was deceptive. He understood that this sparse notation had much in common with the exposed beams and empty sashes of a derelict house. There was enough space and silence here to permit the uncanny to make its presence felt. He glanced at the two beat rests and felt a thrill of anticipatory dread. The little black rectangles were like coffins: the bar lines like shelves in a vault.

The young doctor depressed both the *sostenuto* and soft pedals of the Bösendorfer and placed his fingers over the keys. He relaxed and allowed the force of gravity to draw his hands down. Solemn harmonies became something like a funeral march, composed with such subtle genius that its measured tread also sounded a little like a *berceuse*, a fateful lullaby.

Rheinhardt began the maiden's plea on an anacrusis, and the piano accompaniment immediately became agitated.

Vorüber! Ach, vorüber!
Geh, wilder Knochenmann!

Away! Ah, away!
Away, fierce man of bones!

Rheinhardt leaned against the piano, as if weakened by the approach of the grim reaper.

Ich bin noch jung, geh Lieber!
Und rühre mich nicht an.

I am still young, please go!
And do not touch me.

His voice trailed off and the four chords that followed invited the listener to step into the damp hollow of an open grave. The subsequent fermata was chilling.

When Rheinhardt sang again, he did so in the person of Death.

Gib deine Hand, du schön und zart Gebild!
Bin Freund, und komme nicht, zu strafen.

Give me your hand, you lovely, tender creature!
I am a friend, and do not come to punish.

It was barely a melody — a chant on a single note.

Sie gutes Muts! Ich bin nicht wild,
Sollst sanft in meinen Armen schlafen!

Be not afraid! I am not fierce,
You shall sleep softly in my arms.

The final bars were peaceful, the funeral march, transposed into a major key, progressing inexorably to the second fermata and eternal rest.

After a respectful hiatus, Liebermann said, 'I have heard it a thousand times but it still never fails to touch me. The maiden, begging for her life, and Death, like a lover, taking her in his cold embrace.'

'Yes,' Rheinhardt agreed. 'And it is peculiarly epic, don't you think, for a song of such brevity?'

'Indeed,' Liebermann replied. 'A metaphysical opera condensed into forty-three bars.'

He closed the piano lid and the two men retired to the smoking room, where they took their customary places in front of the fire. Liebermann poured the brandy and they lit cigars. In due course, Rheinhardt produced an envelope and passed it across the cube-shaped table that separated the two armchairs. Liebermann opened the seal and withdrew a set of photographs.

'Good God!' he exclaimed, 'That's—'

'Ida Rosenkrantz,' Rheinhardt interjected.

'She's dead?'

'Yes. It'll be in the newspapers tomorrow. Because she's a singer at the court opera we were obliged to inform His Majesty before notifying the press. Unfortunately, the lord chamberlain experienced considerable difficulty locating him. Our emperor had gone hunting.' Rheinhardt paused before adding, 'In Hungary.'

'What a tragedy,' said Liebermann, shaking his head. 'She had such a fine voice.' He looked again at the first image and his expression communicated both bewilderment and horror.

Rheinhardt described his arrival in Hietzing, the discovery of the dead singer, and summarised the particulars of his interviews with Doctor Engelberg and the housekeeper, Frau Marcus.

'Engelberg was confident that Rosenkrantz's death was accidental.

He expressed a modest qualification with respect to suicide, on account of the singer having seen a psychiatrist last year for a throat condition called *globus hystericus*; however, she did not suffer from suicidal melancholia and the laudanum was only prescribed to help her sleep. Be that as it may, I found myself disinclined to accept his opinion. There was something about the position of the body that wasn't quite right. You see?' Rheinhardt gestured at the photograph Liebermann was studying. 'The way she's lying there, in the middle of the rug and with her arms by her sides. Engelberg insisted that there was nothing irregular about it, but I wasn't so sure.' Rheinhardt paused to draw on his cigar. 'Professor Mathias conducted the autopsy and his findings confirmed that I had good reason to feel uneasy. Rosenkrantz had imbibed a significant quantity of laudanum, but not enough to cause her death. She also had a broken rib.'

'Which one was it?'

'The eighth, on the left side of the ribcage.' Rheinhardt exhaled and watched the smoke from his cigar ascend and disperse. 'There was no evidence to suggest that a struggle had taken place: no marks on her body, no rips in her garments, and no smashed items on the floor of her bedroom.'

'Fräulein Rosenkrantz wouldn't have retired for the evening with a broken rib. She would have called a doctor.'

Rheinhardt nodded. 'I asked Professor Mathias if the injury could have been caused by a fall, but he didn't think so. You see, the rib was completely broken, snapped in two.'

'And apart from this broken rib?'

'Nothing.'

'No other symptoms of pathology?'

'None at all.'

Rheinhardt waited to see if Liebermann would reach the same conclusion as Professor Mathias. The young doctor lit a second cigar, played a five-finger exercise on his knee, and after a lengthy pause said: 'Then the cause of death was compressive asphyxia and the rib was broken unintentionally.'

'Bravo, Max,' said Rheinhardt, raising his glass.

'The perpetrator,' Liebermann continued, 'discovered Fräulein Rosenkrantz either unconscious or very close to the point of losing consciousness. He or she then applied pressure to her chest to ensure that her lungs would not expand.'

'And how do you think that was achieved?'

'Fräulein Rosenkrantz was a small woman. A strong man might simply have pushed down on her chest.' Leibermann stretched out his fingers to demonstrate. 'However, compressive asphyxia would probably have been achieved more effectively — and with greater efficiency — if the perpetrator had simply sat on her.' Liebermann paused, his flow halted by an intrusive image of the opera singer, drugged and laid out on the floor, defenceless. He hoped that she had lost consciousness completely when death finally arrived to take her. 'Unlike strangulation,' Liebermann continued, 'suffocation leaves no tissue damage detectable at autopsy. The perpetrator's expectation was that attention would focus exclusively on the empty bottles of laudanum and that, eventually, a verdict of accidental death or suicide would be delivered. In the absence of any alternative explanation for Fräulein Rosenkrantz's death, this would indeed have been the most probable outcome. Most pathologists would reasonably presume that respiratory failure was in some way connected with the laudanum, even if the common signs associated with an overdose were absent.'

The two men stared into the flickering fire. Liebermann found that he could still hear the introductory bars of *Death and the Maiden*. He was listening to a vivid auditory hallucination and the sombre chords provided a fitting accompaniment to his thoughts. This inner music fell suddenly silent when Rheinhardt asked, 'Can we deduce anything of the perpetrator's appearance from Fräulein Rosenkrantz's injury? His weight and size, for example?'

'I'm afraid not. The eighth rib is not particularly strong. It would be as likely to break under the weight of a small woman as a large man.'

'The method itself is of some significance, surely.'

'One must suppose that the perpetrator had made a thorough survey of the options available to a would-be murderer. Compressive asphyxia would not be the first choice of an uninformed party.'

'Then the murder might not have been opportunistic, as you at first suggested, but planned.'

'Indeed, that is also possible. He or she could have forced the singer to drink laudanum at gunpoint, prior to suffocation.'

Liebermann worked his way through the photographs and returned to the initial image, a full-length view of the opera singer lying within the fringed rectangle of a Persian rug.

'What manner of individual,' Rheinhardt said, 'would leave a room in which they had just committed murder, neglecting to address such an obvious cause for suspicion?'

'Someone in a hurry. Or an obsessive,' Liebermann replied. 'Someone whose fastidious character might find expression in the habitual lining-up of objects: a person — most likely male — who favours well-cut clothes and is prone to pedantic speech; an orderly man of above average intelligence who is careful with money and may own a collection of some kind — a numismatist or philatelist.' Rheinhardt raised an eyebrow at the specificity of his friend's description. 'I am simply listing the features of a certain neurotic *type*,' said Liebermann testily. 'You did invite me to speculate!'

Rheinhardt inclined his head, acknowledging his friend's rebuke. 'Quite so,' he said.

Liebermann extracted a head-and-shoulders portrait of Fräulein

Rosenkrantz from the pile of photographs. The camera had exposed a wealth of detail — the curvature of her long eyelashes and the dimples on her cheeks. Her mouth, pouting even in death, suggested a fragile sensuality, the awkward, self-conscious charm of an ingénue.

'I spent much of today,' Rheinhardt continued, 'perusing Fräulein Rosenkrantz's address book. It contains many names: musicians, bankers, actors, even a Hungarian prince. Some of them might be able to help us with our inquiries. But tomorrow I intend to begin at the opera house. I have an appointment with the director.'

Liebermann sat up in his chair.

'What? You are seeing Director Mahler tomorrow?'

'I am indeed.' Rheinhardt was aware of how much the young doctor venerated the director of the court opera. Such was his devotion to the director's music that he had travelled to Munich for the premiere of Mahler's Fourth Symphony. 'You are welcome to come along with me, if you want, but I had supposed you would be working.'

'Mahler.' Liebermann repeated the name with soft reverence. He stubbed out his cigar and asked, 'What time are you expected?'

'Eleven o' clock.'

'I'll be there.'

'But what about your patients?'

'They . . .' Liebermann's expression became pained. 'They are just as likely to benefit from a consultation later in the day.'

'You won't get into trouble?'

'No,' said Liebermann, extending the syllable expansively but failing to sound very convincing.

'Very well, then,' said Rheinhardt. 'Let's meet at Café Schwarzenburg. Ten-thirty.'

7

Franz-Josef — Emperor of Austria, Apostolic King of Hungary, King of Jerusalem, King of Bohemia, King of Dalmatia, King of Transylvania, King of Croatia and Slovenia, King of Galicia and Illyria, Grand Duke of Tuscany and Cracow, Margrave of Moravia, Duke of Salzburg, Duke of Bukovina, Duke of Modena, Parma and Piacenza and Guastalla, Princely Count of Habsburg and Tyrol, Prince of Trient and Brixen, Count of Hohenembs, Grand Voyvoce of Serbia and Duke of Auschwitz — woke from a nightmare. It had taken the form of a hellish vision: mobs in the street, gunfire, and improvised incendiary weapons spilling fire across the cobblestones outside the palace. Field Marshal Radetzky, in reality dead for over half a century, had burst into the chancellery wing. *All is lost*, he had cried. *It is over. Undone.* These lamentations had been appropriated from a play that the emperor had attended at the court theatre only the previous evening. In the strange permissive world of dreams there was nothing contradictory about Radetzky quoting a line from a tragedy written decades after his own death. Similarly, the emperor had not troubled to question why a large orchestra had been playing a Strauss waltz while Vienna burned.

The awful vision had left him with a sense of foreboding, a portentous dread that sent shivers of unease down his spine.

It was still dark.

After reaching out for some matches, the emperor lit a candle. The clock face showed that it was three-thirty. Franz-Josef doubted that he would be able to get to sleep again. And anyway, there was little to be gained by trying because he rose every morning, without fail, at four, and was never at his desk later than five. It was a custom that he broke with only under exceptional circumstances, and nightmares could no longer be classified as exceptional.

Throwing the eiderdown off, he swung his legs out of bed and his feet made contact with the cold parquet. The bed itself was low and made of iron, a simple truckle bed and an absurdly modest piece of furniture in so large a room. Taking a deep breath, the emperor stood up and pulled the bell cord.

Within moments, a team of servants arrived carrying a rubber bath, which was subsequently filled with lukewarm water. The emperor was relieved of his nightshirt and one of the retainers, an ancient gentleman with a pronounced tremor, remained to perform such essential functions as passing the soap and scrubbing the emperor's back. When His Majesty's ablutions were finished, Ketterl, the *valet de chambre*, emerged silently from the shadows, ready to dress Franz-Josef, as he did every morning, in a military uniform. As soon as the emperor was fully accoutred, Ketterl withdrew, walking backwards through the double doors, leaving his monarch alone to say his prayers.

Franz-Josef knelt, made the sign of the cross, joined his hands, and prayed for the late Empress Elisabeth, his immediate family, his 'friend' — the actress Katharina Schratt — his ministers, and the peoples of his vast empire, united, by a miracle as magnificent as the transubstantiation of the eucharist, in the flesh of his own person.

Rising from his prayer stool, he expanded his chest and, defying the aches and pains of age, marched with a spring in his step to the study. Sitting at his desk, he lit an oil lamp and paused to consider the oval portrait of the late empress. Electric lighting gave him headaches.

The emperor's study was hung with red silk damask decorated with a stylised pineapple motif, and the ceiling was embellished with raised gold tracery. For a royal and imperial apartment, however, the room was unimposing. The rosewood and walnut furniture, sober and practical, might have graced the home of a successful businessman.

There was a knock on the door.

'Come in, Ketterl.'

The *valet de chambre* entered, carrying a tray of coffee, rolls and butter.

'Your Majesty.'

'Thank you.'

Ketterl placed the tray on the emperor's desk, bowed, and backed away through the doors which were shut by unseen hands as soon as he was beyond the threshold. The emperor ate his simple breakfast and watched the sky brighten as he smoked a trabuco.

Resting on a chair adjacent to his desk was a large leather portfolio. He opened it up and took out a wad of documents requiring his signature. Getting through them all would take several hours and like the punishment of Sisyphus his labours were never concluded. Every morning the contents of the portfolio were refreshed. Yet Emperor Franz-Josef refused to deputise. This work was his sacred duty, solemnly performed in his capacity as the *first official* (his wife had mischievously called him the *first bureaucrat*) of the empire. Even so, after only a short period of time the monotony of the work caused his concentration to falter. An image from the nightmare came back to him: fire, broken glass, angry voices.

The emperor circled his fingertips against his temples.

So many peoples, united by my person — as ordained by God . . .

He was a devout man. But over the course of the last fourteen years fate had dealt him blows that might have tested the faith of any saint.

It could all unravel, so very easily.

No, one can no longer trust in divine ordinance alone . . .

The emperor put his pen down, lit another trabuco and, looking out of the window, allowed the violet lucidity of the dawn to cleanse his mind.

8

RHEINHARDT AND LIEBERMANN WERE greeted at the opera house by a severe-looking gentleman with large protruding ears and an impressive moustache.

'Alois Przistaupinsky,' said the man, lowering his head but maintaining eye contact. 'Secretary to Director Mahler. You must be Inspector Rheinhardt?'

'I am indeed,' said the detective. 'And this is my colleague Herr Doctor Max Liebermann.'

Przistaupinsky smiled briefly and said, 'Gentlemen: welcome to the court opera. The director will receive you in his private office. This way, please.'

Their route was complicated and passed through a maze of corridors reverberating with the repetitive beat of hammer blows. The air carried the fragrance of sawdust. At one point they had to make room for three men in overalls carrying what appeared to be a large scaly wing. The secretary took this opportunity to inform them that he was employing a short cut and that they would shortly be arriving at their destination. They subsequently ascended two flights of stairs, whereupon Przistaupinsky halted, adjusted his necktie, and declared, 'You may find the director a little aggravated this morning. Unfortunately, a *situation* has arisen.'

'A situation?' repeated Rheinhardt.

'Yes,' said the secretary, evidently reluctant to elaborate.

Przistaupinsky invited them to ascend a third flight of stairs and, as they neared the top, a curious breathy susurration became clearer, acquiring the limping rhythms of someone weeping.

'Oh, for God's sake!' The wiry figure of Director Mahler came into view. He was standing next to a half-open door, addressing a stout younger man whose plump boyish cheeks were wet and shiny. 'You *must* sing. I absolutely insist!' The director stamped his foot and repeated, 'I absolutely insist!'

As Liebermann approached, he recognised the recipient of the director's wrath. It was the famous tenor Erik Schmedes.

'I can't,' Schmedes replied. 'I am not well enough!'

He emphasised his infirmity by coughing and resting a hand on the wall for support.

'You *have* to sing!' Mahler commanded. 'And if you don't . . .' The director raised a finger as if he were about to draw down retributive lightning from the heavens.

'But it is out of the question,' sobbed Schmedes. 'I am simply incapable of performing. Have mercy on me, Herr Director! I am ill.'

Przistaupinsky moved forward, 'Herr Director?' Mahler acknowledged his secretary, but his expression was blank and distracted. 'Detective Inspector Rheinhardt,' Przistaupinsky pressed, 'and his colleague Doctor Max Liebermann. From the *security office*.' He pronounced the final words with particular emphasis, to ensure that they registered.

The director blinked, sighed and focused on the new arrivals.

'Good morning, gentlemen. You will, I trust, make allowances for my discourteous behaviour. Unfortunately, I have something of a crisis on my hands.' He looked back at the lachrymose tenor. 'Schmedes. Wait here. Przistaupinsky, you wait with him, and make sure he doesn't go anywhere!' The director opened the door wider and made a sweeping gesture with his hand. 'Please, Inspector, Herr Doctor, do come in.'

Rheinhardt and Liebermann both stole glances at the unfortunate Schmedes as they crossed the threshold. The singer was still pressing the wall with his palm and breathing heavily. He looked pitiful.

It was widely rumoured that Mahler ruled the opera house with an iron fist. Indeed, his detractors accused him of bullying. Liebermann had always questioned the accuracy of such reports, believing them to be either exaggerations or malicious gossip. He found it difficult to believe that someone capable of composing the heavenly alto solo from the Second Symphony could possibly be dictatorial or brutish. But now, looking at Schmedes, wretched and broken, he wasn't so sure.

The director's office was large and illuminated by a soft grey light that filtered through high windows. An upright piano stood against one wall, piled high with musical scores.

'Please,' said Mahler. 'Do sit down.'

He offered Liebermann and Rheinhardt two chairs in front of his desk and sat on his own somewhat larger chair behind it.

Gustav Mahler was a small man, but his large head and strong features compensated for his diminutive stature. His long sloping forehead and oval spectacles gave him the appearance of an intellectual. Yet his face had none of the analytic frigidity of a habitual thinker. It was softened by a mane of dark hair, brushed backwards in the style of a romantic poet. Liebermann saw something of his own face reflected in the director's, a certain physiognomic correspondence, a shared intensity of expression. Unusually, both he and the director were clean-shaven.

'I could not believe it when I heard she was dead,' said Mahler, toying with a pen for a moment before casting it aside. 'Ida Rosenkrantz was a rare talent. Her voice was praised by the critics for its power, but she was also capable of performances of great subtlety. The softness of her attack was unique, the way she shaped every note, allowing each pitch to grow into existence, to blossom. Her use of legato was always well judged, and in pianissimo passages her control was second to none. It will be impossible to find another singer to take her place. No one else could do justice to such a wide variety of roles: *Louise, Senta, Violetta* — she could sing them all. Her loss will be felt keenly, not only here in Vienna but wherever great music is loved and appreciated.'

'Were you well acquainted with Fräulein Rosenkrantz?' asked Rheinhardt. 'Were you close?'

The director paused and brought his fingers together, the tips forming the apex of a steeple.

'Inspector, I do not think I am in possession of any facts that will clarify the principal point of issue, which, as I understand it from my reading of the newspapers, relates to whether poor Ida committed suicide or died through mischance. You understand, I trust, that our relationship was strictly professional. We did not socialise. Be that as it may, I can promise you my full cooperation. I am very happy to grant you access to all areas of the opera house and to answer, within reason, any questions you may wish to ask me. However,' Mahler grimaced, 'I cannot give you my full cooperation today. Unforeseen circumstances have created a crisis that requires my immediate attention. If the crisis is not resolved, then this evening's production of *Rienzi* will have to be cancelled and we are expecting the German ambassador to attend. And if the ambassador is disappointed . . .' His sentence trailed off and he produced a nervous little shudder. 'Would you be willing, inspector, to postpone this interview? Could we meet again — tomorrow morning, perhaps? I would consider myself indebted.'

'May I inquire as to the nature of this crisis?' asked Rheinhardt.

The director's foot began to tap on the floor. An irregular burst of rhythms that he terminated with a single loud stamp.

'Really, Inspector, the detail need not concern you.'

'With respect,' Rheinhardt responded, 'I would appreciate an explanation.'

'Very well.' Mahler glanced up at the wall clock. 'But I must be brief.' He pointed towards the door. 'The unhappy gentleman waiting outside is Erik Schmedes.'

'We had the pleasure,' Rheinhardt indicated he was referring to both himself and his companion, 'of seeing Herr Schmedes sing *Tristan* earlier this year under your direction. It was an exceptional performance. The love duet was a revelation.'

'Thank you,' said Mahler. 'And Schmedes is a very great tenor. Indeed, I had chosen him to sing the title role in tonight's new production of *Rienzi*. Hermann Winkelmann was to sing the role tomorrow night.' Liebermann noticed that the director had a small defect of speech: he could not *roll* the letter 'r' correctly. 'As you know, court opera singers attract fanatical devotees, and my choice of Schmedes to sing *Rienzi* in tonight's performance angered the *Hermann-Bündler* — the Winkelmann fans. They said they would demonstrate if their hero was not given the premiere and Schmedes received an unpleasant threatening letter. After much deliberation, Schmedes and I decided that it was probably best to let Winkelmann have the honour of singing the first night. I very much doubt that the threat was genuine, but Schmedes is a sensitive fellow and he was disinclined to take any risks.'

'What was the nature of the threat?' Asked Rheinhardt.

'The author of the letter indicated his intention to follow Schmedes until an opportunity arose to give him a beating.'

'Why did you not call the police?'

'Herr Schmedes assumed that he could not expect the police to protect him indefinitely. Was he wrong?'

Rheinhardt shifted uncomfortably.

'No . . . he was not wrong.'

Mahler nodded and continued: 'Winkelmann was to sing *Rienzi* tonight, Schmedes tomorrow night. Everything was settled. However, about an hour ago I was informed that Winkelmann has been taken ill and that he is now unable to sing. I promptly dispatched several men to search for Schmedes, one of whom found him in a Turkish bath. He was brought here immediately. When I told him what had happened and that consequently he would now be singing in the premiere, he turned pale and started talking a lot of gibberish about having caught a cold on account of leaving the steam room too quickly. He's not really ill, of course, he's just frightened that Winkelmann's followers will carry out their threat if he sings tonight.'

'But if Winkelmann is indisposed . . .' ventured Rheinhardt.

'Exactly,' said Mahler. 'The *Hermann-Bündler* can no longer argue that Winkelmann has been slighted. The danger has passed. But Schmedes will not see reason and instead insists that he has caught a cold and cannot sing. Now, I hope that is enough explanation for you, inspector. May we conclude our business for today and resume again tomorrow?'

Before Rheinhardt could respond, Liebermann interjected, 'Herr Director, what are you going to do with Herr Schmedes?'

'I will urge him, in the strongest possible terms, to reconsider his position.'

'Will that involve more shouting?'

'I imagine so.'

'It didn't appear to be working.'

The director bristled. 'May I ask, Herr Doctor, if you have had any experience of managing the internal affairs of an opera house?'

'No, I haven't.'

'Or if you have ever been responsible for ensuring that visiting dignitaries are not disappointed when they come to see new, eagerly awaited productions?'

'No. I have never been burdened with such responsibilities.'

'As I suspected,' said the director, raising his voice. 'So you will appreciate why it is that I consider your critical remark somewhat inappropriate.'

Rheinhardt threw a distraught glance at Liebermann and then tried to appease Mahler. 'Herr Director, I do apologise for—' He was unable to finish.

'In this particular instance,' Liebermann interrupted, 'I do not believe shouting will achieve very much.'

'But I have no alternative,' said Mahler, thumping the desk. 'And I have found shouting to be the most effective means of communicating with opera singers. Moreover, the *Hermann-Bündler* are not the only ones who can issue threats. I have a few of my own which may encourage Schmedes to be more reasonable.' The director clapped his hands together. 'Until tomorrow, then, gentlemen?'

'Herr Director,' said Liebermann, 'I think I can be of assistance. You see, I am a psychiatrist and frequently called upon to treat patients suffering from anxiety. It may be possible to treat Herr Schmedes's stage fright using similar methods.'

'Herr Doctor,' said Mahler icily, 'thank you for your kind offer, but I fear we do not have the time.'

'What I have in mind would take no longer than twenty or thirty minutes.'

'What are you proposing?'

'Hypnosis. Let us attempt to remove Herr Schmedes's anxiety by hypnosis.'

Liebermann took the metronome from the top of the director's piano, wound the key to its limit, and placed the device on the desktop. He set the rod in motion and the room filled with a ponderous ticking like the inner workings of an enormous grandfather clock.

Erik Schmedes sat in front of the desk, closely observing the weight as it swung from side to side. Liebermann was seated beside him, while Mahler, Rheinhardt and Przistaupinsky stood by the door, beyond Schmedes's line of vision.

'Keep your eyes focused on the metronome,' said Liebermann in a soft monotone. 'Empty your mind — forget your worries — and watch the weight as it traces an arc — this way — then that — this way — then that. As you watch the weight you may find that your eyes are becoming tired, your eyelids heavier. If this happens, do not resist. Just accept and surrender. Listen. How pleasing the regularity of the beat, the gentle rhythm, like the rocking of a cradle — this way — then that. Watch the metronome and allow your mind to become a still surface, calm and untroubled.'

Almost immediately, Schmedes's eyelids began to flicker. The muscles of his face became slack and his lips parted. Liebermann continued speaking in his gentle monotone, occasionally introducing commands instead of suggestions.

'You are feeling sleepy . . . your eyelids are heavy . . . you are struggling to keep your eyes open.'

A few minutes later, Schmedes's breathing had become slow and stertorous.

His head slumped forward.

'On the count of three,' said Liebermann, 'you will close your eyes and sleep. A special sleep, in which you will be able to hear and understand every word I say. One — you are so tired — two — so very tired — three.' Liebermann reached forward and silenced the metronome. 'You are now asleep.'

Liebermann looked at his audience. Rheinhardt was smiling proudly and Mahler's face was rigid with concentration, his hands clasped tensely in front of his mouth. Przistaupinsky was watchful, even distrustful, perhaps.

Liebermann continued. 'Can you hear me, Herr Schmedes?'

The tenor's head rocked backwards and forwards.

'Very good,' said Liebermann. 'Now, I want you to listen to me very carefully. You have nothing to fear. Nothing, do you understand? As I speak, your fear will melt away, like ice in sunlight. And when the fear is gone, you will feel strong and confident. If you sing the role of *Rienzi* tonight, no one will follow you after the performance, no one will attack you. The supporters of Hermann Winkelmann did not want you to sing this evening, but Herr Winkelmann is ill, and now the *Hermann-Bündler* cannot possibly object to you taking his place. None will argue that Herr Winkelmann has been treated disrespectfully. You will sing the role of Rienzi, tonight, because there is no-one else who can do so. It is perfectly safe for you to sing. Repeat after me: *it is perfectly safe for me to sing.*'

'It is perfectly safe for me to sing,' mumbled Schmedes.

'*I have nothing to fear.*'

'Nothing to fear.'

'Excellent.' Liebermann gripped the singer's shoulder. 'Do not worry about the *Hermann-Bündler*, Herr Schmedes. They are not important. Only *your* admirers are important. You must not let them down. You are Erik Schmedes — the *great* Schmedes — giant of the north. Your Tristan was a triumph! How the critics praised your sensitivity and intelligence! How they marvelled at the phrasing and expression of your *cantilena*. And how they will praise you again, after you give them an unforgettable Rienzi tonight! You will be the toast of Vienna.'

'The toast of Vienna,' echoed Schmedes, before adding, rather unexpectedly: 'Giant of the north.'

Shaking Schmedes's shoulder in the spirit of manly brotherhood, Liebermann continued, 'You are feeling full of vigour, fit and healthy, strong as an ox, eager to take to the stage.'

The young doctor paused and watched with satisfaction as Schmedes's chest expanded and his expression set in an attitude of stoic rigidity.

'Listen carefully, Herr Schmedes. Very soon you will awaken from this sleep, fully restored. But you will remember nothing of our conversation. Do you understand?

'I understand.'

'Good. Now, on the count of three, you must open your eyes. One, *waking*, two, *waking*, three! *You are awake!*'

Liebermann removed his hand from the tenor's shoulder.

Schmedes blinked a few times and then turned to face Liebermann. 'Ah, the metronome has stopped. What a shame, I thought I was drifting off just then. The slow beat was certainly helping. Never mind, perhaps we can conduct this experiment another time. I am afraid I must hurry home. You see, I have an opera to perform this evening.' Schmedes stood up, straightened his jacket and addressed Mahler. 'This has been very interesting, Herr Director, but I really must be going.'

The director stepped aside and allowed Schmedes to open the door.

'Schmedes?' said the director.

'Yes?'

'You were worried about that letter.'

'Oh yes,' said Schmedes. 'How stupid of me. Yes, I was being foolish — you were quite right. It's perfectly safe for me to sing. I have nothing to fear. And I have my public to consider. They will be expecting another *Tristan* and I do not intend to disappoint them! Goodbye, Herr Director.'

And with that the singer departed, slamming the door behind him. The company listened to him running down the stairs, singing the overture to *Lohengrin*.

'Well,' said Mahler. 'That was quite remarkable. I am most

impressed, Herr Doctor. Please forgive me for the impatience I displayed earlier.'

Liebermann stood up and inclined his head.

'Now that Doctor Liebermann has dealt with your crisis,' said Rheinhardt, 'could we resume our interview?'

'With pleasure,' said Mahler, laughing out loud. 'With great pleasure.'

9

'Do you realise how many people work here, Inspector?' said the director. 'There are the principal performers, several choruses, choirmasters and répétiteurs, the members of the orchestra, guest instrumentalists, piano accompanists and the prompt. The stage machinery alone requires fifty permanent operators and a dozen electricians, and another thirty-five stage-hands are employed for large productions. There are the administrators, the costume designers, seamstresses, tailors, painters, carpenters, light engineers, porters, ushers, dressers, cloakroom attendants, and box-office staff. We even have our own opera physician. I could go on. The court opera is like a small principality. You wish to conduct an investigation — but where, exactly, do you propose to start?'

Rheinhardt took a slim box of trabucos from his coat pocket and offered one to the director.

Mahler waved his hand in the air.

'No, have one of mine. I owe you two gentlemen this small courtesy, at least.' He opened a desk drawer and removed a canister packed with fat cigars wrapped in silver paper. As he distributed them he added, 'A gift from an archduke who fancies himself a composer. These cigars arrived with an opera score and a request for me to consider it for inclusion in next year's programme. Regrettably, the music was entirely without merit and I had to refuse him. The lord chamberlain wasn't very happy, but what was I supposed to do?'

Rheinhardt struck a match and lit the director's and Liebermann's cigars before lighting his own. The tobacco was of a very high quality and tasted like caramel.

'Very good,' said Rheinhardt, exhaling a yellow cloud that expanded into a haze of pungent sweetness. Crossing his legs, he returned to the original topic of conversation. 'I take your point, Herr Director: many people work at the opera house. But I only want to consult a few of Fräulein Rosenkrantz's associates, preferably *close* associates, and was hoping that you would be able to identify who such persons might be.'

'As I have already stated,' said the director, 'my relationship with Fräulein Rosenkrantz was strictly professional. I did not know her very well and therefore cannot speak with much authority.' He rested his forehead against the knuckles of his closed fist. After a brief pause, he added, 'It was rumoured that she was having some form of dalliance with Winkelmann last year, but I'm sure that it wasn't very much more than a little harmless flirtation. You must understand, inspector, there is always a great deal of gossip at the opera house, and most of it is highly fanciful.' Mahler drew on his cigar and the creases on his brow deepened. 'However, I think I am correct in saying that Fräulein Rosenkrantz had a particular fondness for Herr Schneider.'

Rheinhardt took out his notebook. 'Who?'

'Felix Schneider. Fräulein Rosenkrantz's dresser, although in reality he was more like a factotum. She brought him with her when she came here from Prague.'

'Where can we find him?'

'He will be at home.' Mahler addressed his secretary, 'Przistaupinsky, can you find Herr Schneider's address for the inspector?'

The secretary bowed and left the room.

Rheinhardt wrote the name *Felix Schneider* in his notebook and tapped the pencil against the page.

'I understand that Fräulein Rosenkrantz wasn't very happy at the opera house.'

The director responded, 'How do you mean?'

'She found you . . .' Rheinhardt faltered. 'I apologise, Herr Director, but I must be blunt. I was informed that she found you demanding.'

The corners of Mahler's mouth curled to produce a humourless smile.

'They *all* find me demanding, Inspector. I am perfectly aware of what people say behind my back. I am a tyrant, a monster! But when the singers are getting their standing ovations and the audience are calling for more and stamping their feet, all is forgiven. Under my direction they give the performances of their lives. That is why they stay.'

'I have been told that there is bad feeling between some of the singers.'

'Opera singers are a vainglorious breed. They surround themselves with sycophants and panderers whose foolish talk frequently excites envy. They covet each others' roles and begrudge each others' successes. This business with Schmedes and Winkelmann is typical.' Mahler shook his head, becoming eloquent with despair. 'There are so many factions and divisions in this opera house, the atmosphere is so heavy with rancour and hostility, that if I were transported backwards in time to the court of the Borgias it would seem a model society by comparison.'

Rheinhardt smiled but his gaze remained steady and serious.

'Did Fräulein Rosenkrantz have many enemies?'

The director failed to register the question. He was still thinking about the vanity of opera singers. 'You see, they don't understand that, ultimately, what we do here is not about *them* but about the music. The music *must* come first.' His fist came down on the desktop, causing everything on the surface to jump. 'We must subjugate our individual personalities, our pretensions, and lose ourselves entirely in serving the composer's vision. Did you know there are still some singers who employ the claque? I can't have professional clappers in the opera house! I tried to stamp out this despicable practice as soon as I was appointed. They think it's acceptable to break the spell of the music, destroy the magic of theatre for the sake of a few seconds' contrived applause. But I'll show them. I've recently hired some private detectives. I intend to discover the perpetrators and rid the opera house of the claque once and for all.'

'Herr Director?' said Rheinhardt. Mahler seemed to emerge from a state of self-absorption. 'Herr Director,' Rheinhardt repeated, 'did Fräulein Rosenkrantz have many enemies?'

Mahler tilted his head to one side and his spectacles became opaque with reflected light.

'I can think of many singers who resented Ida Rosenkrantz's success, her popularity. Even cab drivers recognised Rosenkrantz and took off their hats as they passed; however . . .' He changed position and his eyes became visible again. 'I would say that, among her peers, Arianne Amsel resented her most.'

'Why?'

'Because prior to Rosenkrantz's arrival many regarded Amsel as our finest female singer. She does possess a very fine voice, but, if I may express an opinion in confidence, I never considered her the equal of say, Anna von Mildenberg or Selma Kurz. Amsel's voice does not possess Mildenberg's wealth of shadings. Mildenberg's *piano* will yield as much variety as her *forte*—'

'Herr Director,' Rheinhardt interrupted. 'You were explaining why Amsel resented Fräulein Rosenkrantz.'

The director raised a hand apologetically. 'Yes, of course. My reservations concerning Amsel's pre-eminence were not shared by the press. You may recall, perhaps, the outstanding reviews she was getting only a few years ago. The critics had become quite indiscriminate, lavishing commendations on her every performance. She was feted at society events, invited to the palace and presented to the emperor. Needless to say, all this adulation went straight to her head. She became proud and complacent, inflated with self-regard. She started cancelling performances — more often than not, without good cause. I would have terminated her contract but she was so esteemed by the critics, the public and the palace, that my will was opposed. I was summoned by the lord chamberlain and reprimanded for being irascible and overhasty. The situation was intolerable. Yet things were to change and much sooner than I had expected.'

Mahler stubbed out his cigar. 'I appointed Ida Rosenkrantz after seeing her perform in Prague, where she had distinguished herself as Jitka in Smetana's *Dalibor*. In her first season, here in Vienna, she sang well but was rather overlooked by the critics. Then something quite remarkable happened. We were due to perform *The Flying Dutchman*, with Amsel singing Senta, a role which she had made her own. That afternoon I received a telephone call and was informed, yet again, that Amsel was indisposed. As you can imagine, I was furious. And even more so when I learned that the soprano who was supposed to take the role of Senta in the event of Amsel's indisposition had, that very morning, eloped with a Russian prince. It seemed that the public would have to be disappointed, and I was on the brink of making an announcement to that effect when Rosenkrantz came forward and said that she knew the role and was willing to perform it. I was sceptical, and nervous, but in the absence of any other alternative I agreed to her proposal. No one could have predicted the outcome. Rosenkrantz's Senta was sensational. She brought to the role a curiously affecting vulnerability. I have never witnessed anything like it. The opinion of all but the most ardent of Amsel's supporters was that Amsel's hitherto definitive Senta had finally been surpassed. Some critics commented that Rosenkrantz made a very sympathetic female lead on account of her small build. Others were less diplomatic and stated plainly that Rosenkrantz was the prettiest soprano ever to grace the court opera stage. Somewhat insensitive comparisons were made with her *statuesque competitors*. From that night onwards, Rosenkrantz's stock has been steadily rising, while Amsel's has been steadily falling. Amsel has become quite embittered.'

Rheinhardt frowned.

'But Rosenkrantz didn't do anything wrong, as such.'

'Of course she didn't,' Mahler agreed. 'But I suppose Amsel imagined Rosenkrantz secretly learning her best-loved roles in readiness for the moment when she could step into her shoes. And it did make a good story: the shy, diminutive soprano, thrust into the limelight by chance and given an opportunity to demonstrate her prodigious gift. It is the stuff of legends. Not strictly true, of course, but that's what the critics wrote.' Mahler picked up the metronome and slid the weight down the pendulum rod, from *largo* to *presto*. He seemed perplexed. 'I suppose you will want to interview Fräulein Amsel. But I really don't see how she will be able to help you. Amsel and Rosenkrantz were hardly intimates. They never spoke, apart from the exchange of an occasional frigid greeting.'

Rheinhardt did not reply, because at that juncture the director's secretary re-entered the room. He was carrying a square of blue paper on which Herr Schneider's address was copied out in a neat, pedantic hand.

'Thank you,' said Rheinhardt, folding the sheet into his notebook. Then, looking up at the director, he asked, 'Is Fräulein Amsel in the building?'

The director put the metronome down and consulted a massive volume that looked like an accountant's ledger.

'I believe she is rehearsing in the red room.'

Rheinhardt stood up.

'I would like to speak to her, if I may. I won't keep her long.'

'Very well,' said the director. 'Przistaupinsky will take you. But before you go . . .' Mahler turned to face Liebermann. 'Herr Doctor, do you have a card?'

IO

THEY COULD HEAR HER long before they arrived outside the red room. She was repeating the same line. Even though the director had expressed the view that Amsel's gift had, in the past, been over-estimated, she was still an operatic diva, and the proximity of such a powerful voice made Liebermann's heart race. The fragment of melody that she was practising ascended to a beautiful high note that she sustained before gradually introducing a gentle, warm *tremolo*.

Przistaupinsky knocked on the door.

When the singing stopped, they entered.

The red room was clearly so called on account of its overwhelming redness. All four walls were covered with a bright red paint and the large Persian rug laid out on the floor was also red. The effect administered a violent shock to the eye.

At the far end of the room was a grand piano at which a youthful accompanist was seated. Next to the piano stood a woman, and beside her was a short olive-skinned man with a pointed black beard. Przistaupinsky introduced Rheinhardt and Liebermann and then said a few words concerning the purpose of their visit. On hearing Rosenkrantz's name, the olive-skinned man made the sign of the cross and bowed his head.

An arrangement was made to resume the rehearsal in thirty minutes, and Przistaupinsky, the accompanist, and the olive-skinned gentleman left the room.

Liebermann studied the soprano.

She was in her late twenties and possessed an abundance of dark hair, the extremities of which had a tendency to twist into coils. Her eyebrows were high, forming almost semicircular arches, and her nose was, if a little too long, finely cast. The lips beneath the nose were wide and coloured a shade of red that matched the brightly painted walls. She was not overly large, as the critics had implied, but she was certainly tall and had an imposing appearance. The loose-fitting dress that she wore was green and cut from a material that shimmered. Even her smallest movements created vivid coruscations that intimated the contours of her figure beneath — the curvature of her hips, and the full swell of her breasts. A silver and emerald crucifix hung from her neck.

Rheinhardt looked at the score on the music stand. It was an aria from Verdi's *Aida*.

'Do you read music, Inspector?' asked the soprano, seating herself on a chair by the piano.

'Yes.'

'And do you sing?'

'Well,' said Rheinhardt, his cheeks flushing. 'I would hesitate to make such a claim in present company.'

Amsel accepted the compliment tacitly by rippling her fingers.

'Actually,' said Liebermann, 'he's rather good for an amateur. A very competent lyric baritone.'

The diva's eyebrows, already naturally elevated, found further scope for ascent.

'Then perhaps we should try a duet, Inspector.'

'I think not,' said Rheinhardt, lowering himself onto the piano stool. 'Much as I would deem it a great honour.'

Rheinhardt fancied that although Amsel's suggestion wasn't wholly serious, it wasn't made entirely in jest, either. What a story it might

have made, in years to come: how he had sung a duet with the celebrated prima donna. Rheinhardt dismissed the thought and returned
the conversation to the subject of Ida Rosenkrantz.

'Yes, poor Ida,' said Amsel, touching her crucifix. 'How dreadful,
to turn away from God, to rebel against one's maker.' Then, looking
from Rheinhardt to Liebermann and back again, she added, 'But I'm
not sure that I can help you. We were not . . . friends.'

'You must have been acquainted.'

'Well, yes . . . But . . .' Amsel's ample bosom rose and descended
as she produced a lengthy sigh. 'I do not wish to speak ill of the
dead.'

'No one ever does. I will not judge you unkindly for being honest.'

'We were not friends,' Amsel repeated. 'Indeed, it is no secret that
our relationship was somewhat strained. We rarely spoke. I am sure
that von Mildenberg, Förster-Lauterer, Slezak or even Winkelmann
would be much better informed concerning Fräulein Rosenkrantz's
circumstances and state of mind.'

Rheinhardt removed his notebook and scribbled down the names.

'Why was your relationship with Fräulein Rosenkrantz strained?
What was so contentious?'

'Are petty opera house squabbles really of interest to the police,
Herr Inspector?' Rheinhardt did not respond and as the silence intensified Amsel was obliged to supply an answer: 'She turned people
against me.'

'Who?' Rheinhardt asked.

'I trust this conversation is confidential?'

'Of course.'

'The other singers — some of the critics — even Director Mahler.
I do not want to speak ill of her, especially now, and I have remembered her in my prayers.' Again the singer touched her crucifix. 'But
there was something about her . . . something about her appearance,

a kind of fragility, the illusion of childish innocence, that she used to her advantage. She found it easy to manipulate men. And men run the opera house.'

'Why would she want to turn people against you?'

'Jealousy, Inspector.' These words were spoken with decisive finality. Amsel clearly believed that her vocal superiority was indisputable and that only a man whose musical instincts had been horribly corrupted by Rosenkrantz's perfidious charms could possibly think otherwise.

Liebermann crossed the Persian rug and leaned back against the piano, his arms folded.

'Why,' he began, 'did you say that Ida Rosenkrantz turned away from God?'

'Because she took her own life,' the singer replied, a little perplexed. Then, looking narrowly at Liebermann, she added, 'In the Catholic faith, Herr Doctor, self-slaughter is considered a mortal sin.'

'Indeed,' said Liebermann. 'But why do you suppose she committed suicide?'

'I am not *supposing* anything, Herr Doctor. I read that she had committed suicide in the *Zeitung* and the *Tagblatt*.'

'The newspapers reported that Fräulein Rosenkrantz *could* have committed suicide. It was also suggested that Fräulein Rosenkrantz's death might have been accidental. The reports were inconclusive.'

Amsel shrugged. 'I formed the impression that she had killed herself.'

'Do you think that is what happened, then? Do you think she took her own life?'

The diva lifted her hands, her expression showing exasperation. 'I don't know. And what does it matter what I think? My opinion on this matter is surely of little importance. I didn't know her well enough to pass comment.' Then, quite suddenly, Amsel's lower lip began to tremble and she produced a loud sob, an anguished spasm of grief that might easily have reached the upper balcony of the world's largest opera houses. The sob was so theatrical that Liebermann could hardly accept it as sincere, even though tears had begun to course down Amsel's cheeks.

'Madam,' said Rheinhardt, offering her a starched white handkerchief.

'Thank you, Inspector. I'm sorry.' She dabbed at her eyes and spoke between mighty heaves of her chest. 'We were not friends — quite the contrary — even so — it is a terrible thing . . . a terrible, *terrible* thing . . . One *would* . . . one *wouldn't* wish such a thing to happen to anyone.'

Liebermann glanced at Rheinhardt to make sure that he had registered the slip.

The inspector leaned forward and asked softly, 'Where were you on Monday evening, Fräulein Amsel?'

'Monday evening?'

'It was very foggy.'

'Oh, yes, Monday evening. I was at home, entertaining some friends.'

'Who?'

'Herr Eder and his wife, Herr Brunn . . . old friends. I sang for them after supper.'

'And what time did they leave?'

'Oh, I can't remember exactly.'

'Early? Late?'

'About ten o'clock.'

Rheinhardt nodded.

Amsel mopped up the last of her tears and held the handkerchief out, still neatly compressed, for Rheinhardt to take.

'You can keep it,' he said.

*   *   *

It was early afternoon when Rheinhardt and Liebermann finally left the opera house. In addition to interviewing Arianne Amsel, they had interviewed the soprano Bertha Förster-Lauterer, the tenor Leo Slezak, and Rosenkrantz's Czech voice coach Herr Janda. All confirmed that Rosenkrantz had demonstrated no signs of significant mental anguish in the months preceding her death. There was also unanimity concerning Amsel, whose resentment of Rosenkrantz's success was judged to run deep, even by opera house standards.

Rheinhardt and Liebermann retired to the Café Mozart where they discussed all that had transpired over coffee and pastries. Preliminary remarks and observations were succeeded by a lengthy hiatus during which the two men were absorbed by their own private thoughts. In due course, Liebermann lit a cigar and signalled his readiness to share his conclusions.

'Very interesting,' he said, still only half extricated from the inner world.

'Arianne Amsel?' Rheinardt queried.

'All those tears, all that remembering of Rosenkrantz in her prayers ... and then her splendid and very revealing verbal slip! She must have spent the greater part of the last two years wishing Rosenkrantz dead.'

'*Wishing* Rosenkrantz dead, yes,' said Rheinhardt. 'But would she have acted on those wishes? Would she have plotted her rival's destruction?'

'It must have been difficult to bear, the humiliation, her decline in popularity.' Liebermann smiled knowingly. 'And they are hot-blooded creatures, these opera singers. I was once told of an incident that occurred in a provincial Italian theatre, near Naples, I believe. An ageing tenor was so mortified by the ovation his colleague received after performing a *bravura* aria that he stabbed the younger man in the back as he took his bow.'

'Italians,' grumbled Rheinhardt wearily. Then, finishing the dregs of his coffee, he said, 'I suppose you must be getting along to the hospital now.'

Liebermann shrugged. 'Not necessarily. Where does Schneider live?'

II

Amelia Lydgate had come from London to Vienna to study medicine at the university, where she was now enrolled as a student — one of only a handful of women. The prevailing view among the majority of her teachers was that medicine should be an exclusively male preserve, and consequently Amelia encountered prejudice, in one form or another, almost every day; however, she was undaunted by the dismissive remarks directed at her. The ignorance of others amounted to a mild irritation but nothing more, as it was in her nature to approach everything in life with an attitude of rational detachment. Moreover, such outmoded thinking was not ubiquitous. Indeed, she had made the acquaintance of some notable dissenters. Landsteiner, the man who had discovered blood groups, had taken a personal interest in her research, and her former doctor, Max Liebermann, had become — as much as social convention allowed — a close friend.

The public lecture that she was attending had been organised by the Socialist Education Alliance in cooperation with the General Austrian Women's Association. Outside the small hall a poster announced that Frau Flora Eberhardt of the Society for Women's Extended Education would be delivering a talk on the subject of 'Equality and the marriage problem'.

Amelia was seated at the end of a row of chairs approximately halfway down the central aisle. The hall was somewhat austere. A faded portrait of the emperor hung above the entrance but there was little else to enliven the drab interior. A cold, persistent draught stirred the hem of Amelia's petticoats.

Frau Eberhardt was a large woman with broad shoulders and wide hips, all comfortably accommodated in the loose folds of a blue and white reform kaftan. She had evidently dispensed with her corset. There was nothing evangelical about her delivery. She addressed the audience with measured, persuasive oratory.

Amelia noticed that the young woman sitting across the aisle was balancing a copy of Mantegazza's *The Physiology of Woman* on her lap. The young woman had also crossed her feet at the ankles, something rarely seen in polite circles.

Frau Eberhardt had begun by setting out her agenda for change. She demanded the complete revocation of Austrian civil laws that permitted the exercise of patriarchal authority within the institution of marriage. According to existing statutes, a husband was entitled to forbid his wife to take certain jobs. A wife had no right to determine where her family should live, this being the husband's privilege and, unless a prior legal contract had been signed to the contrary, a husband had absolute power to administer his wife's property. Frau Eberhardt deemed all of these things unacceptable in a civilised society. She called for the abolition of all marriages where one party was a young girl and the other a significantly older man. Such marriages were, she maintained, almost invariably arranged to the financial advantage of the bride's family. Thus, they might be legitimately described as a form of prostitution.

Summing up her position, she concluded that the economic independence of women was the first condition of a free marriage.

The speaker received a round of applause, led enthusiastically by the young woman sitting opposite Amelia.

The second part of Frau Eberhardt's lecture was even more controversial than the first.

'To demand economic equality is all well and good,' proclaimed Frau Eberhardt. 'But this will achieve nothing in the absence of sexual equality.'

There was unrest in some quarters of the audience, mutters and the rustle of silk.

'It is the opinion of many leading gynaecologists,' Frau Eberhardt continued, undaunted, 'that the female of the species is *sexually anaes-thetic*, that is to say, not troubled by erotic feelings. Other, more enlightened commentators have suggested that such evidence as exists for this opinion might be accounted for by *cultural* factors. Young women are forced to affect modesty and deny their instincts because of social expectations. Although this is a very plausible hypothesis, it has found no sympathy among the leading lights of the medical community. No less an authority than the late Professor Krafft-Ebing asserted that women have but a shallow interest in sexual activity because of their biology. He tells us in his writings that if *she* — the female of the species — were not passive and submissive,' at this point Frau Eberhardt picked up a book from the lectern and read, '"the whole world would be a bordello, and marriage and the family unthinkable."'

Frau Eberhardt paused before posing some interesting questions: 'Is this true? Can Professor Krafft-Ebing *really* be correct? Is the female of the species sexually anaesthetic? And if she is not, is it really the case that her untrammelled lust and degeneracy would bring about the end of civilised society?'

A smatter of restrained laughter travelled around the hall.

'I will address these issues in turn.'

Frau Eberhardt put the volume down and picked up a sheet of paper. 'I have here the results of a study undertaken in the United States of America, some years ago now, by Frau Doctor Clelia Duel Mosher. Her survey shows that one-fifth of married women achieve a *venereal orgasm* every time they engage in intercourse, and another fifth on most occasions. Her respondents described the experience as *ecstatic* or *delightful*. One of them expressed the simple sentiment that she *would have hated to have omitted the experience*. Are these the responses of sexually anaesthetic women? The conjugal right to satisfactory consummation,' Frau Eberhardt stabbed the air with her finger for emphasis, 'is as much the right of women as it is of men. Economic equality and sexual equality. Nothing less will be acceptable!'

At this juncture a soberly dressed middle-aged woman and her daughter stood up. The daughter had blue eyes and her blonde hair was coiled in braids over her ears. She wore a long dark skirt, a white blouse, a rose-embroidered waistcoat and black suede shoes with silver buckles. She looked like a figure from a traditional German fairy story. In her hand she carried the white carnation of Mayor Lueger's Christian Social Party.

'That is enough!' cried the older woman. 'What you are saying is filth — gutter talk — and doesn't help women at all. There is nothing wrong with wanting to be cared for by a man, a good working man who is willing to labour and support his wife and children. It is unnatural to think otherwise.'

'Sit down,' shouted the young woman opposite Amelia, shaking her copy of Mantegazza in the air. 'Let Frau Eberhardt speak!'

'A woman's place is in the home,' continued the proud housewife, scowling at her critic. 'That is her proper place. We must raise our daughters to be selfless, obedient, and willing to make sacrifices. What is motherhood, if not a sacrifice? What will become of our people if we do not fulfil our duty to husband and country? You . . .' Her face reddened as she brought her mind to bear on the problem of formulating an insult. The result was a single word: '*Intellectual!*' She turned to her daughter. 'Come, Gretl.'

The two women stepped into the aisle and walked briskly towards the exit. Before slamming the door, the older woman shouted back at the stage.

'There are laws about this sort of thing. What you are saying is obscene. They will hear about this at the town hall!'

Frau Eberhardt smiled at her stunned audience.

'Well,' she said finally. 'No one can deny that there is much to do.'

12

Felix Schneider was a diminutive clean-shaven man, with wavy dark brown hair that had begun to turn silver above his ears. He spoke with a lisp, gesticulated excessively, and his cigarettes produced a distinctive fruity aroma which blended with the floral registers of his cologne. His apartment, situated on the top floor of a building in the sixth district, was clean, tidy and tastefully decorated.

Rheinhardt and Liebermann had found Schneider entertaining a young man of dandyish appearance. Rather awkwardly, Schneider explained that his guest was about to leave and immediately hurried the youth to the door. When Rheinhardt had asked Schneider who the young man was, he had answered 'just a friend.' But it was obvious to Liebermann, from Schneider's anxious demeanour, that the guest was an intimate acquaintance, and that the nature of this 'intimacy' was very probably the cause of Schneider's discomfort. Rheinhardt had not wasted time probing Schneider's private affairs and the subject of Ida Rosenkrantz's death was raised without preamble.

After the customary declarations of horror and disbelief, Schneider talked spontaneously about his late 'mistress' with emotion. Indeed, while reminiscing about their years spent together in Prague he became distraught and began to cry.

'I am sorry for your loss,' said Rheinhardt, extending a hand and resting it on Schneider's forearm. 'Please accept my condolences.'

'Thank you,' said the dresser, pathetically grateful for the inspector's sympathy.

Schneider looked drawn and tired, undernourished. He lit another cigarette, and after a short pause seemed to draw sustenance from the tobacco. Words flowed in an unbroken stream of fond recollections. He spoke of his great admiration for Rosenkrantz, the brightness of her smile, the magnitude of her talent, her beauty and good humour. He spoke of theatrical triumphs and the glowing reviews that had followed.

Although Schneider's official title was relatively modest — *personal dresser to court opera singer Fräulein Ida Rosenkrantz* — it was apparent that, during the course of their association, he had been called upon to perform a variety of functions. He had managed her financial affairs (she was famously irresponsible with money), reminded her of coming appointments, smoothed the way for the repair of friendships spoiled by indiscretion, run errands, schooled her in the important matter of opera house politics, and supplied her with safety pins when the fastenings of her dresses broke (usually just before a key stage entrance). And in the privacy of the diva's dressing room he was obliged to hear her confidences and offer her the consolation of a brotherly shoulder to shed tears on. All very unusual for a relationship between a singer and her wardrobe assistant.

'I don't think it was an accident, Inspector,' said Schneider. 'I think she took her own life.'

'Why do you say that?'

'She was not herself . . . unhappy.'

'Doctor Engelberg, her general practitioner, told me that he saw Fräulein Rosenkrantz a few weeks ago and she was in excellent spirits.'

'Doctors . . .' said Schneider, shaking his head and demonstrating his low opinion of the profession with a grimace. Then, remembering that he was in the presence of a medical man, he glanced at

Liebermann and added, 'My apologies, Herr Doctor, I am upset, you understand.'

Liebermann excused him with a magnanimous gesture.

'What did you mean by that?' Rheinhardt imitated Schneider's tone: '*Doctors* . . . '

'She was unhappy about lots of things. I don't think *they* were able to help her very much. '

Schneider had been voluble, talking with natural ease, but now, quite suddenly, he became reticent. He looked across the room at a circular table covered with a purple cloth. A candle flame flickered above three picture frames. The first contained a print of the Virgin Mary, the second a sepia image of an old woman, presumably Schneider's deceased mother, and the third a photograph of Ida Rosenkrantz. The singer was dressed in a medieval costume and had been captured in a melodramatic pose.

'Herr Schneider,' said Rheinhardt. 'You were saying . . .'

The dresser came out of his reverie.

'She was never *right* — in her mind. Well, at least not since this spring.'

'We know that she saw a psychiatrist, a man called Professor Saminsky.'

'She was a consummate actress. It was easy for her to convince her doctor and friends that she was in excellent spirits. But she wasn't.'

'Why? What happened?' asked Liebermann.

Schneider sighed and stubbed out his cigarette.

'Love did not make her happy. This was not necessarily the fault of the gentlemen. She could have made different choices.'

'Forgive me, Herr Schneider,' said Rheinhardt, 'but I am finding it rather difficult to understand your meaning. Would you be kind enough to speak more directly?'

Schneider nodded, and lit another cigarette before resuming. 'What I mean to say is, Fräulein Rosenkrantz was in the habit of becoming romantically attached to unsuitable men, more often than not older men . . . like Winkelmann.'

'Hermann Winkelmann?' asked Rheinhardt.

Schneider did not respond to the question and just carried on. 'It was plain to me that such relationships would never amount to much. The gentlemen were usually married with families. They were never very serious about her. She, however, was always serious about *them*. She would have found happiness more readily in the arms of someone like Schmedes, or a young officer, someone looking for romance rather than a brief amorous adventure.'

'Was she rejected then, in the spring? asked Liebermann.

Schneider turned towards Rheinhardt. 'This is rather difficult for me, inspector. I feel as though I am betraying her.'

'It is extremely important,' Rheinhardt replied, 'that we determine Fräulein Rosenkrantz's state of mind at the time of her death. If you know anything at all that clarifies the issue, then you must say.'

Schneider shrugged. 'I suppose whatever I disclose now cannot harm her.' He sucked on his cigarette and blew the smoke out through his nostrils. 'She got herself pregnant . . . and sought assistance to resolve the predicament.'

'The pregnancy was terminated?' asked Liebermann.

'Yes.'

'Who was the father?' asked Rheinhardt.

'She never told me. But from that time onwards, as far as I'm concerned, she was never herself again. She became sad, preoccupied. She had some kind of throat problem, which got worse. Fortunately, it only became very bad when the opera house closed for the summer. I think she started seeing the psychiatrist about then, too. One must suppose he helped her a little, because she was ready to sing again before the new season started. Be that as it may, she wasn't the same person. I don't know how to describe it.'

'When did she tell you about the termination of her pregnancy?' asked Rheinhardt.

'About three weeks ago, after a performance of *Fidelio*. She burst into the dressing room and started crying as soon as she was through the door. She was beside herself and said all kinds of things about how she was going to hell, and that it was only right given the severity of her sin. I had to give her some slivovitz to bring her back to her senses and then I had to cancel her table at the Imperial.' Schneider flicked a smut of ash from his trousers. 'It was going to be impossible to get her out of the building without being seen and I was worried about what might happen if we encountered anyone important as we tried to leave. But I needn't have worried. She acted her way out. No one would have suspected that only minutes earlier she had been weeping uncontrollably, digging her fingernails into her own flesh . . . horrible.' Schneider shuddered. 'You would never have guessed it. She smiled, accepted compliments, and even stopped to sign a few autographs before getting into her carriage. Remarkable.'

'Was she a religious person?' Liebermann asked.

'Did she go to church? No. But she believed in God and the life everlasting. And she was very superstitious. Although, to be superstitious signifies little in the theatre — all performers are superstitious — but I think it would be fair to say that she was more prone than most. She used to consult a psychic every month. Regular appointments.'

'Do you know the psychic's name?' asked Rheinhardt. 'Or where we could find her?'

'Fräulein Rosenkrantz referred to the woman only as Orsola. I'm afraid I have no idea where she lives. Somewhere near the Prater, I imagine.'

'Who do you think made her pregnant?' asked Rheinhardt. 'Did you suspect anyone? You said that she once had an affair with Winkelmann.'

'Winkelmann was last year, and that particular liaison didn't last very long. But as for the spring . . .' Schneider stroked his chin as he cast his mind back. 'I can remember her mentioning the names of several men with whom I thought there was some *involvement*. Count Wilczek and a wealthy banker, I think his name was Bader. But as to the extent of their intimacy, whether or not these gentlemen . . .' Schneider was evidently embarrassed. 'I really couldn't say.' His arms wheeled in the air. 'She was always mentioning suitors. Besides, what does it matter? How does such information advance your investigation, inspector? Surely, knowing whether it was *this* man or *that* man who made Fräulein Rosenkrantz pregnant is of little consequence now?'

Rheinhardt nodded.

Outside, an organ-grinder began to play, a skipping folk melody that floated up above the sound of the busy traffic. The atmosphere in the room had become intense, and the music, rustic and simple, came as something of a relief. Its naivety was refreshing, like a gust of clean air dissipating the stench rising from a stagnant pool.

'Fräulein Amsel,' said Rheinhardt, bluntly. 'What can you tell us about her?'

Schneider's expression soured. 'One must always respect the achievement of anyone appointed to sing at the court opera, but she is someone for whom I harbour very little esteem or affection.'

'We have been told,' said Rheinhardt, 'that there was much bad feeling between Fräuleins Amsel and Rosenkrantz.'

'There was, indeed,' Schneider replied. 'But Fräulein Rosenkrantz was blameless, believe me. She did nothing wrong.'

Schneider recounted the history of Amsel and Rosenkrantz's feud, beginning, as Director Mahler had, with Rosenkrantz's eleventh-hour substitution as Senta in *The Flying Dutchman*. He tried to contain his bile, but in the end he was unable to maintain even a semblance of civility, and vented his true feelings in a colourful tirade.

'She — Amsel — is puffed-up and arrogant — and how she over-estimates her voice. In spite of her size, it lacks strength. You can hardly hear her over an orchestral *tutti* — it's quite insufficient. Whereas Rosenkrantz . . .' Again his hands conjured hoops in the air. 'Even with the brass section playing *fortissimo*, and the timpani rolling like thunder, you could hear her, floating above — sublime — angelic — clear as a bell.' Schneider's mouth twisted. 'Amsel despised Ida. She could not accept that she had been bettered and in the very role which had made her famous. She was eaten up with jealousy, and she couldn't disguise it. You saw it on her face.' Schneider drew on his cigarette, expelling the smoke as he continued to speak. 'I remember . . . shortly after Ida's triumph in *The Flying Dutchman* she was invited to sing for the mayor at his birthday celebrations. A few days later we were in the Imperial, and who should come in but Lueger himself with his entire entourage. They were all in their uniforms and wearing white carnations. The mayor caught sight of Ida and, brushing the head waiter aside, came straight to our table. He kissed her hand and thanked her for agreeing to sing. A real gentleman — the mayor — so well-mannered. Amsel was seated at a table close by. My God! Her eyes. Let me tell you, if she had picked up her pastry fork and stabbed Ida in the back I would not have been surprised!'

13

As the tram came to a halt outside the town hall, Liebermann looked out of the window and saw a crowd of men standing on the pavement. There were red flags being waved and a banner, drooping between two poles, showed the masthead of a daily socialist newspaper, the *Arbeiter Zeitung*. On a makeshift platform made from wooden crates stood a speaker, angrily jabbing his finger at the seat of municipal power. Every jab was accompanied by a cheer from his supporters. Another group of men, all of whom were wearing white carnations, had gathered close by and were jeering. This second group were smartly dressed, but there was something about them that made Liebermann uneasy. They looked quite menacing.

Two socialists separated from the crowd and marched over to the hecklers. Insults were exchanged and some pushing and shoving followed. It was obviously going to become ugly. The tram pulled away as one of the mayor's supporters landed the first punch.

Liebermann repositioned himself against the curve of the wooden seat and raised the collar of his coat. There could be little doubt that in recent months the atmosphere of the city had changed. It was not an ill-defined change but as tangible as the transition from one season to another. Debate in the coffee houses had become more heated and serious than usual. Words like *overthrow* and *revolution* surfaced from the general mêlée with alarming frequency, and tensions sought release too easily in violence.

It must be the forthcoming election, Liebermann thought.

The prospect of yet another victory for Mayor Lueger seemed to have polarised and intensified opinions. It occurred to Liebermann that the uneasy but dependable compromises so typical of Austrian political life might prove unsustainable. If so, what would happen then? He had always ignored his father's gloomy forecasts. Mendel's pessimism belonged to a different generation, another age, or so Liebermann had hitherto believed. Now he wasn't so sure. Perhaps bad things could still happen in this beautiful, cultured city.

Liebermann jumped off the tram and headed north towards Schotts. When he arrived at the music shop he was greeted by the salesman, Herr Shusetka, who presented him with the scores he had ordered on a prior visit, a volume of Dussek piano sonatas and the *Mephisto Waltzes* by Liszt.

'I don't suppose you have anything by a composer called Brosius?' Liebermann asked.

Shusetka's brow wrinkled. 'Brosius?'

'Johann Christian Brosius.'

'The name is vaguely familiar.'

'I heard his serenade for wind instruments played earlier this week. He's rarely performed these days, but I understand he was once quite popular.'

'Are you in a rush?'

'No.'

'I'll look in the basement. I presume you're only interested in piano pieces?' Liebermann nodded. 'If anyone needs service, ring the bell.'

Shusetka vanished through a door behind the counter. Liebermann heard a dull knocking sound as the salesman made his descent down a wooden staircase. Another customer entered and looked through the lieder collections, but departed without making a purchase.

A considerable period of time elapsed before Herr Shusetka re-appeared. When he did, he looked a little dishevelled.

'You're in luck,' said Shusetka, offering Liebermann a slim volume of piano music. 'I found this.'

Liebermann smiled and read: '*Three Fantasy Pieces* opus eighty-six.'

The pages were yellowing and exuded a dank fragrance. One of them was mottled with green-black mould.

'I'm sorry,' said Shusetka, brushing some dust from the sleeve of his jacket. 'The basement gets damp this time of year.'

Another page was torn slightly.

Liebermann searched for the publication date and found it on the frontispiece: Vienna, eighteen sixty-two. The score was forty-one years old.

'I'll take it,' said Liebermann decisively.

Liebermann walked home through the backstreets. He had not gone very far when he noticed that the stucco wall of one of the buildings had been defaced with black paint. He drew closer and the smudges became crudely executed letters. The slogan read, *The money-Jews have taken our money, don't let them take everything else.* Removing a handkerchief from his pocket, Liebermann tried to clean the surface — but the paint had already dried. It occurred to him that many others must have passed this slogan, but no one — so it seemed — had attempted to remove it. He placed the handkerchief back in his pocket and continued his journey, disturbed and apprehensive.

On returning to his apartment, Liebermann hung up his coat and went straight to the music room. He sat at the Bösendorfer and sight-read through some of the easier sections of the Brosius. There were frequent tempo changes, some interesting modulations, and a fondness for canonic devices. The overall effect reminded Liebermann of Robert Schumann.

Liebermann was satisfied with his purchase. He picked up the volume, held it close to his nose, and breathed in the ripe scent. The pages fell open again, and he noticed a dedication: *To my beloved, Angelika.* He remembered Frau Zollinger mentioning Brosius's wife. What had she said? A great beauty, but superficial. Frau Zollinger hadn't liked her. Presumably Angelika Brosius, like her husband, was now dead. That was how Frau Zollinger had spoken about her. Liebermann felt a subtle melancholy seeping into his soul. It was sad, how people passed into oblivion. Physical death was only the beginning. Thereafter began a process of slow attrition, the gradual dissolution of biographical evidence. Angelika Brosius — the talk of salon society — beauty and muse — was almost gone: a dedication at the front of an old score and a few fading recollections in the head of an old woman. What else of her remained in the world?

'Still,' said Liebermann out loud. 'The music has survived.'

He placed the volume back on the stand and began to work on the first piece, this time concentrating hard to make sure he was getting the fingering right.

14

THE LORD MARSHAL AND the emperor were seated at a large table
in the conference room, on chairs upholstered with green and gold
silk. A rug, decorated with a circular motif, covered most of the parquet
floor. The electric chandelier had not been switched on. Instead, illumination was supplied by two candelabras which stood beneath a
large oil painting. The scene depicted within the ornate frame was a
famous battle that had taken place during the Hungarian revolution.

After some initial business, requiring the signing of certain documents, the two men lowered their voices and leaned towards each
other like conspirators. The conversation that followed was elliptical
and imprecise. An eavesdropper might have concluded that they were
speaking in code.

'And what did the priest say?'

'Everything is in order, Your Majesty.'

'Will he fulfil his obligation?'

'There is no reason to doubt his loyalty.'

'Good.'

The emperor was looking more tired than usual. He sat back in
his chair and pulled at his mutton-chop whiskers. The lord marshal
noticed that the old man was gazing at a white marble bust of Field
Marshal Radetzky — a pale visage, hovering in the shadows like a
ghostly revenant. Franz-Josef's hand stopped moving.

It was not for the lord marshal to disturb the monarch's private thoughts. Being a fastidious observer of court protocol, he never spoke unless spoken to. Minutes passed before the emperor finally stirred. 'Do dreams have meaning?'

'I believe, Your Majesty,' answered the lord marshal, 'that there are some doctors who interpret dreams. It is a new practice among psychiatrists.'

The emperor sighed.

'I've been having a lot of dreams lately, unpleasant dreams. They always begin here, in the Hofburg, and involve some kind of civil disturbance outside.' He described his unsettling vision: agitators in Michaelerplatz, the cobbles awash with fire. As he spoke, he kept his gaze fixed on the likeness of Radetzky. The field marshal's sabre was mounted on the plinth which supported the bust, and the soft lambency of the candles played along its curved edge. When the emperor finished his description, he turned to face the lord marshal and asked, 'Is there any hope, concerning the election?'

The lord marshal shook his head.

When Lueger had first been elected the emperor had vetoed his appointment. In fact, he had done this not once but three times. The city council had been dissolved and Franz-Josef had ruled Vienna through a board of special commissioners. He had hoped that the people would eventually recognise the folly of installing a demagogue in the town hall. But it wasn't to be. During the Corpus Christi procession of 1896 Lueger had received more applause than the emperor himself. Reluctantly, Franz-Josef conceded defeat and sanctioned Lueger's fourth victory. It was a concession that had cost him dearly, a compromise too far.

The lord marshal registered the emperor's glum expression and felt obliged to lift his spirits.

'There is *some* good news, Your Majesty.'

'Concerning the mayor?'

'Intelligence that, if managed correctly, has considerable potential for . . .' the lord marshal chose his word carefully, 'advantage.'

More talk followed, indirect and euphemistic.

The emperor stood and crossed the floor to inspect a clock, suspended on a chain within a lyre-shaped case with windows. He touched the gilt shell mounted on its summit.

'I will leave the matter in your capable hands, Lord Marshal,' said the emperor. 'But remember, time marches on.'

He tapped the glass and indicated the clock face to underscore his exhortation.

The interview was now over.

Gathering the signed documents together, the lord marshal placed them in a leather briefcase. He rose, bowed, and said: 'Very good, Your Majesty.'

15

'I would like to know more of Fräulein Rosenkrantz's medical history,' said Rheinhardt, 'and I am particularly interested in those illnesses that she might have suffered from during the spring and summer months.'

'We have already discussed all that could possibly be relevant,' said Doctor Engelberg testily.

'Even so,' said Rheinhardt.

Engelberg pulled open the drawer of his cabinet and selected a green folder. Returning to his seat, he said, 'What was it you wanted, illnesses in the spring and summer months?'

'That is correct.'

The doctor scrutinised his notes.

'She had a stomach complaint. But nothing else in March and April, other than the problems you already know about. She complained of difficulty swallowing for the first time on the third of February, and I referred her to Professor Saminsky four weeks later.'

'Stomach complaint?'

'A little indigestion, that's all.'

Engelberg's index finger dropped down the margin. He hummed contemplatively.

'What is it?' asked Rheinhardt.

'My entry dated April the twenty-seventh: *fever, lower abdominal tenderness, and vaginal discharge.* A gynaecological problem — an infection of some kind — I advised Fräulein Rosenkrantz to rest.'

'Frau Marcus mentioned that Fräulein Rosenkrantz was confined to her bed because of what she called *a ladies' problem.*'

'Indeed.'

'Did you identify the illness?'

'Not specifically. There was no need. I knew it would clear up soon enough.'

'But you must have examined your patient?'

The doctor appeared outraged by Rheinhardt's suggestion. 'Not invasively, no.'

'But surely it would have been appropriate for you to do so.'

Engelberg shook his head. 'A doctor must have good cause to compromise a woman's dignity.'

Rheinhardt hesitated before continuing: 'Is it possible that Fräulein Rosenkrantz had contracted a venereal disease?

'No.'

'You're quite sure?'

'Yes.'

'Then could the infection have developed subsequent to a termination?'

Engelberg started. 'What are you implying, Inspector?' Rheinhardt did not respond. Engelberg tutted and said, 'Yes, I suppose the infection might have been caused by a termination, but Fräulein Rosenkrantz gave me no reason to believe that this was a cause I should be considering. What have you found out, Inspector? Perhaps you would be so kind as to speak frankly.'

'Fräulein Rosenkrantz fell pregnant in the spring.'

'Who told you that?' said Engelberg, evidently unconvinced.

'An associate of hers.'

Engelberg tapped his notes. 'She didn't complain of these symptoms until late April.'

'Perhaps she felt ashamed, embarrassed? Perhaps she tolerated her discomfort and only came to see you after procrastinating.'

Engelberg shrugged. 'That is possible.' He closed the folder. 'Inspector, I think you should talk to Professor Saminsky.'

'I intend to. He is away at present, but I understand he will be returning shortly.'

'A psychiatrist necessarily touches upon personal matters during treatment. But why must you delve into Fräulein Rosenkrantz's private affairs? I really don't see how it serves the public interest. What if she did terminate a pregnancy? I dare say she has already been judged by her maker. There is no need for a further judgement to be made in the newspapers.'

Rheinhardt stood up and put on his hat. Catching sight of his reflection in a mirror, he straightened the brim and squeezed the upturned ends of his moustache.

'Thank you for your assistance, Herr Doctor. Please don't trouble your servants. I can see myself out.'

16

As Liebermann approached the opera house he inserted his hand into his coat pocket and checked that the letter was still there. The young doctor needed to reassure himself of its existence, to dismiss nagging doubts that he had only imagined its appearance or perhaps misread the signature of the correspondent. Director Mahler had referred to 'a confidential matter' which he wished to discuss 'in person'. Liebermann wondered if the director had developed a psychological problem that he did not wish to disclose to the opera house physician. The director's mannerisms had certainly suggested a restless, neurotic temperament.

Przistaupinsky met Liebermann at the stage door and escorted him to the director's office.

'Herr Doctor Liebermann,' said Mahler, rising from his chair. 'I am so glad you could come.' He glanced at his secretary. 'Przistaupinsky — tea. Please sit, Herr Doctor.'

The surface of the director's desk was obscured by a chaotic jumble of scores and books. Liebermann recognised two titles: a novel by Dostoyevsky, *Crime and Punishment*, and a book of philosophy by Gustav Fechner, *Zend-Avesta, or Concerning All Things in Heaven and the Beyond*.

Director Mahler made no small talk. He produced a newspaper from beneath a battered copy of Mozart's *Jupiter Symphony* and showed Liebermann the masthead. It was the *Deutsche Zeitung*.

'Yesterday's edition,' said the director. He opened it and presented

Liebermann with a lengthy article, the heading of which was stark and unpleasant: *The Jewish Regime at the Vienna Opera*. 'Did you see this?'

'I do not read the *Deutsche Zeitung*,' said Liebermann.

'It is an anonymous article that appears to have escaped the censor's notice, a scurrilous piece of low journalism. Unfortunately, I must ask you to read it.'

Liebermann took the newspaper.

The initial paragraphs concerned Mahler's style of conducting.

What Herr Mahler sometimes does cannot be called conducting. It is more like the gesticulations of a dervish and, when the Kapellmeister has St Vitus's dance, it's really very difficult to keep time. His left hand often doesn't know what the right one is doing . . .

The author then went on to attack Mahler's habit of reinforcing sections of the orchestra with additional instruments.

If Herr Mahler wants to make corrections he should tackle the works of Mendelssohn and Rubinstein . . . But let him leave our Beethoven in peace . . .

The final paragraph claimed that certain members of the orchestra had given Mahler a nickname, the Duty Sergeant, due to his peremptory manner, and had promised rebellion.

Resistance is smouldering, even the most cowardly and submissive musicians will finally join the majority, and one of these days Mahler will find himself without an orchestra . . . it is conceivable to have the Opera without Mahler, but not without the orchestra.

Liebermann was reminded of the civil disturbance he had seen outside the town hall and the hateful graffito. The general atmosphere of volatility had spread even to the philharmonic orchestra. He gave the newspaper back to the director and shook his head.

'Disgraceful.'

'It has obviously been written by an orchestral player and there are some whom I suspect; however, I cannot make an accusation without being absolutely confident that I have the right man.'

'And you want my help?'

'Precisely. I want you to identify the author of this article.'

Mahler tossed the paper disdainfully across his desk.

'Other than the fact that he is an orchestral player and an anti-Semite — which you no doubt already know — there is nothing more I can say.'

The director frowned. 'I thought . . .' He chewed the nail of his index finger. 'I thought a man with your understanding of human behaviour would . . .' He produced a long, disappointed sigh.

'A printed newspaper article is somewhat impersonal,' said Liebermann. 'All the small details which I might find revealing have been removed. It is a sanitised version of the handwritten original. Now, if you had *that* in your possession . . .'

'The editor of the *Deutsche Zeitung* isn't going to give me the original,' said Mahler flatly.

'Perhaps not, but you are the director of the court opera. A man in your position could appeal to the lord chamberlain.'

'Prince Liechtenstein won't want to get involved. Palace aides are always weary of being accused of meddling, and now even more so as the election approaches.'

'Then I am afraid . . .'

The director nodded. 'I understand. Forgive me, Herr Doctor,

I have wasted your time. Please submit an invoice and you will be remunerated.'

'That really won't be necessary,' said Liebermann, a little embarrassed.

'Then I hope you will accept some tickets to the opera with my compliments.'

'I will indeed,' Liebermann replied. Gesturing at the discarded newspaper he added: 'And I would be happy to assist you in due course, should you obtain the original of this offensive article.'

'That is very unlikely,' said Mahler. 'But I will try.' He shrugged. 'One never knows.'

Przistaupinsky arrived with a tray laden with china. He cleared a space on the director's desk, poured two cups of tea and indicated the sugar bowl.

'How did you get on the other day?' asked Mahler. 'Did you and the inspector learn anything?'

'The interviews proved very useful.'

'I'm still rather confused as to the purpose of your visit.'

'Procedures must be observed,' said Liebermann disingenuously.

The director wasn't fooled. He looked at Liebermann sceptically before his features softened. 'Did you read the reviews of *Rienzi*?'

'They were outstanding. I noticed Herr Schmedes was singled out.'

Deep laughter lines appeared on Mahler's face. 'That was a remarkable thing you did, Herr Doctor.' The director raised his teacup as if proposing a toast.

Liebermann inclined his head, hoping very much that he would be afforded another opportunity to impress the director.

17

AMELIA LYDGATE LIVED AMONG a people for whom music was not so much a pleasure as a way of life. In this respect, the difference between the German and English character was most pronounced. Not wishing to appear deficient, Amelia had asked Liebermann to recommend some concerts. He had immediately assumed the role of musical mentor and had taken her to a recital of Bach's *English Suites*. A second concert followed, then a third, then a fourth. In the space of only a few months, attending piano recitals together had become a regular event. Liebermann recognised his own duplicity. These musical outings provided him with a perfect pretext for seeing Amelia. He had previously been obliged to fabricate all kinds of justifications, but now they had found a suitably innocuous reason for meeting and neither party expressed any wish to alter the arrangement.

Pretexts were necessary because Liebermann had once been Amelia Lydgate's doctor. He had treated her at the general hospital for a hysterical illness that had arisen because of a trauma: she had been importuned by a man who was supposed to be acting *in loco parentis*. Needless to say, this unfortunate history complicated Liebermann's relationship with Amelia — a relationship that had continued beyond the termination of treatment.

After attending concerts at the Bösendorfersaal, it had become their custom to stroll down Herrengasse to Café Central, where a candlelit table awaited them in the glass-covered courtyard. First they would discuss the recital, then Amelia's medical studies — anatomy, physiology, diseases of the blood — and finally they would discuss books, philosophy and, very occasionally, psychoanalysis.

Amelia was wearing a plain blouse, grey jacket and matching skirt. She had tied her hair back with a silver ribbon, revealing the luminous red stones of her pendant earrings. The taut whiteness of her neck was completely exposed and her skin gleamed like polished marble. Liebermann made an effort to concentrate more carefully on what his companion was saying. She was praising a book by Goethe called *Elective Affinities*, a work that Liebermann had not read.

'It is a most interesting piece of writing,' said Amelia. 'A romantic novel, but unlike any other I have ever before encountered. In a sense, it is as much about natural philosophy as it is about the lives of the protagonists. In an early chapter the author draws attention to the similarities that exist between chemical reactions and human behaviour, and by doing so raises profound questions relevant to psychology.' She picked up her cup and took a minute sip of Earl Grey tea. When she resumed speaking, her lips were glistening. 'Some substances meet as friends, hastening together, like the mixture of wine and water. Other substances are obdurate strangers and refuse to unite. Oil and water will separate immediately even after they have been shaken together. It is as if preferences are being expressed.' Amelia leaned forward. 'In its day, *Elective Affinities* was the subject of considerable controversy and was regarded as being immoral.'

Liebermann looked perplexed.

'Why was that?' he said. 'Goethe's observation appears harmless enough.'

'Not at all,' Amelia replied, shaking her head. 'Quite the opposite.' The pendant earrings swung and the stones flashed. 'Astute members of the clergy identified in *Elective Affinities* a challenge to Church doctrine. By drawing these analogies Goethe was showing that inanimate matter sometimes appears to exhibit attributes — free will, for example — associated with *higher* explanations. Thus he gives us cause to question their legitimacy.'

'Ah, yes,' said Liebermann. 'I see what you mean. Choices are made by the brain, not the soul.'

'Indeed,' replied Amelia. 'However, the principal objection to *Elective Affinities* concerned the nature of . . .' Amelia hesitated for a moment before saying, '. . . love.' Liebermann tilted his head to one side, adopting the attitude of one eager to hear more. 'Love is the most elevated state,' Amelia continued. 'It was considered almost sacrilegious to suggest that love has a material origin, that lovers are drawn together not by destiny but by the irresistible power of some chemical attraction.'

They gazed into each other's eyes and the moment became uncomfortably intense. A waiter dashed past and the candle between them flickered.

Liebermann looked away. 'Yes,' he said, embarrassed. 'I can see that.'

When he had recovered his composure he turned to face Amelia. She was still staring at him. A vertical line had appeared on her forehead.

'Would you like to read it?' Amelia reached into her reticule and pulled out a slim volume bound in black cloth. She passed the book across the table.

'Yes,' said Liebermann. 'I would.'

They spoke a little more about literature and the conversation became lighter in tone. Amelia mentioned that Frau Rubenstein, the

widow in whose house she lived, was about to embark on a trip to
Germany.

'Really?' said Liebermann. 'Why's that?'

'She's going to visit some relatives in Berlin.'

'I didn't know she had relatives.'

'Neither did I,' said Amelia, tracing a circle with her finger on the
table top.

That night, lying in her bed, Amelia Lydgate was reading a journal
published by *The Socialist Education Alliance*. She discovered that she
could not concentrate. Consequently she got up, crossed the room to
her bookcase and scanned the spines. She found a volume of English
poetry. The well-thumbed pages fell open at 'To His Coy Mistress'
by the seventeenth-century poet Andrew Marvell.

> *Had we but World enough, and Time,*
> *This coyness Lady were no crime.*

The poem took the form of an entreaty: a young man, begging the
object of his love to consummate. The arguments employed were
persuasive.

> *But at my back I always hear*
> *Time's winged Chariot hurrying near.*

Time, thought Amelia. *How the silent hours steal by. Days, months and
years . . .*

> *The Grave's a fine and private place,*
> *But none I think do there embrace.*

Amelia returned to her bed and held the book against her chest. She remembered Frau Eberhardt talking about the research undertaken in America and the answers given by the respondents: *ecstatic, delightful, would have hated to have omitted the experience.* She closed her eyes, but knew she would not sleep.

18

Listening to Constable Drasche on the telephone, Rheinhardt had been overcome by a sense of unreality. The familiar things around him, his desk, pen and bowler hat, had appeared alien, as if they belonged to someone else. The extent of his dissociation had only became apparent when a lengthy, crackling silence was broken by Drasche's anxious inquiry: 'Are you still there, sir?'

'Yes,' he had replied. 'I think I'd better come and interview him myself.'

Rheinhardt had not seen Drasche since the morning when Ida Rosenkrantz's body was discovered. He was waiting with the duty officer at the front desk of the Dommayergasse police station and looked younger than Rheinhardt remembered. After the exchange of some preliminary civilities, Rheinhardt asked, 'Where is he?'

'In our interview room.'

'How long has he been here?'

'About two hours.'

The inspector turned one of the horns of his moustache.

'Tell me Drasche, why did he wish to speak to *you*?'

'He knows me. I'm always running into him on my beat. I used to think he was a thief — out on the streets, late at night, looking at the villas. But I was mistaken.'

'And you consider him trustworthy?'

Drasche's expression was artless. 'I don't see why he would have made it up, sir.'

Rheinhardt nodded, hoping that the constable wasn't as naive as he appeared. Drasche led Rheinhardt to a small, simply furnished room, where a thin, hungry-looking man was nursing a cup of tea.

The inspector took out his notebook. 'Thank you for waiting, Herr . . .'

'Geisler. Achim Geisler.'

He was probably in his early middle years, but looked much older. His hair was prematurely streaked with grey and his face was deeply lined. The coat he wore had been patched at the elbows and a tangle of black thread marked the location of a missing button.

'Where do you live, Herr Geisler?'

'I rent a sleeping berth at the men's hostel.'

'And how much does that cost you?' asked Rheinhardt.

'One krone for the week.'

'Have you found work?'

'Not yet.'

'What is your occupation?'

'I'm a gardener. I thought it'd be easy to get a job up here. You know, what with all the big houses . . .'

'But no one has been willing to employ you.'

Geisler's mouth curved downwards. 'No.'

Rheinhardt made some notes. Before he had finished writing he spoke again. 'Fräulein Rosenkrantz's death was reported almost a week ago.' The inspector looked up. 'Why did you wait so long before coming forward?'

'I didn't know she was dead until today,' said Geisler, his voice rising slightly. 'Last Thursday I picked up a newspaper and stuffed it into the lining of my coat. It helps with the cold. This afternoon my coat got wet and I took the paper out. The headline caught my attention.'

'Are you a devotee of the opera?' said Rheinhardt, narrowing his eyes.

'No. I've never been to the opera. But I knew who Ida Rosenkrantz was and I knew where she lived.'

'How did you come by this information?'

'Timo, her gardener. I used to see him weeding. One day I was passing and asked him if he needed an assistant. He didn't, but we got talking. Decent man, Timo. He said that if he heard about any positions becoming available he'd let me know.'

Rheinhardt nodded. 'Why were you walking the streets on such a night? It was freezing. The fog was impenetrable.'

'Have you ever slept in a men's hostel, Inspector? Each cubicle has just enough room for a bed, a small table, a clothes rack and a mirror. A bath costs fifteen hellers, so most of the men don't wash. The walls are thin and there are arguments. Austrians, Czechs, Hungarians, Poles. They don't get on. This election — you'd think they were all running for office . . . so many opinions.' Geisler placed his hands over his ears and rocked his head from side to side. 'It drives you mad.'

'Why not sit in a coffee house?'

'You can't sit in a coffee house without buying a coffee. It's not a lot, I know, but it all adds up.'

Rheinhardt studied the impecunious gardener. He seemed genuine.

'You're quite sure it was on Monday the seventh. That night?'

'How could I be mistaken? You said it yourself, the fog was impenetrable. I wouldn't forget weather like that.'

'What time was it?'

'I can't say exactly. When I'm walking around out there I lose track of time. But it might have been nine or ten o' clock, no later than eleven — I'm always back at the hostel by eleven.'

'What did you see?'

'A carriage. It was parked right outside. As I approached, the door opened and I saw a gentleman get out. He turned around and I recognised him immediately.'

'You're quite sure?'

'Well, if it wasn't him he must have a double.'

'Did he see you?'

'Yes, he did.'

'Did he react?'

'No. He just hurried through the garden gate and went to the door. The article I read didn't mention him paying a visit. I thought it was something the police might want to know about — and I hoped that,' Geisler grimaced, 'given my circumstances . . .'

Rheinhardt pushed some coins across the table.

'That should see you through the next fortnight.'

'Thank you,' said Geisler, scooping the money up and dropping it into his coat pocket. 'It was definitely him, inspector. It was the mayor: Mayor Lueger.'

Part Two

Demagogue

19

It was a mild evening. Liebermann's footsteps echoed loudly as he marched down the narrow, deserted street. The prospect ahead opened up as he entered a cobbled square overshadowed by the austere façade of the Franciscan church. A full moon, shining with fierce brilliance, bathed the grey stones in pure, argent light. On the gable, pale saints and miniature obelisks were sharply defined against a black sky. In front of the church, surmounting a pedestal, was an imposing statue of Moses, his staff held loosely in his hand. Whenever Liebermann passed beneath the statue's judgemental glare, he always thought of his father. The young doctor kept his eyes fixed on the patriarch as he crossed the square. Perhaps it was for this reason that he only dimly registered the approach of another pedestrian.

'Max'.

The voice was female: a diminutive young woman with dark eyes, delicate features, and full lips. She was wearing a long coat with a fur collar and a Cossack-style hat.

'Clara.'

Time stopped.

Clara Weiss, the woman who he had once been engaged to marry.

They stood, transfixed. Liebermann became aware of his heartbeat sounding loudly in his ears.

'How are you?' asked Clara awkwardly.

Liebermann had never had the opportunity to say goodbye or

explain himself. After informing Clara's father of his decision to break off the engagement, Liebermann had been forbidden to see her. He later learned that she had been sent to a sanatorium.

'How am I?' He found himself unable to answer. He swallowed and said, 'Never mind how I am. How are *you*?'

Clara raised a gloved hand and tilted it from side to side: *so-so.*

Liebermann had not expected such a response. He knew that Clara was being courted by a cavalry lieutenant and the couple were rumoured to be happy. He had seen them together once, getting into a carriage outside the Imperial. The emotion he had felt took him by surprise. Their intimacy had been painful to watch.

'Life goes on,' she said finally, a wry smile twisting her lips.

Another hiatus: each tensile second extending the moment.

'What are you doing here?' Liebermann gestured around the empty square. 'Walking the streets on your own.'

'I've been to see my Aunt Trudi. I was looking for a cab.'

'It's very quiet.'

'Yes, I was heading for the Graben.'

'There's sure to be a cab there.'

'Yes, outside the Peterskirche.' Clara shrugged and seemed about to say goodbye, but instead added, 'I saw your sister Hannah last week. She was at a charity function at the Mandls'. How she's changed and in such a short time. A real young lady, and so very pretty now.'

'I should try to see her more. She's a sweet girl.'

'I suppose you're still always busy with your patients.'

'Things haven't changed much in that respect.'

Liebermann felt obliged to make a reciprocal inquiry about Rachel, Clara's younger sister, and the exchanges that followed were less stilted; however, the strain of keeping their history at bay was impossible to conceal. They both sensed it, like the pressure of a vast body of water sitting behind a dam. The tiniest breach in their defences would be enough to release forces too powerful to manage with artificial civilities.

Liebermann tilted his head: clopping hooves and the rumble of wheels. The reflection of two carriage lamps appeared in a shop window.

'Look. I think it's a cab.'

Gallantly, he stepped off the pavement and was about to raise his hand when Clara called out, 'No, Max!' He turned back to see her looking at him intensely. 'This is ridiculous. I think we need to talk, don't you? Properly, I mean.' She gestured across the square at a tiny café.

Liebermann stepped back onto the pavement.

'Are you sure?'

Clara assented with a curt nod.

The coffee house was illuminated by a thin distribution of candles that fought valiantly against a pressing darkness. All the tables were unoccupied, creating an atmosphere of ghostly dereliction. Clara and Liebermann instinctively chose places at the back. A gaunt waiter wearing squeaky shoes emerged from behind the counter and welcomed them with a melancholy smile. Liebermann ordered a schwarzer for himself and a mélange for Clara.

'Well, Max . . .' said Clara. She did not know where to begin. Liebermann removed a silver cigarette case from his coat pocket and opened it up. 'I'd like one too, please,' Clara added.

They sat smoking until the waiter returned with their coffees.

In due course, Liebermann asked softly, 'What did your father tell you?'

'That you wanted to end it.'

'Is that all?'

'No. He said some other things . . . but really, what else was there to say?'

'I wanted to tell you myself. I wanted to explain why. But your father was insistent that I never see you again.'

'What did you expect?'

'Did you get my letter?' Clara appeared surprised, puzzled. 'No? I didn't think so.' Liebermann drew on his cigarette and exhaled a cloud of smoke. The Egyptian tobacco was pungent. He noticed a slight tremor in his hand. 'When I asked you to marry me, I meant it. You know that, don't you? But I came to have doubts about my own sincerity, the authenticity of my affection. I didn't want to deceive you. And I have hoped, ever since, that one day you would see that I tried to act in good faith. To have married you, without truly loving you, would have been a betrayal of your trust.'

'There wasn't anybody else?' asked Clara bluntly.

'No,' said Liebermann.

The denial sounded curiously hollow.

'Then what made you change your mind?'

Liebermann shook his head. 'I don't know.' Clara raised her eyebrows and Liebermann recognised that he owed her more. A minute appeasing gesture served as an apology. 'We were incompatible. We talked a great deal, but I'm not sure that we were ever very good at listening to each other.'

Clara placed the cigarette between her lips. Its end burned, illuminating her face in the darkness. She looked different: more mature, more composed than the ebullient girlish socialite whom Liebermann remembered.

'When my father told me, I . . .' Her voice caught. 'I really didn't want to go on living. I saw no purpose without you.'

Liebermann found her admission almost unbearable. 'I'm sorry.'

'And I was so angry with you,' Clara continued. 'But you were right, of course.'

'What?'

Tapping the ash from her cigarette she added, 'We wouldn't have made each other happy.'

Liebermann looked at her quizzically — he couldn't quite believe what he was hearing. The conversation that followed was disjointed, interrupted by lengthy lacunae but strangely eloquent. Through the magnifying lens of their mutual discomfort, small signs and hesitations became the principal means of expression. Language ceded its authority to the subtle advocacy of the body — the poetry of sighs and gauche smiles. The process was akin to psychotherapy, both of them struggling towards some indefinable end-point. Their lives had been interrupted and the conversation they were having promised to restore continuity.

'I know what you want to hear' said Clara. 'That I forgive you. Well, there it is — I do.'

Liebermann felt tears in his eyes. He looked away and smeared the moisture down his cheek with a crooked knuckle. The folly of trying to disguise his feelings struck home and he turned towards Clara again, revealing the full extent of his gratitude.

'Thank you.'

For several minutes it seemed that there was nothing left to say. Something unfinished, incomplete, had at last been resolved. Liebermann felt slightly intoxicated.

'I hear that you have found . . .' He was not sure how he should refer to the cavalry officer and opted for the neutrality of 'Someone.'

'Who told you that?'

'My eldest sister, Leah.'

'How news travels.'

'People talk — as you well know.'

It was a pointed remark: Clara was an incorrigible gossip. She took it in good part and prefaced her response with an exaggerated comic pout, reminding Liebermann again how much she had changed. Self-parody was a novel development.

'A cavalry officer.'

'And you're happy?'

Clara shrugged. The casual movement was accompanied by a particular look, a play of features once entirely absent from Clara's expressive repertoire. It suggested cynicism, world-weariness, an unwillingness to take such a question seriously any more.

'Well,' said Liebermann. 'I *hope* you are happy.'

'I'm not sure we are.'

'Then why do you stay together?'

Through the haze of cigarette smoke Clara's eyes supplied her reason. Observing Liebermann's surprise she said, 'Max, you and I, we were so preoccupied with propriety, protecting my honour. If you hadn't been so disposed to respect tradition, convention, we too might have found a reason to carry on — even in the absence of happiness.'

When Liebermann returned to his apartment he played through Brosius's *Three Fantasy Pieces*. He then went to his bedroom where he allowed himself to fall backwards onto the mattress. Staring at the ceiling, he thought about Clara. Her forgiveness had been redemptive, but her candid confession had left him feeling vaguely unsettled. He imagined his former fiancée visiting shabby hotels, the kind where rooms could be reserved by the hour, surrendering herself to dissolute afternoon pleasures and the instructive ministrations of the young cavalry officer, his shiny boots discarded next to hers on the floor. A vivid tableau flooded Liebermann's mind, churning up unwieldy, complicated emotions.

What if I hadn't behaved honourably? What if I had insisted that we become more intimate, prior to marriage?

Clara had not been opposed to the idea. Indeed, she had offered herself, fully, but he had refused, not wishing to take advantage.

Why?

Was it the insidious influence exerted by the religion of their parents, the tacit demand that the rituals of courtship should be respected? Values passed down through generations, God speaking through the mouths of rabbis and fathers. Liebermann had renounced empty dogma, but he understood only too well that the prohibitions of faith had a habit of finding a home in the depths of the unconscious. He remembered the statue of Moses scowling.

If they had pre-empted the ceremony, stealing connubial entitlements before the appointed hour, would they now, as Clara supposed, be husband and wife? Liebermann had seen in her eyes the easy confidence of a natural sybarite, a propensity that it had not been his privilege to discover and encourage. Such delights might have compensated amply for the sterility of their conversations. After all, what defined marriage if not the physical and procreative union at its core? Amity and happiness were incidental, dispensable.

She had asked him if there had been anybody else. Her father had posed the same question. On both occasions, Liebermann had answered *no* — and in a sense this was true. He had not begun an affair, only a friendship.

Amelia Lydgate, from their very first encounter, had fascinated him. Whereas Clara had wanted to talk about social events and famous people, Amelia had spoken with impressive fluency about science, speculative fiction and diseases of the blood. And although it shamed him, Liebermann had to admit that he had always found the Englishwoman desirable, even when she had been a patient in his care: the shadowy curves of her slight body beneath a diaphanous hospital gown, the russet cascade of her untied hair — and such eyes — sky reflected in mercury — glacial, metallic, forensic intelligence.

Had he intended to begin a relationship with Amelia Lydgate? Or had she simply made him realise that Clara was, at that time at any rate, too superficial a person to be his lifelong companion? The latter, he hoped. But even if he was being disingenuous with himself and his intentions had always been suspect, those same intentions had never — *could* never — proceed towards consummation.

In addition to the peculiarity of the Englishwoman's manner, her frosty reserve, there was also her past to contend with. Liebermann had treated her for hysterical symptoms that had arisen from a sexual trauma: unwelcome advances from a person she had trusted, a guardian. How could he, Liebermann, make romantic overtures? To do so would be to put her at risk. And this had always been at the back of his mind: replication of the conditions that had caused her illness might easily precipitate a relapse.

Since ending with Clara, he had lived, for the most part, an unsatisfactory, unfulfilling bachelor's existence . . .

Liebermann got up and left the bedroom. He crossed the hallway and, passing through open double doors, fixed his gaze on the piano. Standing by the Bösendorfer, he let his right hand caress the keys. He picked out one of Brosius's themes. Without the left-hand accompaniment the melody sounded stark and simple. In its exposed state, lifted clear of a dense harmonic context, he saw a feature of its construction that had previously escaped his notice. It filled him with a sense of wonder. The composer, dead for so many years, was speaking to him.

20

THE PRIVATE DINING ROOM was rather shabby and situated in one of the less fashionable suburbs. It contained a round table, a cracked leather sofa and an old piano. Mounted on the wall was an inefficient gas jet that coughed and gasped like an asthmatic vagrant. Arianne Amsel had dressed modestly for the occasion in a subdued ensemble of muted colours; however, the impression of unassuming diffidence that she hoped to create was undermined by the diamond brooch attached to the lapel of her jacket. She had wanted to appear like the other women who frequented the dining rooms, mistresses of older men, but she was obviously not a shop girl. Amsel was an operatic diva and, inevitably, ordinariness did not come easily to her. Her companion was a short, dapper man in his late sixties, somewhat wrinkled and with liver-spotted hands. He possessed unremarkable features, a face easily lost in a crowd and just as easily forgotten. Receding hairline, steel-rimmed spectacles, neatly trimmed beard, he might have been a retired civil servant, university professor or bank manager. If he hadn't become the leader of the claque, Hanno Vranitzky would have made an excellent spy.

They had finished eating and the remains of their *palatschinken* — paper-thin golden-brown pancakes — floated on a half-consumed lake of vanilla sauce and apricot conserve. Although the private dining room was mouldering and dilapidated, the management always seemed to provide good food and wine, a necessary requirement, Amsel supposed, for the well-heeled gentlemen on whose patronage the establishment depended for its survival.

Herr Vranitzky was making notes as Amsel referred to key moments in specific arias: *top* C, *the coloratura passage, a sudden modulation to the relative minor*. The claqueur was so conversant with operatic highlights that he never once asked for clarification. On completing her instructions Amsel said, 'That is all.'

'Very good,' Vranitzky replied, inclining his head and pocketing his notebook. He lit a cigar and sat back in his chair.

The sound of raucous laughter followed by a playful screech penetrated the walls. Neither of them reacted.

'Mahler!' exclaimed Amsel. 'He's driving us all mad with his pedantry. Rehearsals have become a nightmare. Endless repetitions, obsessive attention to detail, a refusal to consider any opinion other than his own — it's all too much. Even the orchestra have had enough. Did you see that article in the *Deutsche Zeitung*? The one about the Jewish regime?'

'Yes,' said Vranitzky. 'I did. Herr Mahler goes out of his way to offend people. Do you know who wrote it?'

Amsel shook her head, barely acknowledging Vranitzky's question before continuing. 'It's impossible to sing without applause. A cold house kills the voice.' She craned her neck and stroked her throat with the tips of her fingers. 'Mahler should know this. A director who forbids the claque knows nothing about singers — their temperament, their psychology.'

'Very true,' said Vranitzky, puffing at his cigar. 'Herr Mahler doesn't know what's necessary in the theatre. Sometimes I wonder whether he has ever stopped to consider its purpose. Audiences go because they want to be delighted, diverted, and above all, entertained.

We know this.' Vranitzky's finger included Amsel in a swift oscillation. 'Our two professions have enjoyed a mutually beneficial relationship for over three hundred years, working to achieve a single aim: the public's pleasure. We create atmosphere, excitement, a sense of occasion. Who could possibly leave a theatre unhappy with the sound of applause still thundering in his or her ears? Mahler is a man who abhors joy.'

Amsel produced a bulging envelope from her bag and passed it across the table.

'In full settlement for services rendered so far this season.'

'Thank you,' said Vranitzky. He took the envelope and slipped it into his pocket. The claqueur tapped the ash from his cigar and shifted in his chair. 'This Mahler business: it has *implications*, you know.'

'Implications?'

Vranitzky sighed and changed position again. 'I trust that you will agree that I have been a loyal servant.'

'You have been more than loyal.'

'I would not forgive myself if you were to think that I harboured doubts concerning your . . .' He paused and his hands juggled as he searched for a suitably diplomatic term. 'Standing.' He was satisfied with his choice and said it again for good measure. 'Yes, standing.'

'Do you have something on your mind, Herr Vranitzky?'

The claqueur ground his cigar stub into a metal ashtray.

'You must have heard me struggling, last night? It seemed like an eternity before the audience followed my example. They are taking longer and longer to rouse. And a lone admirer is very visible.' Vranitzky took a deep breath. 'Perhaps I flatter myself, but I have reason to believe that you value my judgement. Therefore, I say to you — more as your friend than your humble servant — that perhaps the time has come for you to reconsider your position. You have done all that can be done, and . . .'

'I'm sorry?'

Vranitzky reached across the table and placed his palm on the singer's hand. He was like a doctor or a priest and when he spoke he did so in soft, consoling tones.

'The Viennese no longer appreciate your gift.'

Amsel pulled her hand back, shaking her head.

'But Rosenkrantz hasn't even been buried yet! Give them a little more time. They'll soon transfer their affections back to me.'

Vranitzky was silent. His expression collapsed into compassionate folds and creases, tacitly sustaining the pressure of his unwelcome sympathy.

'What is it?' said Amsel, a hint of despair finding weaknesses in her voice. 'Is it more money you want?'

Vranitzky appeared hurt.

'I am a man of honour.'

'I'm sorry. It's just . . .' Amsel's voice rose in frustration. 'This isn't like you. To be so faint-hearted!'

The claqueur refilled the singer's glass and then his own.

'I have heard a rumour. This demon Mahler . . .' Vranitzky swirled the wine and took a sip. 'They say he is hiring private detectives now. He intends to root us out. *All* of us.'

'Oh, he is quite mad.'

'Mad but determined. You will appreciate, I hope, that the future of the claque is my responsibility. I have willingly taken risks for you in the past but, at present, to expose myself or my troops would be foolhardy in the extreme. The entire institution of the claque is in jeopardy.'

'Come now,' said Amsel. 'It's only a rumour. Who told you this?'

'A reliable source. One of the electricians. He overheard the director talking to someone about it on the telephone.'

'I'm sure the director says all sorts of things. Come now, old friend,' said Amsel, smiling through eyes that had begun to glaze with tears. 'We have come so far together. Don't desert me now.'

She revoked her earlier rejection and gave her hand back to Vranitzky. He accepted it, raising her fingers to his moistened lips.

'My dear lady . . . please don't cry.'

The plea was genuine. He hated to see this tall, proud woman humiliated.

'Just until Christmas,' Amsel sobbed. 'Support me until Christmas. Please, that's not much to ask. Rosenkrantz is dead! Things will change for the better. I know they will.'

21

COMMISSIONER MANFRED BRÜGEL was studying Rheinhardt's report. His brow furrowed and his lower jaw jutted out. There was something about the simian perplexity of his expression that reminded Rheinhardt of an orang-utan he had once seen at the zoo. Brügel lifted his large head and began to shake it from side to side.

'No,' he growled. 'No, no, no!' Rheinhardt did not know how he should respond to four consecutive negatives delivered without preamble and with such devastating relish. 'A vagrant,' Brügel continued with sardonic glee, 'walking through fog thicker than potato soup . . .'

'Herr Geisler is a gardener, sir,' Rheinhardt interjected. 'Not a vagrant.'

Brügel swatted the air and pressed on. 'Claims to have seen the mayor visiting Ida Rosenkrantz the night before her apparent suicide, and you expect me to take his word as gospel?'

'It would have been remiss of me not to draw the incident—'

'Alleged incident!'

'—To your attention, sir.'

'Indeed it would.' Brügel snorted like a farm animal. 'However, you have done so now and that is where we shall let the matter rest.'

'But, sir,' said Rheinhardt. 'With respect, I think we should at least—'

'The answer is *no*, Rheinhardt! Think, inspector.' The commissioner jabbed his own temple with a rigid finger. 'Show some judgement. Did you really expect me to endorse your proposal? Good God, man! Have you taken leave of your senses?'

'If Lueger wasn't the mayor of Vienna we would almost certainly question him.'

'But, Rheinardt, he *is* the mayor of Vienna. That is the rather obvious and substantial fact you seem peculiarly unwilling to appreciate.'

'I am perfectly aware—'

Before Rheinhardt could finish his sentence Brügel exploded again. 'You think you can just stroll into the town hall and implicate the mayor in a murder inquiry, on the basis of *this*?' The commissioner flicked Rheinhardt's report with disdain, tearing the paper. 'The testimony of a ne'er-do-well who rents a pallet bed and dines in a soup kitchen?'

'He is not a ne'er-do-well,' said Rheinhardt patiently. 'He has never been in trouble with the police and has simply fallen on hard times. I don't think we can simply ignore his statement.'

'Ah, but we can, Rheinhardt. And very easily.'

Rheinhardt glanced up at the portrait of the emperor. It hung on the wall behind Brügel's desk. Franz-Josef, the old soldier, dressed in his white general's uniform and red sash — on the table beside him, a field marshal's hat sprouting green feathers. Brügel sported the very same oversized mutton-chop whiskers. It was common knowledge that the commissioner was an ardent royalist.

'The mayor and Ida Rosenkrantz were acquainted,' said Rheinhardt.

Brügel tensed. 'What?'

'Rosenkrantz's dresser, Herr Schneider, said that the diva was invited by the mayor to sing at his birthday celebrations.'

'Many others have had that honour.'

'Yes, sir, but the mayor also went out of his way to greet Rosenkrantz when he saw her in the Imperial.'

The commissioner rolled his eyes.

'Lueger likes being seen in public with popular people — singers, actors, the rich and famous. He's a politician.' Brügel leaned forward, 'Listen to me, Rheinhardt, and listen well. They don't call him the Lord God of Vienna for nothing. There would be consequences, grave consequences, for all of us.'

'He is not above the law.'

The commissioner produced a lopsided smile. 'Isn't he?'

'Sir, I know that there are certain constitutional obstacles—'

Brügel cut in vehemently. 'He would have to be removed from office before a case could proceed against him.'

Rheinhardt looked up at the emperor's portrait. 'It is not for me to comment on matters of government and state. But if the mayor was removed from office before the election, there are many elevated persons who would welcome such a development.'

The inspector kept his gaze high.

After a long silence, during which Brügel once again assumed a distinctly ape-like mien, the commissioner clapped his hands together and made a gravelly sound that might have been chuckling.

'A very good try Rheinhardt — you're getting quite slippery these days. But *no*, you cannot interview the mayor. However . . .' The commissioner lowered his voice. 'You raise an interesting issue, a perspective on these matters which I must agree does merit further consideration. Therefore I don't want you to feel discouraged.' The commissioner's grin widened. 'I am not, in principle, opposed to you taking the investigation in the direction you suggest. We just need something more substantial, a little more meat on the bone, eh? Now, if you should come across any further evidence linking Mayor Lueger with Ida Rosenkrantz . . .'

Brügel rubbed his hands together.

'You'll be the first to know, sir,' said Rheinhardt.

'Excellent,' barked the commissioner, glancing over his shoulder at the emperor's portrait.

22

LIEBERMANN PLACED KLASSIKER DES *deutschen Liedes* on the music stand and said to his friend: '"Hope", by David Freimark. Do you know it?'

'Yes,' Rheinhardt answered. 'I do, although I haven't sung the song for many years.'

Liebermann played the introduction. When Rheinhardt's warm baritone came in it reminded the young doctor of chocolate sauce, a dark, delectable, sensuous flowing. Although the melody was simple, beneath its unhurried arc sharp discords imbued the words with depth and tender poignancy.

As they tackled the final stanza, the piano accompaniment became restive and throbbing chords signalled an imminent emotional climax.

> *Est ist kein leerer, kein schmeichelnder Wahn,*
> *Erzeugt im Gehirne des Toren . . .*

> Hope is no vain, flattering illusion,
> Begotten in the foolish mind,
> Loud it proclaims in the hearts of men:
> We are born for better things!

A two-beat rest preceded a hymn-like coda over which the closing lines were plainly delivered.

And what the inner voice declares
Does not deceive the hopeful soul.

Liebermann lifted his hands from the keyboard and released the sustaining pedal.

'Beautiful,' said Rheinhardt. 'I'd quite forgotten those ingenious harmonies. Quite extraordinary.'

Liebermann consulted the contents page. The composers included in the collection were listed with their dates in parentheses. Liebermann ran his finger down the column of names: Robert Franz, Peter Cornelius, Johannes Brahms, Adolf Jensen.

'David Freimark. Eighteen thirty-seven to eighteen sixty-three.'

'He died young.'

'When he was only twenty-six. An accident on the Schneeberg. It happened while he was staying with his teacher, Johann Christian Brosius, and Brosius's wife Angelika. Today, Freimark is remembered only for this one work, "Hope".'

'Always the way. The good and the gifted have a habit of dying young.'

Liebermann rose and took Brosius's *Three Fantasy Pieces* out of the piano stool. He held up the cover for Rheinhardt to read.

'Ah, you've found something by the teacher. Is it any good? I must admit, I've never heard of him.'

'I want to play you some of his melodies.'

Rheinhardt shrugged.

'As you wish.'

Liebermann searched through the score until he came to the second of the *Three Fantasy Pieces* and started to play the right-hand part. Picking out a vague, tonally ambiguous thread of sound, he called out: 'D-A-D-F-E-A.' He then wrote David Freimark at the bottom of the page and underlined the same letters, demonstrating that they occurred within the name.

'You see? How the tune is produced?' Rheinhardt rested a hand on Liebermann's shoulder and stooped to examine the music more closely. The young doctor repeated the melody. 'Let us call this the pupil's theme.' Turning back a page, Liebermann played another melody, again identifying the notes as he struck the keys: 'B-A-C-B-A-B flat.' Glancing up at Rheinhardt, he continued, 'H — of course — is B natural in our German nomenclature. Thus what we have here is a melody derived from the name: Johann Christian Brosius. Let us call it the husband's theme.'

'How very interesting,' said Rheinhardt.

Liebermann then showed his friend that a third melody, consisting of the notes A-G-E-A and B flat, had been constructed from the serviceable letters contained within the name Angelika Brosius.

'The wife's theme. This is how Brosius treats his material.' Liebermann began to play. 'Listen — the husband's theme . . . then the wife's theme. Now you hear them played together — interlinked — united.' He stopped and, resuming at a section marked *nicht zu langsam*, he continued: 'Here we have the pupil's theme, which at first appears on its own. The wife's theme returns, and we hear both, simultaneously. Note, the husband's theme is absent. It is as though the pupil has taken the husband's place. There then follows this rather strange *mysterioso* passage.' Shadowy sonorities in the lower reaches of the Bösendorfer growled beneath softly ringing octaves. 'It sounds like a tolling bell, does it not?' Liebermann turned the page. 'After that eerie central section, husband and wife are reunited but now the pupil's theme is absent — and it does not appear again.'

Rheinhardt smiled.

'You have discovered a programme?'

'I believe the music tells the story of a marital crisis and its resolution. Conjugal bliss, an episode of infidelity and, finally, reconciliation.' Rheinhardt twisted the horns of his moustache. He made a deep humming sound which found sympathetic support from the strings within the piano. He sensed that Liebermann had not finished. 'The accident on the Schneeberg wasn't an accident. Brosius murdered his protégé to save his marriage.'

Rheinhardt straightened up and, after a brief pause, produced a hearty laugh.

'Come now, Max!' He shook his friend's shoulder. 'You are getting carried away.'

The young doctor returned to the *misterioso* passage, with its rumbling bass notes and tolling octaves.

'You can't hear what's happening down there very clearly.' He nodded towards the lower extremity of the keyboard. 'The sound is quite muddy. But if I release the sustaining pedal and play a little faster you'll recognise what's buried in the gloom.'

He played a familiar mournful dirge.

'The *dies irae*?'

'Precisely. From the requiem Mass. The tolling bell declares that the hour of reckoning has arrived. Angelika was Brosius's muse. Not only was she young and beautiful, she was also, so Brosius came to believe, the source of his inspiration. When she transferred her affection to his protégé, Freimark began to produce work like "Hope", a masterpiece. Brosius must have been desperate.'

'How do you know so much about these people? Brosius and his wife aren't exactly Robert and Clara Schumann.'

'I happened to meet an elderly lady called Frau Zollinger who was personally acquainted with Brosius and his circle.'

'Where did you meet her?'

'At a wind-band concert. The ensemble performed a Serenade by Brosius. And I've also been doing a little research of my own in the newspaper archive.'

Rheinhardt pulled at his chin.

'Let me get this clear: you are suggesting that Brosius murdered his pupil and wrote this piece as — what? — a kind of confession?'

'No, Oskar, I am suggesting something far more interesting. David Freimark died in eighteen sixty-three. The *Three Fantasy Pieces* were published a year earlier, in eighteen sixty-two. Creative works originate in the unconscious — the realm of dreams — and Professor Freud informs us that dreams conceal forbidden wishes. This piece,' Liebermann tapped the score, 'expresses a forbidden wish. A wish that was eventually realised.'

'Brosius might have employed the *dies irae* for symbolic purposes. He was alluding, perhaps, to the death of his marriage or the death of love. Not wishing his protégé dead. Besides, it seems unlikely to me that Brosius would have risked detection by leaving such an obvious clue.'

'The programme isn't *that* obvious,' said Liebermann, somewhat peeved. 'Moreover, Brosius was probably unaware of what he was doing. A hysteric has no idea that a useless arm has been paralysed because of a repressed urge to strike out. Similarly, Brosius might have had no idea that his composition was being shaped by a repressed desire to murder Freimark.'

'I find that difficult to accept.'

'Why?'

'Extracting musical themes from people's names requires intellectual engagement. Conscious thought.'

'Mediums have written great works of philosophy while in a trance, supposedly guided by spirits. Of course, such writings are not really the accomplishment of a discarnate author but the product of the medium's own unconscious mind. The unconscious is equal to the conscious mind in every respect, and is in some ways its superior.' Liebermann dismissed Rheinhardt's objection with a gesture. 'The exact mechanism by which Brosius came to encrypt his composition is rather academic. Whether the process was conscious or unconscious, unintentional or intentional, the fact remains that the themes he employed are meant to represent people and what he did with those themes suggests foul play.'

'I take it that Brosius is deceased.'

'He is.'

'And his wife?'

'Yes, she too is deceased.' Liebermann's hand strayed again to the keyboard and he played the pupil's theme. 'Since making these discoveries I have been overcome by a curious need to know whether my speculations are correct.'

'There are some intriguing possibilities here, certainly, and it would be most interesting to establish the facts. But the murder, if there was a murder, was committed some forty years ago. All of the principals are dead. How do you propose to conduct an investigation?'

'I could speak to Frau Zollinger again. She might know more.'

Rheinhardt smiled. 'Forgive me for so saying, but there are other cases more deserving of your attention. More recent cases.'

'There have been some developments?'

'Yes,' said Rheinhardt, with ironic understatement. 'There have been some developments.'

In the smoking room, Liebermann and Rheinhardt took their customary seats. After the brandy had been poured and cigars lit, Rheinhardt recounted what he had learned from Doctor Engelberg. He then spoke of his interview with Herr Geisler. As his narrative approached the point where the identity of Ida Rosenkrantz's visitor was about to be revealed, his friend became quite impatient and made rapid circular movements in the air with his cigar.

'Well?' A flake of tobacco fell, incandescing briefly before landing on the tabletop as a smut of black ash. 'Who was it?'

Rheinhardt delayed the delivery of his answer, savouring Liebermann's irritation, before saying: 'Herr Geisler told us that the visitor was Mayor Lueger.'

Liebermann's reaction was predictable. Shock, followed by disbelief.

'The visitor *resembled* Lueger . . .'

'No. The visitor *was* Lueger.'

'And you accept what Geisler says?'

'I am not a psychiatrist. But Herr Geisler gave me no obvious reason to question the accuracy of his report.'

Liebermann covered his mouth with his hand and, after considering Rheinhardt's disclosure, removed it again to say, 'If it's true . . .' The enormity of the prospect was inexpressible and the sentence remained incomplete. 'What are you going to do?'

'Nothing.'

'*What?*'

Liebermann's incredulity demanded an explanation and Rheinhardt went on to give an account of his conversation with Commissioner Brügel.

'He doesn't think I have enough. The mayor is too powerful. You can imagine what would happen if Herr Geisler's testimony proved to be inaccurate — allegations of incompetence, demands for the commissioner's resignation. However,' Rheinhardt drew on his cigar and produced a wreath of smoke, 'Brügel would be happy to approve further action if I can furnish him with better evidence. He is an ardent royalist and, with a little prompting, I got him to acknowledge that the situation could be played to his advantage. The mayor cannot be prosecuted while in office. A criminal investigation would require him to stand down.'

'And with an election looming . . .'

'Such an outcome would be a cause for celebration at the palace.'

'Well,' said Liebermann, fortifying himself with more brandy. 'What an extraordinary turn of events.'

'We already know that Ida Rosenkrantz was attracted to older gentlemen. We also know that she sang for the mayor on his birthday.'

'It is perfectly possible that they were better acquainted than those around them suspected.'

'Then there is the matter of the termination. If it was the mayor's child and Rosenkrantz had threatened to make their affair public . . .'

'Such a scandal would certainly have injured the mayor's electoral prospects. The traditional Christian voters who support him are harsh in their moral judgements.'

'Precisely.'

Liebermann flicked his glass, tilted his head, and listened to the chime until it had faded into silence.

'But it doesn't make sense.'

'What doesn't?'

'If Lueger had wanted to *silence* Rosenkrantz, he wouldn't have done it himself. Excepting the emperor, he is the most powerful man in the empire. He has loyal lieutenants, bodyguards, a host of men to do his bidding. The idea that he would commit murder, in person, is utterly absurd.'

'Perhaps he didn't intend to commit murder when he left the town hall. Perhaps he was overcome in the heat of the moment. You know how passion compromises reason — people can become unbalanced. If the mayor and Ida Rosenkrantz were lovers, then anything is possible. We can imagine the scene: accusations, provocations, spiteful words, threats . . .'

'Rosenkrantz had imbibed a considerable quantity of laudanum. She wouldn't have been in the mood for a fight. Nor would she have been able to deliver a coherent ultimatum.' Liebermann swirled his brandy and contemplated the jagged rainbows imprisoned in the glass. 'I must say, the more I think about it, the more I am forced to question the reliability of your witness.'

Rheinhardt shrugged.

'I will make further inquiries. Perhaps Schneider or one of the singers knows more.'

Liebermann chuckled. 'I would like to observe the mayor at close quarters. It would be fascinating. They say he can be a paragon of virtue one minute and a raging monster the next. I am reminded of patients who exhibit several personalities.' Liebermann crossed his legs and sat back in his chair. 'I have long subscribed to the view that those who achieve high office cannot enjoy perfect mental health. Such self-belief must be delusional.'

'How reassuring,' said Rheinhardt.

Liebermann smiled mischievously as he refilled the inspector's glass.

'So, what do you propose to do next?'

'I am going to visit Professor Saminsky tomorrow morning. You will recall that it was Professor Saminsky who treated Ida Rosenkrantz's *globus* . . .'

'*Hystericus.*'

'Exactly. Do you know him?'

'I know *of* him. He's very well respected.' Liebermann's expression soured. 'But he hasn't published very much and I'm not altogether sure he deserves the honours he has received.'

'The Order of Elizabeth, I understand.'

'Yes, among many other accolades.'

'You don't like him?'

'I can't say I do. He's one of those medical men whose name appears far too frequently in the society pages. He summers in Karlsbad, where he hobnobs with archdukes, and I cannot forgive him for writing a very disparaging review of Professor Freud's dream book. He's rather conservative in his methods. He seems to disapprove of anything other than sedatives and rest cures.'

'Well, whatever he did with Ida Rosenkrantz it must have worked. She was well enough to sing at the start of the season.' Liebermann conceded the point without grace, letting one of his shoulders rise and fall like a petulant adolescent. Rheinhardt ignored the movement and added, 'I'd be grateful for an opinion.'

'You want me to come?'

'If you would.' Rheinhardt turned towards his friend. 'People tell secrets to their psychiatrists.'

'And good psychiatrists guard them.'

'In which case, I sincerely hope that your low estimation of Professor Saminsky is correct.'

23

Court Opera Intendant Baron August von Plappart was seated in his office on Bräunerstrasse. He opened the drawer of his desk and removed the letter inside. Carefully unfolding the diaphanous paper, he read through one or two paragraphs to refresh his memory. The correspondent was highly critical of Director Mahler and had signed off with the words, 'From a musician who wishes to hear unadulterated Beethoven.'

As a rule, Plappart disapproved of insubordination, but in this instance his indignation was mitigated by a sense of self-righteous vindication. Here was proof, of sorts, that the appointment of Director Mahler had been a grave mistake.

Plappart cast his mind back to the very first occasion when he had become uneasy. The director had invited a large number of celebrated and expensive singers to perform at the opera house without first seeking his, Plappart's, approval. It was a blatant and provocative violation of protocol. Plappart had reminded the director that, in his capacity as financial administrator, it was his duty to issue a caution. Funds were not inexhaustible and the director should observe budgetary limitations. A deferential apology would have been the appropriate response. Instead, Mahler had raised himself up and declared, 'Your Excellency, that is not the right approach. An imperial institution such as the court opera should feel honoured to spend money in this way — it could not be put to better use. Nevertheless, I shall do my best to take your request into consideration.'

Plappart, not accustomed to being addressed like a subordinate, had been horrified. The memory of that rude dismissal was so vivid that it resounded in his auditory imagination as if the words had only just been spoken.

Nevertheless, I shall do my best to take your request into consideration.

How dare he say such a thing? In the intervening years, Mahler had succeeded in making Plappart an implacable enemy. *And now*, mused the intendant, *he's doing the same with the orchestra.*

Plappart had to make a conscious effort to stop smiling when a knock on the door interrupted his thoughts.

'Enter.'

'The director of the court opera has arrived.'

'Show him in.'

The servant disappeared and returned with Mahler. As the door closed, the director bowed and allowed his heels to meet, creating a soft click.

'Excellency!'

'Herr Director, do come in.'

Plappart did not rise from his seat but gestured toward the empty gilt chair in front of his desk. Mahler strode across the floor, sat down, crossed his legs and leaned forward.

'You wanted to see me.'

It sounded like an accusation.

'Yes,' said Plappart. 'I received this letter yesterday.' He held up the sheet of paper. 'The correspondent has chosen to remain anonymous, but it is clearly written by a member of the orchestra. Unfortunately, it is full of allegations concerning your behaviour, particularly at rehearsals.'

'Allegations?'

'Here, read it for yourself.'

Mahler took the letter and studied its contents. When he had finished, he dropped it into the side pocket of his jacket.

'Thank you, Excellency.'

'Thank you?'

'For drawing the matter to my attention. Will that be all?'

Plappart's expression passed from confusion, through amazement, to outrage.

'One cannot simply ignore such allegations.'

'The letter contains nothing new to me. Once again, the same old slanders and smears, the only difference being, perhaps, that this time they are expressed with more venom.'

'This is a worrying development, Herr Director, particularly after the *Deutsche Zeitung* article.'

'Written by the same person, no doubt.'

'Possibly,' said Plappart. 'On the other hand, dissatisfaction in the orchestra may be more widespread than you imagine.'

'There are always certain parties who resist progress and change. I do not believe that their views are very representative.'

'Even so, it might be wise to reconsider your working practices.'

'An orchestra is not a committee. Interpretations are not negotiated and sanctioned by the majority.'

'I am not suggesting that you cede authority, Herr Director, I am merely suggesting that you treat people with more respect.'

'Great music is not created by observing points of etiquette.'

'You forget that the opera house is an imperial and royal institution. It serves the palace and the people. We don't want a mutiny on our hands. The emperor would be most distressed. Unrest of any kind unsettles him.' Plappart paused before adding, 'You understand, I hope, that if problems arise I will have to explain to the lord chamberlain that you *were* advised to be more flexible.'

Mahler lifted his hand and touched his forehead. He held it there for some time, assuming the attitude of someone rapt in deep contemplation. When he finally removed his hand, he sat up and faced the intendant squarely.

'Soon after accepting my appointment I was conducting a performance of *Die Walküre*. In the final act I gave my cue to the timpanist, whom I had carefully rehearsed. He was to produce a long roll. Nothing happened. I glanced in his direction and was astonished to see another man standing in his place. After the performance I demanded an explanation, and was told that because the timpanist lived in Brunn he was obliged to leave early in order to catch the last train. A friend, who lived close by, routinely took up the mallets on his behalf. That is how the philharmonic conducted itself before my arrival.'

'Discipline was required. A firm hand, I quite agree. But perhaps you have gone too far.'

'There are many members of the orchestra who appreciate what I have achieved. Not only has their playing improved but they are considerably better off. Who was it that petitioned for an increase in their salaries?'

Plappart did not reply. He rose from his chair and crossed over to the window. While looking out, he said, 'I have tried to give you good counsel.'

'And I am most grateful for your concern.'

Mahler stood up to leave.

Plappart turned and extended his arm, reaching out. 'Herr Director, the letter, if you please?'

His fingers vibrated, a tremulous beckoning.

'I will return it shortly.'

'The letter was addressed to me.'

'But it concerns me.'

'Herr Director!' said Plappart sternly.

Mahler bowed.

'I will return it shortly,' he repeated. 'Good morning, Excellency!' Mahler bowed and marched to the door. As he pulled it shut, Plappart's cursing followed him into the vestibule. The servant, who was waiting outside, inclined his head politely.

24

'WOULD YOU LIKE SOME TEA?'

The maid's face was narrow and duplicated the weary sadness of an overburdened dray horse.

Rheinhardt glanced at Liebermann. The young doctor shook his head.

'Most kind,' replied Rheinhardt. 'But no, thank you.'

'Professor Saminsky will be with you shortly.'

She bobbed up and down and retreated.

The drawing room in which Liebermann and Rheinhardt found themselves was impressively appointed. Heavy burgundy curtains were tied back with thick yellow cords, admitting shafts of light through high rectangular windows. Wide leather sofas faced each other in front of a fireplace of red marble and on the walls hung romantic landscapes and what Liebermann assumed must be a family portrait mounted in an ostentatious gold frame: the professor, his dowdy wife, and two daughters. It was a rather formal group, lacking warmth and revealing nothing of their personalities. Below this sterile canvas was the gleaming black cabinet of a shiny upright piano. The open lid showed the name Friedrich Ehrbar in silver letters, the first name separated from the second by a double-headed Habsburg eagle.

Liebermann found such an instrument distracting. As a pianist, he was vulnerable to its subtle powers of attraction. It drew him across the floor and he depressed the keys — silently, not allowing the hammers to strike. The physical contact, the feel of cool ivory beneath his fingertips, was accompanied by a curious sense of relief.

'Ehrbar,' he said to Rheinhardt. 'First of the Viennese piano manufacturers to adopt an iron frame for all his pianos.'

Rheinhardt's inability to become excited by this nugget of information was evident in the flatness of his reply. 'Really.'

'The Ehrbar company are purveyors of pianos to the royal household.' Liebermann opened the stool and glanced inside. 'Beethoven piano sonatas.' Lifting the uppermost score to see what was beneath he added, 'Brahms intermezzos.'

'Max, please restrain yourself. It really doesn't do to get caught rummaging through an informant's personal effects. It sets the wrong tone entirely.'

Liebermann tacitly acknowledged the rebuke and closed the stool. He repositioned himself by the fireplace where he inhaled deeply. The air was heady with the mixed fragrances of furniture polish and fresh flowers.

Footsteps presaged the arrival of their host. Flinging open the doors, Saminsky entered the room. He was older, by almost a decade, than the family man depicted in the portrait above the piano. His hair, once brown, was now streaked with silver, and his neatly trimmed beard and moustache were also turning grey. He was wearing a frock coat, a brightly embroidered waistcoat, a white shirt with winged collars, and a blue necktie. The professor's movements were fluid and energetic and when he spoke he did so in a melodious tenor.

'Gentlemen, I am so sorry to have kept you waiting.'

'Professor Saminsky?' Rheinhardt ventured.

'Indeed. I trust Patricia offered you tea when you arrived?'

Rheinhardt guessed he was referring to the maid.

'She did, thank you. I am Inspector Rheinhardt and this is my colleague, Doctor Max Liebermann.'

'Liebermann, Liebermann,' said the professor, squeezing his lower lip. 'I used to know a Liebermann at the general hospital.'

'A cardiologist, I believe,' said the young doctor. 'No relation.'

'And you are the pathologist?'

'A psychiatrist.'

'A psychiatrist?' Saminsky drew back and threw an inquisitive glance in Rheinhardt's direction.

'Doctor Liebermann works in a consultative capacity for the security office.'

The inspector managed to imbue his reply with a certain frostiness which discouraged further questioning.

Saminsky gestured towards the sofas.

'Please.' The two investigators sat opposite the professor, who leaned back, extending his arms. His coat was pulled open by the movement, revealing a gold watch chain with conspicuously large links. 'I know that you have been anxious to speak with me, inspector, but I have only recently returned from Salzburg. A patient of mine, von Kroy, was taken ill. The family were very insistent that I should be present at his bedside.' He then addressed Liebermann, as if only he would understand the next sentence, 'A rather interesting case of religious mania.'

Rheinhardt took out his notebook and coughed to regain the professor's attention. 'I would like to ask you some questions about Ida Rosenkrantz.'

'Ah yes, poor Ida.' The professor's brow furrowed and he clasped his hands together. 'I was shocked, truly shocked, to hear the news of her death. My wife sent a telegram.' He sighed and looked towards the windows, his gaze misting over with reminiscence. 'She had hardly begun her career and showed such promise. And now we will never know what she might have achieved.'

'I was informed by Doctor Engelberg,' said Rheinhardt, 'That Fräulein Rosenkrantz suffered from *globus hystericus*.'

'Yes, she was referred to me . . .' Saminsky stopped to calculate the date. 'Back in March. She responded very well to my treatment regimen and made a full recovery.'

'What method did you employ?' asked Liebermann.

'The standard procedures: general faradisation, baths and a little exercise.'

'General faradisation?' asked Rheinhardt.

'Electrotherapy,' said Liebermann.

'Fräulein Rosenkrantz's mood,' Saminsky continued, undeterred, 'was variable, but I did not think her presentation ever merited the diagnosis of melancholia. Nor did she ever talk of taking her own life.'

'Then you agree with Doctor Engelberg — you believe her death was accidental.'

'I have spoken to Engelberg and, if I have been properly apprised of the facts, then yes, we must suppose her death was a tragic accident.'

'It was you, Herr Professor, who prescribed laudanum for Fräulein Rosenkrantz.'

'Yes, Inspector, to help her sleep: a longstanding problem, and not uncommon among those with weak nerves.'

Saminsky offered his visitors a resumé of the costs and benefits associated with various sleep remedies. When he reached the subject of constipation, Rheinhardt's interruption was resolute, 'Most illuminating, Herr Professor, however . . .'

'Forgive me,' said Saminsky, 'I digress.'

Rheinhardt accepted the apology.

'In your opinion,' asked Liebermann, 'what was the root cause of Fräulein Rosenkrantz's hysterical illness?'

'Root cause?' Saminsky repeated, a hint of irritation creeping into his voice. 'Her constitution, of course, the weakness of her nervous system — what else could it be?'

Rheinhardt tactfully intervened. 'Could you tell us something of Fräulein Rosenkrantz's history?'

Saminsky pulled a face. His features were remarkably expressive. Although he was willing to comply with Rheinhardt's request, it was clear that he viewed the exercise as redundant.

'Ida was raised in upper Austria, near Gmünd. Her father died when she was eleven and her mother took her to Prague. There they lived with her mother's sister, Ida's Aunt Connie, who had three daughters of her own. Connie was married to a civil servant, Herr Stepanek. Ida wasn't very happy in Prague as her cousins never accepted her into the family. They resented her and said hurtful things. She was, needless to say, a pretty child, and I suspect they were jealous of her looks. Young ladies can be very cruel. Ida took piano lessons and it was evident that she was gifted. She was encouraged by a schoolteacher, Herr Bachmeier, and eventually went for singing lessons with a choirmaster called Peter Helbing. I believe he is quite well known in Bohemia. Ida then came to study in Vienna, during which time her mother remarried, leaving Prague to live with her new husband in Italy. Relations between mother and daughter were somewhat strained thereafter. Her mother died quite recently from blood poisoning after being bitten by an insect.' Saminsky shrugged, exasperated by the perversity of fate. 'When Ida had completed her studies, she sang in Hungary for a year and then returned to Prague. Her reputation grew and in due course she was invited to join the court opera by Director Mahler.'

Reinhardt made some notes and, looking up, said, 'Did you ever discuss her private life?'

'Yes.' The syllable was extended, dipping and rising.

'We were informed by one of her associates that the attachments she formed rarely resulted in happiness.'

Saminky's response was circumspect.

'That is probably true.'

'Did she have a lover at the time of her death?'

'She was a striking beauty . . .'

Again, Saminsky's plastic features did the work of language and provided an affirmative answer.

'When was the last time you saw Fräulein Rosenkrantz?'

'Last month.'

'Who was she being courted by?'

'Forgive me, Inspector, but how is this relevant? What passes between patient and doctor is confidential. Even after a patient dies, a physician must endeavour to protect the patient's interests. What is your purpose?'

'Although Fräulein Rosenkrantz's death has been reported in the newspapers as accidental or suicidal, we are not, as yet, entirely persuaded of either possibility.'

The hush that followed was lengthy and disturbed by a series of clucking noises that increased in frequency and volume until Saminsky was able to expostulate. 'What? You think she was murdered? Why?' The professor directed his incredulous gaze at Liebermann, hoping that a medical colleague would be more forthcoming. When the young doctor did not oblige, Saminsky continued. 'Who would have wanted to kill her?'

'I was hoping that you might provide us with some clues,' said Rheinhardt.

Saminsky shook his head.

'There were men in her life. But she was discreet and referred to them in general terms: a *certain* count, the banker, or my composer friend. She rarely disclosed names.'

'Did she mention quarrelling with any of them?'

'She spoke of quarrels at the opera house.'

'With who?'

'Arianne Amsel, Celine Fuchs . . . and she was once slighted by von Mildenberg. But really, inspector, I do not think you can conclude very much from such disclosures. That is how life at the opera house proceeds.'

Rheinhardt tapped his pencil against his notebook.

'Did you know that Fräulein Rosenkrantz consulted Doctor Engelberg on the twenty-seventh of April because of a gynaecological infection?'

'Yes.'

'And do you know the probable cause of that infection?'

'Yes, I do. The termination of an unwanted pregnancy.' Saminsky took a deep breath and continued. 'She must have conceived shortly before I started seeing her. I realised something was wrong immediately. She was anxious about her treatment and asked many questions about the safety of faradisation. One must suppose that at that juncture she was still undecided as to whether or not she intended to have the child. In due course she told me what had happened and what she proposed to do.'

'Who performed the . . .' Rheinhardt hesitated before saying, '. . . procedure?'

'I don't know. I tried to dissuade her, although I must confess on medical grounds rather than moral. Visiting one of these people . . . these abortionists, is highly dangerous. They operate using dirty instruments and the abortifacients they employ are nothing more than a cocktail of poisons. Ida was lucky. The infection cleared up and there were no further complications.'

'Why didn't you share this information with Doctor Engelberg?'

'Ida didn't want me to. I urged her to reconsider but she wouldn't hear of it. Engelberg was not unduly worried by her condition and I did not want to lose her trust.'

'Who was she seeing about that time? February, March?'

Saminsky's frown deepened.

'I don't know whose child it was.'

It was not a convincing denial.

'Professor,' Rheinhardt pressed. 'I must insist on your full co-operation.'

Saminsky removed a handkerchief from his pocket and wiped his brow.

'You are putting me in a very difficult position.'

'With respect, Herr Professor, I don't see how.'

'Do you have a family, Inspector?'

'Yes, I do.'

'Sons, daughters?'

'Two daughters.'

'Ah,' said Saminsky. 'Like me.' He pointed across the room at the vapid portrait. 'Bianka and Claudia. They are older now, twenty-one and twenty-three. My pride and joy.'

'Daughters are indeed a blessing, I am bound to agree; however, you will not think me a dullard, I hope, for failing to appreciate how mention of the rewards of fatherhood makes things any clearer?'

'Ida made me swear to keep the identity of her lover a secret. She made me swear on my daughters' lives.'

'Come now, professor . . .'

'*Come now?* It's easy for you to say that, I'm sure. But if you were in my position, how would you feel?'

'Discomfited, of course. Even so . . .'

'Are you a religious man?' asked Liebermann.

'No, not really,' answered the professor.

'Then what exactly . . .?'

The professor flapped his hands in the air. 'I know that it's irrational, but one cannot break such an oath without pause for thought. I do not want to tempt fate.'

'With respect,' said Rheinhardt, 'I must inform you that with-holding information from the security office is a serious offence. By doing so you also tempt fate in the person of a magistrate. The terms of your pledge were most unfortunate and, as a father, I sympathise with the sentiments you express. Be that as it may, the process of law must take precedence over superstition.' Saminsky's lips remained firmly pressed together. 'Was it Count Wilczek? Bader? Winkelmann? Mayor Lueger?' The professor flinched. 'Lueger?'

Saminsky nodded and whispered, 'Heaven help me.'

'What do you know?' asked Rheinhardt. 'It is imperative that you say.'

The professor stuffed his handkerchief into his coat pocket and answered slowly, as if each word was chafing his conscience.

'The association began after she was invited to sing for the mayor on his birthday.'

'That would have been in October, last year?'

'About that time, yes.'

'Did the mayor know that she was pregnant?'

'I believe so.'

'And he consented to her . . .' Rheinhardt paused to select an appro-priate euphemism, '. . . plan of action?'

'I really can't say. Please, Inspector, you must appreciate that I did not quiz her about the details of this liaison. It was not my business to do so. I do not subscribe to the view that the treatment of nervous disorders is best achieved by talking. Neural deficiencies are not corrected by confession. If that were the case, hysteria would never be seen in devout Catholics. Nervous disorders are plainly caused by disordered nerves!'

This little play on words obviously satisfied Saminsky. A faint smile appeared on his face but it was not sustained. Instead, it flickered and faded.

'Did their association continue,' asked Rheinhardt, 'after the pregnancy was terminated?'

'For a period of time, yes.'

'How long?'

'It lasted until the summer, at least.'

'But eventually it ended?'

'That was my impression. But I cannot be certain. It is possible that Ida maintained her association with Lueger while simultaneously becoming intimate with other gentlemen.'

Rheinhardt glanced at his friend.

'Do you have any questions you would like to ask the professor, Herr Doctor?'

'Yes,' said Liebermann. 'I do.' He paused thoughtfully and pointed towards the piano.

'Do you play, Herr Professor?'

Saminsky looked puzzled.

'When I get the time'

'I notice you own an Ehrbar.'

'A gift from His Majesty. I attended the late empress.'

'How do you think they compare with Bösendorfers? I've been told the action can be a little heavy.'

Rheinhardt closed his notebook and found that his mind was offering him a string of expletives for later use.

'Why on earth did you ask him those ridiculous questions about his piano?'

'The relative merits of the Ehrbar and Bösendorfer actions is a topic of great interest to me. Besides, there's a lot you can learn about a man from such a conversation.'

'And what, may I ask, did you learn?'

'Enough to confirm my existing prejudices.' The two men stepped off the paving stones and began their transit of the wide cobbled road. 'He's a fool. A perfect example of the "physiological psychiatrist": a practitioner whose thinking is stunted by a slavish obedience to historical precedents, an individual who, when presented with the marvel of the human psyche, with its dark continents, power to create dreams, passions and enigmas, sees only a brain trailing threads of nerve tissue: a self-important cretin, looking backwards, resisting progress, while his discipline is straining at the leash, leaping forward, pulling medicine, philosophy and science into the future and the new century.'

'Don't mince your words — eh, Max?' said Rheinhardt.

Liebermann ignored Rheinhardt's sarcasm and continued to vent his spleen.

'General faradisation! A singer walks into Saminsky's consulting room with a throat problem and it doesn't even occur to him to make a connection.'

'I thought *globus hystericus* was associated with difficulty swallowing, not singing.'

'An imaginary obstruction would almost certainly have affected Rosenkrantz's ability to sing.'

'Yes,' said Rheinhardt. 'I suppose it must have, even if the effect was only to damage her confidence.'

'Remember, Oskar, we are discussing a hysterical illness, an illness which has only an *apparent* physical cause. There is, in reality, no lump in the throat, no inflammation of the larynx. The symptoms are perceived, not actual, and as a rule anything produced by the mind has meaning.'

'All right, then, what did Fräulein Rosenkrantz's *globus hystericus* mean?'

They reached the other side of the road. 'Perhaps she wanted to terminate her contract at the opera house, or even cease performing entirely.'

'Nonsense; she loved the applause, the attention.'

'But she didn't love the director's tyranny and the spite of her rival divas. Sometimes when a person cannot make a momentous decision the unconscious settles the issue by other, more subtle means. The person becomes ill, providing convenient exemption from worldly obligations. The fact that Ida Rosenkrantz suffered from a condition affecting her throat is one that no competent psychiatrist would have overlooked.'

Liebermann halted and raised his index finger. 'That is just one possibility, but there are others.' A second finger appeared. 'Perhaps the illness represented a punishment for a past transgression; a transgression that she could only atone for by giving up her most valuable possession, her voice.' A third finger joined the first two. 'Or . . . perhaps the imaginary obstruction in her throat allowed her to avoid performing a sexual act.'

Rheinhardt winced.

'Really, Max . . .'

'All or none of these possibilities might be true. My point is that Saminsky didn't consider any of them. Instead, he tried to strengthen Rosenkrantz's nervous system with electricity because that was what he was told to do when he was a student! The man is an absolute fool.'

Rheinhardt directed Liebermann's attention back across the road to where Saminsky's house and garden occupied a substantial plot. It was a mock-Renaissance edifice not unlike a French chateau. Pitched roofs and turrets suggested aristocratic luxury and the windows were decorated with foliated, volute gables.

'He's doing very well for a fool,' said Rheinhardt. 'Don't you think?'

'It's scandalous,' said the young doctor. 'Freud, a genius, only lately a professor, struggles to achieve recognition, whereas Saminsky, an idiot, collects honours and gifts from the palace.'

'Who said that life was fair?' Rheinhardt slapped Liebermann on the back and they proceeded towards the waiting carriage.

'I take it you will be paying Commissioner Brügel a visit this afternoon?'

'He asked me to return with something more substantial. "A little more meat on the bone" were his exact words.'

'Well, he won't be disappointed.'

'If it really transpires that the mayor . . .' Rheinhardt abandoned his sentence. 'No, one must not think that yet. It is far too early.'

The two men looked at each other and much passed between them. A strange, shared excitement, tainted with the expectation of encountering uncertain dangers.

'You will let me know, I trust, should you succeed in getting the commissioner's approval?'

'Only if you promise not to talk to the mayor about pianos.'

'You have my word. I'll be at the hospital.'

They arrived at the carriage but when Rheinhardt pulled the door open Liebermann made no attempt to get inside.

'Don't you want to come back to Schottenring with me?'

'No. I'm going to catch a train.'

'To the hospital?'

'No, Landstrasse.'

'Why are you going there?'

'To pay my respects to Mozart.'

Liebermann raised his hand, turned sharply, and walked off as though he was suddenly in a great hurry. Rheinhardt took a cigar from his pocket, lit it, and watched his friend's brisk progress down the gentle gradient.

'He does it on purpose,' the inspector muttered.

'What did you say?' asked the driver.

'Nothing,' Rheinhardt replied.

25

IN THE SEVENTEEN-EIGHTIES, Emperor Josef II had decreed that, in order to limit the spread of disease, all interments should take place outside the city walls. So it was that the St Marxer cemetery came to be situated on the south-eastern fringes of the modern metropolis. The new cemetery was so small that it soon became overcrowded and no further burials were permitted after eighteen seventy-four. Standards of maintenance were relaxed and the ensuing decades had imbued the cemetery with a desolate, forlorn aspect.

On previous occasions when Liebermann had ventured out to St Marxer, this general impression of remoteness and neglect had been assisted by the weather. An overcast sky had created an oppressive, eerie gloom. Curiously, the conditions now were, once again, identical. He had never seen, and wondered whether he ever would see, this sad little graveyard in sunlight. It seemed to exist under a pall of perpetual melancholy. Grey clouds had massed on the horizon and the fitful breeze carried with it the harsh laughter of crows.

Liebermann strolled down the principal avenue, occasionally stopping to admire the statuary: an angel, kneeling, hands clasped together, his robes falling in beautifully executed folds from his muscular body; a sweet little child, with curly locks, hands crossed over his chest, and chubby ankles exposed beneath the hem of his baggy nightshirt; an ethereal being, bearing a torch, emerging from the uneven surface of a rough-hewn slab of rock. None of the tombs were very grand, but the understated artistry of their design was eloquent and arresting.

Turning off onto a muddy footpath, Liebermann made his way between more graves until he reached an open space containing a monument of white marble. A stricken cherub, hand held despairingly against its forehead, leaned against a broken pillar for support. The truncated column was symbolic, representing an untimely death. There was no epitaph on the pedestal, only a name in gold letters, and some dates:

W.A. Mozart
1756 — 1791

It was debatable whether the remains of the great composer really were beneath the monument. His body had been wrapped in a sack, sprinkled with lime to prevent contagion, and then tipped off a cart into a mass grave. The residual parts of those buried in this way — bones, teeth, hair — were usually dug up again after eight years. Mozart's monument wasn't erected until eighteen fifty-nine, by which time what was left of him would have been removed and scattered elsewhere. Still, thought Liebermann, there might be some physical remnant, some residuum, some trace yet preserved beneath the cold, wet earth.

Liebermann was, as always, deeply affected by the *Mozartgrab*. His instinct was to pray, but he was incapable of performing such a disingenuous act. He had no belief in God, saints, seraphim and cherubim or childish fantasies of immortality in a heavenly kingdom. It was all such nonsense! Consequently, he was denied a ready outlet for his natural inclination. Nevertheless, the urge to give some form to his feelings was insistent.

Listening to music was the closest Liebermann ever got to an

experience of the numinous, so, very softly, he began to sing a song
that for him served as a substitute for prayer, Schubert's *An die Musik*:

> O blessed art, how often in dark hours
> When the savage ring of life tightens round me,
> Have you kindled warm love in my heart,
> Have transported me to a better world!

The gentle melody, croaked hoarsely above the imagined piano
accompaniment, was cathartic: something inside, something tight and
compact, found release. Liebermann reached out and touched the
broken pillar. In a sense, its symbolism was universal. All lives were
too short. He remembered a ward round he had attended as a student.
The professor had presented the youthful *aspirants* with a cadaverous
ninety-nine-year-old patient who was hanging on to life by a thread.
It was the man's birthday the following week, and he wanted, desper-
ately, to reach the age of one hundred. Who was ever ready to die?
There would always be one more book to read, one more person to
see, one more hour or fleeting yet indispensable minute to spend.

The ninety-nine-year-old patient had died that evening.

Liebermann pressed his hand against the stone. He found himself
thinking of Amelia Lydgate. He had read the book she had given him,
Elective Affinities, a book about love. No, more than that, a book about
inevitable love. He was constantly reminding his dear friend Rheinhardt
that all human action, however trivial, had a deeper meaning. Perhaps
it was time to take heed of his own counsel. Days were not in infin-
ite supply.

Some spots of rain roused Liebermann from his deep musings.
Withdrawing his hand from the truncated column, he chastised
himself for becoming so self-absorbed. He had come to the St Marxer
cemetery with a specific purpose in mind. Mozart was not the only

composer buried within its walls. A few days earlier, Liebermann had visited the city registry in order to discover the final resting place of David Freimark. How fitting it was that the young composer, snatched from life before his time, should be buried so close to Mozart, the patron saint of premature ends and thwarted promise.

Liebermann trudged down the waterlogged avenues, searching for the headstone. Eventually he came to a group of Jewish graves, and one of these belonged to David Freimark. It was a simple arched slab, showing only his name and dates: 1837—1863. The porous stone had crumbled, rendering a brief epitaph illegible. On the raised mound in front of the headstone was a bunch of flowers. The blooms had begun to shrivel and some petals had been scattered by the wind. Other, older bunches, desiccated stems tied together with string, were also distributed around the grave. Liebermann examined each of them in turn to see if any tags were attached. There was nothing.

Rheinhardt, the pragmatic policeman, had challenged Liebermann. What was the point of speculating about Freimark? If the composer had been murdered, all those years ago, and Brosius was also dead, what was Liebermann's purpose?

I want to find out the truth, thought Liebermann. He was a psychiatrist and an acolyte of Freud. His whole professional life was devoted to uncovering truths and it was not in his nature to ignore a mystery.

All these flowers . . .

Was it possible that Freimark still had a coterie of admirers? An artist remembered for a single work, however impressive, did not usually command such respect. No one had left a single bouquet on Mozart's grave!

The rain had begun to fall harder. Liebermann raised his collar and hurried back to the cemetery entrance which was situated next to the gatekeeper's lodge. It was a small, featureless building, the door propped open with an iron weight. Liebermann entered a bare reception room, which contained a table, a well-worn armchair and a small pot-bellied stove. A faded photograph of the emperor hung above a squat bookcase, each shelf stacked with ledgers.

Liebermann called out, 'Hello?'

A grubby-looking man came through the rear door. He was holding a tin cup full of steaming liquid, gripped in both hands to warm his fingers.

'Good afternoon, sir. How can I help?'

'My name is Liebermann. I am currently undertaking some musical research. The composer David Freimark is buried here.'

'Freimark,' said the gatekeeper. He took a sip of his beverage, smacked his lips and added, 'Composer, was he? I didn't know that. Of course, if it's composers you're looking for—'

'Mozart,' interrupted Liebermann. 'Yes, I know. My interest, however, is in Freimark.'

The gatekeeper shrugged: *suit yourself.*

'I noticed,' Liebermann continued, 'that fresh flowers have only recently been laid on his grave. Do you know who put them there?'

'Yes, I do. It was me.'

'May I ask why?'

'Because I was told to.'

'By who?'

'What's it to you?' said the gatekeeper bluntly.

Liebermann took some coins from his pocket and nonchalantly placed them on the table.

The gatekeeper looked at the inducement, produced a melodic fragment using the syllables 'pom-ti-pom' and answered, 'A lady. Frau Abend. We have an arrangement. I buy the flowers and put them on the grave four times a year. She gives me a little something for my trouble.' He glanced again at the coins to indicate that the contract was remunerative.

'Who is she, this Frau Abend?'

'I don't know.'

'Is she related to Freimark?'

'I couldn't say.'

'Has she ever visited the grave herself?'

'She did, a few years back. She didn't stay very long. I think she was just checking up on me.'

'Is she a very elderly lady?'

The gatekeeper laughed. 'No. She's quite young, as I recall.'

'Do you know where she lives?' The gatekeeper offered Liebermann another 'pom-ti-pom' and his expression suggested that something else was necessary before he could proceed. The young doctor found another krone in his pocket.

'Much obliged, sir,' said the gatekeeper. He put down his cup and pulled out a volume from the bookcase. Flicking it open he ran his finger down the page. 'Here we are. Frau Astrid Abend.'

26

THE COMMISSIONER'S EXPRESSION WAS incredulous.

'Lueger knew that Rosenkrantz intended to terminate the life of their unborn child?'

'That is what Professor Saminsky believes, sir,' Rheinhardt answered.

'Well, well, well.'

'The Christian Social Party espouses traditional values: church, fatherland and family. If this unfortunate . . .' Rheinhardt selected an inoffensive euphemism, '. . . *sequel* to the mayor's association with Rosenkrantz had been reported in the newspapers, Lueger would have lost the support of many loyal followers. Rosenkrantz was not stable. Her mood was volatile and she suffered from a medical condition which modern doctors think of as a *mental* problem.'

'Information that could equally have been used to the mayor's advantage, had allegations been made.'

'Rosenkrantz was adored by the public, feted for her portrayal of tragic heroines and doomed lovers. Attempting to discredit her would have been hazardous.'

'True, but not as hazardous as killing her!'

Rheinhardt confronted the commissioner's hard stare.

'Sir: given Herr Geisler's statement, and what Professor Saminsky disclosed this afternoon, it would be an unconscionable dereliction of duty if we failed to pursue the course of action that now *plainly* suggests itself.'

The commissioner picked up a dagger-shaped letter opener. For one horrible moment Rheinhardt thought that his superior had summarily resolved to settle the debate with an act of mindless violence. Instead, Brügel ran his finger along the blunt edge and emitted a low grumbling noise. 'Very well, Rheinhardt, you can go to the town hall.'

Rheinhardt expelled a lungful of air which he had been unconsciously retaining.

'Thank you, sir. I will undertake the interview accompanied by Herr Doctor Liebermann.'

The commissioner's face twisted into an ugly sneer.

'What? I don't think that's such a good idea.'

'His observational skills have served us well on many occasions.'

'Yes, yes, yes,' said Brügel dismissively. 'I know all that!'

'Then why, may I ask, do you object?'

'He's a Jew, Rheinhardt! What kind of reception do you think he's going to get in the mayor's office?'

'I am sure that Doctor Liebermann is fully aware of the mayor's views on the Jewish question.'

'That wasn't my point. Think about what you're hoping to achieve, Rheinhardt, and how best to go about it. You don't want to get the mayor's hackles up as soon as you arrive, do you?'

'With respect, sir, under the circumstances I doubt that the mayor will be very pleased to see either of us.'

The commissioner lifted some papers which earlier had been laid over a bowl filled with *männer schnitten* biscuits. He selected one and bit through the crisp wafers. A change of expression, more than could be reasonably attributed to the effect of hazelnut praline, suggested that some new idea had just occurred to him. Brügel's rigid features softened and, smiling in a way that could only be described as untrustworthy, he declared: 'All right, as you wish. Take Liebermann with you.'

Rheinhardt wanted to ask the commissioner what it was that had made him change his mind, but he decided, on reflection, that it would probably be unwise to ask. He accepted the concession with a brusque nod and the silence that followed was prolonged and awkward. When the commissioner had finished eating his biscuit, he knocked some crumbs from the wiry outgrowths of his mutton-chop whiskers, and said, 'What you're doing, Rheinhardt . . .'

The tentative sentence was never completed and its ambiguity permitted several interpretations.

'Yes, sir?' Rheinhardt prompted, eager for some kind of resolution.

The commissioner placed the letter opener by the biscuit bowl, linked his hands together and shifted his bulk forward.

'You understand, I hope, that this situation must be handled with extreme care. If you have been misled, which is always possible, then the mayor's office will raise questions concerning your competence. I am approving your request, but I do so not without reservation. Please remember that I said that, Rheinhardt: *not without reservation.* At some point in the future it is possible that you will be asked about this conversation, and I need to know that your recollection of my *exact* words will be accurate. A man in my position depends on the judgement of his team. I am assuming that the evidence, as you have presented it to me, is of a certain standard. I cannot be held responsible if it transpires that you have been presumptuous or naive. In the event of a formal complaint being issued by the mayor's office, you cannot expect me to interpose myself between you and the town hall. Is that clear?'

Rheinhardt stood up, bowed and clicked his heels.

'Thank you for your support, sir.'

The remark was impertinent. But Rheinhardt guessed that, this once, he would probably get away with it.

27

Professor Freud reached out and touched an ancient figurine, one of many occupying the desk space between his books and his writing materials. The movement was quick and repeated, like the superstitious ritual of an obsessive.

'Are you acquainted with Professor Saminsky?' asked Liebermann.

'Daniel Saminsky?' Freud's face was impassive. 'Yes, he studied in Heidelberg and was greatly influenced by Erb.'

'I was introduced to him recently.'

'What did you think?'

'I was unimpressed.'

Freud drew on his cigar and opened his mouth, releasing a ring of smoke. 'He wrote a rather unsympathetic review of my dream book.'

'Yes. I remember.'

'And I must admit that since then, on those rare occasions when our paths have crossed, I have been disinclined to exchange civilities. His publications are few but he once wrote a book about diet, exercise, and their effect on the nervous system. If my memory serves me correctly, he championed a certain type of nut-oil and regular sea air. The late empress, a woman easily persuaded by any medical work containing a whole chapter devoted to enemas, consulted him on several occasions. I very much doubt whether his interventions were effective, but in due course he was honoured by the palace.'

'He lives in a very fine house up in Hietzing.'

'Well, there you are,' said Freud, smiling. 'That's what an invitation to the palace can do for you. A physician who has attended the royal family can expect to see his practice thrive — a stampede of society ladies will beat a path to his door. This would be true even if he prescribed nothing but ground shoe leather.' The professor's expression became more thoughtful. 'Still, I can't really criticise Saminsky. We are all, to a greater or lesser extent, dependent on patronage, especially us Jews. I would never have been made *professor extraordinarius* without a little help from Böcklin.'

Liebermann didn't know anybody called Böcklin in the academic, medical or political hierarchies. The only Böcklin he knew of was Arnold Böcklin, the symbolist painter.

'Who?'

'Böcklin. You must know Böcklin. He's best known for *The Isle of the Dead.*'

'I don't understand,' said Liebermann, bemused. 'How could Arnold Böcklin have acted on your behalf? Besides, I thought he was dead.'

'He *is* dead. He came to my aid — indirectly, as it were. Have I not told you the story?' The professor offered his young disciple a third cigar. 'Nothnagel and Krafft-Ebing recommended me for the position of associate professor years ago, but the council of the faculty rejected their proposal and I was passed over.'

'Why did that happen?'

'Oh, because of my views on sexuality — and my race.' Freud sat back in his chair. 'I was passed over again in ninety-eight and ninety-nine. The following year all the names put forward were ratified, with one exception. Mine! I had never considered patronage as a solution. But with a family to feed and bills to pay, the pleasures afforded by high-minded disdain were diminishing. I spoke to my old teacher, Exner, who informed me that the minister on the council was being prejudiced against me.'

'By who?'

'To this day I have no idea. Exner advised that I should seek some . . . *counter-influence.*'

'With respect, Herr Professor,' said Liebermann, scratching his head. 'What has all this got to do with Böcklin?'

Freud requested patience by lifting his finger.

'I have never been personally acquainted with people of power. The only contact I have ever had with *that* class has been professional. Subsequently, I let some of my patients, particularly those possessing wealth or title, know of my predicament. It wasn't an easy thing for me to do, and I felt distinctly uneasy. One of these patients, a very formidable baroness, approached the minister and struck a bargain with him. You see, he was anxious to attain a work by Böcklin — *The Castle Ruin* — for the new modern gallery. Now, as luck would have it, *The Castle Ruin* was owned by the baroness's aunt. My patient mediated between minister and aunt, and after three months the old lady agreed to part with her picture. Shortly after, the baroness found herself next to the minister at a dinner party, and she was the first to hear that he had sent the necessary document pertaining to my associate professorship for the emperor to sign. The next day, she burst into my office and cried "*I've done it!*"'

Freud stubbed out his cigar and his mouth twisted before he continued. 'Congratulations and bouquets rained down on me as if His Majesty had officially recognised the role of sexuality in mental illness, the council of ministers had confirmed the importance of dreams, and the necessity for a psychoanalytic treatment of hysteria had been passed in parliament with a two-thirds majority. Colleagues who had previously crossed the street to avoid me now bowed, even at a distance.' Freud lit another cigar. 'To make one's way in the world, we all have to make compromises. Saminsky, me and, in time, even you.'

Vienna! Liebermann thought. How was it that the most modern and forward-looking city in the world could be so corrupt!

'We shall see,' said Liebermann.

Freud shook his head. The old man's expression was not disapproving, but full of pity. 'A doctor with too many scruples can't make a decent living. And a Jewish doctor must be especially resourceful.' His face brightened with mischief. 'Have you heard the one about Kaplan? No? Good. So Kaplan goes to see his doctor, Birnbaum, for a check-up. After examining his patient, Birnbaum says, "*I'm sorry, Herr Kaplan, but I have bad news. You only have six months to live.*" Kaplan is horrified. He buries his head in his hands and replies, "*That's terrible. Moreover, I have a confession to make: I can't afford to pay your bill.*" Birnbaum responds immediately: "*Very well, Herr Kaplan, I'll give you a year to live.*"'

Freud fixed his inquisitorial gaze on Liebermann. An opinion was required.

'Yes,' said Liebermann. 'Most amusing.' But he was unable to give his mentor a sincere smile.

When Liebermann returned to his apartment he found a letter waiting for him from Gustav Mahler. The director had managed to obtain an original piece of writing by the author of the scurrilous *Deutsche Zeitung* article and wanted Liebermann to examine it as a matter of urgency. Liebermann sighed and composed a brief apologetic response. The earliest he could keep an appointment at the opera house would be the following Monday. He knew that the director would not like this, but there was nothing he could do. Reluctantly, he sealed the envelope and left it on the bureau for his serving man to post in the morning.

28

'WELL, HERE WE ARE,' said Rheinhardt. 'Are you ready?'

'I think so,' said Liebermann.

'Then let us proceed.'

They turned onto the wide boulevard, their heels hitting the asphalt in unison.

The town hall was a grand edifice of pale stone, with a soaring central clock tower flanked by two shorter spires on either side. It was a building rich in Gothic detail, rising up in several layers: columns and arches, mullioned windows, a clerestory and, finally, a pitched grey roof. The long approach gave Liebermann ample time to consider his destination.

In spite of its venerable appearance, the town hall was not an old building. It had been officially opened in eighteen eighty-four, a mere nineteen years earlier. The anachronistic façade was a conceit, designed to evoke a sense of the past, an idealised late Middle Ages in which benign Bürgermeisters protected the rights and privileges of the people, and stalwart, honest guildsmen made the city wealthy with their skill. The town hall was festooned with sculpted figures, denizens of this fabled and prosperous medieval world.

Professor Freud had shown that dreams and fantasies often conceal a darker truth. This civic dream, rendered in stone, was no exception. The mayor did not protect the people of Vienna. Indeed, for those citizens who could not lay claim to an Austrian Catholic pedigree, he was a brooding potentate, surveying the city with malign intent from his high tower. And the townsfolk were not carpenters, furriers and clockmakers, but bureaucrats, speculators and factory workers. Among the statues on the upper parapet, Liebermann did not see any clerks, capitalists, labourers or shop girls.

Liebermann and Rheinhardt ascended the stairs and passed beneath a great archway. On entering the building they were welcomed by a functionary who escorted them through a series of corridors, galleries and shadowy chambers. The interior of the town hall seemed impervious to light. On the first floor the functionary placed them in the custody of a low-ranking official who neglected to introduce himself and recorded their names in a large book before leading them to a spartan waiting room. Half an hour elapsed and another gentleman arrived, this time dressed in the distinctive green tailcoat of a Lueger 'courtier'. He marched them into what appeared to be an antechamber and, gesturing at a pair of double doors, whispered that the mayor would be receiving them in his private apartment. Another half-hour passed before these doors opened, revealing a thickset man, also dressed in green, who beckoned them with a curling finger.

The mayor looked impressive for his age, his lineaments conforming to the classical paradigm of nobility. He was seated behind his desk, writing, and the scratching of his pen nib was clearly audible. The Persian rug which covered the floor was intricately patterned and its fibres were strong enough to add a disconcerting buoyancy to each step. This peculiar sensation, combined with the exceptional nature of the occasion, made Liebermann feel light-headed. Mayor Lueger rose to greet them. He was dressed in an expensive suit and his abundant jewellery glittered as he moved.

'Good morning, gentlemen.'

'Good morning, Mayor Lueger,' said Rheinhardt. 'I am Inspector

Oskar Rheinhardt and this is my colleague Doctor Max Liebermann. Thank you, most kindly, for permitting us to interrupt your busy day. The security office is indebted.'

Rheinhardt and Liebermann bowed together.

'Please sit,' said the mayor. He clearly felt under no obligation to exchange pleasantries. After first consulting what must have been an itinerary, he came directly to the point with alarming bluntness. 'You wish to ask me some questions concerning Fräulein Ida Rosenkrantz?'

'That is correct, sir,' said Rheinhardt. Glancing over at Lueger's servant, he added, 'Some of the questions I must ask you are of a private and personal nature.'

'Pumera,' said the mayor, without turning. 'I'll ring the bell if you're needed.' Making his exit through a door situated behind the mayor's desk, the bodyguard directed a disapproving glance at Liebermann. Had his upper lip risen a fraction more, disapproval would have become contempt. 'Inspector,' continued Lueger, 'it is the duty of every citizen, myself included, to assist the police in their investigations; however, if I am to divulge details of my private life, then I must be confident of your discretion.'

'You have my word,' Rheinhardt replied.

'And what about you, Herr Doctor?'

'You have my word also,' said Liebermann.

'Good,' said the mayor. 'Needless to say, in due course, should I discover that my confidence in you was misplaced . . .'

He paused, allowing his visitors to contemplate the varied forms of retribution that a Lord-God might have at his disposal.

'The office of mayor,' said Rheinhardt, speaking with exaggerated solemnity, 'commands our *complete* respect.'

Liebermann thought that his friend's declaration was too theatrical, too obviously insincere. He was surprised, therefore, to see a muted but satisfied smile appear on Lueger's face. The vanity of a demagogue could never be overestimated.

'Thank you, Inspector,' said the mayor, turning his hands outward and extending his arms. 'I am at your service.'

Proximity did not flatter the mayor. Close up, he cut a less dignified figure. His skin was weather-beaten and wrinkled and one of his eyes showed an alarming independence of movement. He had the yellow fingers of a chain-smoker.

'Mayor Lueger,' said Rheinhardt, 'I understand that you were well acquainted with Fräulien Rosenkrantz.'

'She sang at my birthday celebrations, rather beautifully, I recall — and soon after we became friends.'

'Friends? When you say *friends*, do you mean . . .?' Lueger's frown stopped Rheinhardt mid-sentence. 'My apologies, sir,' said Rheinhardt. 'An insolent question, but it is one that I am required to ask.'

The mayor took a cigarette from a silver box. 'We enjoyed a brief association. What of it?'

'Brief?'

'A few months, that is all. Our liaisons ceased in the spring.'

'March, April?'

'March, although we continued to meet occasionally. Fräulein Rosenkrantz wished that we should remain friends.'

The mayor lit his cigarette.

'And this was not satisfactory?'

'I was very fond of Ida; however, the desire to maintain social intercourse was greater on her part. How did you find out about us?'

Ignoring the mayor's question, Rheinhardt asked solicitously, 'Why did the relationship come to an end?'

Lueger drew on his cigarette and allowed a ribbon of smoke to escape from the side of his mouth.

'I do not see how such information is relevant to your investigation, Inspector.'

Liebermann shifted position to attract the mayor's attention. 'With the greatest respect, Mayor Lueger, in my capacity as medical consultant I must beg to differ. It is vital that we determine Fräulein Rosenkrantz's state of mind in the days preceding her death.'

The mayor's wayward eye found an object of interest some distance above Liebermann's head.

'The liaison ended in March. It is now September.' The tone of Lueger's voice had become brittle.

'In matters of the heart,' Liebermann continued, smiling wistfully, 'the passage of time is no guarantee of recovery.'

The mayor drew on his cigarette, a deep inhalation that expanded his chest. He released the smoke slowly, then shrugged. 'The relationship ended because we were . . . incompatible. She was an artist and, although I enjoy the company of artists, Ida could be very demanding. She wanted us to spend more time in each other's company, more time than I could possibly devote to what was, after all, only a . . .' the mayor's unsteady eye invested his final choice of word with careless disregard '. . . dalliance.'

'Did you quarrel?' asked Rheinhardt.

'Towards the end, all too frequently, I'm afraid. She was remarkably insecure for a creature of such great beauty and talent. I was deeply saddened to learn that she had taken her own life, but I was not, if I am honest, wholly surprised.'

'The precise nature of her death,' said Rheinhardt, constructing a sentence of cunning ambiguity, 'is, as yet, undetermined.'

'Her death could have been accidental,' continued the mayor, 'but I believe suicide much more likely. She was fragile and prone to illnesses. I was forced to conclude that some of these problems might have originated in her mind.'

'Oh?' said Liebermann, tilting his head.

'She used to complain about food getting stuck in her throat. But there was never anything there. She used to imagine it.'

'When was the last time you saw Fräulein Rosenkrantz?' asked Rheinhardt.

Lueger nodded and said, 'She wanted me to marry her. She wanted to be the first lady of Vienna. But Vienna is the only bride I shall ever have.'

He glanced at a picture standing on his desk. It was placed at an oblique angle and Liebermann was able to see the image: an old woman with white hair.

'Mayor Lueger?' Rheinhardt persisted. 'The last time you saw Fräulein Rosenkrantz? Can you recall when it was?'

The mayor stubbed out his cigarette, grinding it into the ashtray until none of the flakes of tobacco were glowing. His expression was neutral, jaw set, lips pursed, but there was something playing about his eyes which suggested calculation.

'I can't remember, exactly.'

'A general indication would serve our purpose. Was the occasion recent?'

'No,' said Lueger, raising his chin up, defiantly. 'It must have been sometime in July.'

'Where did you meet?'

'A private dining room close to the Josefstadt theatre.'

'What was her mood like?' asked Liebermann.

'She wasn't very happy. Throughout the meal she complained about life at the opera house. Although that wasn't so unusual, I'd heard much of it before: how Director Mahler drilled the orchestra like a duty-sergeant and the singers were perpetually plotting against each other.'

'Did she mention any of the singers by name?' said Rheinhardt.

'On that occasion? Yes. Amsel. She claimed that Arianne Amsel had claqueurs in the audience who tried to put her off. It might have been true. It was difficult to determine whether the conspiracies Ida spoke of were real or imagined. Like the lump in her throat.' There was a knock on the door and the mayor called out, 'Enter.'

A 'courtier' opened one of the double doors and, poking his head through the gap, said, 'Mayor Lueger, Herr Steiner has arrived. He wishes to see you with respect to a matter of utmost urgency.'

'Tell him to wait. I won't be very much longer.' The 'courtier' bowed and stepped backwards into the antechamber, closing the door. Looking at Rheinhardt and Liebermann, Lueger said, 'I'm sorry, gentlemen. I'm afraid I must bring this interview to a close.'

'If I could ask just one more question?' said Rheinhardt.

'Very well, but my answer will have to be short.'

'We have learned . . .' Rheinhardt faltered. 'Forgive me, but the matter I must raise is rather delicate. It seems improper to broach such a sensitive subject in so perfunctory a fashion.'

'Please, Inspector,' said the mayor, impatiently shaking his watch chain.

'We have learned,' Rheinhardt began again, 'that Fräulein Rosenkrantz became pregnant, in the first quarter of this year.'

'What?'

'The pregnancy was terminated.'

Lueger waved his hand in the air, attempted to speak, but failed to produce anything approximating language. Taking a deep breath, he recovered his composure and said, 'Terminated? When?'

'April.'

'I am very surprised to hear this.'

'She did not tell you?'

'I knew that she had other admirers, but I did not realise . . .'

The unthinkable prevented the mayor from continuing. Rheinhardt spoke softly, 'You do not consider it possible that the child was . . .'

'Mine? Don't be absurd, Inspector. I would never take such a gamble.'

'Indeed, but accidents happen.'

'Not to me they don't,' said Lueger, his anger flaring. 'Pumera!' The door behind the mayor's desk opened immediately and the bodyguard re-entered. He stationed himself next to the mayor's chair, his arms folded. 'Gentlemen, I am most perturbed by this news. I find it extraordinary that a woman who professed devotion and eagerness to marry should have been so disloyal.'

'It is possible,' said Rheinhardt, 'that she conceived after your association ended.'

'If so, then it must have been within days or weeks, which is equally disconcerting. I can only conclude that Ida's mental problems were more serious than I had supposed. Perhaps she also suffered from some class of moral illness.' The mayor looked at Liebermann for confirmation, but the young doctor could not support his assertion. 'Inspector,' continued Lueger, straightening his back and assuming a more authoritative mien. 'If Ida Rosenkrantz was morally destitute and, as a consequence, she submitted her person to an illegal and irreligious procedure, then that is no business of mine. I know nothing about this and can offer you no further assistance. I trust that you are men of honour and will keep your promise of discretion. There is much that I must attend to this morning. Good luck with your investigation.'

'Thank you again,' said Rheinhardt, 'for granting us the great privilege of a private interview. Your help is greatly appreciated.'

The mayor inclined his head but did not stand.

Pumera escorted Rheinhardt and Liebermann to the double doors.

Before the bodyguard opened them, Lueger called out, 'Inspector?' Rheinhardt turned. 'How did you find out about my association with Ida Rosenkrantz?'

Rheinhardt smiled. 'I am a man of honour, sir, and I gave my word that I would not disclose the name of my informant.'

The mayor accepted Rheinhardt's unenlightening response with an ungracious grunting noise and Pumera ushered the policeman and his companion into the antechamber. Closing the door behind them, the bodyguard returned to his master, where he found the old man deep in thought. The mayor's elbows were resting on the desk, his hands clasped firmly together, the strength of his grip making the knuckles pale. Suddenly aware of Pumera's presence, Lueger looked up.

'She was insane, Anton, quite insane.' He reached for his cigarette box. 'Still . . . they don't know what happened. That's the main thing.'

Rheinhardt and Liebermann crossed the Ringstrasse and walked the short distance to the Volksgarten. The inspector stopped at the gates to buy a bag of roasted pumpkin seeds before they followed a path which took them to a secluded area near the north-east perimeter. They sat on a bench and Rheinhardt encouraged his friend to taste his purchase. The young doctor took a mouthful of seeds and savoured the strong flavours: smoked salt, paprika and some other exotic ingredient that surprised the palate.

'The vendor's Hungarian,' said Rheinhardt, chewing loudly. 'I would also recommend his almonds. They taste of bonfires, liquorice and bacon.'

Liebermann brushed the salt and paprika from his hands, crossed his legs, and began to speak, 'When we passed through the gallery of mayoral portraits, did you notice whose likeness was hanging beside Lueger's?' Rheinhardt shook his head. 'It was the same woman whose photograph was on his desk, a tough, pious *petite bourgeoise*. The familial resemblance was quite pronounced and she is almost certainly his mother. And did you see those items next to the photograph — a rosary, a small purse, and a prayer book with worn edges? We must suppose they once belonged to Frau Lueger. Now, what kind of man would immortalise his mother alongside Catejan Freiherr von Felder and Papa Zelinka? And what kind of man would treat his mother's possessions as though they were holy relics?'

'Ah,' said Rheinhardt. 'I strongly suspect you are about to talk of Greek legends and erotic instincts.'

'What if I am?'

'Well, I was hoping you would have something of a more practical nature to offer, something of direct relevance to the investigation.'

'Unresolved Oedipal feelings are *directly* relevant to the investigation.' said Liebermann. 'The mayor has always cultivated a particular image of himself for public consumption, the bachelor king, dedicated to his work and the city. I had assumed this was politically motivated. Unmarried, he is available to the women of Vienna as an object of fantasy, an idealised husband. He wins their adulation and support more readily. This strategy has been most effective. Who else among our politicians has attracted a nickname like *beautiful Karl*! However, I now realise that another, more fundamental factor must be taken into consideration. He has never married because he is obsessed with his mother.'

'That's all very well,' said Rheinhardt. 'But—'

'A mother's love is a jealous love,' Liebermann interjected, unwilling to entertain objections before his exposition was complete. 'She resents those who seek to usurp her. Thus, no woman, no prospective spouse, can ever be good enough for her *golden boy*. One can imagine the voice of the matriarch, rising from the depths of the mayor's unconscious, warning him about the wily ways of temptresses, vixens and femmes fatales. He described his relationship with Rosenkrantz as a *dalliance*, which suggests toying or trifling, a minor diversion. I suspect that *all* Lueger's relationships with women have been emotionally void, because his unresolved Oedipal feelings prevent him from forming a mature adult attachment. Now, imagine if one of these dalliances went wrong, posing a threat to his career and reputation. Imagine then how loudly the voice of his mother would resound in his head. Her shrill rhetoric, her powerful denunciation of sluts and sirens! And what would he do — what would he be willing to do, I wonder — to appease his mother, to atone?'

Rheinhardt held his hands up. 'Dear God, Max! What are you saying? You cannot make such extravagant claims, just because the mayor has an excess of filial respect.'

'Filial respect! He has put a portrait of his mother up alongside the great and good of Vienna. That is not respect, that is insanity!'

'Come now, Max. You are overexcited! Let us be more considered. In my opinion, we should not be getting bogged down in too much ... theory. There is a simple question we must answer before venturing into such treacherous territory. Was the mayor telling us the truth about the last time he saw Fräulein Rosenkrantz? If he was telling us the truth then Herr Geisler's testimony was nonsense and I have made a grave error of judgement. Commissioner Brügel will not be happy.'

Liebermann turned and studied his friend's face. The inspector looked anxious.

'Lueger was lying,' said Liebermann.

Rheinhardt sighed with relief. 'Yes, that's what I thought. He was evasive, wasn't he?'

'The first time you asked the mayor when it was that he had last seen Rosenkrantz, he acted as if he hadn't heard the question. He seemed distracted by reminiscences and spoke of how Rosenkrantz had wanted to marry him and how Vienna was the only bride he'd ever know. It is possible that he was simply trying to divert you from your purpose, but I am inclined to believe that these musings on marriage were in fact connected with what was discussed during the *real* final encounter — not the one he told us about which took place in the private dining room. The mayor tried to repress the episode and, as Professor Freud's system of psychology predicts, that which was most forcefully dismissed from consciousness was that which most forcefully returned. Lueger could not stop himself from alluding to the truth, albeit indirectly. At that point he glanced at his mother's photograph. He was trying to appease her!'

'Did you notice,' said Rheinhardt, 'how quickly Pumera responded to the mayor's call?'

'The man was clearly waiting,' Liebermann replied, 'listening on the other side of the door.'

'And he made no attempt to disguise this.'

'The mayor certainly knew he was there, eavesdropping.'

'Moreover,' said Rheinhardt, squeezing the tips of his moustache, 'the mayor was perfectly content for us to reach that conclusion.'

'Well,' said Liebermann, tapping his temple, 'he was letting us know something.'

'That he trusts his *courtiers* completely and any one of them would consider it an honour to perjure themselves on his behalf?'

'Exactly.'

'Which means that even if we are now wholly confident that Herr Geisler's testimony is true, his evidence is ultimately worthless. The mayor will have a convincing alibi prepared and God knows how many witnesses ready to come to his aid.'

The two men fell silent as a cavalry officer marched past.

Rheinhardt took out his notebook and began recording his

thoughts. In due course he said, 'What did you make of Lueger's re-action to the news of Fräulein Rosenkrantz's termination?'

'He seemed genuinely shocked.' Liebermann spotted a few grains of salt on his trousers and began flicking them off. 'But he is an accomplished actor.' Indicating a white façade in the distance, he added: 'Good enough for the court theatre.'

'Indeed.'

'Further, the obvious narrative which suggests itself, leading from the mayor's birthday celebrations to Rosenkrantz's death, is much more cohesive if we assume that Lueger made Rosenkrantz pregnant — and had been informed of this.'

Rheinhardt raised his eyebrows. 'What do you mean? *Obvious* narrative?'

Liebermann lowered his voice. 'The mayor had allowed Rosenkrantz to believe that they would be married. How attractive that prospect must have seemed to the singer! How she must have looked forward to the day when she would bid farewell to the opera house, the gruelling rehearsals of Director Mahler and the scheming of her rivals. I suspect that, initially, Lueger himself might have found the idea quite appealing. Rosenkrantz was very popular. She was a vote winner. But the relationship soon began to deteriorate. Demands, arguments, tantrums! And the internalised voice of Frau Lueger was becoming more insistent. You can't marry *her*, she's not good enough! Don't trust her! She's a seductress, a gold-digger, a glorified shop girl! And then: disaster. Rosenkrantz fell pregnant. A lawyer by profession and renowned for his powers of oratory, Lueger made Rosenkrantz accept that it was in the best interests of all concerned if the pregnancy was terminated. It was not the right time. They had to keep up appearances. Besides, there would be many other opportunities in the future. Rosenkrantz — hysterical, highly strung, and vulnerable — agreed. But after the operation, the mayor informed her that their relationship had sadly run its course and Rosenkrantz became seriously ill. The complications caused by the termination might have been life-threatening. During her convalescence the singer had much time in which to reflect on the sorry pass she had reached: long, sleepless, painful nights in which to incubate feelings of resentment and anger.'

Liebermann paused to remove some more grains of salt from his trousers.

'Yes, yes,' said Rheinhardt impatiently. 'Go on . . .'

'They met occasionally, and Rosenkrantz did her best to win back the mayor's heart. But it was hopeless, his heart belonged — and had always belonged — to his mother. As Rosenkrantz became more resentful, she also became more desperate. On Monday the seventh of September she telephoned the mayor and insisted that he come to her house in Hietzing. It was foggy, and he refused. She then issued a threat.'

'What kind of threat?'

'She would create a scandal, ruin his election prospects. She would tell the newspapers about the termination or show them some incriminating correspondence.'

'If she had done that, she would have also ruined her own career.'

'We are talking here about a woman who had significant psychological problems. She wasn't thinking rationally. Whatever the precise nature of the threat, it was sufficient to get the mayor to leave the town hall and travel up to her villa in Hietzing. When Lueger arrived, he calmed her with more false promises and encouraged her to take some of the medication on her bedside table. Laudanum, to help her sleep.'

'You really think he killed her?'

'He is a ruthless individual.'

Rheinhardt finished his pumpkin seeds and screwed up the paper bag.

'I should never have agreed to you coming.'

'Why do you say that? I think I've been extraordinarily perceptive.'

'You have,' said Rheinhardt. 'And that is what worries me. From now on you must be very careful, Max — do you understand?' Rheinhardt glanced over his shoulder. 'He knows who we are now.'

29

Rheinhardt stood in Fräulein Rosenkrantz's parlour, humming the introductory melody of Mendelssohn's Violin Concerto in E minor. He found it particularly conducive to thought.

An upright Bösendorfer piano stood between two windows. There were several sofas and numerous chairs, enough seating to accommodate an audience of at least twenty guests. A large canvas showed an eighteenth-century ship with blood-red sails, listing precariously in the steep funnel of a whirlpool. High above the masts and rigging, in the roiling storm clouds, he detected the features of a satanic face. As far as Rheinhardt could judge, it was not an accomplished work of art. The paint had been applied too thickly.

Lifting the picture off its hook, Rheinhardt scrutinised the wall, but saw nothing irregular. He then turned the picture over. A title had been scrawled across the stiff backing paper: 'The Dutchman rounds the Cape of Good Hope.' The artist's name was almost illegible but might have been 'Schreiber' or 'Schreiner'.

There was a loud knock, a single, decisive strike.

Rheinhardt balanced the painting on a chair and went to admit his assistant.

'Ah, Haussmann. Thank you for coming.' The young man stepped into the hallway, wiping his feet on the floor mat and offering his superior a pinched smile. 'We're going to conduct a search.'

'But the villa has already been searched, sir.'

'We are going to look for places of concealment.'

'Secret compartments?'

'Yes.'

Haussmann produced a visiting card and handed it to Rheinhardt. The inspector held it up and read: *Orsola Salak, psychic.* 'An imaginative suggestion, Haussmann, but I think we can manage without this woman's services.'

'No, that's not what I meant, sir,' Haussmann responded. 'A gentleman was looking for you earlier today. Herr Schneider?'

'Fräulein Rosenkrantz's dresser.'

'Yes, sir. He said that when you interviewed him he had been unable to give you Salak's address.'

'Orsola! Of course. Rosenkrantz's psychic.'

'Herr Schneider found her card in Fraulein Rosenkrantz's dressing room.'

Rheinhardt looked at the address.

'Ybbs Strasse 23. That's close to the Prater, isn't it?'

'Yes, sir. Near the Nordbahnhof.'

'Thank you, Haussmann.' Rheinhardt dropped the card into his jacket pocket and led his assistant into the parlour. When he saw the painting of the Dutchman's vessel again he wondered whether the artist's signature, which looked like 'Schreiber' or 'Schreiner', was, in fact, 'Schneider'.

'Obvious places first,' continued Rheinhardt. 'Beneath paintings and under rugs, then drawers and chests. Books should also be studied very closely. A hollow is often made in the pages of larger volumes. If our initial efforts are unsuccessful, we'll take up some floorboards. Come.' Rheinhardt clapped his hands together. 'Let us begin.'

They set about their task with determined energy. After completing their search of all the rooms on the ground floor they ascended the stairs and entered Fräulein Rosenkrantz's bedroom. The rummaging continued with renewed vigour, but without result.

'Help me with this, Haussmann,' said Rheinhardt.

He was stripping the four-poster bed. Once the counterpane and eiderdown were removed, the two men lifted the heavy mattress. There was nothing underneath. Rheinhardt then began tapping the bedposts, which proved to be disappointingly solid. When they had finished, Rosenkrantz's exotic chamber looked as if it had been ransacked and Rheinhardt was feeling a creeping sense of frustration.

The adjacent room was small and seemed to have no specific purpose. It contained a cupboard full of linen, two wooden chairs, a table and an enamel stove. A pile of old songbooks were stacked in the corner. Rheinhardt slumped down on one of the chairs and removed a cigar from his pocket. After lighting it, he opened the stove door in order to dispose of the extinguished match. He leaned forward — and froze.

'Sir?' his assistant ventured.

'Haussmann, when we were here last, the day we found Fraulein Rosenkrantz's body, I asked you to prepare a floor plan of Rosenkrantz's bedroom and check the other rooms. Do you remember looking in this stove?'

'No, sir.' Haussmann squatted next to Rheinhardt and discovered that his superior was staring at some blackened papers. The young man turned to face Rheinhardt, his expression perplexed, puzzled.

'It's always a good idea to check stoves and grates, Haussmann.'

The young man struggled to understand the insinuation. 'I'm sorry, sir?'

'These papers, Haussmann.'

'They're completely burned, sir.' He reached out to touch the crumbling remains. 'What use could—'

'Stop!' Rheinhardt cried, grabbing his assistant's wrist. Rheinhardt closed the stove door gently with his foot. Then, releasing Haussmann, the inspector rose from his chair and examined the polished metal pipe which connected the stove to the chimney. He took from his pocket a pair of pliers, which he then used to loosen the bolts which kept the pipe and stove joined together. 'Be a good fellow and fetch me some linen from the cupboard.'

The pipe came away from the stove and Rheinhardt, taking the material from Haussmann, plugged the circular hole. 'At least we don't have to worry about the wind now.' Rheinhardt opened the window and flicked some ash from his cigar. 'One big gust and there would be nothing left, just a pile of ashes. Now, run to the post office and telephone Schottenring. I need a few items.' Rheinhardt scribbled in his notebook, tore out the page and handed it to his bewildered assistant.

30

AFTER RETURNING HOME FROM the St Marxer cemetery
Liebermann had written a note to Frau Astrid Abend. He had declared
an interest in the music of David Freimark and explained how he had
learned of her provision of flowers for the composer's grave. Further,
he had asked if she was prepared to reveal her connection with the
composer. Liebermann justified this inquiry by claiming, somewhat
disingenuously, to be an amateur musicologist with an interest in
Freimark's life and works. Frau Abend had dispatched a prompt reply,
inviting Liebermann to her apartment in the fourth district.

When Liebermann arrived he was received by a manservant who
escorted him into a cluttered parlour. Most of the surfaces were festooned
with flowers and family photographs. The scratched furniture and torn
upholstery suggested not poverty but, rather, the invasion — past and
present — of young boys whose destructive behaviour was tolerated
by indulgent parents. Liebermann noticed that a tin soldier had been
hidden among the green branches of a potted plant. A rocking horse
was poking its head out from behind a leather chair.

After waiting only a few minutes, Frau Abend entered the room
and introduced herself. She was in her late thirties and wore a simple
green dress and white blouse. Although wrinkles were gathering
around her eyes, her skin had a youthful bloom and her easy smile
reinforced a strong impression of gentle forbearance. Tea was served
and the conversation flowed without awkwardness.

'I am not sure that I can tell you very much,' said Frau Abend, 'I suspect that you probably know more about Freimark than I do.'

'Actually, I know very little,' said Liebermann. 'I have only recently begun researching his life.'

'But why Freimark? He isn't very . . .' Frau Abend rotated her hand in the air '. . . fashionable.'

'A chance encounter. I met an elderly lady who once knew him. Frau Zollinger? Do you know of her?'

'I'm afraid not.'

'She was a patron of the arts. Freimark was a member of her circle.' Frau Abend poured the tea. '"Hope" is a very lovely song, Herr Doctor. But I don't know anything else by Freimark. Do you?'

'Nothing else he wrote is published. What is your connection with Freimark? Are you related?'

'No.'

'Then why—'

'The flowers? Because of my mother. It was my mother's wish that I continue an existing arrangement. She is dead now — two years passed.'

'Oh, I'm sorry.' Frau Abend made a gesture to suggest that sympathy was not required. 'May I ask,' continued Liebermann, 'your mother's name?'

'Carolin Fuhrmann — née Cronberg.'

'And what was she to Freimark?'

'Nothing,' said Frau Abend. Liebermann scratched his head and Frau Abend smiled, mildly amused by his perplexity. 'I am sorry, Herr Doctor. It was not my intention to confuse. Allow me to explain in full. My mother, Carolin, had a sister, Angelika. It was Angelika who paid for the flowers originally. My aunt died almost ten years ago. However, before her death she asked my mother to ensure that the flowers continued. Naturally, my mother agreed. When my mother

was dying, she, in turn, asked me to honour the promise she had made
to my aunt, and I have done so to this day.'

'Angelika. That would be Angelika Brosius?'

'Ah, so you do know something about my family.'

'Only that your aunt was married to Johann Christian Brosius,
Freimark's teacher.'

'Indeed.'

Frau Abend brushed a loose strand of hair from her face.

'Do you remember your Aunt Angelika?'

'Of course I do.'

'What was she like?'

'Striking,' said Frau Abend. She plucked a frame from a small table
and handed it to Liebermann. 'This photograph was taken when she
was in her fifties.' Liebermann studied the portrait: a woman with
long grey hair, high cheekbones and eyes of peculiar luminosity. There
was something unearthly about her appearance, detached, immaterial
— a natural muse. Frau Abend continued, 'I was very fond of my
aunt, but she lacked *something*.'

'Whatever do you mean?'

'She wasn't a very warm person. She wasn't like my other aunts,
the aunts on my father's side of the family.'

'You didn't like her.'

'Oh, no,' Frau Abend exclaimed. 'You misunderstand me. I liked
her very much. She took me to concerts and exhibitions and for rides
on the Prater. She was a good aunt. And she always treated me like
a young woman, never as a child.'

'Did she ever talk to you about Freimark?' Frau Abend shook her
head. 'What about her husband?'

'Yes, she spoke about him sometimes. Although Uncle Johann didn't
die until—' She stopped suddenly and her brow furrowed.

'Eighteen seventy-eight,' said Liebermann.

'Yes. I must have been about thirteen at the time. I went to the funeral, a grand affair at the Zentralfriedhof. But I remember him well, Uncle Johann, a big, sullen man — like a bear. He smoked enormous cigars. My mother always insisted on the highest standards of behaviour when we visited Aunt Angelika. We had to be very quiet because Uncle Johann was usually in the music room, working. I thought it most unfair. We had to be quiet while Uncle Johann could make as much noise as he wanted. He used to bash the piano like his life depended on it. Well, in a way, I suppose it did. My mother told me he would become incensed if disturbed. He was reputed to have quite a temper, which might have been true, although I never saw him angry. In fact, I remember him as a rather subdued man.' Frau Abend sighed. 'It always struck me as a sad place. Their apartment felt like a tomb. It always felt cold, empty. They didn't have any children. When Uncle Johann died my aunt carried on living there. She should have moved — somewhere smaller, brighter.'

'When did your aunt die?'

'Almost ten years ago.'

'Can you remember if there was anything among her effects which concerned Freimark?'

'There might have been.' Frau Abend winced. 'We threw a lot of things away.'

'Letters? Papers?'

'Yes, but I don't remember anything specifically to do with Freimark. And there was certainly no music, if that's what you're looking for. All the unfinished manuscripts were by Brosius.'

'What did you do with them?'

'We gave them to the conservatoire. My aunt used to copy out his scores. They were very neat.'

'She was a musician?'

'Yes, and a good one, so my mother said. But I never heard her play the piano. Not once.'

Liebermann handed the photograph back and took a sip of tea.

'Frau Abend, do you know how Freimark died?'

'An accident, I believe. My mother mentioned a mishap on the Schneeberg.'

'Did she say anything else?'

'About the accident? No, not that I recall.'

Liebermann paused before asking his next question.

'Why did your aunt arrange to have flowers placed on Freimark's grave? And why was she so anxious for this to continue?'

Frau Abend looked at Liebermann with wide eyes. A certain mischievousness played around her lips.

'Oh, isn't it obvious, Herr Doctor?'

'They were . . .' Liebermann hesitated before adding, '. . . lovers?'

'My mother said that Aunt Angelika would probably have left Uncle Johann had Freimark lived.'

'Fascinating.'

Frau Abend smiled. 'Affairs of this kind are commonplace among artists. Is it really so fascinating? I must suppose that you came here today hoping to discover the whereabouts of some lost Freimark songs or piano pieces. But I'm afraid all I can offer you is some very old gossip. If, today, Uncle Johann was held in higher regard, or if Freimark had written more, then perhaps these private details might merit a chapter in a volume of biography. But neither composer is very significant. No one is interested in them any more. Uncle Johann is sometimes mentioned as a footnote in articles on Brahms, and as for Freimark — well.' Frau Abend sighed. 'Perhaps, Herr Doctor, you should find a more worthy subject?'

'I am a psychoanalyst,' said Liebermann. 'A disciple of Professor Freud.' Frau Abend shrugged to show that the name meant nothing to her. 'We psychoanalysts believe that there is much to be gained by studying small things, the things that are usually overlooked by others. I am not in the least deterred by the fact that only one of Freimark's songs seems to have survived. Most of us live and die without leaving anything of value behind. Freimark bequeathed humanity one very beautiful song. That is sufficient reason, as far as I am concerned, to continue my inquiries.' Imitating his friend Rheinhardt, Liebermann lowered his voice and added: 'You have been very helpful. I am most indebted.'

31

'Now, HAUSSMANN, STAND BY the table, and for heaven's sake keep still,' said Rheinhardt. 'This is a very delicate procedure.'

Rheinhardt knelt by the stove, opened the door, and inspected the blackened papers within. The charred remains looked very much like a bundle of letters. Unfortunately, the lowest sheets in the bundle had been reduced to ash and most of the surviving sheets had fused together. Only the upper leaves looked as if they might be saved. Rheinhardt slipped a clean square of paper beneath the uppermost sheet. Holding his breath, he lifted the brittle remnant off the top of the carbonised bundle and stood up. He then took a few misjudged steps and watched in despair as the blackened sheet glided lazily towards the floor. It shattered as it landed, giving Rheinhardt cause to swear with uncharacteristic ferocity.

Haussmann looked on with sympathy.

'Bad luck, sir.'

'Nothing to do with luck, Haussmann — that was sheer incompetence!'

Rheinhardt returned to the stove and repeated the manoeuvre, insinuating the clean paper again beneath the uppermost leaf. As he withdrew his hand, only half of the leaf came away. This time, the pace of his departure from the stove was funereal. He crossed to the table and allowed his precious cargo to slide onto a rectangle of glass that had already been prepared with gum. The burnt paper was horribly warped and he pressed the crisp surface with his fingers. He was able to depress some of the blisters but others broke up, creating jagged mosaics. It wasn't ideal but it was better than nothing. Moreover, when he examined his handiwork his spirits lifted at the sight of some ghostly lettering.

'We've got something.'

'Well done, sir.'

Rheinhardt repeated this painstaking process several times, but the task of removing sheets from the top of the bundle became increasingly difficult. It became impossible to slide the clean paper into the crumbling mass without causing extensive damage. In the end, he had to settle for the retrieval of a few 'corners' before it became impossible to proceed further.

'Observe,' said Rheinhardt to his assistant. 'The ink appears grey, or a different shade of black against the dull black of the paper. This doesn't always happen when letters are burned. One must assume that the outcome depends to a very large extent on the chemical composition of the ink. Be that as it may, as you can see, our efforts have not been wasted.'

Rheinhardt lifted the first pane of glass and turned it towards the window. The writing manifested in grey loops.

'See, Haussmann: *best interests . . . in the meantime . . . we should . . . and thereafter I earnestly hope that . . .*'

The young man frowned.

'Not very—'

'Informative?' Rheinhardt cut in. 'No. However, a word of advice: dripping water hollows a stone.'

'I beg your pardon, sir?'

'So said a Roman poet. Oh, never mind . . .'

The second sheet of paper was blank, but the third contained phrases that made Rheinhardt's heart quicken: *affection for you is not in doubt . . . constancy and truth . . . our meeting when . . .*

Rheinhardt indicated the text and beamed at his assistant.

'A love letter, sir?'

'I would say so.'

The next two fragments contained nothing more than a few words, but the final fragment, a triangular piece with two straight edges, showed the correspondent's name. Rheinhardt allowed the light to play over the signature. There was something magical about the way in which the script flashed in and out of existence. The characters were black, a black of preternatural depth. They stood out in sharp relief against the pitch neutrality of the scorched background.

From your dearest Karl

'Sir?' Haussmann had detected Rheinhardt's sudden change of expression. The older man's cheeks had become flushed with excitement.

'Haussmann. Tell me — what does that say? Can you see the letters?'

'From your dearest . . . Karl.'

'That's what I thought. Dripping water, eh?'

32

LIEBERMANN FOUND HIMSELF SEATED, once again, opposite the daunting figure of director Mahler.

'I am sorry I couldn't come earlier,' said Liebermann. 'Other commitments, I'm afraid.'

Mahler accepted the apology and handed Liebermann a letter.

'The correspondent signs himself *a musician who wishes to hear unadulterated Beethoven*,' The director could not conceal his disdain. 'It was sent to Intendant Plappart and is almost identical in style to the heinous article that the editor of the *Deutsche Zeitung* saw fit to publish. I have assumed that both article and letter are the work of the same author. He is almost certainly a member of the orchestra. There can be little doubt now, as his complaints are very specific. For example, he objects to my addition of an E flat clarinet for performances of Beethoven's *Coriolan Overture* and the *Eroica Symphony*.' Mahler looked at Liebermann with renewed intensity. 'Before you proceed, Herr Doctor, I must take you into my confidence so that you will fully appreciate the importance of this matter. My personal relations with Intendant Plappart, the opera house administrator, are somewhat strained. His Excellency and I disagree on almost everything. A dissenting orchestra would suit his purposes.' Liebermann required further clarification. 'He would like,' Mahler added, 'to have me dismissed.'

'He can't do that — surely.'

'He can try. And that is reason enough for me to make the detection of troublemakers a priority. They provide Plappart with justifications for his cause.' The director changed position, crossing his legs and throwing an arm over the backrest of his chair. 'You must be aware that Emperor Franz-Josef is not a very discerning patron of the arts. He is much more comfortable sitting on a horse than in the royal box. And it is rumoured that His Majesty thinks that I take music too . . .' Mahler grimaced, '. . . seriously.'

'Ah,' said Liebermann. His instinct was to console, but under the circumstances he thought that it was probably best to offer only tacit support.

'And one more thing,' said Mahler, raising his index finger. 'I must beg your indulgence.'

'For what?'

'When I learned that you could not come immediately I consulted a graphologist, Professor Skallipitzky — do you know him?'

'No, I don't.'

'A gentleman of some renown in his field. Even so, I did not find his comments very illuminating.'

'What did he say?'

'He drew my attention to the slant and shape of the letters and made some inferences about the writer's character. He said that the correspondent was opinionated and held rigid beliefs concerning what is right and wrong. This, of course, is self-evident from the text. I was not impressed and Professor Skallipitzky's fee was, I am sorry to say, exorbitant.'

Liebermann gestured, indicating that he was not offended.

'I am happy to assist; however, now that you have a sample of the culprit's handwriting, my services are surely redundant. All that you have to do now is ask the musicians to write a few lines and compare scripts. Even if the culprit attempted to disguise his handwriting, it is probable that an expert like Professor Skallipitzky would be able to make a positive identification.'

'The solution you suggest would take time, Skallipitzky's time, which is costly. I have already included his initial bill among my official expenses and a subsequent, even larger bill would *not* meet with Plappart's approval. I would then have to defray — personally, you understand — a quite preposterous sum. But the issue of Skallipitzky's remittance is really a secondary consideration. I am obliged to be wholly honest with the orchestra. If I were to do as you suggest, it would be necessary for me to stand in front of them and explain why such an unorthodox request was being made.' The director paused before continuing. 'I do not want the guilty party and his supporters — there will inevitably be supporters — to see that I am worried. It will only encourage them and then they will attempt to stir things up even more.'

Liebermann accepted the director's reasoning and began to read the letter. The content was much the same as the *Deutsche Zeitung* article, a ranting, labile invective littered with anti-Semitic slurs and crude flights of fantasy masquerading as wit: *Yes, Mahler has E flat clarinets on the brain. Not content with adding one to the Eroica, he has also reinforced the trombones and double basses, and it is even being said that he will send his brother-in-law to Jericho to rediscover Joshua's trumpet, because Aryan trumpets are not loud enough for him.*

When Liebermann had finished reading he looked at the director. The great man was biting his fingernails and his high forehead was scored with horizontal creases.

'Well?' said Mahler eagerly. 'Do you detect anything of interest?'

Liebermann stroked the letter flat. 'I am of the opinion that inferring character traits from writing is a dubious pursuit. It may be that certain features of a hand are more common, let us say, in men than in women, but apart from such crude distinctions it is difficult to say very much else with certainty. One cannot assert that a well-rounded "O" betrays perfectionism or a jagged "W" impulsivity! It is possible, however, to draw some modest conclusions about the writer's state of mind by examining the effects of pressure during the act of writing.' Liebermann raised the letter. 'The nib has broken the paper in several places, which suggests a high degree of muscular tension.'

'Meaning?'

'Anxiety or anger. In this instance, most probably the latter.' Liebermann lowered the letter again. Mahler's face showed palpable disappointment. The young doctor was not deterred. He ventured a smile and continued: 'Let us abandon our consideration of the physical properties of the script and adopt a more psychological approach. The letter is anonymous. This is an important fact because certain things follow from it. The author was anxious to conceal his identity and, curiously, what we try to conceal frequently finds alternative and involuntary means of expression. The truth leaks out, as it were, in the form of subtle signs and aberrations.'

'With respect, Herr Doctor, I am not altogether sure what you are talking about.'

'Mistakes merit close inspection, as they often reveal an underlying preoccupation.' Liebermann ran his finger down the page. 'The author refers here to a philharmonic concert on the tenth of March, which he describes as a fiasco. Beethoven's *Egmont Overture* and Seventh Symphony were performed. The programme also included Weber's Second Piano Concerto. Needless to say, you were conducting. Actually, I recall that concert well. I attended with my mother and younger sister. And it did not take place on the tenth of March but the tenth of April. Such transpositions usually represent a kind of distancing, a denial. There was something about that concert that made the writer uncomfortable. The author then refers to Burkhard's review. But notice, he spells the critic's name incorrectly: B-U-C-K-R-H-A-R-D. When he was writing the name, the movement of his pen was disrupted by a disturbing association. It would be most interesting to read the review to which he refers. I would suggest that you find a copy and examine it very closely.'

'There is no need.' Mahler was grinning.

'Why?'

'I can remember what Burkhard wrote. He was very critical of the wind players — and with good cause. They did not acquit themselves well.' Mahler pulled his arm out from behind the chair and leaned forward. 'That is very interesting.' He raked his hair back. '*Very* interesting,' he repeated with more emphasis.

'Displacement,' said Liebermann, more to himself than to his companion. 'Unwilling to accept responsibility, the blame is transferred — projected.'

'Among those in the orchestra I suspect,' said Mahler, 'there is no one whom I consider more untrustworthy and potentially disloyal than Thomas Treffen, the principal flute player.' The director suddenly slapped his thigh. 'The culprit is Treffen! It must be!' Springing up from his chair, he paced up and down before coming to an abrupt halt. 'Once again, Herr Doctor, you have provided me with an invaluable service. Could I remind you that I am perfectly happy to remunerate — assuming that your fee is reasonable, of course.'

'The complimentary tickets that you have already offered are quite satisfactory.'

'As you wish, but I feel I owe you something more,' said Mahler. 'Particularly given how much Professor Skallipitzky was paid.'

Liebermann handed the letter back to Mahler. 'The tickets will be more than adequate recompense for my time. Thank you.'

He began to stand.

'Forgive me,' said Mahler. 'But we are not quite finished. How am I to proceed? Perhaps you have an opinion?'

* * *

When Liebermann arrived back at the hospital he was surprised to find Rheinhardt waiting outside his room.

'Oskar? What on earth are you doing here?'

The inspector answered his question with a blunt statement.

'We must return to the town hall.'

'I can't go to the town hall. Not now — I have patients to see. And there's a ward round this afternoon with Professor Pallenberg.'

'I have taken the liberty of negotiating your release from clinical duties for the rest of the day.'

'You did *what?*'

'The professor was very accommodating. Come, there is a carriage waiting outside and the mayor is expecting us at eleven-thirty.'

Liebermann noticed that his friend was less composed than usual. Indeed, his eyes were wide open, giving him a slightly wild look.

'What's happened?'

'We found something. I'll tell you on the way.'

33

THIS TIME THERE WERE no delays. Liebermann and Rheinhardt were escorted straight to the antechamber adjoining the mayor's private apartment in the town hall. At eleven-thirty precisely, one of the double doors opened and they were ushered in by Pumera. Again, Lueger was sitting behind his desk, but this time he had abandoned the pretence of industry. He was smoking a cigarette and he watched their approach with predatory interest.

'Good morning, Inspector.'

'Good morning, sir.'

The mayor silently acknowledged Liebermann but did not trouble to greet him personally. He then dismissed Pumera with a hand gesture.

'Thank you for your note, Inspector. Please, do sit down.'

Liebermann and Rheinhardt bowed before taking their places.

'It is very good of you to see us at such short notice,' said Rheinhardt. The mayor accepted the compliment but felt it necessary to add, 'Regrettably, I can only spare a few minutes.'

'We appreciate,' said Rheinhardt, 'that for one who occupies so high an office there can never be sufficient hours in the day.'

The mayor flicked the ash from the end of his cigarette and said, 'Some new evidence has come to light?'

'Another search was made of Fräulein Rosenkrantz's villa in Hietzing and some burned letters were recovered from a stove.' The inspector reached into his pocket and produced a blackened scrap of paper sandwiched between two rectangles of glass that had been taped together. He handed the object over to the mayor.

'What's this?'

'Part of a letter.'

Lueger peered at the scorched remnant and grunted.

'How do you know it's a letter?'

'Look closely. Some writing has been preserved. Do you see it?' The mayor opened his drawer and took out a magnifying glass. He studied the carbonised paper though the hoop of silver. 'Would you confirm for us that the writing is yours? It appears to say: *From your dearest Karl.*'

The mayor set the magnifying glass aside.

'Yes,' he said, 'That is my handwriting.' Lueger's deviating eye made his expression difficult to interpret. 'Were any other letters recovered?'

'Yes.'

'Intimate letters?'

'That is what they appear to be.'

Lueger drew on his cigarette and allowed the smoke to escape through his nostrils. 'Then you must return them to me.'

'I'm sorry. I am afraid they must be retained by the security office.'

'Why?'

'Ida Rosenkrantz's case is still open — ongoing.'

'Really, Inspector,' The mayor shook his head. 'You were already aware that Fräulein Rosenkrantz and I were . . . friends. Is it so very remarkable that we corresponded? If you are in possession of what are, in effect, my private papers, then I demand that they be returned.'

'Strictly speaking, the letters I have in my possession belong to Fräulein Rosenkrantz.'

'She is dead, Inspector.'

The mayor said these words with an air of finality, as if this stark declaration obviated further discussion. He was breathing heavily. Liebermann leaned forward to capture the mayor's attention.

'The letters seem to have been burned close to the time of Fräulein Rosenkrantz's death . . .'

The sentence hung in the air, suspended, oddly incomplete.

'She was obviously unwell, Herr Doctor,' said Lueger. 'Isn't that just the sort of thing that suicides do?'

'Not exactly,' said Liebermann. 'The typical suicide composes a brief explanatory note and begs for forgiveness.'

The mayor shrugged.

'It seems to me that this *discovery* supports everything I have already told you. Ida was a sick woman. She got herself into a state — burning old love letters — and then killed herself.'

An uncomfortable silence ensued.

Rheinhardt took out his notebook and turned a few pages.

'Mayor Lueger, are you absolutely sure that the last time you saw Fräulein Rosenkrantz was in the summer?'

For the first time, the strain of interrogation began to show on Lueger's face. The illusion of handsome nobility that he was so adept at creating suddenly dissolved. He appeared haggard and drawn. A slight tremor shook the yellow smoke-stained fingers. Liebermann almost felt sorry for him.

'Inspector,' said the mayor. 'What, precisely, are you trying to make of all this?'

Rheinhardt feigned surprise. 'I'm sorry?'

'What manner of story are you attempting to piece together here? That I compromised her? That she then died of a broken heart? That I am responsible for her death? Before you and your associate proceed any further I would strongly suggest that you review your thinking. May I remind you that the election is approaching.' He struck the table with a clenched fist. 'I cannot — *will not* — tolerate a scandal.'

'With respect,' said Rheinhardt. 'It was not our intention to imply—'

The mayor stood up and pointed an accusatory finger at Rheinhardt.

'Don't treat me like a fool, Inspector!' His voice was loud and his eyes glittered with fury. 'Better men than you have done so before and suffered the consequences.' A thin thread of spittle escaped from his mouth and clung to his beard. The door behind the mayor's desk opened and Pumera appeared. 'The inspector and his companion are leaving,' said the mayor.

Rheinhardt rose from his chair and with surprising elegance removed the letter from the mayor's desk and dropped it into his pocket. The bodyguard stepped forward but the mayor extended his arm, halting his progress.

'Show them out, Pumera.'

Part Three

The Kiss

34

ARIANNE AMSEL WAS LYING in a vast four-poster bed, her eyes wide open, gazing into the darkness. The air was redolent with cigar smoke, the pungency of which failed to smother a feral undertow of post-coital fragrances. Floating in space, somewhere vaguely above her line of vision, was the glowing terminus of the cigar. It flared and crackled, revealing the aquiline nose and shrewd eyes of the lord marshal. His expression was typically severe. There was no slackening of the jaw, no benign indifference, no sign of the inebriate idiocy which stuns the spent male into satisfied silence before the precipitate onset of sleep.

They had originally been introduced by the lord chamberlain. The occasion had been a celebration of German culture at the palace, in the presence of His Majesty the emperor, Franz-Josef.

How long ago was it now? Arianne asked herself. *Two years?*

A few memories flickered into existence. Glamorous women, the Bosnian Guard, and the *Hochmeister* of the Teutonic Knights in his gleaming white cape. She had been invited to the function with other eminent members of the Richard Wagner Association, Baron von Triebenbach and a charming young composer called Aschenbrandt. It seemed to her that an age had passed since those heady days when she was loved by everyone.

At that time she'd had no idea how the lord marshal's office served the emperor, but she had quickly guessed from the lord marshal's manner (and the sycophantic behaviour of those around him) that he occupied an elevated station in the imperial hierarchy. He was certainly more commanding than the lord chamberlain. However, unlike Prince Liechtenstein, the lord marshal knew almost nothing about opera and his manner was rather cold and stiff. She had flirted with him, albeit in a rather half-hearted way, and when Aschenbrandt had appeared, providing her with an excuse to leave, she had welcomed the opportunity.

Flowers had followed and in due course the lord marshal had come to hear her sing in *The Flying Dutchman*. Friends told her how powerful he was, but even then she had only responded with polite interest to his romantic overtures. It wasn't until Rosenkrantz had sung at the mayor's birthday party that Arianne had cause to review her position with respect to the lord marshal. It wasn't until then — far too late, in fact — that she came to appreciate the extent of Rosenkrantz's iniquity.

When, finally, Arianne and the lord marshal did become lovers, their illicit couplings were an unexpected success. Even so, their assignations took place infrequently. The lord marshal exercised extreme caution in all his affairs and he made no exception when it came to the management of his private life.

'Have the police been again?'

Arianne was aware that he had said something, but she was so deeply submerged in reminiscences that she was unable to identify the exact words.

'I'm sorry? I was drifting off,' she lied. 'What did you say?'

'The police? Have they been to the opera house again — asking questions?'

'They haven't spoken to me.'

'What about the others?'

'The police doctor, I've forgotten his name, he's been back a few times to talk to the director.'

'You saw him?'

'No.'

'Then how do you—'

'It's the opera house!' said Arianne, sitting up. 'We make it our business to know such things. Nobody enters the director's office without news spreading.' She paused before adding, 'I hate him!'

'Who?'

'The director.'

'Why? What's he done now?'

'The roles he has given me for the spring season are . . . demeaning. More Mozart! Who wants to sing Mozart! He does not give me the roles I deserve.' Arianne turned on her side and nestled against her lover's body. 'Couldn't you speak to Liechtenstein?'

'I did.'

'No, again, I mean.'

'He said that Mahler doesn't listen to anybody. He's completely inflexible.'

'But surely . . .'

'The palace doesn't like to be seen interfering.'

Arianne sighed and let her fingers play on the lord marshal's inner thigh.

'But the palace *does* interfere, doesn't it?'

Arianne felt the lord marshal's leg muscles tightening.

'Whatever do you mean by that?'

'People try to please the emperor, don't they? And I've heard that, privately, His Majesty has said things about the director. He doesn't approve of the way he runs the opera house.'

The lord marshal relaxed again. 'That's probably true.'

'Well then . . .'

The lord marshal drew on the cigar and closed his hand around one of Arianne's large breasts. The flesh only began to resist further compression when he was squeezing quite tightly. Arianne gasped.

'I'll think about it,' said the lord marshal.

Arianne was not convinced that he would. Consequently, she disappeared beneath the bedclothes, where she began to perform an act which would ensure his compliance. She had come to accept, belatedly, that a singer's career depended on more than just a good voice. Ida Rosenkrantz had obviously reached the same conclusion, but many years earlier.

35

PROFESSOR FREUD HAD POSITED the existence of a general phenomenon of childhood in which possessive feelings for the parent of the opposite sex were combined with hostile — sometimes murderous — feeling directed towards the parent of the same sex. In the desires and rage of infancy he had seen Greek tragedy recapitulated: the drama of King Oedipus. Freud had once suggested to Liebermann that a failure to resolve these primal urges might be an important determinant of mental illness, but he had been unable to specify how this resolution might be accomplished. In the intervening months he had given the matter much thought and was now regaling his disciple with some speculative hypotheses.

'The Oedipal situation casts the father in the role of an angry rival, competing for the mother's affection. In the already troubled infant mind, fears develop concerning the nature of paternal retribution. The child already has some inkling that his sexual feelings towards his mother are futile; the threat of castration — by his father — settles the issue and Oedipal desires are repressed. In due course, the syndrome disintegrates. Sexual interest in the mother wanes and hostility towards the father diminishes. The child is free to enter adolescence unencumbered by infantile material, which has served its purpose by orienting the libido towards its appropriate object. For girls, maturity is reached by a more circuitous route.'

Professor Freud threw his head back, opened his mouth, and allowed a spire of smoke to ascend.

'All infants,' he continued, 'irrespective of gender, are profoundly attached to their mothers; however, the ultimate orientation of female libido requires a transfer of affection from mother to father. How does this happen — and why — since mother has hitherto been the principal source of nourishment, tenderness and care? It happens because, at this juncture, little girls make a momentous discovery. They learn that they are anatomically deficient, incomplete. Boys have something which they don't have. This dramatic realisation creates feelings of inferiority and envy. The little girl rejects her mother and becomes devoted to her father, whom she now believes has the power to rectify her deficiency. Normal development then proceeds, with the wish for a penis being gradually replaced by a wish for a baby.'

Freud waved his cigar in the air, creating a diaphanous blue-grey screen.

'Unlike her brothers and opposite-sex play-friends, the little girl is free from worries about retributive castration: subsequently, forbidden ideas are repressed with less vigour. Thus it may be the case that women never achieve the moral strength of men. Moreover, they are prone to suffer from unresolved sexual feelings towards their fathers.'

The old man peered through the dissipating smoke.

'Ah,' he said, his lips buckling to form a lopsided smile. 'I see that you are not persuaded.'

Liebermann, embarrassed by the transparency of his reaction, felt an uncomfortable warmth rise from beneath his collar to his cheeks.

'You seem to have made a number of . . .' Liebermann stretched his fingers nervously and said, '. . . assumptions.' Freud made a gesture, inviting Liebermann to continue. 'With respect, where is the evidence for these processes?'

'You aren't married yet,' said Freud. 'Wait until you have children. Little girls are always asking why it is that their brothers have a *widdler* and they don't.'

'And boys,' said Liebermann, 'three-year-old-boys — you really think they fear castration?'

'Yes, and with good reason. A common threat employed by parents to discourage little boys from playing with themselves in public is — *if you carry on doing that I'll cut it off!* And when a little boy chances upon a little girl urinating, and observes a conspicuous absence in the location where he is endowed, what is he to think? It is perfectly reasonable for him to conclude that castration is not an idle threat but a real punishment.'

Liebermann thought about his father. They had always been, for as long as he could remember, uneasy in each other's company. There was something problematic, elusive, and frankly inexpressible at the root of their inability to communicate. He wondered whether some vestige of infant anxiety was still lurking in his unconscious.

'These are challenging ideas,' continued the professor, 'and it may be some time before the world is ready to accept them. Indeed, I must resign myself to the publication of several preparatory works before I risk setting yet more unpalatable truths before an already recalcitrant public. I am conscious of the fact that they have hardly digested my dream book. They will not welcome further threats to their complacency so soon after.'

The two men continued to discuss 'Sophoclean psychology' for several hours. In due course, Freud glanced at his desk clock, stifled a yawn and said, 'Forgive me, I am a little tired.'

Liebermann stood and unhooked his coat from the back of his chair.

'Thank you, once more, for a very stimulating evening.'

Freud made a languid papal benediction with his cigar.

'Strange that you should have mentioned Saminsky the other day.'

'Oh? Why's that?

'I ran into him at an auction. We were both bidding for the same unguentarium.'

'The same what?'

'One of these.' Freud turned and lifted a bottle from his bookshelf. It was mottled with patches of iridescent blue and green. 'Roman: first century. It was used to keep perfume in. I couldn't compete, of course. Saminsky's resources exceed mine by several orders of magnitude.'

'He's a collector?'

'Yes, and a very serious one too.' Freud rotated the bottle. 'Notice the long narrow neck, how it flares out — the swelling mouth. Beautiful.'

He could have been describing a woman. Freud found sex in the most unlikely places.

36

RHEINHARDT LOOKED UP AT the shabby apartment block and wondered whether it was derelict. No gaslights flickered in the windows and two weary caryatids, streaked with bird droppings, grimaced beneath the weight of heavy capitals. There was no concierge and the foyer stank of sewage. Rheinhardt picked his way across broken tiles and ascended the staircase. He could not imagine Ida Rosenkrantz in this place. He could not imagine her lifting the hem of her expensive dress and stepping over old newspapers and smashed glass.

Perhaps Herr Schneider was mistaken?

The phrase was forming under his breath just as he arrived at Orsola Salak's door. It stood wide open. Rheinhardt rapped the woodwork and an unnaturally deep female voice croaked, 'Who is it?'

'My name is Rheinhardt. I am a detective inspector.'

'Police?'

'Yes. May I come in?'

'Do as you please.'

Her German was heavily accented.

'Your door is open.'

'I know.'

'Shall I close it?'

'Open — closed. It makes no difference.'

Rheinhardt wiped his feet on a floor mat and stepped into a gloomy hallway. Through another open door he saw a woman, seated next to

a small table. The late-evening light was failing and all he could make
out was this hunched figure.

'Orsola Salak?'

'Come in, Inspector.'

She was very old, in her eighties perhaps. Her hair was a grizzled
mass of wisps, filaments and braids of varying sizes. Embedded in this
unkempt tangle were filthy ribbons and broken fetishes. Rheinhardt
saw discoloured copper rings, a miniature horseshoe, and a dried-up
palm frond folded to make a cross. The general effect reminded him
of a magpie's nest. Salak didn't look like the psychics and mind-
readers who sat in booths on the Prater. Their posturing and
theatricality was reassuringly absurd. Orsola Salak was something
quite different, something more grave and disturbing — a reversion
to an ancestral primitive type. Rheinhardt became aware of an eerie
grinding sound emanating from her person. He noticed her clawlike
right hand, the spidery action of her fingers, kneading whatever it
was that she held.

'It isn't safe, leaving your door open like that.'

She produced a dry cackle. 'I am protected.'

'I didn't see anyone.'

'Well, *you* wouldn't.'

She raised her head and the appearance of her eyes made Rheinhardt
draw breath. The pupils were an opaque, malignant white: milky
discs, rimmed with the remains of what had once been dark brown
irises. Her skin was like parchment. When she smiled, deep seams
opened up, segmenting her face and giving it the deranged appearance of a wooden puppet.

'What's the matter? Never seen a blind woman before?'

'I'm sorry, I didn't mean . . .'

'Come in, sit.'

She reached across the table and shook an empty chair.

Rheinhardt glanced around the room.

Faded wallpaper, dusty curtains, a rug that covered only a small area of the floor. Beside the old woman was a battered ebony chest with a tarnished silver hasp. On top of it was a pile of charms made from hair and beads. They were like small effigies. Memories stirred. Rheinhardt recalled seeing an identical totem among Fräulein Rosenkrantz's jewellery and cosmetics.

He sat down. 'Thank you.'

'I'd offer you something to drink, Inspector, but I have only some herbal remedies.' Orsola Salek kicked the chest which produced a muffled clink. 'You wouldn't like them.'

'Perhaps not.'

The grinding continued.

'You're not here for your fortune, are you?'

'No.'

'A professional visit, eh?'

'I'm afraid so.'

Orsola Salak thrust her head forward and her calcified eyes caught the light.

'You want to talk to me about Ida?'

Rheinhardt was surprised, and replied, somewhat redundantly, 'Yes, Ida Rosenkrantz.'

The old woman nodded to herself. 'I heard about what happened.'

'She used to consult you.'

'Yes.'

'Did she come often?'

'Very often.'

'Then you must know a lot about her.'

'I do.'

Rheinhardt placed two kronen on the table. The old woman had no trouble locating the inducement. She snatched up the coins and secreted them in the voluminous folds of white lace that hung from her body. She then began a gravelly monologue.

Once again, the picture of Rosenkrantz that emerged was of an insecure, hysterical women, inclined to form relationships with un-suitable partners. Salak was unable to identify any of Rosenkrantz's paramours by name. In the time-honoured tradition of fortune-tellers, she was evasive and spoke only in general terms. At one point she implied that it was *she* who had been responsible for Rosenkrantz's success, that by wise counsel or the exercise of her divinatory gift she had engineered Rosenkrantz's celebrity. Rheinhardt ignored the in-sinuation and asked Salak more questions about Rosenkrantz's private life. The old woman's tendency to digress was testing, and throughout the interview her motile fingers sustained a grinding accompaniment. There was something about this persistent, chalk-on-blackboard scraping that put Rheinhardt's nerves on edge.

'You know she fell pregnant?'

'Yes.'

'Who was the father?'

'A powerful man.'

'How do you know he was powerful?'

'He didn't want the child. He persuaded her to get rid of it.'

'What happened?'

'She went to see an angel maker.'

'Do you know which one? Do you know who? Please. This is important. If you know, you must say. If you are protecting someone, then have no fear. I am not interested in making an arrest. I am only interested in piecing together Fräulein Rosenkrantz's history.'

The ensuing hiatus was filled by noises which carried from the nearby train station: the screech of metal, a whistle, and the acceler-ating rumble of a steam engine leaving for Prague. Eventually, Orsola Salak spoke. 'Do you give me your word?'

'I do.'

'Do you swear by all that is most precious to you?'

Rheinhardt thought of his family, his wife Else, his beloved daughters, and felt a frisson of discomfort.

'I swear by all that is most precious to me.'

Salak accepted the oath with a grunt and continued, 'She was in a terrible state. I told her to see someone, a Jewess. Her name is Judit: Judit Gardosh. She lives near St Leopold's.'

The old woman gave Rheinhardt an address and he wrote it down in his notebook.

'How is it that you are acquainted?'

'Judit comes to see me occasionally, for a reading. She's from the old country. Would *you* like a reading, inspector?'

'I think not.'

'It's no trouble — and you have been generous.'

The old woman raised her arm and shook her fist like a gambler dicing. Rheinhardt recoiled with disgust as five or six small bones scattered across the tabletop. They looked remarkably like the phalanges of a human hand; however, they were very small, and Rheinhardt had the sickening thought that they might have once belonged to an infant.

'Where did you get those?'

'They were my grandmother's. She taught me how to read them. She had the gift, and so did *her* grandmother.'

Salak's hands played over the bones, her fingers trembling above the arrangement. Rheinhardt felt peculiarly vulnerable. The sun had set and the room was now filled with shadows. His eyes were playing tricks on him. In certain places the darkness seemed peculiarly unstable.

'Three women,' said the old woman, her words expectorated rather than spoken. 'They bring you such happiness. Ah, you are a lucky man to have three women in your life.'

'What about them?'

'Who are you? *That* is the question: the policeman or the man with three women in his life.'

'What do you mean?'

'What are you? A policeman? Or a father and husband? The time is approaching, very soon, when you must ask yourself such questions. Be true. Otherwise . . .'

'Otherwise what?'

Orsola Salak scooped the bones back into her hand and the grinding started up again.

'Be true,' she repeated.

The temperature in the room had dropped and Rheinhardt's rapid breathing was leaving a faint trace of vapour in the air. The shadows, particularly those gathered in the corners of the room, seemed even more restless. Rheinhardt shook his head to free himself of the illusion — but the impression of movement persisted.

'I must go,' he said firmly.

'Yes, I think you should now.'

Rheinhardt placed another krone on the table and marched towards the door with undignified haste.

37

ALTHOUGH FRAU ZOLLINGER HAD agreed to see Liebermann, her tight-lipped suspicious expression did not betoken recognition. She was sitting in a chintz armchair and her features were even more severe than Liebermann had remembered: hooked nose, sharp chin — brittle lacquered hair. She picked up her walking stick and waved it towards a chaise longue.

'Sit down, Herr Doctor. Do you know anything about bunions?'

'A bunion is an enlargement of bone or tissue around the joint of the big toe.'

'What do you do with them?'

'You mean, how are they treated?'

'Yes.'

'I am a psychiatrist. It would be better to follow the advice of your specialist.'

'He wants me to sit with my feet in a bucket of ice.'

'Then that is what you should do.'

'A woman of my age? I'd get a cold.'

'I cannot suggest an alternative.'

At least Frau Zollinger knew who he was.

Liebermann sat down, glancing around the room. It was filled with ornaments and *objets d'art*. The walls were covered with oil paintings — one of which looked like an allegorical work by Hans Makart — and a rosewood grand piano occupied the far corner.

'Do you play, Frau Zollinger?'

'No. My husband did, but very badly. He was good at making money but not much else. He would sit for hours at that piano, murdering Chopin.' She shook her head. 'When he developed arthritis he had to stop. He was devastated but I was relieved. I used to get such headaches.'

Liebermann had written to Frau Zollinger, explaining that he had developed an interest in Brosius's music since hearing the Wind Serenade at the concert where they had met. He had requested an interview in order to discover more about the composer and his circle. The request had been granted in spindly handwriting on paper that smelled of violets.

Frau Zollinger did not take much prompting. She spoke readily about her soirées, recalling the artists and poets whom she and her husband had entertained. Many of them were no longer famous, but Liebermann permitted himself the humane dishonesty of pretending to know of their reputations. Frau Zollinger had obviously over-estimated the significance of her salon, and Liebermann did not want to disabuse her of this harmless delusion. In due course she spoke of musicians, and once again linked the names of Brahms and Brosius together.

'They were friends,' said Frau Zollinger, 'but it was only a matter of time before they argued. Brahms argued with almost everyone in the end, even with his closest associates. He had a colossal temper. And Brosius was just the same. It was remarkable that the friendship lasted as long as it did.'

'What was the cause of the argument?'

'I don't know. Something to do with Bruckner, I think.' She paused and added, 'I have a recording of him somewhere.'

'I beg your pardon?'

'Brahms. You know — a wax cylinder? My husband was much

impressed by Edison's machine and brought one back from America. He recorded Brahms playing one of the Hungarian Dances.'

'Where is it?'

'In a box with all the others. My husband made many recordings — mostly of himself, unfortunately. Everyone thought the phonograph was a miracle, but I found its scratchy sound rather irritating.'

'Do you have any recordings of Brosius or Freimark?'

'No. They died long before my husband visited America. He didn't talk to me very much.'

'Your husband?'

'Brahms. He exhibited a peculiar attitude with respect to women. If they did not appeal to him, he was incredibly awkward and ungracious; if they were pretty, he had an unpleasant way of leaning back in his chair, pouting, stroking his moustache, and staring at them as a greedy boy stares at cakes. He never gave me that greedy stare.' The old woman paused and added without sentimentality and with a modicum of pride: 'Few did.'

'I expect he must have given Angelika Brosius that look.'

'Well, yes,' said Frau Zollinger. 'Of course.'

Her lips twitched but failed to sustain a smile.

Liebermann crossed his legs and leaned forward.

'Did you know that Angelika Brosius has a niece? Frau Abend?'

'No, I didn't.'

Liebermann explained how he had learned of Frau Abend's existence. When he had finished telling the story of Freimark's grave he added, 'She agreed to see me last Sunday. I was hoping to find some of Brosius's manuscripts. But they've all been given to the conservatoire.'

The old woman seemed to withdraw and her eyes became glassy.

'I was there — at Freimark's funeral.'

'Were you?'

'Yes. A modest affair.'

'Was Brosius there also?'

'Yes. And Angelika.'

Liebermann tried to make his next statement sound innocuous.

'Frau Abend said something very intriguing. She said that Angelika Brosius and David Freimark were . . . lovers.' The old woman nodded. 'You knew this?'

'It was suspected.'

'Did Brosius know of his wife's infidelity?'

'He couldn't leave her. She was his inspiration.'

'Frau Zollinger,' said Liebermann, 'the accident on the Schneeberg . . .'

'Yes?'

'Was it an accident?'

'Men are maddened by beauty. I was never beautiful, which is just as well. Who wants to be surrounded by madmen?' Her eyes narrowed. 'Apart from psychiatrists.'

'Frau Zollinger,' said Liebermann, a hint of urgency hardening his voice. 'Is it possible that Brosius killed David Freimark?'

The old woman examined her walking stick. She wasn't disturbed, merely preoccupied. Eventually she changed position and said, 'I asked the very same question myself — at the time.'

'Did you speak to anyone?'

'Yes. My husband.'

'How did he respond?'

'He became angry. He told me I was being ridiculous. He told me I should keep thoughts like that to myself. It was shameful, he said, to doubt the integrity of Brosius, a man whom we counted among our friends. I know why he was so agitated.'

'Why?'

'It had crossed his mind too.'

38

DIRECTOR MAHLER HAD PROVIDED Liebermann with two tickets to see *Così fan Tutte*, a comic opera by Mozart. There was never any doubt about who Liebermann would take as his guest. Once again, the pretext of Amelia Lydgate's continuing musical education served his ulterior purpose. Within hours of issuing the invitation he was holding her reply in his hands. She had found the prospect of a night at the opera *most agreeable*.

The box they occupied was well positioned and exclusive.

'Do you know *Così fan Tutte*?' Amelia asked.

'I am familiar with some of the arias,' said Liebermann, 'but have never attended a complete performance. It isn't produced very often.'

'Why is that?'

'One must assume that previous directors have not been persuaded of its merits. Director Mahler, however, is a great champion of Mozart's operas, particularly those that are less well known. Last year he programmed the first-ever performance of *Zaide* on the emperor's name day.'

'First-ever?'

'Yes. It was never performed in Mozart's lifetime.'

'Remarkable, that an opera by Mozart should be neglected until the early years of the twentieth century.'

'Indeed. There are still some who question his genius. They find him too . . . light. But they miss the point. That is his gift. Only Mozart can make sadness so sweet. Even when a libretto demands that he represent something horrible, he does so with charm and natural grace.'

Amelia craned over the edge of the box in order to study the audience. She was wearing a skirted décolleté green velvet gown. Liebermann had seen her wearing it on a previous occasion, at a ball, and he was reminded of the time they had danced together — the warmth of her body, accidental brushes, her pale shoulders exposed and unbearably close. The hem of her gown rose up, revealing a pair of black boots. Her feet were slim and the soft leather emphasised the contours of her shapely ankles. Liebermann recalled what Frau Zollinger had said about Brahms, and wondered if he too was now exhibiting that 'greedy boy' look. Embarrassed, he lowered his head and flicked through the programme. He noticed that Arianne Amsel was singing the part of Fiordiligi.

Arpeggios and fragments of melody signalled the arrival of musicians in the pit. In due course, the leader of the orchestra played an 'A' and all the instruments converged on this single note. The house lights dimmed and Director Mahler appeared. He marched to the podium, barely acknowledging the applause, and raised his baton. The chords that he summoned from his players were congenial, sympathetic, winsome and irresistible. Eight stately bars preceded the arrival of a playful tune that chased across the orchestra. The scurrying motif evoked the tropes of comedy with miraculous precision: characters donning disguises, confused identities, secret assignations and hasty concealments. Mozart had deftly informed the audience that they were about to be amused and a wave of infectious anticipation swept through the stalls.

The curtain rose on a café scene where two young men, Ferrando and Guglielmo, were praising their fiancées, Dorabella and Fiordiligi; however, their companion, an older man, Don Alfonso, was scornful. He accused them of naivety and was soon proposing a wager of one hundred guineas. He would prove that Dorabella and Fiordiligi — like all women — were inconstant. The conventions of farce were assiduously observed, yet, as the drama progressed, the music expressed much more than wit and humour. It exposed a poignant fragility at the heart of human affairs and, beyond that, the hopeless absurdity of life itself. Liebermann was forced to consider the sad comedy of his own predicament, his desire for the woman seated next to him and his mounting frustration.

Undulating strings introduced a trio for two sopranos and bass. It was absolutely exquisite, a prayer for the safety of departed friends and lovers crossing a distant sea. The female voices floated in celestial suspension over the gentle lapping of the orchestral accompaniment. Liebermann did not believe in heaven. But if there was such a thing, then it was easy to imagine such music welcoming weary souls as they passed through its gates.

When the trio came to its sublime conclusion the audience burst into spontaneous applause. Amelia turned and looked directly at Liebermann. He struggled to understand the meaning of her expression, which was unusually open. She looked helpless and a little bemused, as if the music had been the cause of her undoing. He leaned forward and said: 'Is something the matter?'

'No,' she replied. 'It was just . . .' she hesitated and her chest rose and fell. 'Beautiful.'

Later in the first act, Ferrando sang an aria about love. Once again, Mozart transcended the limits of *opera buffa*, producing music of great poignancy. Ferrando's tenor was full of tenderness: '*The heart that is nourished by hope and by love has no need of better food.*' Love was essential, and a life without love could only ever be a pale imitation of what life is supposed to be. Liebermann found himself thinking of Mozart's grave. He remembered the truncated marble column and the stricken cherub. Life was so woefully short. Emotion tightened his throat.

In the second act, Arianne Amsel performed the famous rondo aria, 'Have pity, my love, forgive.' It was something of a showpiece, consisting of several sections in different tempi and clearly composed to display technique. The melody was full of large intervals, requiring the voice to drop suddenly from high soprano to contralto. Liebermann enjoyed the aria as a piece of theatre but the music did not move him. When Amsel stopped singing, a solitary clap could be heard over the orchestral coda. It continued into the silence that preceded the next *recitativo*, provoking only a smattering of restrained applause. Evidently the house shared Liebermann's opinion.

At the end of the opera, when the lovers were reunited, the cast came together to sing a strange valedictory. It was as though they were stepping out of the drama and into the real world. 'Happy is the man,' they sang, 'who always looks on the bright side of everything and through life's ups and downs lets himself be guided by reason.' Liebermann considered himself a natural optimist and someone who venerated Enlightenment values; yet he couldn't say that these things had brought him happiness. He knew that true fulfilment depended on something quite different.

They collected their coats from the cloakroom and walked the short distance to the Café Schwarzenberg where they ordered coffee and pastries. Sitting by a window through which they could see the Karlskirche, they talked about the opera and Liebermann spoke of his recent visit to the *Mozartgrab*. He spoke about the symbolic meaning of the truncated column and Amelia listened intently. When he had finished, she said, very seriously, 'None of us can know the number of days we are allocated on this Earth. Time passes and death comes suddenly. Therefore one must seize all the opportunities that life offers. It is dreadful to contemplate how it must be to spend one's final hours regretting what might or could have been.'

*   *   *

Liebermann hailed a cab.

For much of the journey they were uncharacteristically silent. It was a silence that they had reached not merely because the evening's conversation had run its course. It was a silence that they had *earned* after the labour of all their previous conversations. A boundless silence, tolerated without discomfort and against which their intimacy might be tested. They had had so many conversations, and about so many things: diseases of the blood, Nietzsche's theory of eternal recurrence, automata, literature, reform fashion houses, therapeutic nihilism, secessionist art and design, Renaissance architecture, women's rights, literature and, of course, the nature of love.

Liebermann recalled Ferrando's aria, with its simply worded statement of love's necessity, and realised that the very same sentiment had been expressed by Goethe in *Elective Affinities*: 'A life without love, without the presence of the beloved, is only a *comédie à tiroir*.' And that was precisely how Liebermann had experienced his life since his first encounter with Amelia Lydgate, a series of unconnected episodes, superficial and unsatisfying.

Liebermann's thoughts were racing.

Outside, a thin rain had begun to fall.

In matters of the heart women could not express themselves freely. It was not permitted. They relied on more subtle means of communication. When Amelia had handed him her copy of *Elective Affinities* she *must* have done so knowingly.

They arrived in the ninth district and the carriage stopped outside Amelia's house. Liebermann offered her his hand and helped her to alight onto the pavement, before paying and dismissing the driver. The street was empty and the atmosphere was hazed with a fine mizzle.

'Will you not need a cab to get home?' asked Amelia.

'No,' Liebermann replied. 'I think I'd prefer to walk. My head is still full of music. I must walk, otherwise I shan't sleep.'

It was so easy to hide behind words, make excuses and mislead. He yearned again for the restoration of silence, the honest silence that had enfolded them in the carriage.

They walked to the door and Amelia turned to face him. The water vapour diffused the gaslight, making her face appear soft-edged and ghostly. Liebermann felt inebriated, as if he'd been imbibing too much absinthe.

'Once again,' said Amelia, 'I must thank you for a wonderful evening.'

Liebermann did not reply. He stood very still, returning her intense gaze. He was aware of the distant clatter of hooves and the muted hum of the city, but the world seemed to be receding. Amelia's eyes had always held a peculiar fascination for him. They were such an unusual colour, neither blue nor grey but some indeterminate hue in between. Their preternatural luminosity was contained by a dark rim which circulated each iris. For a moment he thought that he might be falling, but soon realised he was mistaken. Amelia's eyes were becoming larger because she was moving closer. She had taken a step towards him. Her head fell backwards and her lips formed a tentative, experimental pout. Quite suddenly — as if a moment of intervening time had been excised — her mouth was opening beneath his and they were kissing.

39

RHEINHARDT WALKED UNDER AN archway and found himself in a small empty courtyard. The building was old and crumbling — but not unclean: an able demonstration by the residents that squalor need not be an inevitable consequence of poverty. There was none of the usual rubbish which typically cluttered the entrance of such dwellings, no broken carts, rusting metal or fallen masonry. A broom, standing by a water pump, was clearly used to sweep mud from the cobbles with some regularity.

The first door Rheinhardt examined proved to be the address he was looking for. He noticed a *mezuzah*, a small receptacle containing holy words on parchment and attached to the painted frame. Its presence identified the household as Jewish. Glancing along the other doors, Rheinhardt saw that all but one of the occupants were similarly observant. A quivering curtain presaged the appearance of an inquisitive face behind the window and Rheinhardt indicated that he wished to enter. Seconds later the door opened, revealing a diminutive woman in a colourful embroidered dress and white blouse. She was middle-aged, with brown hair and a swarthy complexion. Her cheeks were wide and the flesh beneath her eyes had begun to mottle and sag.

'Yes?'

'Frau Gardosh?'

'Yes.'

'My name is Rheinhardt. I am a detective from the security office.' Frau Gardosh pursed her lips and attempted — unsuccessfully — to conceal her trepidation. 'May I come in?'

'What's it about?'

'I need to ask you some questions.'

'But it isn't very convenient. I'm . . .' She hesitated before going on, 'I'm looking after a friend. She isn't very well.'

'I won't keep you long.'

'But she needs my constant attention.'

'Frau Gardosh,' said Rheinhardt impatiently. 'If you are trying to keep me out of your home because you fear that I will discover the nature of your business, then I must ask you to desist. I have already been informed.'

'Business . . . I don't run a business.'

'You are an *angel maker*,' said Rheinhardt, with heavy emphasis. He saw that Frau Gardosh was about to deny the allegation and swiftly added, 'Orsola Salak told me.'

At the mention of Salak's name the woman's expression changed. It was as though she had been slapped round the face.

'Orsola Salak told you?' Her voice was weak with disbelief.

'I have not come here to arrest you. I only want to ask you some questions about one of your . . . clients.' Frau Gardosh remained silent. 'Of course, should you refuse to cooperate . . .' He allowed the implied threat to register before adding, 'May I come in now?' Frau Gardosh consented and ushered him into her parlour. 'Would you like to check that your ailing friend is comfortable before we begin?' asked Rheinhardt. Gardosh raised her hand and touched her lips. Her body swayed backwards and forwards, pulled this way and that by the conflicting currents of her own indecision.

'Forgive me, Inspector . . . but—'

Disinclined to prolong her misery, Rheinhardt said, 'I see. There *is* no friend. It doesn't matter. Shall we sit? Good.' His clipped delivery did not permit the woman to dwell on her shame. 'If I might suggest you come a little closer. Thank you. Do you live here on your own, Frau Gardosh?'

'Yes. My husband died many years ago, soon after we came to Vienna.'

'I'm sorry to hear that. Do you have any children?'

'Two sons.'

'And where are they?'

'One is apprenticed to a carpenter in Hernals. The other is in the army.'

Rheinhardt took out his notebook.

'Tell me, how long have you been assisting young women in difficulty?'

'It was hard, Inspector, without a husband and with two hungry boys to feed.'

'Yes, I can imagine.'

'And they're not always so young, the ones who come here. Older women can make mistakes too.'

'I'm sure.'

'Inspector . . .'

'Yes?'

'Why aren't you going to arrest me?'

'I promised Orsola Salak that I wouldn't.'

'And you intend to keep that promise?'

'I do.'

Frau Gardosh was clearly suspicious of Rheinhardt's casual dereliction of duty. Her wrinkled brow suggested that she wanted a more substantive reason to believe him. Rheinhardt was happy to oblige. 'And there is the matter of your religion.'

'What of it?'

'I am not eager to further the cause of certain parties unsympathetic to your people. If I arrest you, elements of the press will make much of a Jewish angel maker.'

'Why should you care about that?'

'There is an election coming. Things are bad enough as it is. I don't want to give the belligerents another excuse to march into Leopoldstadt.' He ventured a self-congratulatory smile. 'Good police work isn't just about arresting people.'

Frau Gardosh considered the point. A subtle movement of her head suggested that she found it plausible enough, although a residue of scepticism continued to corrugate her brow.

'What do you want to know?'

'In the spring,' said Rheinhardt, 'Orsola Salak sent a woman to you. Her name was Ida Rosenkrantz. Do you remember her?'

'Yes, of course I remember her. She was an opera singer, a famous one, too.'

'Unfortunately, she died recently. Did you know that?'

'No, I didn't.'

'It was in all the newspapers.'

'I don't read them. It's been years since I last sat in a coffee house.'

'Can you remember the date when she came to see you?'

'No, not exactly.'

'Then approximately?'

Frau Gardosh paused to think. 'Late March, early April . . . perhaps. She was very young. How did she die?'

'An accident. How many months pregnant was she?'

'She came to see me as soon as she realised. It was very early.'

'How did she present? Was she sad, relieved, tearful?'

'They're all sad, Inspector, the women who come to me for help.'

'Then how did she compare?'

'She was very distressed. She cried a great deal. I had to encourage her to be brave.'

'She didn't really want to go through with it?'

'They all have second thoughts.'

'And you encourage them to be . . . *brave*.'

Frau Gardosh sighed.

'You think me a bad person, Inspector. But most of the women who come to me aren't like Fräulein Rosenkrantz. They don't have fine dresses and plenty of money. They are poor, with husbands who get drunk and can't hold down a job. These women come to see me because they don't want to bring another child into the world — a child that they can't provide for — they don't want to nurse another baby through coughs and fevers, only to see it die when the weather turns cold. I know what people say . . . that what I do is wrong, sinful. But is it so wicked? To spare a sweet little infant from suffering?'

'I have not come here to judge you, Frau Gardosh.'

She looked down and studied her hands.

Rheinhardt waited until she looked up again before continuing. 'When you were comforting Fräulein Rosenkrantz, did she say anything about her circumstances?'

'It was a long time ago, inspector. Six months.'

'Indeed, but I am interested in every detail. Did she, for example, give you any indication as to who the father might be?'

'Yes.'

'She did?'

'Yes. A doctor.'

'I beg your pardon?'

'In fact, I seem to recall her saying that the father was *her* doctor.'

'Engelberg? Saminsky?'

'I don't remember her mentioning those names.'

Rheinhardt leaned forward.

'You're quite sure of this, Frau Gardosh?'

'Yes. A family man — naturally. I think he must have been quite rich. She said he'd given her the money to pay me with. It was a lot. More than I usually see in months.'

'Why so much?'

'Largesse, I imagine.'

Rheinhardt's pencil hovered above his notebook, but he was too stunned to write anything down.

40

LIEBERMANN WAS FAMILIAR WITH most of the songs in *Klassiker des deutschen Liedes* but he was making a number of small and irritating mistakes, such as bad fingering and forgetting the prior introduction of accidentals. Rheinhardt didn't seem to mind (indeed, he didn't even seem to notice): he was clearly enjoying himself, belting out one popular song after another — Schubert's *Ständchen*, Weber's *Reigen*, Franz's *Für Musik* — his voice spirited and booming.

The cause of Liebermann's poor performance was a stream of vivid and intrusive recollections. He could not stop thinking about Amelia Lydgate: her mouth yielding to his ingress, enfolding her in his arms and drawing her close, the coolness of her white neck, and the sweetness of her perfume. The whole experience had left him in a state of ecstatic remove, light-headed and slightly delirious. Something of their coming together had remained with him — in one form or another — since their parting on Thursday night. These memories were constantly vying for attention, interrupting his thoughts or waiting for an opportunity to inhabit every part of his conscious mind. They seemed to achieve this by ingenious associative pathways. Even an innocuous lyric could serve as a starting point.

'I'm sorry,' said Liebermann after a mechanical rendition of Beethoven's *Adelaide*. 'I am not playing very well this evening.'

'Oh, I don't know,' said Rheinhardt. 'A little lacking in energy, perhaps, but otherwise perfectly acceptable.'

'No. This really won't do. One more song and then we will have to bring our music-making to an end.'

Rheinhardt stood behind his friend and gripped his shoulder.

'Sometimes you take it all too seriously, Max.'

'You sound like the emperor.'

'Do I?'

'That's what he said about Mahler.'

Rheinhardt smiled, leaned forward, and turned the page. The next song in the collection was Freimark's 'Hope'. Liebermann placed his hands on the keyboard and played the introduction, emphasising the sharp discords scattered like treacherous barbs among the dense harmonies. It was an apposite choice, and the sentiment expressed in Schiller's poetry found his susceptible heart with the swift and direct certainty of a well-balanced arrow. Liebermann hoped that Amelia Lydgate would not regret their moment of abandon and decide against further intimacy, he hoped that their first kiss would lead to others, he hoped that he would see her again soon . . .

Liebermann had written Amelia a letter as soon as he had returned to his apartment. Among the gentlemanly obligations of the age was a requirement that he should compose a pre-emptive request for forgiveness. It was always possible that a woman might, on reflection, conclude that she had been treated disrespectfully or, even worse, exploited. However, even as he was composing his propitiatory sentences, he was acutely aware that it had been Amelia who had stepped towards him and not he towards her. When Amelia's reply arrived he was relieved to find, among the cautious, allusive, discreetly worded paragraphs, the desired gentle assurances.

The intensity of his feeling found an easy outlet in the pliant keys. As 'Hope' approached its emotional climax he felt a charge of energy coursing down his arms, animating his fingers. As the final chord faded into silence he was satisfied that he had done justice to the composer's genius.

'Well,' said Rheinhardt. 'There was nothing wrong with that.'

'Even so, I am not inclined to continue. Now that I have, at last, delivered an acceptable accompaniment, that is where we should finish.'

'As you wish,' said Rheinhardt.

They entered the smoking room and took their customary seats. Brandy was poured and cigars distributed. Rheinhardt made some introductory remarks and proceeded to describe his encounter with Orsola Salak — although he neglected to mention his undignified escape. The memory of the sudden drop in temperature and the moving shadows still unnerved him. He then recounted his interview with the angel maker, Frau Gardosh.

'Fräulein Rosenkrantz went to see Frau Gardosh in late March or early April. She couldn't remember exactly when. One must suppose that Frau Gardosh gets a lot of custom. I asked her if she had any idea who had made Fräulein Rosenkrantz pregnant, and to my great surprise, she said yes.' Rheinhardt sipped his brandy. 'According to Gardosh, Fräulein Rosenkrantz was in a distressed state. A very distressed state, even when measured against the standards of misery that Frau Gardosh is accustomed to. The gentleman in question had given Fräulein Rosenkrantz the money to pay for the procedure and had urged her — perhaps against her will — to terminate the pregnancy. Gardosh said that this gentleman, a family man, was her doctor.'

Liebermann whistled through his teeth.

'Engelberg or Saminsky?'

'Frau Gardosh didn't know. Names weren't mentioned. But she must have been referring to the latter.'

'Why not Engelberg?'

'Engelberg isn't a family man. He's a widower. Further, when I met with Engelberg we discussed Fräulein Rosenkrantz's gynaecological symptoms. I asked him if he had examined her, and he hadn't. Indeed, he seemed horrified by the thought of doing such a thing! He said that a doctor must have good cause to compromise a woman's dignity. His tone and manner were sincere. I do not believe that Engelberg would seduce a patient.'

Liebermann lit his second cigar and adopted an attitude of one deep in thought. Turning to his friend he said, 'Professor Freud has suggested that women are predisposed to find older men attractive because they harbour unresolved sexual feelings for their fathers.' Rheinhardt grumbled into his brandy. 'This *natural* inclination,' Liebermann continued, 'was obviously amplified in Fräulein Rosenkrantz, and one must suppose that this amplification was due to her history. You will recall that her father died when she was young, she was rejected by her female cousins — and even her mother eventually abandoned her to begin a new life in Italy. Her talent was discovered and nurtured by older men. Her schoolteacher and the choirmaster, Peter Helbing. What, we must ask ourselves, might older men have come to represent for such a person?'

'Kindness, protection, security?'

'Exactly, and, at a deeper level, the recovery of that precious relationship, lost so tragically early. As a sexually mature woman, when she fell into the arms of an older man she did so as much in the role of a daughter as that of a lover. Her needs were complicated.'

'I find that thought rather . . . distasteful.'

'The unconscious, the seedbed of our desires, has scant regard for conventional morality. It finds satisfaction however it can.'

'All of which suggests that she would have been easy prey for Saminsky.'

'Indeed. The relationship between doctor and patient has much in common with the relationship between parent and child. Saminsky would have made a powerful appeal to Rosenkrantz's need for a surrogate father.' Liebermann flicked his brandy glass, producing a soft chime. 'And there is another factor which should be taken into consideration when assessing the plausibility of Gardosh's allegation.' Liebermann paused before adding: 'The nature of Saminsky's treatment. It was one which provided him with ample opportunity to err, necessitating — as it does — prolonged physical contact.'

'Electrotherapy? I thought it was administered with a machine.'

'During general faradisation the patient is nude or partially clothed. The current can be delivered through electrodes or passed through the doctor's hand. The *electrical hand method* is recommended for sensitive persons, and given what we know of Rosenkrantz — her artistic temperament, her *globus hystericus* — I think it safe to assume that Saminsky would have identified her as a member of that group. Which means that he would have spent a great deal of time stroking her throat,' the young doctor paused before adding on a knowing cadence, 'and chest.'

Liebermann suddenly thought of Amelia Lydgate as he had first seen her, as a patient in the general hospital. This memory, which trespassed onto the hitherto uncluttered terrain of his deductions, took the form of a mental picture. He remembered her white cotton gown, the subtle curve of her small breasts beneath the thin material, and the sight of her exposed feet on the tiled floor. This image aroused in him a discomfiting mixture of concupiscence and guilt.

Rheinhardt stood up and walked over to the mantelpiece. He flicked some ash into the fire and said, 'Saminsky told us that the mayor was to blame for Rosenkrantz's pregnancy.'

'He was trying to divert attention away from himself.'

'Yes, but to implicate the mayor . . .'

'Lueger and Rosenkrantz *were* lovers.'

'I know, but such a strategy is fraught with dangers.' Rheinhardt raised his hands in disbelief.

'Indeed, but the boldest lies are often the most effective. We are obliged to believe them on account of their magnitude. *No one —* we reason — would dare make up such a thing.'

'The man must be some kind of fool.'

'That was my impression also.'

Rheinhardt began to pace in front of the fire.

'What are we to make of this new intelligence? If the mayor did not make Rosenkrantz pregnant, then your previous speculations must be wrong. You imagined Rosenkrantz threatening the mayor with a scandal, the most significant element of which was his prior insistence that she terminate her pregnancy.'

'She could have led him to believe that he was responsible for her condition, even if the guilty party was in fact Saminsky.'

The inspector looked doubtful.

'When we informed Lueger of Rosenkrantz's pregnancy he was shocked. I am convinced that he wasn't feigning surprise. He really didn't know about her pregnancy until that precise moment. I am also inclined to believe that the mayor, as he suggested, would have been diligent in his efforts to avoid such an unfortunate eventuality.'

'Oskar, the only prophylactic known to be completely effective is celibacy!' Liebermann sat up in his chair. 'Even so, let us — for the sake of argument — accept that Lueger was completely ignorant of Rosenkrantz's condition. Does this really change how we should view the material facts? The mayor visited Fräulein Rosenkrantz, letters were destroyed, and the following morning she was found dead.'

Rheinhardt resumed his pacing. 'What if Rosenkrantz had threatened to expose Saminsky? He is a rich man and has much to lose . . .'

'Not as much as our illustrious demagogue.'

'Men have killed for less.'

Liebermann puffed on his cigar and after a few moments said,

'Didn't Saminsky say he was away when Rosenkrantz's body was discovered — something about a religious maniac in Salzburg?'

'Yes, he did. Be that as it may, I'd like to pay Professor Saminsky another visit. There are clearly some issues here that need to be clarified. Are you available on Monday?' Liebermann nodded. 'Good.'

41

On arriving at Saminsky's Hietzing mansion, Liebermann and Rheinhardt had been received by a gaunt serving man who did not — as they had expected he would — show them into the drawing room. Instead, he had escorted them down a corridor and deposited them in a small but comfortable waiting area.

They sat on leather armchairs, listening to the muffled sounds of voices that came through the double doors. A pile of men's and women's journals had been left on an oriental table. Liebermann picked up a fashion magazine and looked at the illustrations. A clock struck the quarter hour — twice.

Like most physicians, Professor Saminsky saw a number of his patients at home. Before entering the mansion, Liebermann had registered an emblazoned coach parked on the road outside. He had supposed that the professor must be occupied with the care of an important person. Another fifteen minutes passed before the double doors opened, confirming Liebermann's surmise. Standing next to Saminsky was an elderly woman whose sombre dress was countered by the glitter and flash of diamonds. She looked frail and her head drooped beneath a dowager's hump, yet when she spoke her voice was loud and clear, each syllable precisely articulated. 'Thank you, Professor. You have performed a miracle. I am feeling stronger already.'

Saminsky's palm was hovering close to her lower back. He was making small circular movements, impatiently willing her to move forward.

'I am delighted to hear that, Countess.'

'The same time tomorrow?'

'Indeed, Countess, the same time tomorrow.' Saminsky's serving man was approaching from the opposite end of the corridor, his emaciated face a frozen mask of impassivity. 'Ah, there you are, Hans-Peter.'

The aristocrat offered Saminsky her hand. As he bowed to deliver his kiss, she looked away, as if favouring him with a private moment in which to appreciate the honour.

'Good evening, Herr Professor.'

'Good evening, Countess.'

The old woman followed Hans-Peter, affecting an air of languid indifference as she rustled past the two gentlemen who had respectfully risen from their seats.

Saminsky made a dramatic supplicating gesture with open arms.

'I am so dreadfully sorry, gentlemen. But there was nothing I could do.' He glanced down the corridor to check that the countess was making satisfactory progress and muttered under his breath, 'She just wouldn't go.'

'Never mind, Herr Professor,' said Rheinhardt. 'It is no matter.'

'You are very kind, Inspector. Please, come this way.'

They stepped from the waiting area into a very spacious consulting room. It was unusually large, with high windows overlooking a parterre and medical charts mounted on the walls — the human body, in different poses, excoriated so as to expose the underlying muscle groups. Among these anatomical drawings was an oil painting of the late empress, based on the famous portrait by Winterhalter.

In addition to Saminsky's desk and a trolley bed there were numerous pieces of technical equipment: a mechanical chair for strengthening wasted legs, several batteries for the administration of electrotherapy, and an octagonal wooden frame (large enough to admit a standing person) around which hoops of conducting wire had been wrapped.

'Ah,' said Saminsky to Liebermann. 'You are interested in my D'Arsonval Cage. It was constructed by Richard Heller in Paris. Beautiful workmanship, don't you think?' Saminsky tugged a strut, demonstrating that one of its eight sides was a door. He held it open, smiling.

There was something about Professor Saminsky's appearance that reminded Liebermann of a showman. With his pointed beard and colourful waistcoat he might have been a stage magician, inviting a member of the audience to inspect an apparently empty box.

'Yes,' Liebermann agreed. 'It is very well made.'

Saminsky closed the cage and marched towards his desk. 'This way, gentlemen. Would you like some tea?'

'No, thank you,' said Liebermann.

'How about you, Inspector?'

'No, thank you,' Rheinhardt replied.

'A shame. I have some very fine black tea from Ceylon. Please . . .' He gestured towards some chairs. Like Professor Freud's, Saminsky's desktop was littered with ancient artefacts, including several glass and clay unguentaria. 'Now, gentlemen, how can I help you?'

Rheinhardt made some preliminary remarks about the purpose of their visit and produced his notebook. He asked Saminsky to confirm a few details from their earlier interview, none of which were, in reality, terribly important. He then requested the precise dates of all Rosenkrantz's treatment sessions, which Saminsky supplied after perusing her case notes. Occasionally, the professor's eyes showed a trace of suspicion, otherwise his manner was relaxed and confident. In due course, Rheinhardt said, 'The night Fräulein Rosenkrantz died, you were away in Salzburg — is that correct?'

Some lines of consternation appeared on Saminsky's forehead.

'No. I'm afraid it isn't. Why do you say that?'

'When we were here before you said that you were recently returned from Salzburg.'

'Well, yes, that's true. I'd just been to see von Kroy. But the night when Fräulein Rosenkrantz died, I was still here in Vienna. I'm sorry . . . I didn't mean to mislead you.'

'Where were you, then, that evening?'

'I was with a patient called Kluge, Udalbert Kluge, an elderly gentleman who suffers from hallucinations.'

'Did you go to his residence?'

'Yes. It was something of an emergency — his wife was most upset.'

'And where does Herr Kluge live?'

'Not very far. Near the train station.'

Rheinhardt continued questioning the professor for a few more minutes, then looked at Liebermann.

'Herr Professor,' said Liebermann, 'I have been giving some considerable thought to Fräulein Rosenkrantz's history.'

'Oh?'

'I know that you believe symptoms originate in the body; however, would you accept that some aspects of character are shaped by experience?'

'How do you mean?'

'Fräulein Rosenkrantz's father died when she was very young. Is it not possible that this loss might have produced in her a predilection for the company of older men? That she sought in her relationships with them not only the satisfaction of her physical needs but a surrogate?'

'I suppose so, although, as I have already made clear, I did not discuss her private life very much. I only learned of her relationship with . . . the mayor, when she told me of her predicament.'

'But the other men she mentioned, you must have formed a general impression of their age?'

'They were, I believe, more established gentleman. Yes.'

'Father figures . . .'

'Yes. Possibly.'

Liebermann paused for a moment before continuing.

'Professor Saminsky, did you treat Fräulein Rosenkrantz's *globus hystericus* using the *electrical hand* method.'

'Yes. As a matter of fact I did.'

'Inspector Rheinhardt was asking me about the procedure as we travelled here. Would you please explain it to him?'

'Certainly,' said Saminsky. 'The patient sits on a chair with feet placed on a large flat electrode, which is connected to the negative pole of a magnetic coil. The positive pole is held in the physician's left hand. The current passes through his body and he touches the patient with the right hand, thus delivering the charge.'

'I see,' said Rheinhardt.

'The patient must remove her shoes and stockings?' asked Liebermann.

'Obviously,' said Saminsky.

'And her other garments?'

'Of course, although a lightweight gown is provided to preserve modesty.'

'Which muscles did you stimulate?'

'The *sternocleidomastoid* — the *splenius capitis* and *cervicis* — the *levator scapulae* — the *trapezius* — the *pectoralis major* . . .'

'The muscles of the neck and chest?'

'And upper back, yes.'

The professor reached out and picked up one of his unguentaria — a clay bottle, the neck of which was pinched, creating a shape vaguely reminiscent of the female form.

'We are agreed that Fräulein Rosenkrantz had a weakness for father figures. Therefore the therapeutic situation you describe must have had a particular but predictable effect on her.'

'I beg your pardon?'

'Did she not become . . . excited? After all, you, a distinguished psychiatrist, must have appealed to all her expectations of what a father figure should be. Successful, suave, cultured, caring.'

Saminsky's mouth dropped open.

'Doctor Liebermann, what are you suggesting?'

'She became aroused, did she not?' The professor was speechless. 'It must have been an extremely testing situation. Fräulein Rosenkrantz was a renowned beauty. You are a physician, but being medically qualified does not make you inhuman. We understand this. You are still a man, with a man's needs. Yes, it must have been very testing indeed to touch her and feel her responding, to feel the soft warmth of her flesh beneath your fingers, to observe the quickening of her breath: a kind of torment.' Liebermann found that his words had conjured in his mind an image of Amelia Lydgate. He had meant to build towards a condemnation, but when he reached his final sentence it was forgiving. 'More than a mere mortal man could reasonably expect to resist.'

'That is enough!' cried Saminsky. He directed a fiery look at Rheinhardt. 'What is the meaning of this outrage, Inspector?'

Rheinhardt produced a cigar, lit it, and said calmly, 'We have reason to believe that the mayor was not responsible for Fraulein Rosenkrantz's pregnancy.'

'*What?*' said Saminsky.

There was an odd cracking sound. Saminsky opened his clenched fist. The tiny bottle had been snapped in half.

The carriage rolled past the Kaiser Pavillion and followed the railway line towards the centre of Vienna. For most of the journey Liebermann and Rheinhardt were isolated from each other by the heavy folds of a contemplative silence. It wasn't until they crossed from Fünfhaus into Neubau that the inspector stretched his legs and said. 'Well?'

Liebermann removed his spectacles from his pocket, cleaned the lenses with a handkerchief, and put them on.

'I am inclined to believe,' he began with scholarly aplomb, 'that when Fräulein Rosenkrantz confided in the angel maker she was telling the truth.'

Rheinhardt made a grumbling noise, the elements of which eventually came together as speech: 'I suppose I should go and see Herr Kluge.'

'If you discover that Professor Saminsky does not have a satisfactory alibi . . .' Liebermann allowed the incomplete sentence to terminate at a precipice beyond which there existed a host of possibilities.

'Then that will definitely complicate matters.' Rheinhardt blew out his cheeks and let the air escape slowly. 'I couldn't help noticing that you were unusually direct with Saminsky.'

Liebermann shrugged.

'It seemed the right approach to take.' He didn't want to discuss Saminsky or the illicit goings-on between doctors and patients. Turning to gaze out of the window he produced a jarring non sequitur. 'Is it very difficult to get a corpse exhumed?'

'What?'

'I suppose there are forms to be filled.'

Rheinhardt's expression darkened. 'Quite a few of them, actually.'

'You could get permission, though — I mean, as a senior detective you have the authority.'

'If an exhumation is pertinent to a murder inquiry, yes.'

Liebermann spun round to face his friend. 'I would like you to get authorisation for the exhumation of David Freimark's body.'

Rheinhardt groaned.

'Max, we've got more important things to worry about than the fate of David Freimark!'

'A murder is a murder.'

'Indeed. All human lives are of equal value. Be that as it may, a diva of the court opera has been murdered, Karl Lueger, the Lord God of Vienna, is our prime suspect, and the late empress's physician has just given us good reason to doubt his integrity. It is not the time to be chasing around cemeteries digging up dead composers of thwarted promise!'

'He was murdered. I'm sure he was.'

'Let this Freimark business go, Max. It's becoming a morbid preoccupation. There are more pressing matters.'

Liebermann shook his head and repeated stubbornly, 'A murder is a murder.'

42

LIEBERMANN ENTERED HIS APARTMENT clutching the day's mail. He sorted through the letters looking impatiently for one that had been addressed in Amelia's distinctive hand, but was disappointed. Overwhelmed by tiredness, he dropped the unopened envelopes into his writing bureau and found himself drawn towards the featureless cabinet in which he kept his spirits. He angled his head to study the contents: slivovitz, becherovka, vodka, and a quarter-full bottle of absinthe. He picked up the absinthe, held it up to the light and, after a moment of perilous indecision, sensibly decided against the idea. Instead, he poured himself a glass of slivovitz and sat down at the piano.

Brosius's *Three Fantasy Pieces* stood on the music stand. He played through the second of these, before essaying a few of Zemlinsky's *Rustic Dances*. He then felt a strong urge to hear some Chopin and lifted the Opus Nine *Nocturnes* out of the piano stool. After a satisfactory rendition of the B flat minor, he rewarded himself with a warming swig of alcohol and positioned his hands in readiness for the opening bars of the E flat major. His mental preparations were interrupted by the sound of someone knocking at the front door. His first thought was that it must be one of Rheinhardt's emissaries. However, he immediately dismissed the idea, having only recently bid the inspector goodbye at the Schottenring station.

Liebermann rose from his seat and went to investigate. He was amazed to find his erstwhile fiancée leaning nonchalantly against the door jamb.

'Clara?'

'You look surprised to see me.'

'Well . . . I am.'

'Didn't you get my letter?'

'Your letter?'

'I sent you one this morning. Didn't you get it?'

Liebermann remembered the unopened correspondence in the bureau. 'I might have.'

'What do you mean, you *might* have?'

'I've only just returned from Hietzing. I haven't had time to open my letters yet.'

'No time? You were playing the piano. I could hear you.'

'Yes.' Liebermann extended the word until its thinness aroused suspicion.

'I see.' Clara took a step backwards. 'This isn't quite the welcome I was expecting. I will write to you again and—'

'No. Don't go!' He had not forgotten the gratitude he had felt when she had generously forgiven him, the sweet relief, the heady release from oppressive guilt. The last thing he wanted now was to offend her. 'I'm so sorry, Clara. Whatever will you think of me? Please, do come in.'

'Are you sure?'

'Yes. Of course.'

Liebermann took her hat and coat. As she turned he was enveloped by her perfume, a heavy scent that recalled the overlarge exotic blooms and humid heat of a greenhouse. Clara was wearing an impressive gown of blue silk, trimmed with silver. The neckline was low but a crescent of diaphanous gauzy material covered the swell of her breasts. Liebermann's expression must have betrayed his appreciation. She looked up at him with dark eyes that communicated quiet amuse-ment and satisfaction.

Liebermann ushered Clara into the music room.

'So . . .' he said, as she lowered herself onto the sofa. 'It is good to see you again.'

Clara pointed towards the cigarette box.

'May I?'

Liebermann came forward — performing a little leap — eager to be hospitable. He flicked open the box's lid. Clara took a cigarette and allowed him to light it for her. She then looked meaningfully at the bottle.

'Slivovitz?' said Liebermann.

'Please.' He collected a second glass from the cabinet and poured his guest a generous measure. 'Thank you. What were you playing? Chopin?'

'One of the nocturnes. Do you still play?'

'I stopped for a while but I've started again. The easy preludes and one or two of the mazurkas. Herr Donner thinks I'm making very good progress.' She narrowed her eyes suddenly. 'What were you doing in Hietzing?'

'I was with Inspector Rheinhardt.'

Clara nodded and proceeded to talk about a concert that her piano teacher had recommended. When she paused, she drew on her cigar-ette and looked at Liebermann with searching intensity. He was reminded of how much she had changed. He found this more worldly, mature incarnation of Clara somewhat disconcerting. She spoke fluently and easily — as she always did — gliding from one subject to the next, but beneath her monologue ran an elusive undercurrent, another level of communication that resisted interpretation.

Liebermann was distracted by the brightness of her lips — and by the poppy-red stain that had appeared on her cigarette.

Even after their chance meeting, the likelihood of ever again seeing Clara in his apartment had seemed so very remote that he had not given the possibility any prior consideration. Mentally unprepared, he found himself struggling to accept the reality of her presence: a problem which was compounded by injudicious nervous drinking.

As Clara continued talking, the reason for her visit did not become any clearer. Liebermann was tempted to ask outright, *What are you doing here?* But he was far too polite. It even crossed his mind that he might excuse himself and read her letter, but Clara could see the bureau from where she was sitting and such a manoeuvre would almost certainly invite comment. Time passed, and their conversation remained in a curious state of unresolved suspension. The dialogue had circled through a number of topics, none of them very consequential, and had arrived back at the starting place: music.

'Let's play a duet!' said Clara. Her words were slurred. Since she had not imbibed enough slivovitz to get inebriated in his company, Liebermann concluded that she must have been drinking prior to her arrival. The excessive use of perfume had perhaps been a ploy to disguise the smell of alcohol.

'I don't know . . .' he responded warily.

'Oh, come now, Max! It'll be fun.' Her exclamation was strained as she forced gaiety into each word.

'I'm not even sure I have any duets.'

It was a weak lie. 'At least take a look,' Clara pleaded.

Liebermann found an edition of the Opus 39 *Waltzes* by Brahms and held it up. 'Could you manage these?'

'Yes, of course.'

They sat at the Bösendorfer and Liebermann set the tempo by counting aloud. Clara attempted a bar or two of the B major and then abruptly stopped playing. 'No, not this one, something a little slower.' She turned some pages. 'Number three. Let's play number three.'

The G sharp minor was short and poignant, typically Viennese in its blending of emotions, happiness and sadness brought together by the magic of a musical truce. The bitter-sweet melody, full of delicious regret, kept a wistful smile on Liebermann's face until the final bars resolved all ambiguities in favour of undiluted melancholy. They played a few more of the slower waltzes, and Liebermann became acutely aware of the warmth of Clara's body, the heat generated by their thighs touching. Her proximity, her heavy perfume, the slivovitz and the music were beginning to have an effect.

Liebermann listened to the whisper of Clara's skirts as she changed position. She said nothing, but there was a tacit command in the protracted silence, a demand for attention. He turned slowly. Clara's hair was slightly dishevelled and the gauze that covered her breasts was damp with perspiration.

'Max . . .'

She said his name and brushed his cheek with the back of her fingers.

Liebermann remembered seeing Clara with her cavalry lieutenant outside the Imperial. He remembered the way the man had touched her and the proprietorial feelings the sight of their intimacy had aroused. He still found her very attractive. Clara tilted her chin, offering her parted lips. For a moment Liebermann experienced a kind of metaphysical torture as his emotional instincts were pulled in opposite directions. Then, quite suddenly, something snapped in his mind and he found himself clumsily rising from the stool.

'I'm sorry,' said Liebermann, not quite sure how he should behave. 'I think we should stop there.' He moved to the table and automatically filled his glass. 'Would you like another?'

Clara shook her head.

'Oh, Max. Please don't go through some silly act, pretending that nothing's happened. What are you trying to do? Spare my feelings?'

'I can't . . .' he said, vainly hoping that another swig of slivovitz might help.

Clara crossed the floor and stood in front of him. 'I know you want to. We were stupid . . . we denied ourselves for no good reason.'

'I can't,' he repeated again. 'It wouldn't be right.'

There was something in his tone that gave away more than he had intended.

'My God — you're not . . . you're not involved with someone, are you?' Liebermann did not deny it, but the hesitation was enough. Clara made a gesture in the air, a kind of pushing away. 'I know where my coat is,' she added with unnatural self-control.

When she got to the door Liebermann called out: 'Clara . . . I'm sorry.'

She repeated the same distancing hand gesture and said, 'Mazel tov.' He couldn't tell what she meant by this. Her voice was still neutral.

On the landing outside his apartment Liebermann leaned over the hand rail and watched her running down the the stairs. Her blue skirt flickered in the gaslight and suddenly vanished.

Liebermann leaned back against the landing wall and, addressing the ceiling, said: 'That went well . . .'

43

'FRAU KLUGE?'

'Yes?'

'Inspector Rheinhardt.'

'Oh yes, do come in.' She was a frail woman in her seventies, with wild hair and half-moon spectacles that sat behind the terminal bulb of an elongated nose. 'Did you catch the train?'

'No.'

'Very wise. They built the Hofpavillion for the emperor — but he never uses it. There must be a reason, eh?'

'Possibly.'

'One can never be too careful.'

Rheinhardt wondered whether Frau Kluge, as well as her husband, might not have benefitted from Professor Saminsky's help. The old woman showed him into a book-lined room which was redolent with the stale odours of decrepitude, ammonia, mould and rotting leather. In the centre of the room sat a gentleman with a long white beard who was wearing a quilted jacket and a traditional Chinese hat. The silk dome was decorated with luminous dragons and chrysanthemums. He was reading intently.

'Inspector Rheinhardt,' said Frau Kluge, drawing her husband's attention to their visitor. Kluge put his book aside and squinted at his guest.

'Inspector Rheinhardt, you say?'

'Yes,' said Frau Kluge. 'He wants to talk to you about Professor Saminsky.'

'Does he?'

'That's what the note said.'

The old man rose by pushing down on the chair arms. He stood, rather shakily, for a second or two during which he excecuted a bow and declared himself to be 'Herr Udalbert Kluge.' He then fell back into the chair.

Rheinhardt clicked his heels.

'Thank you so much for agreeing to see me, sir.'

Frau Kluge sat next to her husband and took his hand.

'Udalbert has not been well.'

'Indeed. I was informed of this by Professor Saminsky. Would you object to me sitting down?'

'No.'

'That is most generous.'

Rheinhardt found himself a stool and drew it up in front of the couple.

'What is the nature of your illness, Herr Kluge?'

The old man grumbled. 'They say that I observe things in the world that have no material reality.'

Frau Kluge stroked her husband's sleeve. 'Don't fret, my dear.'

'Good Christians believe in the existence of angels and demons — and no one says that they are mad.'

'No one has said you are mad, my dear.'

'But that is what they think: that is what Saminsky thinks.'

'He says that you have weak nerves.'

'I've had enough of his electrical therapy. It's unpleasant. He said it would just tingle — but the rods are hot. They burn. And those pills of his, they make me all confused.'

Rheinhardt coughed to attract their attention.

'I understand that Professor Saminsky came to see you on the evening of September the seventh.' Kluge's moist eyes were unrespons-ive. Rheinhardt turned to address the wife. 'Is that correct, Frau Kluge? Your husband was very unwell and you called Professor Saminsky?'

'The professor has had to come on several occasions,' Frau Kluge answered. But I can't remember exactly when. He came in August . . . and early September. It could have been the seventh.'

'You keep no records?'

'No.'

'On those occasions when he came, can you remember what time Professor Saminksy arrived?'

'It was quite late, I think.'

'How is it that you can remember the time, but not the date?'

'When Herr Kluge has a turn it is usually after dinner. We eat at half past eight.'

Herr Kluge raised a wrinkled finger: 'The point is this, Inspector. We live in a Christian country.' His voice had become querulous. 'Belief in non-material entities is Church doctrine. Did not Jesus cast out demons, and did He not transfer them into the herd of Gadarene swine? One cannot question the word of God. Given the choice between Saminsky and God, who would you believe? The old man paused, bit his lip and added, 'They say he's Jewish.'

'God?' Rheinhardt replied. 'He may very well be.'

44

RHEINHARDT RANG THE DOORBELL. It was was answered by the maid, who looked even wearier than she had on the occasion of his first visit with Liebermann.

'I would like to see Professor Saminsky.'

'I'm afraid he is not in.'

'Do you know when he's expected back?'

'I will have to ask the mistress.'

'Frau Professor is at home?'

'Yes.'

'Then perhaps I could speak to her?'

Rheinhardt was shown into the drawing room where he was once again at liberty to contemplate the opulent decor and trappings of Saminsky's success. His gaze lingered on the Ehrbar piano before it climbed to the family portrait — the professor, his dowdy wife and two daughters. Rheinhardt crossed to the window and looked out onto a lawn aggrandised with classical statuary. From the serpent that coiled around his hefty staff, Rheinhardt recognised Asclepius, the god of medicine and healing. The deity had so far favoured and protected the Saminsky household, but Greek gods were notoriously fickle.

The double doors opened and Frau Saminsky entered, followed by the maid.

'Inspector Rheinhardt?'

'Frau Professor.'

Rheinhardt was surprised to discover that Frau Saminsky had aged rather well. She had lost some weight and her appearance was no longer dowdy, quite the opposite. She wore a red and purple striped blouse with a yellow dress which was as vivid as dandelions — clashing colours that announced her arrival like a cymbal crash. The dull matronly expression of the portrait had been replaced by the wide professional smile of a woman accustomed to hosting dinner parties.

'I am so sorry, but my husband isn't at home.'

'Then perhaps you could help me?'

Frau Saminsky delivered a sympathetically modulated reply: 'But I'm not sure that I can.' Rheinhardt's unyielding expression made her add, 'Of course, I'll try to help . . . Would you like some tea?'

'No, thank you.'

Without making eye contact with the maid, Frau Saminsky raised a finger and made a flicking movement. It was all that was required to communicate the maid's redundancy. A general sagging of the young woman's body sufficed as a curtsey before she departed from the room.

'Please sit down, Inspector.'

As Frau Saminsky lowered herself onto the seat she fanned out her dress. A glimmering in the fabric suggested that a metallic thread had been woven into the silk.

'Where is Professor Saminsky?'

'He cancelled his clinic.'

'An emergency?'

'Not a medical emergency — no — but, nevertheless, a matter of some importance. You are still investigating the death of Ida Rosenkrantz?'

'Yes.'

'So sad . . .' said Frau Saminsky. 'She was such delightful company.'

'Did you know her?'

'She came to dine with us on many occasions.' Rheinhardt did not show his surprise. 'Professor Saminsky thought it would be good for her. She had no family of her own. Not here in Vienna. I think her mother went to live in Italy.'

'What was she like?'

'The girls adored her.' Frau Saminsky looked over at the family portrait. 'They were devastated when they heard what had happened.'

'Frau Professor? Your husband — where can I find him?'

Frau Saminsky straightened her back and raised her bosom. Adopting an attitude of haughty pretension she replied, 'The palace.' The effect she had worked so hard to achieve, however, was immediately ruined when her powdered face broke into a self-satisfied smile.

'The palace,' Rheinhardt repeated.

'Yes. My husband is often called to the palace. He is a trustee of several charities patronised by the late empress.'

'When are you expecting him to return?'

'I am not. I will be going to the palace myself, this evening. We have been invited to a ball in the Redoutensaal.'

'A great honour.'

'Indeed.'

Rheinhardt produced his notebook. 'Frau Professor, what were you doing the night Fräulein Rosenkrantz died?'

'Nothing. I was at home.'

'And what about Professor Saminsky?'

'He was at home too.' She reflected on her answer and added, 'Well, for most of the evening. The telephone kept on ringing and in the end my husband had to go out.'

'To see a patient?'

'Yes. Kluge, I think. It was all very inconvenient. My poor husband was leaving for Salzburg the following morning and had booked an early train.'

'What time did your husband return?'

'I don't know. I went to sleep and when I awoke he had already gone.' Frau Saminksy frowned. 'With respect, Inspector, I think it would be advisable to ask my husband these questions.'

'Of course,' said Rheinhardt, rising from the sofa. 'Would you be kind enough to tell Professor Saminsky that I need to speak with him again — at his earliest convenience.' Rheinhardt handed Frau Saminsky his card. 'I can be contacted at the Schottenring police station.'

45

ONLY THE CHANDELIERS ABOVE the stage of the Grosser Saal were illuminated. The rest of the concert hall was in shadow. Liebermann was seated in the back row of the balcony, peering through opera glasses at the wind section of the orchestra. It consisted of Herr Treffen — the principal flute — two oboes, two clarinets and two bassoons.

Director Mahler was rehearsing Beethoven's Fourth Symphony: the trio section of the third movement. The music was lively and exciting, its equine gallop carrying the listener forward with the buoyant energy of its skittish syncopations. Mahler's left hand was planted firmly on his hip, while his right hand beat the air with casual ferocity. Sweat had collected on his brow, his hair sprouted vertically from his head, and his pince-nez were tilted at such a crooked angle that Liebermann felt sure they they would fall off at any moment. Suddenly the director stopped conducting and stamped his foot on the podium. The booming sound he managed to create was apposite, being very Beethovenian in its power to evoke fateful associations.

'No, no, no,' Mahler cried, glaring at the wind section. 'Gentlemen, would you kindly observe the composer's phrasing. Again please.' Through the opera glasses Liebermann observed Herr Treffen's expression. He did not look very happy.

The orchestra repeated the passage but their efforts failed to appease the director. He stamped his foot again. A single ceremonial beat that found dramatic longevity in the hall's acoustically munificent niches.

'This is intolerable!' Mahler cried.

His face was distorted with rage. His eyes flashed with a diabol-
ical light and his mouth twisted into an ironic, malevolent smile. The
right corner drooped down to create an expression of such menace
that the offending parties became rigid with fear.

'Who did it?' Mahler shouted at the wind section, jutting his head
forward. 'Come on. Own up! Which one of you did it?'

'Herr Director?' ventured one of the bassoons, his voice quavering
and uncertain. 'Who did what?'

'I heard an F.' Mahler slashed the air with his baton. 'Who played
the F?'

The tension mounted. Mahler's face darkened, turning a shade of
red that augured an outburst of volcanic magnitude. The tension
created by the imminence of this cataclysm was unbearable, causing
those musicians closest to the director to cringe. The second oboe, a
young man with a fuzzy blond beard, courageously raised his hand
and said, 'It might have been me, Herr Director.' There was a
communal holding of breath, an expectant pause, during which it
seemed perfectly possible that Mahler would pounce on the oboist
and devour him. Instead, the director nodded at the young man and
said, 'Let us continue.' Mahler tapped the music stand with his baton.
'From the *pianissimo* — and please, gentlemen, pay attention to the
dynamics. It doesn't say *crescendo* on the score. It says *crescendo poco a
poco.*' He rotated his head, slowly, taking in every member of the
orchestra. '*Poco a poco.* Little by little.'

The rehearsal continued in this manner for over an hour, with
Mahler attending to every minute performance indication with
pathological exactitude. At one point, he insisted that Herr Treffen
play a single phrase, on his own, six times. Afterwards, Liebermann
scrutinised the wind players and was gratified to see small gestures
of consolation and solidarity. The subtle exchange of complicit

glances was encouraging and gave him reason to believe that his plan just might work.

When the rehearsal was over, Liebermann quickly left the concert hall and stood in the vicinity of the stage door. The musicians soon followed, spilling out onto the pavement. A few walked off immediately, but the majority stopped to smoke and talk with their colleagues. They hung around in a large amorphous group that gradually fragmented into smaller groups and a ribbon of stragglers. The dispersal of the orchestra was a slow process, but in due course Herr Treffen, the second oboe and one of the clarinettists separated from the throng and drifted off in the direction of the Ringstrasse. Liebermann stepped from his place of concealment and commenced his pursuit.

The trio of musicians crossed Karlsplatz and turned along the Naschmarkt. They chose a side street and after taking a few more turnings arrived at their destination, a grubby little beer cellar. Liebermann congratulated himself on his perspicacity. After such a gruelling rehearsal, during which the wind instruments had been thoroughly humiliated by Director Mahler, it was inevitable that Treffen would call a meeting of his war council. Liebermann waited for a few minutes and then walked down the steps and opened the door. On entering, he was surprised and delighted to find that the beer cellar was quite full. The clientele were a strange mix of professional men and labourers. Some political pamphlets on the tables suggested a common cause.

Liebermann located the players. They had taken off their coats and were now sitting at a table. The landlord — a man with a spectacularly oversized turned-up moustache — presented them with three steins and slapped Treffen on the back. They were obviously regulars.

Mounted on the wall next to their table was a blackboard displaying the menu: *salonbeuschel* (veal lung and heart), *gebackene Schweinsohren* (fried pig's ears), *grenadiermarsch* (infantryman's stew) and *tafelspitz* (boiled beef). There were only two desserts, *apfelstrudel* and pancakes. Liebermann stood with his back to Treffen's cabal and studied the menu carefully. Over the general hubbub he was able to catch a few angry words: *outrageous, unacceptable*. A gentleman at an adjacent table rose and Liebermann took his place. As he did so, a woman advanced from behind the counter and wiped the dirty surface with a damp rag.

'What can I get you?' she said, giving Liebermann a rather peculiar look.

'The boiled beef,' he answered.

'And anything to drink?'

'A *dunkel*.'

'Which one?'

'I'm not fussy.'

The woman walked off, her broad hips swaying as she negotiated a course through the crowded cellar. Liebermann saw her say something in the landlord's ear which prompted the man to throw a glance in Liebermann's direction. This prompted Liebermann to consider his surroundings more carefully and he was soon able to guess the nature of what had been said. He was the only Jew present. However, none of the patrons seemed to have noticed and the landlord showed no further interest in him.

Liebermann turned his head slightly and strained to hear the musicians.

— *Did you understand what he wanted?*

— *No, not all.*

— *He is insane. He tries to make distinctions where there are no distinctions to be made. I've never known anything like it.*

— *We cannot go on like this.*

A group of labourers burst out laughing, drowning out the

musicians' talk with their loud guffaws. When their racket had subsided, Liebermann heard just one further snippet of conversation, but it was enough.

— *What are you going to do now, Thomas?*

— *I'm going to write to Plappart again.*

The waitress returned with Liebermann's boiled beef and beer. She put the plate in front of him and flicked open the lid of the stein.

Liebermann took some coins out of his pocket and placed them in the woman's hand. 'Actually,' he said, standing to leave, 'I'm not very hungry after all.' The look of disappointment on the waitress's face suggested to Liebermann that she had either spat in the food or adulterated it with something worse. 'You eat it,' he added, with a kindly smile.

46

RHEINHARDT HAD CLOSED HIS eyes, meaning to rest for only a few
minutes, but the gentle rocking of the carriage had lulled him to sleep.
He had dreamed of visiting Orsola Salak. His slumbering brain had
created a very realistic approximation of the old witch's apartment.
It was identical in almost every detail — except for one: the presence of Fräulein Rosenkrantz. The opera singer had been sitting next
to Salak, eating a piece of *Sachertorte*. She had suddenly stopped
chewing. It was evident that she had discovered something hard and
inedible in her mouth. Pushing the object forward with her tongue,
she plucked one of Orsola Salak's fortune-telling bones from between
her lips. Rosenkrantz had offered the tiny phalanx to Rheinhardt,
saying: 'Go on, take it. I think this one might be very useful.' He had
replied: 'I couldn't. We hardly know each other.'

The atmosphere of the dream had been difficult to dispel. It had
left Rheinhardt feeling strangely dislocated. Indeed, on waking he
hadn't been sure where he was. He had nervously pulled the curtain
aside, the light hurting his eyes: a wide road, grand villas. As soon as
he had realised that he was in Hietzing it all came flooding back —
the telephone call and the duty officer's voice.

Rheinhardt lit a cigar. Each inhalation helped to restore his mental
equilibrium. Outside, the splendid residences had disappeared and
in their place were the skeletal frameworks of buildings under
construction. A few façades were nearing completion. The absence

of ornament did not appeal to Rheinhardt. He found their economic lines uninviting and without warmth. A constable was standing by the roadside, waving his hand in the air. It was Drasche.

The carriage came to a halt and Rheinhardt stepped down onto the cobbles. Drasche bowed and clicked his heels.

'Inspector Rheinhardt.'

'Constable Drasche.'

'Well, sir. I didn't think we'd be meeting again — not so soon, anyway.'

'Indeed, Drasche. The good people of Hietzing seem to have become remarkably accident-prone of late.'

Drasche pointed across an open field. 'The lake's beyond those trees, sir.'

'Then you had better show me the way.'

'Of course, sir.' They began walking. 'I'd say he's a professional gentleman by the look of his clothes, sir.'

'Where did you find them?'

'In the cabin, sir. It's where the bathers get changed.'

'Did you search the pockets?'

'Empty, sir.'

'And presumably you found a bicycle?'

'Yes, sir,' said Drasche, surprised. 'How did you know that?' Rheinhardt pointed to the rather obvious and prominent single track that had flattened the grass. 'Well, I never,' said the constable.

They fell silent for a short time. Eventually Drasche said, 'With respect, sir, did you pursue,' he searched for a euphemism and came up with two, 'that *matter* — that *business* — after you spoke to Herr Geisler?'

'I took Herr Geisler's testimony very seriously,' Rheinhardt replied, giving Drasche a look that he knew would discourage further inquiry. On seeing the young man's brow furrow, Rheinhardt felt a pang of regret. He did not want to discuss the mayor with Drasche but neither did he wish to intimidate the poor fellow. Rheinhardt adopted a heartier tone and smiled. 'Have you seen Herr Geisler recently?'

'Yes, sir. He's still at the hostel.'

'And has he found a job yet?'

'Not that I know of, sir.'

'Well, let's hope his luck improves — eh, Drasche?'

'Yes, sir.'

They passed through a line of beech trees beyond which was a small circular lake. It was perfectly still and mirrored a canopy of unbroken white cloud. Set back from the water was a small wooden hut. Beside it stood another constable and a man whose stooping posture betrayed his advanced age. At their feet lay an inert figure dressed in a blue and white swimming costume. Rheinhardt and Drasche walked around the water's edge. It was preternaturally quiet. Even the birds were silent.

As they drew closer, Rheinhardt increased his speed. Something instinctual — a frisson of anticipatory excitement — sharpened his senses. He became aware of the stagnant smell rising from the rushes, the sound of his shoes grinding the gravel beneath his feet. He could feel his heart in his chest, palpitating, unnaturally enlarged, denying his lungs the extent of their full expansion.

'God in heaven . . .' he muttered under his effortful breath.

He broke into a trot and soon found himself standing over the body, staring into the bleached, lifeless face. The damp material of the bathing suit clung to the man's torso and exposed the vulnerable contours of his shrunken genitalia. It was Professor Saminsky.

The elderly man came forward. 'I found him out there.' He gestured across the lake. 'He was floating, face down.'

'What is your name?' asked Rheinhardt.

'Herr Ebersbacher. Arnim Ebersbacher.'

'And what time did you discover the body?'

'Six-thirty.'

'That is a very early hour.'

'I get up early.'

'In order to swim?'

'I do so every morning. It keeps me in good health. I'm seventy-five, you know.' The old man pushed his chest out to emphasise his fitness. 'He's usually here at about the same time.'

'You've seen this gentleman before?'

'Yes, many times. I don't understand how he drowned. He was such a good swimmer.'

Part Four

The Last Song

47

WHEN RHEINHARDT HAD BROKEN the news of Professor
Saminsky's death to Frau Saminsky, she had fainted. A doctor was
called and it wasn't until the early hours of the afternoon that the
inspector was finally admitted into her bedchamber. By that time
the nature of her grief had changed and the doctor's sedating tinctures had begun to take effect. The keening and sobbing had subsided,
but what had replaced this mental anguish was — for Rheinhardt —
more disturbing. Frau Saminsky's expression was now devoid of
emotion. She seemed numb, hollowed out.

'I'm sorry for your loss,' said Rheinhardt. Frau Saminsky turned to
look at him. Her bloodshot eyes communicated nothing of her inner
state.

'What do you want, Inspector?'

Rheinhardt sighed. He did not wish to intrude upon this woman's
private suffering. Yet there was no alternative.

'I gave Daniel your message.' She said this as if she thought that
the inspector might have come merely to confirm that she had
complied with his prior request.

'Thank you.' He was tempted to get up and leave. It felt wrong
to be there. Instead, he took a deep breath and asked his first question. 'Frau Professor, did you meet with your husband last night —
as planned?'

'Yes.'

'And you attended the function in the Redoutensaal?'

'Yes.'

'May I ask, what frame of mind was your husband in?'

One of Frau Saminsky's eyebrows rose a fraction. 'Actually . . . he was rather preoccupied.'

'Oh?'

'He said very little.' She hesitated before adding, 'He was anxious to speak with the lord marshal.'

'And did he?'

'What?'

'Speak with the lord marshal?'

'Yes.' Frau Saminsky opened her hand, revealing a crushed hand-kerchief. She stared at it with drugged detachment, then asked, 'Where is he?'

'The body has been removed to the pathological institute.'

'Have my daughters returned yet?'

'No.'

'I do not think I can tell them. I cannot bear to see their faces. Will you ask Doctor Rzehak to . . .' Her sentence trailed off and her lower lip trembled slightly.

'Yes, of course.'

Frau Saminsky blinked at her inquisitor. 'Drowned.' The word seemed to hang in the air, resonating like a struck gong. 'How did it happen?'

'We don't know yet. When the autopsy is completed we will know more.'

'He loved swimming. He said that I should swim too, but I have never been a very active person. I have heard it said that opposites attract. That was certainly true in our case.'

She closed her eyes and a tear trickled down her cheek. Raising her hand, she dabbed her face with the screwed-up ball of her handkerchief.

'What time did your husband rise this morning?'

'I don't know. He didn't come to bed.' She opened her eyes. 'When we got back from the palace last night he went straight to his study.'

'Why?'

'He said that he was too agitated to sleep. He wanted to read before retiring.'

'And when *did* he retire?'

'He didn't. He must have been up all night — or perhaps he dozed in his study before leaving the house this morning.'

'Do you have any idea why he was so anxious to speak with the lord marshal?'

'No.'

'Did they speak for long?'

'Yes, they did.' Frau Saminsky raised a hand. 'I cannot answer any more of your questions, Inspector.' This was not a protest but a simple statement of fact. 'I really can't.' She let her arm fall and it landed heavily on the counterpane.

Rheinhardt stood up, bowed, and made his way to the door.

48

FROM THE POST OFFICE in Hietzing, Rheinhardt had sent a telegram to the *Obersthofmarschallamt* — the lord marshal's office. Under the emperor's personal direction, the *Obersthofmarschallamt* oversaw all the House of Habsburg's legal business. Rheinhardt had hoped (somewhat optimistically, he knew) that — given the *Obersthofmarschallamt* and the security office were both, in the broadest possible sense, legal organisations — his request might be given special attention. To his great surprise, he discovered later that day that his optimism had been vindicated. At the Schottenring police station he was handed an envelope bearing an imperial seal, and inside was an invitation to the palace written in the lord marshal's own hand. Rheinhardt had rushed to the pathological institute to collect Professor Mathias's autopsy results, and then home in order to get changed into his evening suit — palace protocol demanded that visitors wear either a suit, military uniform or national costume. His carriage had rolled under the massive dome of the Michaeltract with only seconds to spare before the appointed time.

Rheinhardt was led by a liveried servant through a series of rooms. He was conscious of a general impression of opulence, flowing past him on either side as he followed his guide: red, cream and gold, illuminated by the pendant brilliance of chandeliers. The atmosphere was redolent with the scent of freshly cut flowers. Rheinhardt kept his eyes fixed on the servant's shoulder blades. He was sure that looking around in the awestruck manner of a country bumpkin, newly arrived in the city, would be in breach of palace etiquette.

After what seemed like an eternity they emerged onto a landing. The servant invited Rheinhardt to sit on a Louis XIV sofa and tapped lightly on the first of two sets of double doors. A voice called out and the servant entered the room. Shortly after, the servant re-appeared and said, 'Please come forward.' Rheinhardt stood up, checked that the tips of his moustache were sufficiently sharp, and marched towards the open doors. As he entered the room, the servant introduced him with a pompous declaration. 'Detective Inspector Oskar Rheinhardt of the Viennese security office.' As soon as he had stepped over the threshold the doors closed behind him.

Rheinhardt found himself standing in a modestly proportioned room, albeit one with a gilt ceiling and a Gobelin tapestry hanging on the wall. The lord marshal was a hawkish man in his late fifties. His beard was neatly trimmed and his moustache projected outwards beyond his cheeks. He was dressed, like Rheinhardt, in an evening suit and white bow tie. However, his chest was decorated with various ribbons and medals. He was sitting behind a writing desk with curved, spindly legs.

'Inspector Rheinhardt,' said the lord marshal, gesturing towards a chair. 'Do sit down.'

'Lord Marshal.' Rheinhardt bowed. 'Thank you for granting me this interview. I am indebted.'

'Not at all,' said the lord marshal, rearranging the papers on his desk. 'I knew Professor Saminsky. I want to know what happened.'

Rheinhardt lowered himself onto the chair and took out his note-book. 'May I ask, sir, how it was that you and Professor Saminsky were acquainted?'

'Saminsky assisted with the management of the late empress's medical charities. My bureau was frequently consulted vis-à-vis the ratification of documents related to his work with them.'

'Then you will permit me to offer my condolences.'

'He was a fine fellow, a man of industry and intelligence. He will be greatly missed. You said in your telegram that he drowned?'

'There is a small lake near his villa in Hietzing. It was his custom to swim there in the early hours of the morning. His body was discovered by a fellow bather.'

The lord marshal squeezed his lower lip. 'Some kind of accident?'

'There was nothing to suggest that his death was attributable to misadventure. Moreover, the autopsy results showed that he was in good health, which means that we are obliged to consider other possibilities.'

'What? You think he might have killed himself? Why ever would he do such a thing?'

'I was hoping that you may be able to help answer that very question.'

'Me?' The lord marshal touched his chest. 'How should I know? We were acquainted, but not intimately so.'

'I spoke with Frau Professor Saminsky this afternoon. She told me that Saminsky was in a rather agitated state last night and anxious to speak with you. There was a function in the Redoutensaal?'

'Yes, there was.'

'And Saminsky *did* seek you out.'

'Yes, he did.' The lord marshal assented. 'And I have to say, now that I think about it, he *was* out of sorts. Saminsky was usually a jovial, lively fellow, but yesterday he was definitely not himself.'

'Depressed?'

'No, I wouldn't say depressed — more distracted.' The lord marshal stroked his beard, 'Restless, unable to keep his mind on one thing.'

'What did he want to speak to you about? It was Frau Professor Saminsky's view that her husband wished to speak to you concerning a *particular* matter.'

'None of what we discussed required urgent attention.'

'Forgive me, but may I inquire as to what it was, exactly, that you discussed?'

'Saminsky was somewhat preoccupied with the possible financial implications of his status as charity trustee. He wanted to know what would happen if any of the charities amassed debts. Would he, for example, be called upon to pay them?'

'And what did you advise?'

'I told him that I would get my assistant Ackermann to review the relevant contracts.'

'And was Saminsky satisfied with that answer?'

'No, but it was the only answer I could give under the circumstances. He also wanted to know whether his work for the charity board was going to be brought to the emperor's attention. He was not unambitious.'

Rheinhardt made some notes and said: 'But did Saminsky say anything that now, with the benefit of hindsight, you recognise as being significant concerning his mental state?'

The lord marshal pressed his hands together. 'He was distracted, but I cannot say any more than that. It would be misleading to imply that I saw in his demeanour a presentiment of coming tragedy.' The lord marshal frowned. 'I will inform the emperor of Professor Saminsky's death in due course. You will appreciate that suicide is a sensitive subject where His Majesty is concerned.'

Only four years had passed since the emperor's son had shot himself in a hunting lodge at Mayerling.

'Was His Majesty also acquainted with Professor Saminsky?'

'They met a few times when Saminsky was treating the late empress. And Saminsky has been presented at court on many subsequent occasions. It is only right that I inform His Majesty.'

'I see.'

'Well, Inspector, I'm sorry I haven't been much help.' The lord marshal rose from his seat. 'But that is all I can tell you — a sad business.'

Instead of calling the servant, the lord marshal escorted Rheinhardt to the double doors. They both walked out onto the landing.

Rheinhardt inclined his head. 'Thank you, once again.'

The lord marshal made an indulgent sign and mumbled an unintelligible platitude. At that precise moment, the second set of double doors opened, and out walked the emperor, accompanied by two generals. Rheinhardt stiffened and his heartbeat accelerated. The emperor was wearing blue trousers and a white tunic with gold flashes. He was a little shorter than his companions, who were also brilliantly attired but in red uniforms decorated with yellow braid. All were equipped with sabres. Rheinhardt looked to the lord marshal and the rising terror must have shown in his eyes.

'It's all right,' whispered the lord marshal. 'Stay exactly where you are.'

More people emerged, following the emperor and his generals: an entourage of palace aides and adjutants — and behind them a swarm of serving men. The emperor was marching straight towards Rheinhardt and the lord marshal. As the emperor approached, the lord marshal bowed low and Rheinhardt did the same. He was in this position, looking down at the floor, when he became aware of a pair of extremely shiny shoes occupying the uppermost arc of his visual field. The shoes were motionless, and the general kerfuffle that had previously accompanied the emperor's advance had now been replaced by a restive hush. When Rheinhardt lifted his head, he discovered that the shiny shoes, as he had feared, belonged to the emperor. Rheinhardt swallowed and tried to keep perfectly still.

It was a face that every citizen of the empire knew: the bald head and the massive oversized mutton-chop whiskers, the round chin and prominent nose, an inescapable face, reproduced, as it so frequently was, in paintings and postcards and on commemorative tea services and chocolate boxes. Rheinhardt was dimly aware of the entourage piled up behind that familiar visage, but most of all he was aware of the emperor's clear blue eyes. They were looking directly at him.

Rheinhardt could hear the roar of his own blood in his ears, the remorseless pounding of his heart. Suddenly, the emperor threw an inquiring glance at the lord marshal.

'Your Majesty,' said the lord marshal, 'may I introduce Detective Inspector Oskar Rheinhardt of the security office.'

Franz-Josef . . .

The great empire and all its disparate peoples were held together by this one man. From Bohemia to Galicia, Transylvania to Bosnia, Dalmatia to the Tyrol — Germans, Magyars, Czechs, Slovaks, Croats, Serbs, Slovenes, Italians, Ruthenians, Poles and Little Russians, all of these citizens — from those who dwelt in the grandest Schloss to the humblest peasant hut — revolved around this pivotal figure of power. And he, Rheinhardt, was at that very moment closer to him than any other human being. He felt as though he was standing at the very hub of the universe.

'Rheinhardt,' said the emperor. 'Security office, eh?'

'Indeed, Your Majesty,' said the lord marshal.

Behind the emperor his entourage were waiting with bated breath. It seemed to Rheinhardt that his destiny was in the balance, his fate hanging by a thread. It was well known that one of the architects of the opera house had hanged himself after the emperor had made a disparaging remark about its 'lowness'. The curling of the emperor's upper lip had destroyed careers and ruined lives.

The emperor nodded, as if a process of inner deliberation had come to an end.

'Where would we be without our fine security office?'

The generals muttered their approval.

'Very good, very good,' said the emperor, addressing no one in particular. He swept his arm forward. 'Carry on.' With these words, the passage of time, which had hitherto been held in a state of suspension, was permitted to proceed again. There was an almost physical sensation of unlocking and release.

Reflexively, Rheinhardt bowed again. He could hear the entourage marching past. When he raised his head, he could see the aides, adjutants and servants chasing after the emperor and his companions as they trotted down the staircase. One of the generals was talking about manoeuvres in the east.

Rheinhardt was stunned.

'Well, Inspector,' said the the lord marshal. 'You have been honoured.'

Rheinhardt didn't feel like he'd been honoured. Rather, he felt as if he had narrowly missed being crushed beneath a juggernaut.

49

THE DIRECTOR HAD NOT offered the flautist a seat. Mahler opened a desk drawer and removed a sheet of paper. As if to avoid contamination he held it between his thumb and forefinger and signalled that he wished Treffen to take it from him.

'What am I supposed to do with this?' asked Treffen.

'Read it.'

Treffen studied the letter. As his eyes oscillated his neutral expression was unchanging. When he had finished reading, the flautist stepped forward and placed the letter on the director's desk. He then stepped back to his original position.

Mahler tapped a distinctive rhythm on the cover of a score. Liebermann, who was seated on the piano stool, thought it sounded like one of the director's funeral marches.

'Well,' said Mahler. 'Who do you think wrote such a letter?'

'I have no idea.'

'Then you won't mind providing us with a sample of your handwriting.'

Mahler pushed a blank card and a pencil towards Treffen.

'I beg your pardon?'

'For a graphologist to look at.'

Treffen's eyebrows rose a fraction, but it was enough to convert neutral indifference to surprise.

'Herr Director, are you accusing me?'

'No. I am giving you an opportunity to demonstrate your innocence.' The director picked up the pencil and held it up. 'A few phrases
will suffice, or a poem that you have committed to memory. Schiller's
"Ode to Joy", perhaps?'

'I am afraid I cannot comply with your request, Herr Director.'
Mahler feigned puzzlement. 'If I *were* to provide you with a sample
of my handwriting, which would, needless to say, prove my innocence, you would then summon another member of the orchestra.
And if it transpired that he too were innocent, you would be obliged
to summon others. Where would it end? There is a principle at stake
here. You cannot treat members of an imperial and royal institution
with such casual contempt. When you disrespect the rank and file,
you also disrespect the institution, and, when you disrespect *this* institution, you disrespect the emperor.'

'I couldn't agree more,' said Mahler, 'and ordinarily I wouldn't
dream of making such an impudent demand. I only do so now because
I am absolutely certain of the outcome.' Mahler placed the pencil on
the blank card with exaggerated care. 'I know where you go after
rehearsals, Herr Treffen. I know where you plot and scheme. This
gentleman,' he gestured towards Liebermann, 'overheard you. There
really is no point pretending otherwise. You have been found out.'

Treffen peered at Liebermann and a flicker of recognition appeared
in his eyes.

The director continued: 'I do not wish to humiliate you, Herr
Treffen. Nor do I have the slightest desire to make an example of you.
All that I want is an orchestra comprised of musicians willing to share
my vision, men from whom I can expect, within reason, a measure
of loyalty.' Treffen was about to speak but Mahler raised his hand to
silence him. 'This unsatisfactory situation in which we find ourselves
can be resolved, I believe, in a civilised manner without unnecessary
embarrassment to all concerned — and I think you know how.'

Treffen moved awkwardly, shifting his weight from one foot to the other. After a protracted silence during which it was evident that his internal deliberations had been both difficult and painful, he said in a strained voice, 'Herr Director, I wish to tender my resignation.'

'Accepted,' said Mahler. He sat back in his chair. 'I trust you will soon find another position more suitable for a man with your,' he paused before adding, 'very *particular* views.' The emphasis was heavily ironic.

Treffen turned and marched briskly to the door. His hand had barely made contact with the handle when Mahler called out, 'One more thing, Herr Treffen. Please inform your co-conspirators that I intend to take no further action. I believe, perhaps wrongly, that they are impressionable young fellows who have had the misfortune to come under your influence. Be that as it may, any more of these,' Mahler snatched up the letter, 'and I will not be so forbearing.'

Up until that juncture, Treffen had managed to control his anger; however, the resentment and bitterness that he had been suppressing suddenly found expression.

'They don't need your magnanimity!' Treffen sneered. 'You think yourself so very superior, don't you? Touched by greatness! Well, you're not, by any stretch of the imagination. The old director was twice the conductor you'll ever be. And as for those symphonies of yours, well, the less said the better! You may think yourself above us all, but really you're nothing but a pathetic little . . .' Treffen collected the bile of his own prejudice in his mouth, savouring its acidity as he prepared to spit out the inevitable unimaginative insult.

'Don't spoil things for yourself, Herr Treffen,' Mahler interjected. 'I am indeed in a magnanimous frame of mind but, as you know, I am prone to sudden mood swings. This letter,' Mahler stabbed the sheet of paper with his finger, 'is slanderous! If you want me to instruct a lawyer then by all means continue.'

Treffen fumed for a few moments, his suppressed rage producing a rash which climbed up his neck and mottled his cheeks. He growled something unintelligible, a throaty curse, and left the office, slamming the door so hard that the window panes rattled.

'Well, Herr Doctor, that was most satisfying.' The director produced a broad grin. 'Thank you so much for your assistance.'

Liebermann inclined his head. 'I thought you were very lenient, all things considered.'

'I meant what I said. I have no interest in exacting revenge. Revenge would be just one more distraction and there are too many of those already in my life. At present, there is only one thing that merits my full attention.' He raised his arms heavenwards. 'Music.'

Mahler called Przistaupinsky and ordered tea. When the secretary returned, his tray was also laden with two dishes of *Marillenknödel* — apricot dumplings.

'Excellent,' said Mahler.

'From Café Mozart,' said Przistaupinsky.

Mahler observed Liebermann closely. 'I take it you like *Marillenknödel*?'

'I do.'

'I am always a little suspicious of those who profess indifference to *Marillenknödel* — it is beyond my comprehension. My sister Justi has an old recipe which is truly wonderful.' Mahler said these words with the same conviction he might have used to describe the transcendent beauty of Wagner's *Liebestod*. 'Even so,' he continued, 'the chef at Café Mozart usually acquits himself well. Wouldn't you say, Alois?'

'Indeed, Herr Director.'

Przistaupinsky poured the tea, distributed the plates and served the dumplings. They were golden brown, sprinkled with icing sugar and still steaming slightly. Liebermann sliced through the breadcrumbs with his fork. The exterior broke open, revealing a whole baked

apricot inside: the vertical incision and moist interior created a discon-
certingly sexual impression.

When Przistaupinsky departed, the two men talked for a time
about their victory over Treffen, but in due course the conversation
became more general. It was while they were discussing the songs of
Alexander Zemlinsky that Liebermann sought Mahler's opinion with
respect to Freimark's 'Hope'. The director agreed that it was a remarkable piece of lieder writing and, with some subtle prompting from
Liebermann, was soon reflecting on the relationship between Freimark
and Brosius.

'I find early Brosius quite dull, lacking in originality; however,
there was a kind of flowering in his middle years, the influence of
which I think is detectable in Freimark's "Hope". Those poignant
discords.' Mahler tilted his head as if he were listening to the song
being performed. 'But Brosius never continued with his harmonic
experiments. After the second string quartet he reverted back to the
comfortable, derivative style of his youth. The *Rustic Symphony* is
execrable.'

'Brahms respected him,' Liebermann ventured.

'Well, they were friends — for a period, anyway. Brahms was
obliged to be complimentary.'

The talk shifted to a concert series in which the director had
programmed Brahms's *Variations on a theme by Haydn*. Mahler spoke
with passion, slicing the air with his nail-bitten fingers.

'Brahms takes the seed from the pod and nurses it through all
the stages of development to its highest degree of perfection. In fact,
he has no rivals in this field, not even Beethoven, whose inventive-
ness makes him soar into other distant realms. The *Andante* of my
own second symphony and the *Blumenstück* from the third are also
variations . . . Rather than a continuous development of the same
sequence of notes, mine are decorative arabesques and garlands

{ 299 }

woven around the theme.' The director got up from his seat, crossed to the piano and began playing to illustrate his point. 'Brahms's variations,' he continued, 'are like an enchanted stream, with banks so sure that not a single drop gets lost, even at the sharpest bends.' Again, he provided an example.

As the director played, Liebermann noticed that a four-hand arrangement of an untitled piece was already on the music stand.

'What is this?'

'Oh, something I was working on the summer before last, an *Adagietto*. It'll be the slow movement of my fifth symphony.' Mahler detected Liebermann's interest. 'Can you read it?'

'Yes,' said Liebermann.

'Would you like to . . .' Mahler wriggled his fingers in the air.

'Oh, I couldn't. I mean, not with . . .'

'Nonsense,' Mahler cut in, making a dismissive gesture and urging the young doctor to make room for him on the piano stool. Liebermann could not quite believe his situation. Anxiety made his fingers feel cold and inflexible. He rubbed his hands together to generate some warmth. 'You may be familiar with some of the material,' Mahler continued, unaware of his companion's sudden crisis of confidence. 'The introductory theme is derived from one of my Rückert songs. Are you ready?'

Liebermann looked at the notation so closely that the staves began to blur.

Liebermann swallowed and said, 'Yes.'

They began to play, filling the room with a sound of such beguiling beauty that Liebermann instantly forgot himself. The melody was weightless and unhurried, hovering, occupying a tonal universe that was at once both ecstatic and painfully sad. It was like nothing Leibermann had ever heard before, touching him in some deep place, finding subtle and sympathetic registers of emotion. This music was peculiarly eloquent, suggesting the numinous in its oceanic pitch and swell. Here, unmistakably, was the weary soul, bidding adieu to earthly existence. Yet the lure of eternal peace was not so great as to mitigate mundane attachments, the recollection of simple human pleasures: sunlight on an upturned face, a child's smile, mountain air in the morning, the smell of flowers after summer rain, the immediacy of physical love. The soul was leaving for a better place, but not without a backwards glance and the reluctant acceptance that some things would be lost for ever. Throughout, the aching melody was held in a state of suspension, striving for but repeatedly denied resolution. The effect of this was to make the music unbearably intense. When the final phrase desended, step by step, Liebermann was fighting to hold back tears. An F major chord, pure and translucent, consigned the soul to heaven, and the silence that followed lasted for some time.

The director removed his hands from the keyboard and said: 'Well, what do you think?'

Liebermann was speechless.

50

As usual, Café Central was busy. Even so, Rheinhardt and Liebermann had found a table where they could talk without being overheard. A group of littérateurs were arguing loudly about poetry and the pianist was thumping out a medley from Strauss's *Die Fledermaus*. Liebermann noted that his friend had failed to order a pastry: a reliable indication that something was amiss.

'I feel responsible, somehow,' said Rheinhardt, stirring his Türkische coffee and staring glumly into the black whirlpool that he had created. 'Don't you?'

'Oskar,' said Liebermann, sighing, 'we didn't drive Saminsky to commit suicide!'

'But how can you be so sure?'

Liebermann turned away and gazed towards the corner where the chess players had gathered. It was remarkable how they could concentrate, given the noise. 'Professor Mathias is quite certain that it *was* suicide?'

Rheinhardt nodded. 'Frau Saminsky said her husband was preoccupied. He didn't go to bed after returning from the palace. The lord marshal also said Saminsky wasn't his usual jovial self. I think we may have been a little too . . . '

'Emphatic?'

'Yes.'

Liebermann shrugged. 'It's all very odd, though, don't you think? That Saminsky should drown — at this particular juncture?'

'Yes. And ordinarily we would be obliged to consider the possibility of foul play. But Professor Mathias was unequivocal with respect
to his conclusion.' The crescents of loose skin under Rheinhardt's
eyes had darkened due to the absence of sleep. He shook his head
and added, 'I'm not sure we went about things in the right way.
Those blunt accusations. He couldn't face the prospect of scandal
and ruin.'

Liebermann pushed his *Topfenstrudel* across the table.

'Eat this. It'll make you feel better.'

'Aren't you hungry?'

'I'll order another.'

Rheinhardt sliced the pastry with his fork and placed a small piece
in his mouth. He began to chew, slowly, and Liebermann hoped
that it would have the desired effect.

'Did you go to see Herr Kluge?'

'Yes. The poor fellow is old and plagued by supernatural visita-
tions.'

'Does he live on his own?'

'No, with his wife who is also very peculiar.'

'Did they remember Saminsky paying a call on the seventh of
September?'

'Frau Kluge remembered Saminsky visiting in August and early in
the following month, but she couldn't provide dates. She was, however,
confident that Saminsky had arrived late. Apparently Herr Kluge is
most vulnerable to hallucinations after eating his evening meal which
is served at half past eight.'

Liebermann remembered Saminsky opening the D'Arsonval cage.
He had looked like a stage magician, a creator of illusions. In a way,
his whole life was misdirection and deception. He had concealed his
mediocrity behind a screen of smoke and mirrors.

The pianist finished the Strauss medley and received a vigorous round of applause. Liebermann waited for the noise to subside. 'I think I might have been mistaken about Lueger.'

Rheinhardt put down his fork.

'Good God! I don't think I've ever heard you say such a thing.'

'The mayor is shrewd. And I wonder, would a shrewd man have chosen such a course of action . . .' The sentence trailed off and Liebermann grimaced.

'What about the voice of Frau Lueger, sounding in her son's head, her possessive love, her denunciation of sluts and sirens? What about all that?'

Liebermann ignored Rheinhardt's taunt.

'The very fact that Geisler saw the mayor outside Rosenkrantz's villa should have given us pause for thought. If he had intended to kill her, surely he would have taken better care not to be seen.'

'Men with murder on their minds are, not surprisingly, somewhat absorbed by their thoughts and therefore prone to incautious behaviour. It was a foggy night. Lueger might not have seen Geisler approaching.'

'And those letters in the stove? Would he really have tried to destroy them after killing his erstwhile mistress?'

'We don't know that he *did* try to destroy them. Perhaps they were placed in the stove by Rosenkrantz. However, if it *was* Lueger, his behaviour cannot be considered entirely unreasonable. Most people are completely unaware that certain inks survive fire.'

Liebermann pulled at his chin.

The pianist began to play again, a Slavic melody that Liebermann didn't recognise. 'What if Fräulein Rosenkrantz's rib wasn't accidentally broken?'

'I'm afraid I'm finding your reasoning a little difficult to follow, Max. Are you suggesting that the perpetrator broke the rib on purpose?'

'Yes.'

'Why would he have done that? If it wasn't for the broken rib he would have almost certainly got away with it!'

'Exactly.'

'Oh, I see,' said Rheinhardt. 'The broken rib was broken because of an unconscious wish to be caught and punished.'

'No. I believe the perpetrator was fully aware of what he was doing.'

'Forgive me, Max, but you really aren't making much sense.'

Liebermann took a sip of his schwarzer coffee.

'Whoever killed Rosenkrantz wanted us to conclude that she had taken laudanum, lost consciousness, and that her rib was accidentally broken while she was being asphyxiated. And why wouldn't we reach such a conclusion? It's so very plausible.'

'But to what end?'

Liebermann caught the attention of a passing waiter.

'Another *Topfenstrudel*, please.'

The waiter bowed and dashed off towards the counter.

Rheinhardt frowned at his friend: 'Well?'

51

Commissioner Brügel had arranged an arc of photographs on his desk. Each of the images showed a different view of Professor Saminsky's drowned body. Some of the photographs, especially those taken at a distance, possessed a modicum of artistic merit. They showed the still surface of the lake, the ring of trees, and the pale uniform sky overhead. If it had not been for the corpse in the foreground, some of these landscapes would have been suitable for display at an exhibition.

'Why,' said the commissioner, 'did you request an audience with the lord marshal without consulting me first?'

Rheinhardt straightened his back.

'Sir: I tried to speak to you before I wired the *Obersthofmarschallamt*, but you were unavailable. I telephoned from the post office in Hietzing.'

'Then you should have waited for me to return.' There were several arguments that Rheinhardt could have proferred to justify his actions, but he knew that to do so would very likely make matters worse. The commissioner was famous for his intransigence. Once he had taken a view there was little point in trying to persuade him otherwise. 'You can't just go blundering into the palace,' Brügel continued. 'There are procedures, protocols, and customs that must be observed. Fortunately, the lord marshal was not offended by your impertinence. A less gracious individual might have taken umbrage and issued a complaint.'

The commissioner proceeded in this vein for some time, his invective becoming more heated until he finally began to rant. Rheinhardt
remained calm, knowing that the storm would eventually pass. When
it did, the commissioner fell back in his chair, exhausted by his own
choler.

'I'm sorry, sir,' said Rheinhardt, lowering his head deferentially. 'It
won't happen again.' A show of remorse usually helped to expedite
matters.

The commissioner, who was still breathing heavily and whose nose
had darkened to the shade of a ripe plum, made a grunting noise
which Rheinhardt took to be a sign of reluctant approval. After
making some adjustments to his clothing, Brügel turned his attention
to Rheinhardt's report. He flicked the pages backwards and forwards
and finally said, 'Your conclusions are equivocal, but it's obvious what
happened. Isn't it? Saminsky made Fräulein Rosenkrantz pregnant,
she agreed to see the angel maker, but subsequently made demands
that Saminsky was not prepared to meet. Perhaps she wanted him to
leave his wife and family? The crime was well thought out, and had
it not been for the broken rib we might easily have concluded that
Rosenkrantz's death was accidental. When Saminsky learned that we
suspected foul play he impulsively tried to implicate the mayor. In
due course, he recognised the direction the investigation was taking
and elected to take his own life in order to escape the scaffold and
public disgrace.'

Rheinhardt nodded. 'Indeed, sir. However, I am still of the opinion
that Herr Geisler's statement is accurate. I believe that the mayor was
with Fräulein Rosenkrantz the night she was killed, a fact which
cannot be overlooked, and recommend caution with respect to what
we are at liberty to conclude.'

'No, Rheinhardt,' said Brügel. 'It is clear now that your witness
must have been mistaken.' These words were spoken with an air of

finality. The commissioner had evidently lost his appetite for indicting the mayor. 'On reflection, it is most unfortunate that *you* decided to pursue that particular line of inquiry.' Brügel's hard stare dared Rheinhardt to object to his use of the personal pronoun. 'Let us hope that the mayor is a man who does not hold grudges.'

'Sir: this is most unsatisfactory.'

'On the contrary, Rheinhardt, the mystery of Ida Rosenkrantz has been solved and when the newspaper reports appear, I promise you, the security office will be warmly congratulated.' The commissioner's face contracted as if in response to a sudden attack of indigestion. 'I suppose I should congratulate you.'

'Thank you, sir,' said Rheinhardt. 'That is most kind. However—'

'There is nothing more to discuss,' Brügel cut in. He collected the photographs of Saminksy, slid them into a buff folder and snapped it shut. Looking up at Rheinhardt with peculiar intensity he added, 'The case is closed.' Brügel's severe expression declared that he was not in the mood to be contradicted.

'Very good, sir.'

Rheinhardt felt that some kind of bargain had been struck, although he couldn't specify what exactly. He also sensed that the commissioner might owe him some small favour in return for his acquiescence.

'Sir?'

'What is it, Rheinhardt?'

'I would like to conduct an exhumation.'

Rheinhardt returned to his office where he found a message from Professor Mathias. The old man wanted him to visit the pathological institute as soon as possible. Paying less attention than he should have, Rheinhardt rushed through some outstanding paperwork and was soon waving down a cab on the Schottenring. Within minutes he was sitting in the morgue, next to the autopsy table. Professor Mathias was still working on a corpse. Rheinhardt registered the pretty and youthful face: golden braids, gemstone eyes, and translucent skin. She couldn't have been more than sixteen.

The professor stroked the girl's smooth forehead. 'Voltaire once wrote that it is one of the superstitions of the human mind to have imagined that virginity could be a virtue: witty, of course — as one would expect — but woefully wrong-headed. Why is it that the French, whose medieval courtiers invented romance, have become so cynical in modern times? A German writer would never make jests at the expense of modesty. I fear that, now, we alone among the peoples of Europe carry the flame.'

'Perhaps you haven't been to the theatre lately, Herr Professor. Our young writers show little respect for the old ways. They mock romance.'

'God help us, then. We'll go the way of the second empire. You mark my words.' Mathias put down his instruments and covered the girl's face with a green sheet.

'Why did you want to speak to me, Herr Professor?'

The old man took off his spectacles and began to clean them with his apron.

'Something's been troubling me.'

'Oh?'

'Was the lake in which Saminsky drowned very muddy?'

'I didn't pay much attention to the lake. I was rather preoccupied with Saminsky. Why?'

Mathias put his spectacles back on and reached for a small bottle. Holding it up to the electric light he said, 'What do you see?'

'Water? A brown sediment of some kind has collected at the bottom.'

'Correct.'

'Watch.' The Professor gave the bottle a vigorous shake and held it up again. The water was now cloudy and opaque.

'Herr Professor, what has this got to do with Saminsky?'

'I obtained the contents of this bottle from Saminsky's lungs — which isn't always possible. You may be surprised to learn that sometimes the lungs of a drowned man are dry. Now, observe the particles. They are fine and take a long time to settle. I must confess, I didn't notice how much precipitate there was at first.' Mathias appeared somewhat embarrassed by the admission.

Rheinhardt made a forgiving gesture. 'What does it mean?'

'Unfortunates who drown themselves don't usually thrash around. They simply lie back, allow their lungs to fill, and lose consciousness. Drowning isn't as unpleasant as you might imagine. Individuals who have been saved from drowning often describe having experienced a feeling of detachment and peace after an initial stage of panic. The fact that there's so much mud in this bottle suggests to me that it was kicked up.'

'Saminsky was struggling?'

'Indeed.'

The two men looked at each other. Professor Mathias's eyes blinked behind the thick lenses of his spectacles.

'Are you saying, Professor, that Saminsky might not have committed suicide after all?'

'I am saying that you had better take another look at that lake. If the water is relatively clear . . .' Mathias allowed the implications of the incomplete sentence to multiply.

Rheinhardt took the bottle from the old man. 'May I ask you to compose a brief supplementary report, Herr Professor?'

'Of course.'

Saminsky had made Rosenkrantz pregnant. He had attempted to

implicate the mayor, and now there was reason to believe that Saminsky might — like Rosenkrantz — also have been murdered.

The case was far from closed.

Rheinhardt tilted the bottle and a rainbow of colours appeared beneath the dark blue stopper. He was obliged to continue the investigation. If Commissioner Brügel challenged him, he could always blame Professor Mathias.

52

Apart from the occasional rustling of reeds and leaves, the lake was, once again, shrouded in absolute silence, the surface a sheet of glass beneath a white void. Rheinhardt passed through the beech trees and followed the gravel path until he reached the changing hut. For a few moments he stood quietly, contemplating the hushed scene. He placed his hands on his thighs and, leaning forward, peered into the water. He couldn't see very much, only the sky's pale reflection.

In the hut he stripped off his clothes and donned a black and green swimming costume. He hadn't been swimming for months and was quietly excited by the prospect. The door hinges needed oil and bellowed a bovine protest as he made his exit.

Rheinhardt edged down the gentle incline until his feet were covered in water, and then began to wade out slowly into the lake. It was cold, but not cold enough to make him shiver. When the water was lapping around his waist, he bent his knees and pushed off, launching himself into a horizontal glide before initiating a languid breast stroke. Occasionally he would allow his legs to descend in order to test for depth, and he discovered that the lake was generally shallow. Only when he was in the very middle was there a place where the bottom was beyond the reach of his toes. Taking a deep breath he dipped his head beneath the surface and stared at the bed of the lake. The water was pellucid. He saw flat stones and some bricks embedded in the mud. Coming up for air, he took another deep breath and lowered his head again. He scissored his legs, creating a disturbance, and watched dark nebulae rising. They expanded until the agitated water was opaque. Rheinhardt undertook various experiments of this kind, and when he was satisfied that he had gathered enough evidence to support Professor Mathias's hypothesis he swam a few circuits of the lake for pleasure.

As he followed the bank opposite the wooden hut, Rheinhardt caught a glimpse of someone walking beyond the beech trees. He expected to see a man emerging onto the path at any moment — another swimmer, perhaps? But no one did emerge. His instinct was to go and investigate, but he resisted the urge and continued to circle the lake. Where had the man gone? Rheinhardt became acutely aware of his vulnerability. The lake was a lonely place. Moreover, he had just established that Saminsky had very probably been murdered there. Rheinhardt's carriage was parked some distance away. He wondered whether the driver would hear him if he called for help.

Feigning indifference, Rheinhardt rolled onto his back and allowed the buoyancy of the water to support his body. He continued to observe, and did so for some time, but saw nothing unusual. In fact, he was beginning to question whether he had seen anything at all when, quite suddenly, out of the corner of his eye, he saw a man wearing a coat and hat leap from behind one tree to a new hiding place behind another.

Rheinhardt decided that it was unwise to remain passive. He was a sitting target. Rolling over, he immediately began a fast crawl, hoping that an element of surpise might work to his advantage. He made directly for the bank, which at its nearest point was quite steep. Finding some purchase, he heaved himself out of the water. He stood up, crossed the path, and made his way through the trees. When he arrived at the location where he expected to discover a man crouched down in the scrub and brushwood, he found nothing. Nor, when he

looked across the grass towards the road, did he see anyone attempting
to make their escape.

The inspector scratched his head.

After Rheinhardt had dried himself off and changed back into his
clothes he conducted a quick search of the area and then made his way
back to the road. His carriage was waiting for him near one of the
unfinished villas. Rheinhardt looked up at the driver.

'Did you see anyone by those trees?' He pointed towards the
beeches.

The driver shook his head.

'There was a man skulking around up there. He was wearing a
coat and hat — you must have seen him!'

The driver shrugged.

'I didn't see anyone.'

53

THE DIRECTOR LOOKED AMSEL directly in the eye and said, 'I am afraid that your contract will not be renewed next year.'

At first, the singer looked as if she was going to cry. Her haughty expression lost its integrity as her lower lip began to tremble. But then she touched her crucifix and seemed to draw strength and inspiration from its substance. Suddenly she was like a martyr, bravely accepting her destiny as the faggots ignited and the flames licked at the hem of her gown. Arianne Amsel shook her mane of dark curls and raised her chin. 'I am not surprised, Herr Director. You have been undermining me for years now. It was inevitable that you would one day deliver the final blow.'

'That is a very serious allegation, Fräulein Amsel.'

The singer responded by assuming an expression of pure contempt. 'You men are so weak.' Mahler drew back, his quizzical expression intensifying. 'So easily manipulated.'

'What?'

'She turned you all against me.'

Mahler laughed incredulously.

'Are you referring to Ida Rosenkrantz?'

Amsel reached across the director's desk, pointing.

'You were duped, just like the rest of them. Prince Liechtenstein, Intendant Plappart, Mayor Lueger! Yes, even you fell for her act.' Amsel jabbed her rigid finger. 'Even you were seduced by her counterfeit innocence.'

'I can assure you,' said the director with earnest authority, 'Ida Rosenkrantz played no part in my decision to end your contract.'

'That is something I find very hard to believe.'

'Perhaps so, but it is true. There is only one person responsible for your fate.' Mahler produced a knowing look. A subtle movement was sufficient to clarify his meaning. 'You have given me many reasons to terminate your contract — your frequent indispositions, your tantrums and your tiresome objections to being cast in perfectly good roles. All these I have overlooked. But there is one thing that I could not, and cannot, overlook — your stubborn refusal to accept my prohibition of the claque.'

'You are mistaken, Herr Director. I have never required services of that kind. I can hardly be blamed if my supporters are moved by the beauty of the human voice and choose to show their gratitude for artistry with applause.'

Mahler sighed.

'I might have been persuaded otherwise last year, but this . . .' Mahler's hand revolved in the air as he searched for the right word, '. . . *nuisance* has become particularly conspicuous of late.'

Amsel motioned as if to speak but then suddenly changed her mind. She shook her head and her curls bounced before settling. This gesture, which usually betokened pride and vainglory, was now devoid of confidence. It had been reduced to a nervous tic, little more than an involuntary spasm.

'I have employed some professional gentlemen of my own,' Mahler continued. 'Private detectives.' He allowed Amsel a moment in which to register the implications of this admission: 'The likes of Herr Vranitzky have no place in the opera house of the new century.'

The look of defeat on Amsel's face was unmistakable. She rose from her chair and walked to the door. Mahler stood up and bowed. The gesture was entirely redundant but it was unthinkable for him to remain seated. It was important to observe the customary courtesies. Amsel turned. Her lips were pressed tightly together and her eyes glinted with moisture.

'I am sorry,' said the director. 'But the score is sacred, and the music must come before everything.'

'You'll never win, you know. '

'I beg your pardon?'

'The claque. You'll never get rid of them.'

'Perhaps not. But I intend to have a very good try.'

'A word of advice, Herr Director?'

'Oh?'

'You are making yourself very unpopular. You are making your-self enemies in high places.'

The director smiled.

'I know.'

54

Rᴇɪɴʜᴀʀᴅᴛ ʟᴏᴏᴋᴇᴅ ᴅᴏᴡɴ ᴛʜᴇ hallway and saw light spilling from his youngest daughter's bedroom. He poked his head round the door and saw Mitzi, sitting in a nest of pillows, studying the contents of a book.

'You should be asleep.' Mitzi made an appeal for clemency with her large dark eyes, and Rheinhardt was immediately disarmed. A permanent half-smile, inherited from her mother, softened the child's expression and provoked a sympathetic flowering of good humour that expanded in the vicinity of her father's heart. 'What are you reading?'

'*Strange Tales from Transylvania.*'

Rheinhardt sat on the edge of the bed and Mitzi handed him the book. The cloth cover was faded and the pages were brittle with age. Rheinhardt flicked through the volume, registering titles: 'The Jealous Vampire', 'The Six-fingered Hand', 'The Wicked Queen'. Each story was illustrated with a surprisingly good mezzotint.

'Where did you get this?'

'From one of the market stalls in Leopoldstadt.'

'Are the stories frightening?'

'Not really.'

Only a year earlier this volume would have given Mitzi nightmares.

Rheinhardt felt a pang of regret. He was keenly aware of Mitzi's childhood slipping away.

The book fell open at a story titled 'The Gypsy Fiddlers'.

Although the responsible course of action at that moment would have been to tuck Mitzi up and put out the light, Rheinhardt could not deny her the pleasure of a bedtime story.

'Once upon a time, there lived a boyar—'

'A what?' asked Mitzi.

'A boyar,' Rheinhardt repeated. 'A landowner.'

Mitzi nodded, wriggled out from beneath the eiderdown and sat next to her father. Rheinhardt placed his arm around her shoulders and continued.

'Now, this boyar was old and mean. He was a miser and didn't want anyone to have his money. He was so mean that even the possibility of others enjoying his money after his death made him unhappy. He resolved that this should never happen. So he sold most of his land for gold and collected all of his wealth in wooden chests. He then went off to find some gypsies who he had learned were encamped nearby. When he arrived, the gypsies were in the middle of a celebration. A great feast had been laid out and they were dancing to a tune played by five fiddlers. The merrymakers invited the boyar to join them, but he refused. He asked them if they would transport some chests for him and promised to pay them well. The job didn't sound very difficult and the gypsies agreed.'

Rheinhardt buried his face in his daughter's thick hair and planted a kiss among her curls. The love that he felt for her never ceased to surprise him. There was something breathtaking about its sheer excess. A small elbow found his ribs, reminding him to continue.

'The gypsies went back with the boyar to his castle and the boyar ordered his servants to bring ten wooden chests up from the cellar. "Inside these chests," said the boyar, "are magic books. They are evil and can do much harm. I don't want them here any more. Load them onto your wagons and we'll hide them in a safe place." The gypsies followed the boyar to a cave in a deep wooded ravine, and there the boyar ordered them to place the chests inside. They then built a brick wall to seal the entrance and disguised it with dirt and bushes. The boyar made the gypsies swear that they would tell nobody about the hiding place, and he rewarded them with a purse full of coins. But dark thoughts were occupying the boyar's mind. When he returned to his castle he commanded twenty of his most loyal servants to steal upon the gypsy camp and kill them. So that was what they did. They killed the men, the women, and the children. They killed the five fiddlers and smashed their violins before trampling the broken instruments into the ground. They burned the wagons, drove the horses into the forest, and took the purse full of coins that the boyar had given the gypsies in payment for their help. When the servants told the boyar what they had done he was well pleased. He opened the purse and gave each of his men a coin. A rumour spread that it was robbers who had killed the gypsies and, in the fullness of time, the terrible massacre was forgotten.'

Rheinhardt felt his daughter nestling in the arc of his protective arm. He squeezed her closer.

'The boyar grew very old, and as the years went by he wanted to be near his money again. His wealth was the only thing he had ever cared for. One summer night, when a full moon was shining brightly in the sky, the boyar travelled to the cave in the ravine, parted the bushes, and pressed his ear against the wall. He sighed with relief. His chests were still safe. But his relief was shortlived. From inside the cave he could hear the sound of fiddlers and singing. The boyar was horrified. "Someone's found my treasure," he cried. The boyar beat his fists against the wall until his hands were cut and bleeding. Suddenly the wall parted, and inside he saw a band of gypsies making merry. They looked familiar. The music was wild and their faces reflected the red flames which leaped up from a campfire. The boyar threw himself between the wooden chests and the gypsies and stood in readiness to defend his possessions. Standing thus, he watched as the wall closed, sealing the entrance of the cave once more — and trapping him inside.'

Rheinhardt paused for dramatic effect.

'What happened to him?' Mitzi asked.

'There are those who say,' Rheinhardt continued, 'that on summer nights, as they have walked through the deep wooded ravine, they have heard the sound of gypsy fiddlers playing a wild dance. Others have searched for the boyar's cave but no one has ever found it. As for the boyar himself? Well, he did not return to his castle and he was never seen again.'

Rheinhardt let his cheek rest on the crown of Mitzi's head. He inhaled the distinctive fragrance that came off her hair, a soapy scent but with a feral undertow, like civet or the soft musk of a kitten's fur.

'Good?'

'Yes.'

'Now it's time for you to get some sleep.' Mitzi disengaged herself from his arm and slid beneath the eiderdown. He stood over her, marvelling at the perfection of her small features and the healthy glow that emanated from her peachlike skin. 'Goodnight, my dear.'

Rheinhardt kissed his daughter's forehead, placed the book on a chest of drawers, lowered the gas jet, and closed the bedroom door gently behind him. He walked down the hallway and entered the sitting room, where his wife Else was making a shopping list and his eldest daughter Therese was doing some schoolwork. Else looked up and caught Rheinhardt's eye. Such was the intimacy between husband and wife that no words were necessary. Her tacit inquiry was answered with a reassuring smile and she continued adding items to her list. Rheinhardt lowered himself into an armchair and began to twirl his moustache.

What are fairy tales?

He was sure that his friend Liebermann would be able to supply him with an erudite answer, in which the unconscious and infantile sexuality would very probably play a significant part; however, as a layman he immediately arrived at what he considered to be a more plausible view. Fairy tales were educational. Set in distant lands and among peoples comfortably removed from everyday life, fairy tales introduced children to the idea of badness existing in the world. They helped prepare children for the harsh reality of human iniquity.

Rheinhardt remembered the witch, Orsola Salak.

Who are you? That is the question: the policeman or the man with three women in his life?

Rheinhardt could have offered Orsola Salak many answers to that question, but all of them, he realised, would be secondary to the one fundamental answer which took precedence over all others. He did his job to make the world a safer, better place for his wife and children. Interposing himself between the badness of the world and his family had become his *raison d'être*.

The uncanny atmosphere of 'The Gypsy Fiddlers' and the intense love he had felt for Mitzi while reading it had affected his state of mind. It was as if he had been opened up, released from the internal straitjacket of rationality. He found himself curiously willing to accept Salak's prophecy.

'What are you? *A policeman? Or a father and husband? The time is approaching, very soon, when you must ask yourself such questions. Be true. Otherwise . . .*'

Salak's implied threat sent a shiver down Rheinhardt's spine. He was committed to the security office, but his commitment ended with the protection of his family's interests. He did not want his wife to become a widow and his daughters to grow up without a father.

If I continue to play the part of the good policeman and continue this inves-
tigation, it might end in the grave for me . . .

The witch had advised him to be true, and that meant putting his
role as a husband and father before his duty as a policeman. In the
Café Central, Liebermann had presented him with a chilling scenario.
The Rosenkrantz case was more complex and more dangerous than
he had even imagined.

Rheinhardt stood up. He crossed to the window and moved the
curtain aside. There was nobody waiting for him on the street below,
no suspicious figure loitering.

'What is it?' asked Else. As usual, she had sensed his unease.

'Nothing,' he replied. He moved to the table and rested his hands
on Else's shoulders. 'I thought I heard rain.'

55

Professor Freud lit a cigar and produced a flotilla of clouds that floated slowly over Liebermann's head. Their conversation had touched upon several weighty subjects — masochistic impulses, psychasthenia, eurotophobia, and the mechanisms of repression — but as the evening progressed the atmosphere had become less collegiate and more convivial. Unusually, Freud had loosened his necktie prior to sharing some reminiscences of his early medical career.

'One day,' said the professor, between puffs, 'I had a friendly message from Chrobak.'

'The renowned gynaecologist?'

'Indeed. He wanted me to take on a patient of his. You see, he'd just accepted a new teaching appointment and didn't have enough time to care for her. I arrived at the patient's house before him and found that she was suffering from attacks of meaningless anxiety and she could only be soothed by the most precise information about where her doctor was at every moment of the day. When Chrobak arrived he took me aside and told me that the patient's anxiety was due to the fact that although she had been married for eighteen years she was still *virgo intacta*. The husband was absolutely impotent. In such cases, he said, there was nothing for a medical man to do but to shield this domestic misfortune with his own reputation and put up with it if people shrugged their shoulders and said of him: *He's no good if he can't cure her after so many years.*

The sole prescription for such a malady, he added, *is familiar enough to us, but we cannot order it. It runs . . .'*

Freud picked up a pen and scribbled something on his prescription pad. He tore off the sheet and handed it to his young disciple.

Liebermann took the slip of paper and read:

R   *Penis normalis*

Dosim

Repetatur!

Liebermann looked up and smiled.

'Chrobak recommended this?'

'Like many of his colleagues, Chrobak was perfectly aware of the link between *eros* and emotional disturbance. A year earlier I had overheard Charcot discussing a similar case.' Freud reproduced the hand movements of the great French neurologist, '*It's always a question of the genitals — always, always, always!* I thought to myself, if he knows that, why does he never say so? In due course my own clinical observations confirmed what had hitherto been merely anecdotal. I was convinced that many mental disturbances — and not just those affecting women — were attributable to problems arising in the bedroom, and subsequently concluded that, without satisfactory release, the accumulation of libido in the nervous system has a tendency to turn into anxiety. At that time, I viewed this transformation as a purely physical process, like wine going bad and becoming vinegar, but I have since, of course, rejected this simplistic view in favour of a more sophisticated etiological theory.'

Freud continued talking, but Liebermann was distracted by a line of thought not unconnected with the professor's reflections. The room seemed to recede as he was drawn inwards and a ghostly image of Amelia Lydgate formed in his cranium. She was stepping towards him, moving closer, her head falling backwards in readiness to receive his kiss. He had been so cautious, indecisive and dilatory. He had supposed that because Amelia had once been assaulted the prospect of intimacy would be unwelcome to her, and even psychologically damaging. But perhaps he was wrong. Perhaps intimacy, real intimacy, could be corrective, healing.

'Listen to this.' Freud's voice impinged upon Liebermann's reverie. The old man was evidently about to tell a joke, although how this had come to pass was a complete mystery to Liebermann on account of his distraction. 'Frau Weinberger,' said Freud, tapping his cigar on the edge of an ashtray, 'accompanied her husband Jacob to the doctor. After the doctor had given Jacob a complete medical examination, he called Frau Weinberger into his office, alone. *I regret to inform you,* said the doctor, *that Jacob has been overworking and his health has suffered. His condition is critical and unless you take the following advice he will surely die. Each morning, wake him gently with a kiss. Be pleasant to him at all times and make sure he is always in a good mood. Cook him only his favourite meals and don't burden him with chores. Never nag or make unnecessary demands. And, most importantly, never deny him his conjugal rights. A satisfactory erotic life is essential for his well-being. If you do as I advise for the next six months, I am confident Jacob will regain his health completely.* On the tram home, Jacob asked his wife: *What did the doctor say?* Frau Weinberger assumed a grave expression and replied: *He said you're going to die.*'

Liebermann laughed, but his laughter died when he noticed that the prescription slip was still in his hand. The words written upon it were as portentous as an ancient prophecy, and had many implications concerning his past and future conduct with Amelia Lydgate.

56

RHEINHARDT AND LIEBERMANN'S MUSIC making was over, but a fragment of Schubert's *Abends unter der Linde* — 'Evenings under the Lime Tree' — had lingered in Liebermann's mind, transparent but curiously persistent.

'Commissioner Brügel was unimpressed by Mathias's supplementary report,' said Rheinhardt. 'He said he thought that the results were inconclusive.'

'I suppose there's an element of truth in that,' said Liebermann. 'A man committing suicide might have kicked up some mud.'

Rheinhardt sipped his brandy and replied, 'I was advised, in no uncertain terms, to leave the Saminsky affair alone.'

'What are you going to do?'

The inspector turned to his friend and said, 'I keep thinking of the Crown Prince.'

'Another *suicide*,' said Liebermann with suggestive emphasis.

'Did you know he was seen at the opera shortly before his demise? The overture had already begun when the curtain was pulled aside and his father joined him in the royal box. A significant occurrence: the emperor rarely patronises the opera. They say the two of them were whispering throughout the performance. The conversation they were having was apparently very serious. Expressions were grave. After the second act the emperor rose abruptly and departed. A week later the troublesome prince was dead.' Rheinhardt emptied his brandy glass and placed it on the table. 'I think, on this occasion, I will obey orders.'

The silence that followed was deep and protracted. Liebermann could still hear the Schubert melody, endlessly repeating. Beneath it he discerned the beat of his own heart. Liebermann offered Rheinhardt a cigar but the inspector refused.

'Another brandy, perhaps?' Rheinhardt ventured.

'Yes, of course,' said Liebermann, obliging.

The inspector took the replenished glass and swirled the contents. 'I have some news that will make you happy,' he said, without turning. 'I have received authorisation to exhume the body of David Freimark.'

57

Low, dark clouds hung over the St Marxer cemetery. Everything seemed colourless, bleached to a vapid greyish monochrome by an obstinate drizzle. Two gravediggers and their assistants were standing in a hole, only the upper halves of their bodies visible. Although spades descended with mechanical regularity, progress was slow. The ground was so wet that it was necessary to shore up the sides of the grave to prevent the walls from falling in. Clots of viscous mud oozed through the vertical timbers, creating an alternating pattern of faecal extrusions.

Rheinhardt and Liebermann had tired of watching this dismal scene, and had walked the short distance to the *Mozartgrab*. Beneath the stretched fabric of their umbrellas they smoked cigars and made some desultory conversation about the composer's genius. The truncated column and the statue of the despairing cherub, his hand pressed pathetically against his brow, had never appeared more poignant. They returned to Freimark's grave, made some encouraging remarks to the men (even though the hole didn't look any deeper) and then walked up and down an adjacent pathway, stopping occasionally to read headstones.

Eventually they heard a cry. Turning, they saw one of the gravediggers waving his spade in the air like the pendulum of a metronome.

'Come,' said Rheinhardt.

They hurried towards the swinging blade, their route necessitating a disrespectful leaping over the final resting places of the dead. When they arrived at their destination they stood on some planks that had been placed at the foot of Freimark's grave and peered down. The distinctive shape of a coffin had been revealed. A section of the lid had rotted through, and Liebermann thought that he could see something white inside. He also fancied he could smell corruption, decay, the release of foul vapours, but he checked his imagination and realised it was only the fetor of waterlogged earth.

The exhumation continued under a pall of silence. In due course the coffin was heaved out of the grave. Liebermann could see, quite clearly now, a fixed, skeletal grin through the aperture.

'The top's rotten,' said the chief gravedigger. 'But the rest is sound. We could carry it to the mortuary van.'

Rheinhardt nodded.

The rain intensified and the gentle background susurration, hitherto ignored, suddenly increased in volume, becoming a continuous thrumming. There was something minatory about the downpour. Liebermann should have felt eager, excited, but the bleakness of the landscape and the miserable weather had lowered his spirits. The grave looked as if it had been violated rather than simply opened. He was filled with terrible doubts about the entire enterprise.

'Well,' said Rheinhardt, demonstrating remarkable perspicacity. 'It's too late to put him back again.'

'There won't be much left of the poor fellow,' said Professor Mathias. 'Putrefaction and maggots: they eat everything.'

Liebermann and Rheinhardt helped the old man take the lid off the coffin. Inside were Freimark's jumbled bones and some shredded remnants of fabric. A considerable amount of soil had accumulated around the skeleton. Where it was deepest, the surface trembled on account of the activity of burrowing insects. One of them, a creature with a ribbed carapace and agitated flagella, was crawling along the ridge of Freimark's hip.

Mathias stood at the head of the coffin and, assuming a solemn expression, began to recite a poem.

"'The warder looks down at the mid-hour of night, on the tombs that lie scatter'd below.'" He raised his hand up, like an actor, and added, "'The moon fills the place with her silvery light, and the churchyard like day seems to glow. When see! First one grave, then another opes wide, and women and men stepping forth are descried, in cerements snow-white and trailing.'" Behind the thick magnifying lenses of his spectacles, Mathias's eyes seemed to be floating outside his body. They fixed on Rheinhardt and the professor issued a challenge. 'Well, Inspector?'

'That was the first stanza of Goethe's *Totentanz*,' Rheinhardt replied.

'Too easy, wasn't it?'

'There's something in the coffin,' said Liebermann.

'Yes, the remains of David Freimark,' Mathias responded with alacrity.

Liebermann ignored the remark and pointed at an object half-buried in the soil. His extended finger directed the gaze of his companions through the baroque curves and arches of Freimark's ribcage. 'Look.'

Mathias craned over the coffin's edge. 'So there is.' He reached under the sternum and pushed the soil aside, uncovering a long wooden box. A tiny rusted key projected from the lock.

The three men exchanged glances. Professor Mathias gave the box to Rheinhardt, who turned it over and examined it from all sides. The surfaces were unmarked. There was no beading or inlay. It looked, to the inspector, like an elongated pencil case.

'Oskar?' said Liebermann, impatient to discover what was inside. 'What are you waiting for?'

Rheinhardt sat down on a stool and placed the box on the bench in front of him. The key resisted the force of his knuckle for a few moments, then suddenly capitulated. Its rotation produced a click that sounded disproportionately loud — amplified by the morgue's commodious acoustics. Rheinhardt raised the lid. Liebermann was aware of a faint breath of air and registered a fragrance, the merest trace of lavender. Inside the box lay a cylinder of paper, speckled with musical notation and tied with a piece of red ribbon. With great care, Rheinhardt removed the roll and slipped off the binding before flattening it out on the bench.

'A song,' said Rheinhardt.

The staves were arranged in groups of three, a vocal part and piano accompaniment. The tempo indication was *Langsam, andächtig.* Slowly, devoutly, Rheinhardt read the title: '*Nearness of the beloved.*'

'Ah yes,' said Professor Mathias. 'I know it well. Once again, Goethe, I believe.'

'Schubert also wrote a setting,' said Rheinhardt.

Without looking at the text, Mathias began to recite, '"I think of you when the sun's shimmer gleams from the Sea: I think of you when the moon's glimmer is mirrored in streams . . ."'

'Yes. That's it.'

'Are you sure it's not a copy of the Schubert song?'

'Quite sure.'

Liebermann pulled up a stool next to Rheinhardt, sat down, and stroked the edge of the paper. All the notes had straight stems and the heads were neatly executed. Beneath the vocal stave Goethe's poetry shadowed a melody which was ostensibly in C minor but swiftly slipped through a series of bold modulations. Rheinhardt turned the sheet over and held its extremities to stop the paper from curling. In the bottom right-hand corner was a date. 1 September 1863.

'Eighteen sixty-three,' said Liebermann. 'The year he died.'

'His last song?' Rheinhardt ventured.

'Possibly,' Liebermann replied.

'I'm very fond of 'Hope,'' said Mathias. 'I wonder if this setting is as affecting. You sing, don't you, Rheinhardt? Would you care to give us a flavour . . .?'

'Not now, Professor.'

'Come now, don't be shy. I'm told that you have a fine singing voice.'

'With respect, Herr Professor, although I also am eager to hear Freimark's swansong, given our purpose right now, I would very much like you to proceed.'

'As you wish,' Mathias grumbled and shuffled back to the coffin. Rheinhardt released the paper and allowed it to curl. He rolled it up tightly, replaced the ribbon, and pushed it back in the box. As the lid fell, Rheinhardt caught Liebermann's eye. The young doctor looked feverish with excitement.

'We'll find a piano later,' said Rheinhardt under his breath.

'You do realise,' said Mathias, 'that the chances of discovering anything significant are vanishingly small.'

'Yes,' said Rheinhardt. 'Even so . . .'

The professor picked up a femur and studied its ballooning terminus and the *Greater trochanter*: 'I'll clean the bones and take a closer look at them in due course; however, if the facts you have presented me with are correct, then much will depend on the condition of Freimark's cranium.' Mathias put the femur back in the coffin and lifted the hollow white skull. He held it in both hands and stared into the eye sockets. 'My poor, dear fellow. That it should come to this.' Mathias sighed and held the skull beneath the electric light which hung over the dissection table. 'See here,' Mathias said. 'A very substantial insult, radiating fractures, located in the right parietal bone and a smaller, centrally placed insult, located in the frontal bone. The right zygomatic arch is also cracked. However, the occipital and temporal bones are intact, as are the maxilla.' He paused and ran his finger over the parietal injury. 'Interesting.'

'What is?' asked Rheinhardt.

'Come closer. What do you see?'

'An indentation, some splintering.'

'And what about this?' Mathias poked his finger into the damaged area.

'What about what?'

'It's a right angle, Oskar,' said Liebermann.

'Straight edges,' said Mathias. 'Most unusual. Now, it's perfectly possible that a man falling off the Schneeberg might land, unhappily, on a rock, the tapered summit of which just happened to be square-shaped; however, most natural structures are irregular or rounded. Ergo: I would suggest that this parietal insult was produced by a mallet or hammer.' The professor turned the skull around. 'The other injuries are unremarkable.'

Rheinhardt had heard Mathias's words and understood their meaning. Nevertheless, he felt an irrational desire for confirmation. 'Freimark was killed with a hammer?'

'Or a mallet. Yes.'

'He was struck down first,' said Rheinhardt, 'and then pushed off the mountain?'

'That is very likely,' said Mathias. 'Congratulations, gentlemen. I must admit that I was rather sceptical about this escapade. I thought that you might be wasting my time. But I was wrong. I do not know how you came to suspect foul play, but your methods have been vindicated. Again, congratulations.'

'Professor Mathias,' said Rheinhardt. 'Why do you think it was that no questions were raised after the original autopsy? Why didn't the pathologist mention an anomalous impression on the skull in his report?'

'Why?' Mathias responded. 'Because he never saw it, most probably. He didn't undertake a thorough examination — and why should
he have? Accidental falls are common enough in lower Austria. The
cause of death is almost always a head injury. In Freimark's case, a
superficial inspection of the scalp would have sufficed to locate the
fatal trauma. There would have been little reason to look further.
Besides, we are talking about a pathologist who practised forty years
ago. If he was anything like the men who taught me, he would have
been eager to finish his work and return to his club.'

Rheinhardt turned to face his friend.

'Well done, Max.'

'I was wrong,' said Liebermann distractedly.

'I beg your pardon?'

'In the second of the *Three Fantasy Pieces* I thought the repeated
octaves represented a bell, tolling.'

'And they don't?'

'No.'

'Then what do they represent?'

'Hammer blows. Brosius had it all planned.'

58

It was past midnight when Rheinhardt finished his paperwork. He opened the drawer of his desk and took out a tin of *Vanillestern* biscuits, baked by his wife. Unfortunately, there were only two left. The tin had been full when he had sat down earlier. Although he could remember consuming biscuits as he wrote his report, he was not conscious of having eaten quite so many. Yet the evidence was irrefutable. He shrugged, and decided that abstinence, at this late stage, would constitute a deplorable act of self-deception. Besides, two more biscuits would not expand his waistline very much further.

Leaning back in his chair, Rheinhardt rested his feet upon the desk and placed a whole *Vanillestern* in his mouth. He savoured the appeasing sweetness and the slow release of flavours. His wife had added some unusual essences that blended harmoniously with the traditional recipe and left a pleasing, zesty aftertaste. The second biscuit was even more satisfying. Rheinhardt thought of his wife with affection, gratitude and a modest frisson of desire before closing his tired eyes. Some thirty minutes later he awoke from a disturbed, chaotic dream in which he had been chased around a lake by a gang of gypsy fiddlers.

Rheinhardt tidied his desk and made a half-hearted attempt at shaking the creases out of his trousers; however, he paid more attention to his moustache, and checked with his fingers to make sure that the points were still upstanding. He left his room and walked down several empty corridors and a staircase. The door that he eventually came to had a sign hanging outside which read 'Records Office'. Rheinhardt fished a key out of his pocket and entered.

The light, when it came on, was not very powerful. Its weak illumination revealed a room full of cabinets and a station which was usually occupied by a clerk. The air smelled frowsty and institutional. Rheinhardt went directly to the cabinets in which cases designated as 'closed' were stored and began to search through the shelves. It did not take him very long to find Professor Saminsky's file.

Sitting at the clerk's station, Rheinhardt opened the folder and began to examine the contents. There were the photographs of Saminsky's body and there were his own preliminary reports and case summary. Beneath a wad of official correspondence held together with an elastic band he found the results of Professor Mathias's first autopsy. The results of the second autopsy had been removed.

59

LIEBERMANN WALKED THROUGH THE streets of Alsergrund, his hands plunged deep in the pockets of his astrakhan coat. He could feel the gift he had bought Amelia Lydgate, wrapped in crepe paper and tied up with a silver bow. Initially he had considered buying her flowers, but such an offering had seemed too ephemeral. He had then considered buying her a piece of jewellery, but on reflection that hadn't seemed appropriate either. It wasn't that she did not like jewellery (she often wore earrings and brooches when they attended concerts together), but rather it was that jewellery did not demonstrate an appreciation of her essential character. She was attracted to meteorites more than to precious stones. He had observed her behaviour in the Natural History Museum. A lump of iron that had travelled between worlds held much more fascination for her than the largest diamond.

After much deliberation, he had decided to buy her a book, *Psychology from an Empirical Standpoint* by Brentano, a rather abstruse work of philosophy concerning the discrimination of mental and physical phenomena. Liebermann closed his fingers around the volume's spine and laughed. To an onlooker, such a gift would seem entirely misjudged: dry, technical and, worst of all, unromantic. But it was a gift that he knew Amelia would like.

She was such a remarkable woman. So unlike any other woman he had ever encountered. He adored her. Every feature of her person: the line that appeared on her forehead when she was deep in thought, the sound of her voice and the shape of her hands. Just thinking about her made him feel ridiculously happy.

He crossed the road and passed through a knot of people who had gathered around a pedlar. They were making a lot of noise, haggling over prices. A Ruthenian, wearing a sheepskin jacket and high boots, was standing close by, considering whether or not to investigate.

Liebermann turned off the main road into a quieter side street. He had been reluctant to admit it to himself, but his joy was definitely laced with feelings of nervousness. Two weeks had passed since they had attended the performance of *Così fan Tutte* at the opera house; two weeks, during which they had maintained a tender correspondence. Until only a few days earlier it had been impossible to arrange another rendezvous because of their respective commitments and their newfound intimacy had presented Liebermann with a fresh logistical problem. Where should they meet? A café was too public, a private dining room too louche, and it still felt improper for Liebermann to invite Amelia to his apartment. The obvious solution was for them to meet, as they had always done, in Amelia's rooms. For as long as Liebermann had been visiting Amelia, Frau Rubenstein's presence downstairs had provided a comforting illusion of propriety, performing, as she did, the functions of a discreet duenna. Now that Frau Rubenstein was abroad, visiting relatives in Berlin, even this disposal had become more complicated.

The situation had been resolved when Amelia issued an invitation for Liebermann to visit her at home, that evening, making no mention of Frau Rubenstein's absence. Her note had provided him with a welcome exemption from responsibility.

As Liebermann drew closer to his destination, he found himself thinking of Klimt's Beethoven Frieze. He had gone to see this extraordinary wall painting the previous year (with Clara — then his fiancée — and Hannah, his younger sister). Among the many complex allegories and symbols, the artist had painted a kissing couple. They were both naked and locked in a passionate embrace. This image, which Liebermann's mind reproduced with eidetic clarity, revived a host of tactile memories: the softness of Amelia's lips, the curve of her hip and the narrowness of her waist. He yearned to kiss her again.

When Liebermann arrived outside Frau Rubenstein's house, he stopped to compose himself. Eagerness had accelerated his step, and he was now a little out of breath. The door looked strangely different, all the details in high relief, as though illuminated by brilliant sunlight.

Liebermann knocked and waited.

Her face, when it appeared, was smiling. She ushered him into the hallway and they stood for a moment, staring awkwardly at each other. Amelia was wearing her reform dress. It hung loosely around her slender body like a kaftan, falling from her shoulders to the floor. The red of the fabric was patterned with circles of gold that glittered when she moved. She had unpinned her hair, creating a cascade of complementary russet and copper waves.

Liebermann extended his hand. She took it — and he pulled her gently towards him. As she moved closer, her head tilted backwards to receive his kiss.

In the Beethoven Frieze the surrendering female figure is barely visible behind the muscular solidity of her paramour. Only her arms appear around his neck, but the rest of her body is economically suggested by a pale, featureless border. The couple are situated in an arch of blazing light, behind which stand ranks of serene yet alluring angels. Around the host, the flowers in the gardens of paradise are blooming . . .

Once again, this remembered image flared up in Liebermann's mind, and it was as though he and Amelia had been magically transported into Klimt's rapturous vision. They had unwittingly assumed the positions of the man and woman and were no longer individuals but universal principles, male and female, as fundamental as night and day, destined, inescapably, to come together. Amelia's frame felt fragile beneath the soft fabric, and Liebermann's arms, as they closed around her, promised strength and protection. He was acutely aware that she was not wearing a corset. There was no artificial barrier between them, no whalebone cage imprisoning her flesh. The sense of her nakedness intensified his desire and his hands swept down her back, mapping each exquisite curve, conveying every minute discovery through thrilled nerves to his excited brain.

When they finally drew apart they were both stunned by the ease with which they had resumed their intimacy. It was as though the intervening two weeks had been a momentary interruption of a single continuous kiss. Liebermann realised, with some embarrassment, that they had still not spoken to each other.

'I've got you a present,' he said, producing the crepe paper parcel.

Amelia took it, smiled, and replied, 'Thank you. I'll open it upstairs. Would you like some tea?'

'No, thank you.'

Their exchange sounded peculiarly stilted in the wake of what had just transpired. On their way up to Amelia's rooms, Liebermann was confident that very little of the evening would be spent discussing the strengths and weaknesses of Brentano's system of philosophy. And he was right.

60

RHEINHARDT CRANED HIS HEAD around the bedroom door. Else was sitting at her dressing table, brushing her hair. Each downward movement of her arm was accompanied by a crackle of static electricity. She sensed him there, watching, and turned.

'I've got to go back to Schottenring,' said Rheinhardt.

'But it's eleven o'clock.'

'Yes, I know.'

'I didn't hear the telephone.'

'Nobody called, my dear.' Else threw him a quizzical look. 'I neglected to prepare a document for the commissioner. It completely slipped my mind. I'd better go.'

'Can't it wait until morning?'

'Sadly not.'

Else shook her head: 'How could you forget such a thing?'

'Senility,' said Rheinhardt. He was about to leave, but his wife's disappointment made him linger. Crossing the floor and approaching her from behind, he leaned forward and wrapped his arms around her shoulders. Their gazes met in the mirror.

'What time do you think you'll be back?'

'Oh, I don't know. Before two, I expect.' Else's lips contracted. Rheinhardt responded with an affectionate squeeze. 'I want you to know something.' He smiled and kissed the crown of her head. 'I love you. I know you've probably suspected that for some time now, but all the same . . . '

He watched Else's eyes narrow in the glass.

'Is something the matter?' she asked.

Rheinhardt sighed. 'It comes to something, my dear, when a man can't tell his wife that he loves her without causing consternation!'

She was not to be fobbed off so easily.

'Oskar?'

He kissed her again and stroked her face.

'Sweet dreams.' He released her from his grip and strode to the door where he allowed himself one last backwards look. The image of Else, sitting at her dressing table, produced a swell of emotion that almost cracked his voice, 'Sweet dreams,' he repeated, and set off down the hallway. He did not dare to look in on Mitzi and Therese. He knew that their angelic slumbering faces would present him with too great a challenge, and that his fragile resolve would falter.

Rheinhardt put on his coat, stepped out of his apartment, hurried down the stairs and let himself out onto the streets of Josefstadt.

It was a clear, bright evening. A cloudless sky glittered with stars and a gibbous moon floated high above the rooftops. Rheinhardt breathed in the chill air and looked up and down the empty road. He could not see the man who had been following him but he knew that he was hiding somewhere in the vicinity. It was a mystery how policemen acquired this sixth sense; however, its existence was indisputable. The stranger had been following Rheinhardt for almost a week, a situation that ordinarily would not have caused Rheinhardt excessive anxiety. But an auxiliary intuition had been persistently warning him to exercise caution, and at the back of his mind Orsola Salak's prophesy refused to be dismissed.

Rheinhardt set off, weaving through cobbled streets until he found himself near the old theatre. He turned into Piaristenstrasse and glanced up at the baroque complexities of the Maria Treu Kirche. Its two spires thrust upwards with impressive vigour. Between them was a gable on which winged figures perched and gesticulated with a commensurate surplus of energy. The exuberance of the architecture contrasted starkly with Rheinhardt's sober mood. He began to walk faster.

When Rheinhardt neared his destination he thanked God for a piece of good luck. A carriage came rattling down the narrow passageway, making enough noise to cover the sound of his footsteps. He came out on a road that terminated in a high wall to the left. It was only possible to go one way. Rheinhardt walked a few metres along the pavement and then slid between two bearded caryatids which stood on either side of a deep porch. Positioning himself behind one of the stone giants, he held his breath and waited. The brisk tread of the stranger could be heard over the fading rattle of the carriage, becoming louder as he turned the sharp corner. It was obvious that the man had been following Rheinhardt very closely — a professional, without doubt.

As soon as the stranger stepped into view Rheinhardt leaped forward and hooked his elbow round the man's neck. He pulled the man backwards into the porch and held him fast. As his prisoner struggled, Rheinhardt felt something heavy collide with his hip.

'Keep still and I'll let you breathe.' The man didn't stop moving so Rheinhardt applied more pressure. 'Keep still, I say.'

Although his captive had a slim physique, he was remarkably strong and limber. Rheinhardt felt his hold loosening and to his horror the man slipped down and out from beneath his armlock. A moment later, Rheinhardt was deflecting punches that came at him with great force and speed. He wasn't fast enough to maintain an adequate guard and he got caught on the chin. Another punch drove into his stomach, winding him badly. With bovine determination Rheinhardt snapped his head forward again and butted his assailant in the face, before pushing him with considerable force against one of the caryatids. The man's hat fell off and rolled across the pavement and into the gutter. Rheinhardt grabbed the man's lapels but, once again, he could not keep hold of him. The villain escaped, stumbling out of the porch before righting himself and turning to confront Rheinhardt. It was a hard face — expressionless — sharp features, cropped hair, and cold reptilian eyes. The man thrust his hand into his coat pocket and his expression flickered with doubt and uncertainty.

'I believe you are looking for this,' said Rheinhardt, producing the man's gun. He pointed it directly at the man's heart. They were both breathing heavily. Somewhere, out on the streets, some people were carousing. A woman was laughing as two men sang *Trinke, Liebchen, trinke schnell* from *Die Fledermaus*. 'Tell your master that the case is closed. His secret is safe with me. I am fully aware that it is no longer in my interests to continue the investigation.' The man's eyes darted from the gun barrel to Rheinhardt's eyes and back again. 'Do you understand?'

The man nodded and edged backwards to the kerb where he bent his knees and scooped up his hat. After replacing it on his head, he showed Rheinhardt that his hands were empty, turned on his heels, and walked off into the night. Rheinhardt leaned back against the building and massaged his jaw. It hurt a great deal, but there was no blood. Suddenly he was overcome by a profound tiredness. He felt drained of energy and would have liked nothing more than to just lie down on the ground and rest. Rheinhardt peered into the darkness. The man really had gone.

'Dear God,' Rheinhardt sighed. 'I'm getting too old for this.'

The voices of the carousers could still be heard, but they were already fading.

61

THE EMPEROR AND THE LORD marshal were seated at the conference-room table. A sudden draught made the candles flicker, and the unsteady light created a general illusion of movement. The bust of Field Marshal Radetzky seemed to leap forward. Franz-Josef was unnerved by the phenomenon. He frowned, drew on his cigar, and fell into a state of meditative contemplation.

They had been discussing the mayor — a subject which reliably lowered the emperor's spirits. Franz-Josef's humiliation at the 1896 Corpus Christi procession still haunted him: the crowd, applauding Lueger and slighting their Habsburg sovereign.

Emperor of Austria, Apostolic King of Hungary, King of Jerusalem, King of Bohemia . . .

Franz-Josef tacitly enumerated his many titles, until he came to *Grand Voyvoce of Serbia*. He felt an acid burn in his chest and the pain made him grip the arm of his chair. Gradually the discomfort subsided and he continued smoking.

Corpus Christi.

This year's procession was even worse.

Back in May he had been fulfilling his obligation to God and the people, walking beside the Cardinal Archbishop, when Count Goluchowski had appeared at his side. It was immediately obvious that the man was distressed. '*Grave news from Serbia, Your Majesty — a group of rebel officers have brutally murderered King Alexander and* the Queen.' Franz-Josef had straightened his back and asked, '*Is there anything we can do?*' He had hoped that Goluchowski would answer in the affirmative, that he would disclose a clever response strategy. Instead, the minister had adopted a regretful expression and replied, weakly, '*Nothing, Your Majesty.*' Even though the sun was shining and Franz-Josef had — up until that point — felt hot in his uniform, a chill seemed to settle around his shoulders. Where would it all end? He had thanked the minister and continued walking.

The emperor exhaled and stared in an unfocused way through the dissipating cigar smoke.

'One must suppose that, once again, the mayor will be re-elected.'

'Sadly, Your Majesty, that is the outcome we must anticipate.' The lord marshal made an apologetic gesture.

'I take it that the delicate matter you have previously referred to has now been resolved?'

Their speech became more elliptical.

'An unforeseen difficulty did arise, Your Majesty, but it was promptly dealt with by my office.'

'I'm glad to hear it.' Franz-Josef stubbed out his cigar and pulled at his mutton-chop whiskers. 'Even so . . .'

The lord marshal detected the emperor's unease.

'Your Majesty?'

'I think, perhaps, we should take measures to ensure that the waters remain untroubled. Loyalty should be rewarded.'

'Indeed, Your Majesty.'

'One wouldn't want . . .' The emperor did not feel it was necessary to be explicit.

'Of course, Your Majesty.'

'Well then,' said the emperor, indicating with a change of intonation that, as far as he was concerned, their business was concluded.

The lord marshal placed some signed documents in his leather brief-case, bowed, and crossed the floor.

'Good evening, Your Majesty.'

The emperor responded with a barely perceptible nod of his head.

As the doors closed Franz-Josef lit another cigar. It was his custom to be in bed by eight or nine, but he was disinclined to retire. He suspected that he was going to have one of his bad dreams again. Flames, breaking glass, the Hofburg stormed by agitators. The emperor looked at the bust of Radetzky.

'Is there anything we can do?' he said aloud.

The silence that followed was enough to bring a tear to the old man's eye.

62

WHEN RHEINHARDT FOUND THE envelope bearing the mayor's seal in his mailbox, his heart faltered. He stood for some time, immobilised by anxiety, supposing that the letter inside must contain a list of the mayor's grievances. A second letter — demanding Rheinhardt's dismissal — was probably awaiting the commissioner's perusal. Bracing himself, Rheinhardt began to read; however, he was surprised to discover that it was not a letter of complaint, filled with allegations of professional incompetence, but a plainly worded invitation written by a municipal secretary. The mayor respectfully requested Detective Inspector Rheinhardt and his colleague, Herr Doctor Liebermann, to attend a private meeting at the town hall two days hence.

Thirty minutes prior to their engagement, Rheinhardt and Liebermann sat in the Café Landtmann, drinking pear brandy and speculating on the mayor's purpose.

'I don't like it,' said Rheinhardt. 'Whatever can he want?'

Liebermann was concerned that Rheinhardt had imbibed more liquor than was strictly necessary to steady his nerves.

'Come on, let's go,' said Liebermann, 'We'll walk around the park a few times before going in. Some fresh air will clear our heads.'

They left the coffee house, crossed the Ringstrasse, and wandered around the green avenues in front of the town hall. In due course Rheinhardt looked up at the clock tower and said, 'We'd better go in.' Ascending the stairs, they stepped beneath the Gothic archway and entered the building. On this occasion they were met by one of Lueger's green-coated *courtiers* who escorted them straight to the antechamber outside the mayor's apartment. Soon after they were seated the double doors opened and Pumera appeared, gesturing for them to come forward.

The mayor was sitting behind his desk and stood as they entered.

'Good morning, gentlemen.'

Rheinhardt and Liebermann crossed the wide expanse of the Persian rug, bowed, and sat down in the two chairs that had been placed in readiness for their arrival.

Lueger offered them cigarettes, which they refused, before lighting one for himself.

'Well, gentlemen,' he said, smiling. 'Congratulations. You got your man. Professor Saminsky, eh? And who would have thought it? I never encountered the fellow but I am given to understand that he was well thought of by his peers and a favourite of the late empress. I've been following the revelations in the *Wiener Zeitung*. Have you read the latest? No?' The mayor picked up a newspaper and pointed at a column. 'Not only was he a murderer but an embezzler too. It's all coming out now. Apparently, he pocketed thousands from palace charities. Extraordinary, that he got away with it for so long. No wonder he took his own life. I suppose he knew that his days were numbered.' The mayor dropped the paper and drew on his cigarette. 'Gentlemen: would you care for a cognac?'

'No, thank you,' said Rheinhardt.

'Please. You are my guests and I will be offended if you do not accept my hospitality. Pumera? Some cognacs, please.'

The bodyguard moved silently to a cabinet and began to prepare a tray.

'Mayor Lueger,' said Rheinhardt, 'why did you wish to see us today?'

The mayor appeared astonished by Rheinhardt's question. 'To congratulate you on solving the Rosenkrantz murder and to thank you for exercising discretion. Things could have turned out very badly for me, had certain sections of the press,' he smiled benignly at Liebermann, 'been informed of my . . .' he hesitated before adding, '. . . involvement.' The *certain sections of the press* to whom he referred were Jewish journalists. Showing no sign of embarrassment, the mayor continued: 'Yes, a scandal could have been very damaging just before an election; however, as things stand, my campaign is proceeding well and I have every reason to expect a favourable outcome.'

Rheinhardt bowed his head. 'Commissioner Brügel will be delighted to hear that you are satisfied with our conduct.'

'And so he should be. One more thing, Inspector.' The mayor puffed at his cigarette. 'My letters, the ones that I wrote to poor Ida: given that the investigation is now over, I assume that they can now be returned to me?'

'Only a few scraps survived.'

'Still, I would be grateful for their return.'

'I am sure that the commissioner will not object to such a request.'

'Good man.'

Pumera appeared by the desk and the brandies were distributed. Lueger raised his glass. 'Prost! Gentlemen. Your good health!'

Rheinhardt's glass came up, but Liebermann's remained resolutely still. 'I am most surprised . . .' he said softly.

'What?' The mayor frowned.

Rheinhardt threw a quizzical glance at his friend.

'Surprised,' Liebermann repeated, 'that you are happy to drink *my* health.'

Rheinhardt sensed Pumera bristling. The mayor smiled and said: 'Herr Doctor, in these rooms, I decide who is a Jew. Your good health!'

With evident reluctance, Liebermann raised his glass.

'Prost,' said Rheinhardt, starting to breathe again.

63

Liebermann fancied that he could still detect a hint of lavender coming off the manuscript paper. He took a deep breath, which had the effect of intensifying the fragrance, and leaned into a resonant chord. After depressing the sustaining pedal, he then played a glittering figure in which triplets in the right hand were set against pairs of quavers in the left.

Rheinhardt began to sing:

> *Ich denke dein, wenn mir der Sonne Schimmer*
> *Vom Meere strahlt . . .*

> I think of you when the sun's shimmer
> Gleams from the sea;
> I think of you when the moon's glimmer
> Is mirrored in streams.

> I see you when dust rises
> On the distant road;
> At dead of night, when the traveller
> Trembles on the narrow footbridge . . .

The music modulated continuously, never finding repose, its unpredictable progressions creating a sense of nervous agitation. After an exquisite third verse the harmonies dissolved into silence, leaving the vocal line to proceed without accompaniment.

> I am with you; however far away you are,
> You are near me!

The chord with which the song began was repeated and the glittering figure hovered, once again, above the final couplet.

> The sun sets, soon the stars will shine on me.
> O that you were here.

Liebermann's hands travelled down the keyboard until all sense of tonality was lost in the soft thunder of the piano's lowest octave.

It was the fifth time they had performed 'Nearness of the Beloved.'

'Wonderful,' said Rheinhardt. 'The more we play it, the better it gets. Freimark surpassed himself. Yes, I would go as far as to say that 'Nearness of the Beloved' is better than 'Hope'. It is more daring and atmospheric. Those discords are so characteristic of his art, and how easily they find the heart.' He rested the palm of his hand on his chest. 'I wonder who decided that Freimark's last great accomplishment should go with him to the grave? Imagine, consigning a song of this merit to oblivion. No music lover could have performed such a heinous act without a troubled conscience. One can only suppose that Freimark specified that it should be done prior to his death, and that someone close to him felt compelled to make good a promise.'

Liebermann indicated the date: 'The first of September 1863.'

'The year he died. What of it?'

'Freimark was murdered on the twenty-eighth of August.'

Rheinhardt bit his lower lip. 'Perhaps he had some reason for dating the work prospectively.'

'Such as?'

'Oh, I don't know. He might have originally intended to present the work as a gift . . . a birthday present.'

'Dates on manuscripts almost always show when a work was completed.'

'But Freimark was dead on the first of September.'

'Indeed.'

Rheinhardt puffed out his cheeks, scratched his head, and said: 'No. This song was undoubtedly written by Freimark. His style is unmistakable. What are you suggesting, that Brosius wrote "Nearness of the Beloved"?'

'Yes,' said Liebermann. The young doctor paused before adding: 'Not Johann Christian Brosius, of course, but his wife, Angelika Brosius.'

'Max, that's ridiculous — she wasn't a composer!'

'Wasn't she?'

'You have never, until this moment, given me any reason to think that she was anything other than a muse.' Rheinhardt stroked the manuscript with his finger. 'Besides, even if Angelika Brosius was a very competent musician, she still couldn't have written "Nearness of the Beloved". It isn't just a clever piece of mimicry — a pastiche of Freimark's "Hope". "Nearness of the Beloved" employs the musical language of "Hope", but then takes it so much further. One can see development, novel use of signature discords, progress! Given that the authorship of "Hope" has never been called into question, I cannot see how you can possibly make such an assertion.'

Liebermann sighed.

'Look at the words of "Nearness of the Beloved". So full of yearning: *O that you were here . . .* This song is a love letter, written by Angelika Brosius to David Freimark while she was in the throes of grief. The recently departed are laid out as part of Jewish ritual. Angelika Brosius wrote "Nearness of the Beloved" and then concealed it in his coffin. It is a private communication, which she meant for Freimark, and Freimark alone.' Liebermann reached out and played a part of the vocal line. 'Yesterday I visited the conservatory archive. Nothing of Freimark's work survives but I was able to inspect several of Brosius's original scores. Angelika sometimes made fair copies of her husband's compositions. The handwriting is identical.'

Rheinhardt drummed his fingers on the side of the Bösendorfer.

'She might have extended the same service to Freimark.'

Liebermann shook his head. 'Brosius's early work is completely inconsequential; however, in his middle years — after marrying Angelika — we see a marked qualitative improvement. The music he composed at this time was not unlike Freimark's "Hope". There are, I have been informed, certain similarities.'

'You think Angelika was responsible for Brosius's music as well?'

'I don't think she sat at the piano, writing fantasies which she then handed to Brosius for him to endorse as his own. I suspect the process was rather more subtle. She probably discussed his music and expressed opinions, encouraging some features while discouraging others — perhaps she made explicit suggestions — she may have even intro- duced a few accidentals while copying. And when she fell in love with Freimark, she did the same for him. Angelika Brosius was a very practical muse; however, I am convinced that she could not work her magic unless she was in love. That is why, after she met Freimark, the quality of Brosius's music deteriorated. His *Rustic Symphony* is execrable, apparently.'

'If she was such a great talent, why did she not write more?'

'Perhaps she did.'

'Then where are her scores?'

'Hidden, destroyed? Or perhaps "Nearness of the Beloved" is her single conventionally executed composition. Not all artists are prolific.

It is possible that she was one of those who only write when moved to do so by deep feelings, and that after Freimark's death she was never deeply affected again.'

'Individuals endowed with such talent usually seek public recognition.'

'Men do, certainly, but I'm not so sure about women. Can it really be the case that only men have been able to compose great music through the ages? Yet I would wager that, excepting Clara Schumann, you cannot name a single female composer. Women are not as motivated as men to pursue standing in the world. It is even possible that Angelika Brosius was unaware of the magnitude of her gift.'

Rheinhardt twisted one of the horns of his moustache and made a grumbling noise. Eventually the grumbling became inflected and comprehensible. 'Very interesting: very interesting, indeed. When you take "Nearness of the Beloved" to the conservatory, will you inform them of this theory of yours?'

'Yes, but I don't suppose they'll take any notice. The professors will register the stylistic similarities between "Hope" and "Nearness of the Beloved" and attribute the work to Freimark. Like you, they will seek an alternative and more conservative explanation for the post-mortem date. And when the song is published, the name of Freimark will appear next to the title in all the catalogues.' Liebermann allowed his hands to find the dissolving chords after the third verse. 'I don't know . . .'

'What?'

'She didn't want anyone to hear it. I wonder . . . shouldn't her wishes be respected?'

Rheinhardt's expression had become minatory: 'I hope you're not thinking of—'

'No,' said Liebermann curtly. 'No. You're quite right. "Nearness of the Beloved" is a wonderful song, whoever wrote it, and wonderful songs must be heard.' Liebermann rolled up the manuscript paper and placed it in its box. 'I'll take it to the conservatory tomorrow.'

The two men retired to the smoking room and sat in their customary places. Liebermann poured the brandy and cigars were lit. They did not speak for several minutes, choosing instead to gaze into the fire. Liebermann found that the melody of "Nearness of the Beloved" was still sounding in his mind. Its deeply expressive harmonies were suggestive of the eternal. A chivalrous urge to respect Angelika's wishes still lingered. The song was as private as pillow talk, as confidential as an intimate letter. Yet he knew that in the morning he would rise and deliver the manuscript to the conservatory archive. The grave was no place for great art.

In due course, Rheinhardt stirred and said, 'Commisioner Brügel called me into his office today.'

The sinuous melody began to fade and Liebermann emerged from his reverie.

'Did he want to know what the mayor had to say?'

'Yes, but that wasn't his principal concern.' Rheinhardt exhaled a cloud of smoke. 'We had a rather strange conversation, somewhat allusive and punctuated by artful *looks*, the kind that superiors are inclined to employ when they say one thing but *mean* another. It took me a while to grasp the purpose of the interview. The commissioner said that he was very pleased with how the Rosenkrantz investigation had been prosecuted and, if I continued to heed his good counsel, I might reasonably expect a promotion next year.' The tone of Rheinhardt's voice was matter-of-fact. 'He then disclosed that he is shortly to be honoured by the palace.'

'What are they going to give him?'

'The Order of the Iron Crown, third class. Brügel then proceeded to deliver a rather long speech, which I couldn't help thinking was a kind of rehearsal: privilege of public service, the friendship of colleagues, allegiance to the crown, and so on. When he reached the end of this interminable oration he declared that, if I continued to demonstrate valued qualities such as good judgement and discretion, eventually I too might receive some official recognition for loyal service.'

Liebermann played a five-finger exercise on his chair arm. When the drumming ceased, he said: 'I would offer you my congratulations, if I thought this news gave you a true sense of achievement.'

'How could it?' said Rheinhardt.

They looked at each other with grim expressions.

'Well,' said Liebermann, 'I was right.'

'In the end,' said Rheinhardt. 'Yes.' Liebermann frowned but Rheinhardt took no notice. 'Although it is a pity that we were denied bringing the perpetrators of such heinous crimes to justice.'

'Indeed,' Liebermann replied. 'But life is not like a piece of music, structured, logical, and concluded with the precise finality of a perfect cadence. No, life is more like the unconscious — murky, strange and unpredictable.' The young doctor stood and walked to the fireplace. He took a pair of wire-rimmed spectacles from his top pocket, hooked the arms behind his ears, and adopted a professorial attitude. 'When Ida Rosenkrantz's association with the mayor ended, her dreams of escaping the opera house and becoming the first lady of Vienna were shattered. She developed a hysterical throat condition, a telling symptom arising as it did in an unhappy singer, and transferred her libido — a libido that became attached all too easily to father figures — from Lueger to her psychiatrist, Saminsky. When she became pregnant with Saminsky's unborn child, she accepted his *paternal* authority and obediently went to see an angel maker. Afterwards, when Saminsky declared, with considerable regret, that he had come to realise that it was not in their interests (for her as a patient and for him as a married man) to continue seeing each other as lovers, she acquiesced once again. Time passed. The infection she contracted due to the termination flared up and she was confined to her bed. Isolated, with only her maid for company, she became resentful and angry. Although she recovered from her physical problems, her psychological state was not good: she brooded on her sorry personal circumstances, becoming depressed and eventually desperate. On Monday the seventh of September she telephoned Lueger and demanded that he come to her villa in Hietzing. For reasons which are still unknown to us, he agreed. He did not try to conceal himself when he was seen by your witness Geisler, because the mayor was not contemplating murder.'

Liebermann flicked some ash into the fire. 'Obviously, when the mayor entered Rosenkrantz's villa there were emotional scenes. But he used his famous powers of persuasion to calm her. Soon he was satisfied that the situation was under control and felt confident enough to leave. But Rosenkrantz was still deeply distressed. She felt alone, abandoned. She burned the mayor's love letters and telephoned Saminsky. When Saminsky arrived she was probably beside herself. She told him that the mayor had recently departed and complained about her lot: she was sick of being the pretty plaything of older men. All she had ever wanted was their love, but all she had ever received were empty promises and shabby treatment. Her condition worried Saminsky. She was out of control. The last thing he wanted was a scandal.'

A burning piece of wood cracked and a shower of sparks illuminated the hearth. 'Saminsky was doubly motivated,' Liebermann continued. 'He realised that in one fell swoop he might rid himself of Rosenkrantz and perform a great service to the crown. If the mayor was implicated as a suspect in a murder investigation, just before an election, it might bring about his downfall. The man responsible for accomplishing such a coup could expect the shadowy powers that operate in the Hofburg to show their gratitude with a generous dispersal of honours and rewards: a carriage with a coat of arms on the door, a Schloss overlooking the Danube.' Liebermann threw his cigar stub into the flames. 'Saminsky must have delivered a performance the likes of which we rarely see outside the court theatre. Yes, he had been weak. Yes, he had been a fool, an insensitive coward, and if only *dearest* Ida could find it in her heart to forgive him he would make amends. He would leave his wife — whom he had never really loved — and take Rosenkrantz away to a better place. The vulnerable singer succumbed to his kisses and caresses, his gentle ministrations, and finally complied when he suggested that she should take a little laudanum to calm her nerves and help her sleep. Only minutes later he encouraged her to take a few drops more . . . and then a few drops more.'

Liebermann rested his elbow on the mantelpiece and continued: 'When Rosenkrantz lost consciousness, Saminsky set her down on the floor and sat on her chest. Her lungs could not expand and she quickly suffocated. Saminsky then bounced on her chest until he heard one of her ribs snap. I am not sure whether he placed Rosenkrantz's body in the middle of the rug to arouse suspicion, or whether that was merely the result of his obsessiveness. He was fastidious in dress and was a collector. Individuals of this personality type have a distinct tendency to line up objects, often automatically and without thought. Whatever the case, he informed the lord marshal's office of his actions and was probably praised for showing initiative. Rewards would follow.

'When we first interviewed Saminsky, he misdirected us concerning his whereabouts on the night of the murder — claiming to have recently returned from Salzburg — and led us to believe that the mayor was responsible for Rosenkrantz's pregnancy. He must have felt quite pleased with himself; however, when we reappeared, challenging the accuracy of his testimony and accusing him of unprofessional conduct, the experience understandably unnerved him. Saminsky was an opportunist, not a hardened criminal. He panicked and immediately went to the lord marshal for assistance. Unfortunately, Saminsky's discomposure did not impress the lord marshal, who began to doubt whether the psychiatrist had the stomach to carry through the undertaking he had embarked upon. What would happen, he wondered, if Saminsky went to pieces during questioning? The consequences, so soon after the Crown Prince's demise at Mayerling, were unthinkable. The lord marshal's agents were dispatched, and the following day Saminsky was no longer a problem. The same, however, could not be said of Detective Inspector Oskar Rheinhardt. Even though your superior gave you a clear indication that the Saminsky case was best left alone — you continued to investigate. You were put under surveillance, and the resulting intelligence was not good. Had you not dealt with the lord marshal's agent so deftly, I very much doubt you would be sitting here now, drinking brandy and enjoying my excellent cigars.'

Liebermann crossed the floor and returned to his seat.

'The commissioner was, of course, quick to endorse the most expedient account of Saminsky's death.' Liebermann's voice became laboured: 'Rosenkrantz had insisted that Saminsky leave his wife. She had started to issue threats. To avoid a scandal Saminsky killed her, taking care to make it look as if she had committed suicide. Unfortunately, he accidentally broke one of her ribs, thus drawing attention to his crime. When Saminsky realised we were catching up with him, he took his own life.' Liebermann returned to his professorial mode of address. 'Commissioner Brügel made sure that Saminsky's file was in order, removing and presumably destroying the supplementary autopsy report by Professor Mathais. Within a few weeks, the palace had discovered *evidence*,' Liebermann raised his eyebrows, 'that Saminsky was an embezzler, giving the public reason to contemplate the effect that the prospect of imminent exposure might have had on a man who already had a murder on his conscience. The commissioner was rewarded for his cooperation with the Order of the Iron Cross, and you, my friend, have been offered promotion and future honours as a reward for demonstrating *good judgement and discretion.*'

Rheinhardt poured himself a brandy, threw his head back, and drank it down like a shot of schnapps.

'God in heaven,' he sighed. 'What will become of us!'

Liebermann produced a sardonic smile. 'I dare say we'll carry on. There will be the usual festivities at Christmas, dances, and then more balls in the new year. We will give each other bunches of violets next March, and then there will be concerts and operas and the Corpus Christi Day procession.'

'But it can't go on for ever,' said Rheinhardt. 'Not with so much corruption. *Protektion* is one thing, but this . . .'

'I have always been sanguine about the future,' said Liebermann. 'But I am not so sure now.'

'The mayor, the palace!' Rheinhardt shook his head violently. 'And if that wasn't enough, now there's Serbia to worry about.'

'Serbia?'

'The assassinations! My colleague Hohenwart thinks there will be a war.'

'Oh, that's impossible. Serbia isn't important enough. A few skirmishes, perhaps.'

Rheinhardt shrugged his shoulders. 'One might start over again, I suppose, but I can't think where. Vienna is our home.'

Liebermann sipped his brandy and his expression lightened.

'How about London?'

'London? Why London?'

'There's a place to the north of the city called Highgate, which

I understand is a little like Grinzing. The pastries, music and weather could be better, but still, the people are of a similar type. I always think of the English as polite Germans. Yes, London wouldn't be *so* bad.'

64

THE TOWN HALL ROSE up above the Christmas market in all its Gothic splendour and its soaring spires, patinated with early evening frost, sparkled beneath a crescent moon. Liebermann pulled Amelia closer to him, and when she turned her head he kissed her quickly on the lips. She was wearing a long green coat, embroidered with elevated black curlicues, and a hat, artfully worn so as to display waves of luxurious red hair.

They laughed at their own audacity.

There had been a Christmas market held in Vienna for over six hundred years, and the Viennese were old hands at transforming seasonal commerce into a fine art. The little park in front of the town hall was filled with people, the crowd constantly fed by an endless stream of humanity pouring in off the Ringstrasse. Above the stalls and traders, paper lanterns swung beneath the branches of tall trees, and the air was suffused with fragrances: roasted chestnuts, mulled wine, exotic spices, frankincense, chocolate, Arabian teas, sugared fruit, almonds, pumpernickel, scented soaps, cologne, mustard, and scorched sausages. The olfactory mêlée was overwhelming.

The couple passed by a vendor selling spirits from a miniature alpine cabin, its interior crammed with multicoloured bottles. Liebermann's gaze travelled across the alcoholic spectrum, slowing for a moment as it passed over the eldritch glow of the absinthes.

In a tiny enclosure, small children were riding ponies around a circular track.

Squeezing through the throng, they came upon a group of musicians playing *Schrammelmusik*. The small band, consisting of a zither player, accordionist and two violins, were giving a lively account of a popular drinking song. A group of noisy revellers had gathered around the musicians and were attempting the yodelling chorus, which required a dropped beat to be supplied by the collision of steins — a requirement that was causing much spillage and merriment.

'Come,' said Liebermann. 'Let's move on.'

Eventually they arrived at the arched entrance of the town hall, where an enormous Christmas tree had been erected. It was bedecked with ribbons and candles and exuded a fresh resiny smell. A small choir of six gentlemen — wrapped up in woollen scarves, red-cheeked, and with bright, fervid eyes — were standing next to the tree, fully exploiting a portamento which climbed to the very highest note of *Stille Nacht*.

'Liebermann?'

The young doctor turned and almost reeled back when he discovered who had spoken his name.

'Director Mahler.'

'My dear fellow,' said the director, smiling warmly and shaking Liebermann's hand. 'How are you?'

'Very well, thank you.'

Before Liebermann could reciprocate, the director was gesturing at the woman standing next to him. 'Allow me to introduce my wife.'

Alma Mahler was reputed to be one of the most beautiful women in Vienna. Liebermann was rather surpised by her appearance. Although very pretty, she was not as striking as he had supposed. She had rather soft rounded features, and a winning if rather cautious smile. Groomed eyebrows traced delicate arcs above her large inquiring eyes, and, like Amelia, she too wore her hat at a precipitous angle to show off her hair to best advantage.

Alma raised her arm, allowing her gloved hand to fall at an angle from the wrist.

Liebermann bowed and brushed the fawn leather with his lips.

'Frau Director.' Then urging his companion to come forward, he said: 'My fiancée, Miss Amelia Lydgate.'

Amelia inclined her head.

'You are English?' asked the director.

'Yes.'

'And where are you from, exactly?'

'London.'

'Ah, London,' said the director. 'I travelled there once to conduct a German season at Covent Garden. I learned a little of your language — not a great deal, I'm afraid — and gave your countrymen a second opportunity to hear Wagner's *Der Ring des Nibelungen.*'

'Was it well received?' asked Amelia.

'Yes, the audiences were very enthusiastic. I left exhausted, but also convinced of a deep affinity between the English and German peoples.' The director addressed his wife. 'This is Herr Doctor Liebermann, my dear. Do you remember me mentioning him back in the autumn? The fellow who managed to get Schmedes back on stage when there was that awful business going on with the Hermann-Bündler: the one who helped to weed out Treffen.'

Alma's face brightened with recognition.

'Ah yes, the psychiatrist, of course. You are a man possessed of remarkable talents, Herr Doctor.'

Liebermann was embarrassed by the compliment and made a humorous self-deprecatory remark.

'So,' said the director. 'Where are you going?'

'Nowhere in particular,' Liebermann replied. 'We just came to see the market.'

'Well, why don't you join us? We were on our way to meet some friends at Café Landtmann.'

'Yes, *do* join us,' said the director's wife, stepping forward and clutching Liebermann's arm.

Liebermann looked to Amelia to see what she thought. She was nodding her head.

Extricating himself from Alma's eager grip, he reached out and took Amelia's hand.

'Thank you, Herr Director. We would be delighted to join you.'

The two couples made their way down the wide boulevard that led to the Ringstrasse. As was often the case, Liebermann thought that he might be dreaming. He was going to the Café Landtmann, with Amelia Lydgate on his arm, in the company of Director Mahler and his wife.

Sometimes the city in which he lived seemed to be a place of boundless possibilities.

He glanced back at the town hall, and wondered if the newly re-elected demagogue was ensconced in the clock tower, gazing down from behind one of those many black windows on his domain.

There might be difficult times ahead . . .

But he wasn't prepared to ruin the evening thinking about them now.

Acknowledgements and Sources

I WOULD LIKE TO thank: Kate Elton, Clare Alexander, Steve Matthews and Nicola Fox for their valuable comments on the first and subsequent drafts of *Death and the Maiden*, Nick Austin for a thorough copy-edit, Simon Dalgleish for identifying German errors in the text, Luitgard Hammerer for translating my research questions into German and making contact with various institutions in Vienna, Harald Seyrl at the criminal museum in Vienna for answering questions on the mayor's immunity to prosecution and early twentieth-century abortion law, and Dr Yves Steppler, consultant pathologist, for advice on compressive asphyxia.

The opening scene in which Karl Lueger presents officers of the anti-Semitic German-Austrian Writers' Association to the emperor is based on an image which can be found in the Austrian National Library Photograph collection. Descriptions of Karl Lueger — including small details like his offset eye — can be found in *Karl Lueger: Mayor of Fin de Siècle Vienna* by Richard S. Geehr. 'I decide who is a Jew' is a direct and now quite infamous quote. Descriptions of Franz-Josef were informed by passages found in *The Emperor and the Actress* by Joan Haslip. The emperor's routine and living quarters are detailed in the Hofburg Palace Guidebook, *Imperial Apartments, Sisi Museum, and Imperial Silver Collection*, by Ingrid Haslinger and Katrin Unterreiner. There is a long tradition, going all the way back to Bach, of composers

representing themselves in their own music with themes constructed
from the letters of their names. Later composers have dramatised their
personal relationships using the same principle. The *Lyric Suite* by the
Second Viennese School composer Alban Berg is a notable example.
In 1976 George Perle discovered that Berg had worked his own initials,
and those of a woman with whom he was having an affair, into the
central motif. My descriptions of Gustav Mahler are based on many
sources: however, the first and second volumes of Henry-Louis de la
Grange's four-volume biography, *Gustav Mahler*, were invaluable. The
tenor Erik Schmedes refused to sing at the premiere of *Rienzi* because
of threats made by the fans of Hermann Winkelmann — although
in January 1901, not 1903. The red room at the court opera is
mentioned by de la Grange and was used for auditions. My red room,
however, is entirely imagined. An anonymous article criticising Mahler
was published in the *Deutsche Zeitung* in 1898, early in his career at
the court opera. I have quoted directly from the original, making no
changes. Critical letters were also circulated at the time, one of
which Mahler obtained. In order to establish the identity of the
author, Mahler persuaded the opera house to pay a graphologist,
Professor Skallipitzky, to analyse the handwriting. He also paid a
second unknown expert out of his own pocket. Mahler's response to
Plappart's request for more judicious expenditure of opera house funds
is a direct quotation. The incident of the timpanist leaving the opera
house early to catch the last train took place in 1897. Mahler's views
on Brahms as a composer of variations are authentic. *Marillenknödel*
(apricot dumplings) was indeed Mahler's favourite dessert. I have been
unable to trace his sister Justi's much-loved recipe but an acceptable
substitute can be found on page 101 of *Viennese Cuisine: Cook and Enjoy*
by Martina Hohenlohe (Pichler Verlag). Mahler's strong views on
Marillenknödel were originally expressed to Karpath. Although Mahler
hired private detectives in an effort to rid the court opera of the

claque, he was never entirely successful in achieving this aim. They were still there when he left the court opera in 1907. The content of Frau Eberhardt's speech on marriage and female sexuality was based on information found in *Schnitzler's Century* by Peter Gay. The statistics on female orgasm are from a study conducted by Dr Clelia Duel Mosher in the USA in 1892. The Kleines Café in Franziskanerplatz (which also appears in *Mortal Mischief*) did not exist in 1903. In fact, it didn't appear until the 1970s — but its location and ambience suited the purpose of my plot. Translation of *Death and the Maiden* was taken from Richard Stokes's *The Book of Lieder*; the *Così fan Tutte* excerpt was translated by Jonathan Burton; *An die Musik* by William Mann, Goethe's *Totentanz* by Edgar Alfred Bowring, and Goethe's *Nearness of the Beloved* was taken from a booklet accompanying a CD of Schubert songs and attributed to *Deutsche Grammophon GmbH, Hamburg*. The story of how Freud obtained his professorship is taken from Ernest Jones's biography of Freud. The account of Oedipal processes is a bowdlerisation of my own précis in a non-fiction book called *Changing Minds: the History of Psychotherapy as an Answer to Human Suffering*. Strictly speaking, these ideas weren't expressed in this way by Freud until the 1920s. Even so, many of the elements were current so it isn't inconceivable that a conversation like the one described could have taken place. Brahms's way of looking at women was originally observed and noted by the composer Ethel Smyth, and Brahms really did make a recording of Hungarian Dance No. 1 on an Edison phonograph. The symbolism of the town hall in Vienna, as described in *Death and the Maiden*, reflects views expressed by Professor Joseph Koerner of Harvard University in *Vienna: City of Dreams*, a television documentary shown on BBC4. The electrical-hand method of administering electrotherapy is described in *Freud, Dora, and Vienna 1900* by Hannah S. Decker. A reproduction of an illustration showing a physician applying current to the spine with an 'electrical hand' can be found in *Healing the Mind: A History of Psychiatry from Antiquity to the Present* by Michael H. Stone. The lord marshal is an entirely fictional character, although the lord marshal's office (*Obersthofmarschallamt*) is not. The lord marshal's office and its agents executed the legal business of the House of Habsburg and some historians believe that this bureau played an active role in covering up the 'truth' behind Mayerling (see *A Nervous Splendour* by Frederic Morton). *The Gypsy Fiddlers* is an authentic Transylvanian folk tale. I have made a condensed version of the original, which can be found in *Ghosts, Vampires, and Werewolves: Eerie Tales from Transylvania* by Mihai I. Spariosu and Desz Benedek. Freud's anecdote about Chrobak's prescription for female maladies can be found in *The History of the Psychoanalytic Movement* by Sigmund Freud. Needless to say, I do not subscribe to Chrobak's view that female psychiatric ailments would swiftly evaporate using this 'panacea'.

Frank Tallis
London, 2010